THE
SHADOWS

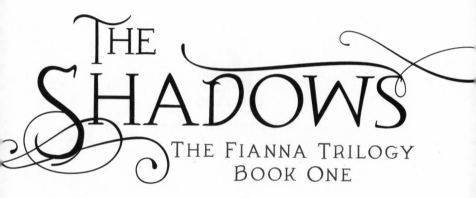

THE SHADOWS

THE FIANNA TRILOGY
BOOK ONE

MEGAN CHANCE

SKYSCAPE

For Maggie and Cleo, with love

Text copyright © 2014 by Megan Chance
Author Photo copyright © 2014 C.M.C. Levine
All rights reserved.

Published by SKYSCAPE, New York

www.apub.com

Amazon, the Amazon logo, and SKYSCAPE are trademarks of Amazon.com, Inc., or its affiliates.

ISBN-13: 9781477847183 (hardcover)
ISBN-10: 1477847189 (hardcover)
ISBN-13: 9781477816233 (paperback)
ISBN-10: 1477816232 (paperback)

Book design by Abby Kuperstock

Library of Congress Control Number: 2013923549

Printed in the United States of America

There she weaves by night and day
A magic web with colours gay.
She has heard a whisper say,
A curse is on her if she stay
To look down to Camelot.
She knows not what the curse may be,
And so she weaveth steadily,
And little other care hath she,
The Lady of Shalott.

And moving thro' a mirror clear
That hangs before her all the year,
Shadows of the world appear . . .

. . .

"I am half-sick of shadows," said
The Lady of Shalott.

"The Lady of Shalott"
—Alfred, Lord Tennyson

❦ Cast of Characters ❧
[AND PRONUNCIATION GUIDE]

─────── THE KNOX FAMILY ───────

Grainne Alys Knox [GRAW-nya]—*Grace*

Aidan Knox—*Grace's brother*

Maeve Knox—*Grace's mother*

Brigid Knox—*Grace's grandmother*

─────── THE DEVLIN FAMILY ───────

Patrick Devlin

Lucy Devlin—*Patrick's sister*

Sarah Devlin—*Patrick's mother*

─────── THE FIANNA (FINN'S WARRIORS) ───────

Diarmid Ua Duibhne [DEER-mid O'DIV-na]—*Derry O'Shea*

Finn MacCumhail [FINN MacCOOL]—*Finn MacCool,
the leader of the Fianna*

Oscar

Ossian [USH-een]—*Oscar's father*

Keenan

Goll

Conan

Cannel Flannery—*Seer*

──── THE FENIAN BROTHERHOOD [FEE-NIAN] ────

Rory Nolan

Simon MacRonan

Jonathan Olwen

──────── THE FOMORI ────────

Daire Donn [DAW-re DON]

Lot

Tethra

Bres

Miogach [MYEE-gok]

Balor

──────── IN LEGEND ────────

Tuatha de Dannan [TOO-a-ha dae DONN-an]—*the old, revered gods of Ireland, the people of the goddess Danu*

Aengus Og [ENGUS OG]—*Irish god of love, Diarmid's foster father*

Manannan [MANanuan]—*Irish god of the sea, Diarmid's former tutor*

Lir [LEER]—*god of the sea, Manannan's father*

Brigid [BREED]—*Irish goddess*

The Morrigan—*Irish goddess of war; her three aspects:*
Macha [MOK-ah], Nemain [NOW-nm], and Badb [BIBE]

Danu—*Irish mother goddess*

Domnu—*Mother goddess of the Fomori*

Cuchulain [COO-coo-lane]—*Irish hero*

Etain [AY-teen]—*Oscar's wife in ancient times*

Neasa [NESSA]—*the Fianna's Druid priestess*

Cormac—*ancient High King of Ireland*

Grainne [GRAW-nya]—*Cormac's daughter,*
promised in marriage to Finn, eloped with Diarmid

Fia—*Finn's son*

Senach Síaborthe [SEN-awk SEE-bora]—*legendary demon warrior*

King of Lochlann—*Miogach's father*

Tadg [TYG]—*Diarmid's Druid teacher*

————— OTHER PEOPLE —————

Rose Fitzgerald—*Grace's best friend*

Timothy Lederer—*neighbor and friend of the Knoxes*

Mrs. Needham—*"friend" of Mrs. Knox*

the O'Daires—*investors in the Irish uprising*

Jerry—*Patrick Devlin's stableboy*

Leonard—*Patrick Devlin's driver*

Dr. Eldridge—*Grandma Knox's doctor*

————— OTHER WORDS —————

Almhuin [Allun]—*the keep of the Fianna, aka the Hill of Allen*

ball seirce [Ball searce]—*the lovespot bestowed on Diarmid*

Beltaine [BAL-tinna]—*ancient Celtic festival, the first of May*

cainte [KINE-tay]—*one who speaks/sees, Druid poet*

dord fiann [Dord FEEN]—*Finn's hunting horn*

Dubros—*an ancient woods in Ireland where*
the legendary Diarmid and Grainne find refuge

geis [GISE]—*a prohibition or taboo that compels the person to obey*

Magh Tuiredh [Moytirra]—*location of the great battle between the*
Dannan and the Fomori

milis [MILL-ish]—*sweet, an endearment*

mo chroi [Muh CREE]—*my heart*

ogham—*ancient form of Irish writing*

Samhain [SOW-in]—*ancient Celtic festival, October 31*

sidhe [Shee]—*fairies*

Slieve Lougher [Sleeve Lawker]—*location in ancient Ireland*

veleda—*ancient Druid priestess*

THE
SHADOWS

Ancient Ireland

I t is given to you," the archdruid said, handing her Finn's
hunting horn. "It is put into your care and that of your
descendants."

The *veleda* curled her fingers around the horn and felt the
power, an ancient energy. She caressed the crack at the base
where it had been trampled in the battle that had mortally
wounded its owner, Finn MacCumhail, the great leader of the
Fianna warriors. The bronze decoration had been stripped
away, replaced and mended with hammered silver etched
with ogham, the symbols that infused it with magic.

The power was hers. The privilege of sacrifice. She looked
up into the blue eyes of her teacher and mentor.

He asked soberly, "Do you accept the task, my child?"

She glanced at the men lying on the biers surrounding
her, the soldiers of the Fianna, with Finn at the center. They
were as still as death, clad in the raiment of battle. They were

the most elite warriors and bodyguards of the High King of Ireland. These men had served gods and kings; they were the subjects of countless stories, poems, and ballads. Everyone knew of the Fianna. There was not a boy who did not dream of becoming one of them, nor a girl who did not yearn for their kisses.

But now a new world had come.

"I accept the task," she said.

"They will return when the horn has known the *veleda*'s blood, when the incantation is sung and the horn is blown three times," the archdruid continued. "When Ireland is in need, they will return as young men in their prime to fight for her. That is the spell that is laid. That is the word that is spoken."

"But they have grown arrogant and greedy these last years," she joined in, singing the spell she'd labored to master, not just the words but how to *say* them. "They have misused their power, and they have not always served the honorable. And so we place upon them this *geis*, this prohibition: the *veleda* must decide if their new fight is a worthy one. If it is not deemed so, they will fail, and die."

The magic of the words threaded through the branches of the overhanging rowan tree. She clutched the horn tight between her fingers. The power reverberated through her like thunder heard beneath the water.

"The *veleda* will see the path," the archdruid sang. "She will weigh the task and choose the worthiest side. And on Samhain, when the doors between worlds open, her death will release her power to the chosen, and they will win. If this condition is not met, the Fianna will disappear, never to return to any world. This will be done. This is complete."

The spell would pass through her blood and down through the generations, from one Druid priestess to another. One day her descendant would blood the horn. One day the daughter of her daughter's daughter would know the joy and power of self-sacrifice.

She smiled and echoed, "This is complete."

The moon turned the color of blood. The rowan tree trembled, and the earth shook beneath her feet and opened, swallowing the Fianna. The men were there and then gone, and the great maw closed again, leaving no seam, nothing to show what had been, nor what lay beneath.

Beltaine, May 1, 1874

Diarmid

First was the darkness—or no, not the darkness itself but rather his awareness that it *was* dark, and that it had been so for a very long time. Next came memory, only bits and pieces: golden hair and eyes the color of a spring morn. Her voice cautioning him not to go without his great sword. Then the boar, charging, tusks red with blood. Pain, there had been pain. And thirst. And ... death. And then, from far away, his foster father's voice, conversations held in a gray twilight.

Now Diarmid heard murmurings, young men's voices. He opened his eyes, blinking at the daylight peeking through an unshuttered window. He saw the ceiling first, spotted with mildew, in one place black with soot, and then the rest of the room: seeping walls, a potbellied iron contraption in one corner. Pallets of straw, his friends dressed as he was: in linen shirts, capes, and boots. The Fianna. He knew a moment of swelling pride.

And then he realized that the undying sleep was broken. They had been called back as foretold. Ireland had need of them again.

He saw the white-blond head of his best friend, Oscar. Then Ossian, Oscar's father, looking strangely young, no more than twenty-four, as if there were only a few years between him and his son instead of more than twenty. Some of them had died old men, some of them in war, some—like Diarmid—by other means; but they were all young now. Most of them, like him, eighteen or nineteen; some a bit older. Goll, no longer haggard. Keenan, still thin but not yet gaunt and gray. Conan—bald as always, but then he'd been bald in his youth, and still wearing that stinking sheepskin about his shoulders.

And then there was ... Finn. His golden-red hair glistened in the pale light, his gaze was as sharp and blue as ever. Finn, whom Diarmid had betrayed. Finn, who'd had the means to save him but had let him die.

Diarmid rose to one elbow, trying to gain his bearings. Yet nothing was familiar but these friends he'd known the whole of his life.

"A restorative sleep, it seems," Finn said with a smile, rising, flexing arms and shoulders. "It looks to be all of us together again, lads. The horn's sounded at last."

"Where is she?" Ossian asked. "Shouldn't she be here? The priestess?"

Diarmid looked around. No woman anywhere, no *veleda*. He remembered hearing the spell through his dreams, the archdruid's booming voice and the *veleda*'s soft one, though still powerful. Even then he'd felt a foreboding, and now he looked for her with dread.

There was another part of the prophecy that had a special role for him. He didn't think the others knew of it—he wished he was ignorant himself.

"She's not here," he said, hoping no one heard his relief.

"Who blew the horn?" Finn asked. "Where is she who blooded it? She should be—"

There was the sound of rapid footsteps, a clatter, and the door sprang open. A boy burst inside. Threadbare coverings on his legs, short boots revealing bare ankles, a shirt with buttons, a small cap. The boy skidded to a stop, his breath coming fast. "You'd best get up! Get up! Get up! You got to get outta here! The Whyos are coming, and they're gonna take your hide for bein' in their panny!" The boy spun on his heel, racing out again.

They were silent, staring at one another.

Finn frowned. "By the gods, what was that?"

Diarmid ignored Finn's question. He went to the single window and looked out. This was no world he knew. He stared in shock at tall buildings blocking the sky, with metal ladders twining around them and narrow streets below; chariots with four wheels; horses—the only thing familiar—and the stink of mud and piss and piles of garbage. People dressed in outlandish costumes. More people than he had seen in one place since the battle against Daire Donn and the son of Lochlann. But these people were not fighting.

And these were not the green hills and glens of Ireland.

"We're not home," he said, his voice gravelly from long sleep. He cleared his throat, said again, more loudly, "'Tisn't Ireland." He turned back to his friends. "Where are we? *When* are we?"

Then they heard the shouting.

ONE

May 15, 1874

Grace

"Wake up, Gracie. Come on, wake up now."

My brother's voice broke through my dream. His words were slurred; I knew before I was fully awake that he was drunk—again. I squeezed my eyes more tightly shut and buried my face in my pillow. "Go away, Aidan."

He only shook my shoulder harder. "Get *up*, Grace. I nee' yer 'elp."

I opened my eyes, wincing at the sudden pain. Too bright. The world was too bright, and Aidan was a sickening flare within it. I put my hand to my forehead. "Ouch—my head."

"Come on. There's a man a' the door."

I knew if I took a headache powder right this moment the pain would go away. But we couldn't afford even powders, and believe me, it made me miserable. I'd been having these headaches much more often lately, along with nightmares full of thunder and weird, glowing lights. Mama said both would fade in time once the excitement was over.

Excitement. As if bill collectors and the constant threat of being put on the street were something *fun*. As if there was any hope of it ending soon.

Aidan wavered before me, his dark hair falling into his face, his beautiful blue eyes—which I'd been jealous of since I'd been old enough to know mine were brown—wide and anxious and afraid. He was only twenty, but already he had the sickly pallor of a constant drunk, which he was.

"Who's at the door, Aidan? Someone else you owe money?"

"The do'tor," Aidan said. "Saw 'im through the window. I'm in no condition—"

"No, you never are."

"He won't lissen to me anyway," he said. Which was also true. The whole world knew not to trust Aidan anymore. "You know whata say to 'em, Gracie. You always do."

I groaned. This one would not be easy. Dr. Eldridge had been sending us messages for months now. Bills that had gone onto the stack with all the others though we could no longer pay anything. It was all we could do to eat.

For a moment my resentment of my brother overwhelmed me. I would be seventeen in a month, and I should have been doing things like going to teas and shopping with my friends. But it wasn't just Aidan's fault. My father's business—Knox's Clothing Emporium, a ready-made clothing shop—had gone under. We would have done all right after his death if all our savings hadn't disappeared when Jay Cooke & Company's huge banking firm failed, sending the whole world—not just us—into despair. It had been only late last year. There had been plenty of suicides then. Shanties sprung up at the edges of the city overnight; suddenly the streets were full of the hungry and homeless. We weren't the only ones suffering in this terrible depression, but somehow knowing that didn't help when you were struggling to keep everything from falling apart. Soup kitchens were everywhere, run by churches feeding the poor, which we were now. But we weren't just *any* poor. We had been well-to-do once, and most of our friends still were, and what would they say to see the Knoxes standing in line at a soup kitchen? Mama wouldn't allow it, and I had my pride, too, though sometimes when I walked past a line stretching into the street and smelled soup and bread, my stomach growled so horribly I knew everyone must hear.

And since then, Aidan's drinking had increased. There was something wrong with him, I knew. But I didn't know what it was, and I didn't know how to cure him or how to make him care again about anything but drinking and gambling. Grandma was too ill to help—she'd been the reason for the doctor in the first place. Mama was no good with any of it. It had been two years since Papa had died, and she still couldn't cope at all. *Someone* had to take care of things, and that someone was me.

I sighed. "Let him knock. He'll go away soon enough."

"'e's not goin' anywhere. Mama's abed. Don' let 'er be upset. Please, Gracie."

I took a deep breath and waved him away. "All right. Go. I can't greet the doctor in a dressing gown, now can I?"

Aidan smiled with relief. He pulled himself into an unsteady stand.

"I'll stall Mama if she wakes," he said.

He left, and I rose carefully, my head pounding. The morning was warm, but the floorboards were cold beneath my feet, the thick Aubusson carpets long since sold, along with every painting, vase, wall hanging, and almost all the furniture. Now my bedroom held only my bed, a rickety table and chair I'd scavenged from the attic, and a trunk with a washbasin and a chipped ewer on it and a tiny cracked mirror above it.

I stepped to the mirror and undid my braid, then caught my dark curls with a frayed ribbon and tied them back. The pounding from downstairs set a rhythm with my growing headache. I threw off my nightgown and put on my chemise and corset and gown, stockings and boots—I'd had to learn to dress myself since we'd let the maid go—and went downstairs.

I opened the front door so quickly Dr. Eldridge nearly fell into me. His gaunt face was red with frustration. He regained his balance, tugging at his coat. "Miss Knox, might I have a word with your brother?"

"My brother's not at home." I had become very good at lying. Not something to be proud of exactly, but sometimes I felt as if it should be. "I'd be happy to pass along a message."

I wasn't surprised when he said, "Then perhaps I could speak to your mother about a sensitive matter."

"I'm afraid she's still abed."

"I see." He hesitated. I knew he was trying to decide whether to speak to me, but everyone knew of my brother's weakness and my mother's frailty. Who else was there to speak to? Dr. Eldridge cleared his throat. "I've been privileged to serve your family—"

"Yes, indeed. Grandmother's feeling much better." Another lie, but what was one more when a whole trunkful of them was already at my feet?

"I'm glad to hear it." His expression went grim. "It is, however, customary, when one is feeling better, to pay one's bill."

"She's not *that* much better."

"Miss Knox—"

"I will speak to my brother about it." I put my hand on the door.

He blocked it with his foot. "Your brother is avoiding me, Miss Knox. I've sent several letters. I'm afraid I have no choice but to proceed with legal measures."

I let my eyes fill with tears. This wasn't hard. "Please, Doctor. Things are so very difficult just now, what with my father's passing."

He glanced away uncomfortably. "I do understand, miss. But your father's been gone some time, and the talk is . . . well, I know this is indelicate, but one hears. From other merchants."

Clearly, my tears weren't having the desired effect.

"As I said, I have no choice, Miss Knox. You will be hearing from my lawyer."

We would lose the house and all that was left. "Please, Doctor—"

"I *am* sorry, miss."

He was halfway down the steps. Beyond him, a horse and carriage went by with the *clackity clack* of hooves on cobblestones and a curious stare from the driver. I retreated into the darkness of the doorway. In spite of the fact that everyone knew of our situation, I did not think our neighbors were aware of quite how bad things were, and Mama would be horrified if they discovered it. Desperately, I said, "Doctor, have you any interest in antiquities?"

He turned around. "Antiquities?"

"I have . . . one thing." Already I regretted this, but what else could I do? "It's very old. I don't know what it's worth, if anything. My grandmother said it was ancient."

"What is it?"

"A hunting horn. From Ireland."

He sighed. "Let me have a look at it."

I closed the door and grabbed my skirt to hurry up the stairs, my heart heavy and my head aching. I had no real hope that the doctor would accept the horn. It *was* old, tarnished and cracked; its value lay more in the stories my grandmother had told me of it, the old Irish tales of gods and fighting men and miraculous feats. It was my most treasured possession. I'd spent hours lying on my bed and turning it over in my hands, closing my eyes, imagining the battles it had seen, heroes sweeping me into their arms and carrying me far away from empty rooms and Mama's tears and Grandma's growing dementia. I didn't want to give it up. But it was all I had, and we could not lose the house. We had no place else to go.

I pulled the papier-mâché box from under my bed. *You have to,* I told myself. If Dr. Eldridge took the horn, it would ease things for a while. And that was all I needed. Just a little more time to find a way out of this mess that was my life. I opened the lid.

The horn was gone.

It couldn't be. I tried to think of the last time I'd seen it. Only a few weeks ago, I'd cut myself on a ragged edge of the silver and bled all over it. I tried to remember what I'd done then. Wiped it clean and then . . . I'd put it away, hadn't I? Or perhaps I'd—

"I'm so sorry, Gracie."

My brother's voice.

Oh no. No, no, no.

I looked over my shoulder at Aidan, who leaned against the door frame. His apologetic smile was crooked and sweet. "Was a game a few weeks ago. I didn' think I'd lose it. I planned to win it back before you noticed it was gone. I *will* win it back, I promise—"

I launched myself at him, slamming into him so hard he lost his balance and we both went sprawling onto the floor, me on top. He put up his hands to fend me off.

"You drunken . . . *bastard*," I hissed, hitting him with all my strength. "That horn was *mine*, Aidan. It wasn't yours to take. Damn you! Damn you, *damn* you!"

"Grainne Alys Knox! Your language!"

My mother's voice was tight with horror. I looked up to see her standing in the hallway, her hand at her throat, her face pale.

I gave my brother a final shove and pushed off him. "He stole my horn. He stole it and lost it at dice."

"Act'ally, it was faro," he said.

I kicked him hard.

"Step away from your brother, Grace," Mama said. "You'll wake your grandmother with all this noise, and you are hardly behaving like a lady."

Because I was furious, I said, "Doctor Eldridge is downstairs, waiting for me to return with the horn I've bartered to keep him from lodging a suit against us."

My mother's glance went quickly to Aidan, who was rising onto his elbows. "You've paid him nothing?" she asked.

"What was I to pay 'im with?" Aidan replied bitterly.

"How do you pay for your drink?" I asked him.

My brother's face shuttered. "You don' wanna know."

"That will be enough," Mama said. She was trembling.

My headache flared. I put my hand to the wall to steady myself.

Mama noticed. "Another headache?"

I nodded.

"I'll try to win back the horn," Aidan said, sounding more sober now than he had all morning. "I never meant to lose it. I didn' think I would."

"That won't help us today, will it?" I tried to blink away

the ache in my head. "Well, I'll have to tell him. He'll lodge a suit, and *you'll* be the one who must manage that, Aidan."

"I think we can put this off no longer," Mama said. "There are things we must talk about, Grace."

I knew the "talk" she meant. When I turned seventeen, I would be old enough for an early debut. Old enough to find a rich husband—though no one said *rich*, of course. To talk about money was crass and beneath us. No, what everyone said was *well*, as in *You must marry well, Grace.*

Mama and I had talked of it before, and I knew she was right. But I was afraid. Not of marriage, really; in finishing school, every conversation was about who would marry first, what dresses we would wear to our debut, engagements and weddings and the boys who were possibilities. But then, I'd never imagined that my own marriage would be for anything less than true love. Breathless sighs and stolen kisses. The whole world opening up like an oyster, just waiting for me to grab the bright, shiny pearl of it—

From the door below came a knock. Dr. Eldridge, waiting.

So much for dreams. "Yes, Mama, we'll talk."

And then I went downstairs to tell Dr. Eldridge the bad news.

That night, Mama waited for me in the parlor. The room had once held settees and upholstered chairs. There had been carpets on floors that were now bare and scuffed. In that corner had been a glass-fronted whatnot filled with porcelain figurines; in the other a pianoforte, with sheaves of music.

Paintings had hung from golden cords, filling nearly every space; now there were only darkened spots on the red toile wallpaper where they'd once been and one worn settee and an old rocker where my mother sat, which I couldn't look at without wondering if we might have to burn it for firewood this winter. My grandfather had made it out of pine, and carved in it a hunting horn and a tree branch with berries.

My mother was embroidering handkerchiefs again, made from a linen tablecloth that had been too worn and stained to sell. As if any of us needed more handkerchiefs. One could only cry or sneeze so often. I watched as she plied the needle in the dim light of a single lamp. Her golden-red hair, as straight and fine as mine was thick and curling, was swept up elegantly, her bones delicate and sharp beneath her freckled skin. Once she'd worn satins and silks. She'd had gowns of every color. Now I saw her only in the brown she had on today, and a black silk she'd worn the entire year after Papa had died, following the rules of mourning to the letter. Black-swathed windows, mirrors turned to the wall, black-edged calling cards and stationery.

Even in the dated gown, Mama looked every inch a lady. But her poise only hid despair and indecision. She had let Aidan gamble and drink away everything we had left, and I was angry with her even as I knew I might have done the same. My brother was charming and feckless. He won forgiveness easily with a smile. I loved Aidan, but he infuriated me. I didn't understand how Mama never seemed to be the least bit angry.

Because he was her favorite, of course, as he had always been.

I bit back my resentment and clasped my hands tightly as I stood before her. "You wanted to speak with me, Mama?"

She glanced to the windows that fronted the street, which had once been hung with three sets of curtains—sash and lace and then damask on top—and now had only thin chintz. She set aside the handkerchief. "Grace, it's time we considered your debut. You're a pretty girl. There's no reason you couldn't win a good husband."

"You mean an old, rich husband."

She winced. "The things you say sometimes."

"Well, it's true, isn't it?"

"The doctor's lawsuit is only one of what will be many."

I started. She knew how bad things were?

As if she'd heard my thoughts, she said, "Oh yes, I know, though you try to keep it from me. We *will* lose the house if something is not done. And then where are we to go? What about your grandmother, who is too ill to leave her bed?"

"Aidan could—"

"I've lost hope that Aidan will ever change."

The shock of my mother's admission silenced me. She had never before said a word against him.

"You are my responsible child, Grace. You no longer have the luxury of waiting for love, as your father wished for you. You must marry."

"So because I'm responsible, I must be the one to pay the price? That's hardly fair."

"We will all end up in the poorhouse otherwise. Life is not one of your fairy tales, Grace, but I believe that, with some luck, you can find a white knight to save us."

White knight. I did have a sometimes embarrassing romantic streak—but truly, was it so wrong to want a fairy-tale ending?

"I've spoken to Mrs. Needham," Mama said. "We've come to an arrangement."

"Mrs. Needham?" I asked, and then, suspiciously, "What arrangement, Mama?"

Mrs. Needham was a vicious tyrant of a woman who, along with my mother, was on the board of the Charity Hospital. She had long been jealous of Mama, I knew, though exactly why was a mystery to me. That Mama spoke of my debut and Mrs. Needham in the same breath was worrisome.

"She has offered to loan us the money to pay for your debut. And to sponsor you as well."

Now I was more than suspicious. "Why ever would she do that?"

"In return for me giving pianoforte lessons to her daughters."

And I understood. This was the chance for Mrs. Needham to lord it over my mother. The chance to humiliate her every time she was there, to gloat because my elegant, beautiful mother had fallen so far that she must teach Bach and Mozart to Mrs. Needham's dull, untalented daughters.

"Mama, no," I said. "You can't do that."

"I have already agreed."

"You can't mean it. You can't want to be beholden to *her.*"

My mother met my gaze. "I have hopes that you will make a good enough match that I shall never have to set foot in Mrs. Needham's parlor again."

"And if we can't pay her back?"

"Oh, I think we should see that we can, don't you?"

"Mama, if we must borrow, it should be to pay the bills and save the house, not for gowns and receptions."

"And then what, Grace? There will be more bills, and still no way to pay them or pay off another debt. Your debut is an investment, darling. I don't believe it will be a wasted one."

Slowly, I nodded. What else was I to do—run away? Leave my family to ruin? It was not just my future at stake, but my mother's, my grandmother's. My brother's. I loved my family. And I would do what was best because I could.

Mama said softly, "You might end up very happy, you know, Grace. Your father and I were. There are worse things in life than being a wife. You'll know that when you hold your first child in your arms."

But that seemed a hundred years from now, a life that belonged to someone else. I'd never even been kissed, and that seemed the worst thing, suddenly—that I would never know what it felt like to be in love.

"There's a supper tomorrow night at the Devlins'," Mama went on patiently. "A small thing, meant to welcome back Patrick."

"Patrick's back from Ireland?"

I had known the Devlins all my life. Mr. Devlin's

business—Devlin Hatters and Tailors—had been in friendly competition with Knox's Clothing Emporium, and our families were close. Aidan and I had played with Patrick and his younger sister, Lucy, when we were children. But after Patrick's father had died in a carriage accident four years ago, he'd gone to Ireland to learn the business.

"He returned a few weeks ago," Mama said. "There will be several people there. Some of his friends but also more important men."

Richer men.

"You'll wear the dove-gray silk," Mama added, as if I had a choice, as if it wasn't my only supper gown.

I turned away from her and made my way blindly from the parlor and up the stairs. I wanted to lock myself in my room and scream.

But even as I thought it, I knew I would never do it. The way things were going, it would only bring the police and the neighbors, and wouldn't *that* be one more perfect thing to add to an already exceptional day?

I was halfway down the hall when I heard my grandmother's weak call. I wanted to ignore her. Let her call Mama. But then Grandma called again, and, obedient as ever, I went to her room.

It was as empty as the others. A bed and a nighttable and a chair and nothing more. It was hot, too, and stuffy, with that closed-in invalid feel. No fresh air ever reached this room— my grandmother would not allow the windows to be opened. It was dangerous with all the fairies and creatures running about, she said often. What had once been charming child-hood stories were only exhausting nonsense now.

The room was dark, the calico curtains closed against day-light or moonlight. I went to her bedside table and lit a gut-tered tallow candle. "A little light would be nice, Grandma," I said with false cheer. "Why do you sit here in the dark?"

"Sit down, *mo chroi*," she said, her accent still heavily Irish though she'd been in this country forty years. *My heart.* The endearment warmed me, as always.

I did as she asked, and she grasped my hand with her wrinkled, bony one. Her gray hair lay in a straggling braid over her shoulder; her nightcap was askew, the ribbons trailing over her sunken cheek. But her eyes were lively. She had dark eyes, like mine. *Black Irish*, she would say to me. *There's good to come of that*, mo chroi, *you'll see.*

"Your head hurts," she said.

"I did have another headache. But it's gone now."

"They've come. 'Tis the reason."

She had been saying things like this more and more often. I feared that one day I would enter this room to find her completely fallen into madness.

"I hear them." Her gaze went distant. "Such confusion."

"I—"

She gripped my hand hard. "The hunting horn. Did you blow it?"

"No. Why would I? You told me not to. And it's gone anyway, Grandma. Aidan lost it in a bet. Weeks ago now." I wondered even as I said it why I told her the truth.

"Aidan . . . lost it?" Her brow furrowed.

"He said he'd try to win it back," I reassured her, though the chances of that were as good as me stumbling into a leprechaun and a pot of gold in our backyard. I would never see that horn again.

"You will find it, *mo chroi*. You'll be the saving of us all."

"Yes." I tried to smile. "Mama's planning my debut as we speak. I'm to find a husband. I expect that will turn everything around."

My grandmother shook her head. "No, lass——"

"Yes," I said firmly. "I'm quite resigned to it. So you see, there's nothing for you to worry about."

Grandma went silent. I rubbed my thumb over her swollen knuckles. So frail. I remembered when she had nearly frightened me with how alive she was, when she had seemed somehow bigger than everything else in the world.

And now she was just an old woman confined to bed, and I was afraid. I couldn't bear to think of her in a poor asylum. She would die there.

She whispered, "Do you see them, lass?"

"See who?"

She squeezed my hand again, not answering, and then she closed her eyes. I sat with her, watching the moonlight creep past the crack in the curtains, slanting across the floor—a tiny glowing sliver.

I felt its call just as I always had. There was something about moonlight, as if it were sent just for me, as if it were a voice in my head saying, *Come. I've something for you. Come.*

I laid Grandma's hand on her chest, which barely rose and fell as she slept, and I went quietly from her room. My mother had gone to bed already; there was no light downstairs. Who knew where Aidan had gone?

I slipped down the stairs. The back door was locked against the thieves and the homeless that filled the city. I turned the key and stepped out into the small backyard. The night air was soft and cool; I closed my eyes and lifted my face to it, and then I stepped to where I could see the moonrise over the roof.

The moon was huge tonight, blue white in a deep-blue sky. I stared up at the shadows of its face, and my yearning rose until I thought I might burst. In that moment, I felt part of every legend and romantic tale I'd ever heard. Like Tennyson's Lady of Shalott in her tower, imprisoned by a curse, unable to look upon the world except through a mirror. I whispered, "'*I am half-sick of shadows*, said the Lady of Shalott.'"

The air seemed to pulse around me with music only I could hear. I wanted to dance in it. I wanted . . . what? I didn't know. I didn't know what I wanted or who I was, just that I was meant for something *more*.

Wasn't I?

I looked back at the moon, begging her, as I always did, for answers. *Tell me your secrets. Tell me what I am.*

But she was as silent as ever.

TWO

May 16

Grace

I dressed slowly for Mrs. Devlin's supper. The dove gray looked well on me, I knew, with its lace-edged sleeves and polonaise. I couldn't put up my hair until my debut, but I had become rather good at fixing it without a maid, and I arranged it as best I could to disguise my lack of jewelry, which had all been sold. Still, I thought the style too plain; I would not stand out in the least from the other girls there, who would have jewelry and ribbons. I'd look a poor church mouse beside them. But I had gloves, at least, and if I turned my hand just so, you couldn't see the grease stain that marred the palm.

Aidan waited for me in the parlor. Mama would not be going; Grandmother was too ill to be left alone. "You must serve as her chaperone," Mama was telling him as I came in. "Don't lose yourself in drink and forget."

Aidan wasn't drunk now, but there was a look in his eyes that I recognized: pinprick pupils. He'd been into Grandma's laudanum, no doubt. But his walk seemed steady as he led me down the railed stoop and past the wild-looking shrubs—no gardener now either—that lined the cast-iron fence of our redbrick row house.

There was no carriage, of course, and so we walked the few blocks to Madison Square. The day was warm; I had to ask Aidan to slow down so that I didn't arrive sweating and bedraggled.

"It will be good to see Patrick again," Aidan said. "Though now that he's one of the Brotherhood, I expect there'll be no living with him."

"The Brotherhood?"

"The Fenians," Aidan said, as if I were the most stupid girl in New York City. "You've heard of them, haven't you?"

I had—there wasn't an Irishman in the city who hadn't. The Fenian Brotherhood had formed to help Ireland win its independence from Britain. It had been one of my father's favorite topics of conversation. But I hadn't been interested then and was less so now. I'd been born here in New York City; the problems of Ireland seemed very far away, and nothing to do with me.

"Yes, I've heard of them," I told my brother haughtily. "Is that what Patrick was doing in Ireland these last years?"

"The Devlins have business interests there. But I'm certain Patrick was trying to raise funds for a rebellion as well."

The thought irritated me. It meant the conversation at supper would be mostly politics. But perhaps we'd be lucky and the men would save such talk for after supper.

I glanced at the street, at the passing carriages, the horses raising clouds of dust that settled between the cobblestones, and I wished I were in one of those carriages, going anywhere.

But then we were at the Devlins'. Aidan took me up the steps that led to the white marble-fronted brownstone. Much finer than our house. I felt a little stab of envy that Devlin Hatters had stayed so successful when our own fortunes had fallen so far.

A butler welcomed us into the beeswax-and-rose-scented foyer. Old Irish-made tapestries hung the length of the hall. Statuettes of horses and serpents—all ancient and Celtic—held places of honor on highly polished sideboards and tables. Patrick's late father had been a collector of all things Irish. It was small wonder that his son was involved in the Fenian Brotherhood.

Our footsteps were muffled by a rose-patterned carpet as the butler led us to the parlor. People were there already; some I recognized: The Lederers and their son, Timothy. Mrs. Devlin and Lucy, who was two years my senior, and blond and pretty. She'd had her debut last year and tonight wore a gown that I thought daringly low-cut, with fabric roses on the neckline that fluttered with her every breath. She was flirting rather obviously with Timothy, who looked pleased and flushed—well, no chance for me there, not competing with Lucy. Beyond them were the MacDoyles, with their son Michael in tow—pimply faced and my age but looking barely grown into his own skin. Maisie O'Doul, one of Lucy's friends, who had no sense of humor and a distracting habit of blinking constantly, stood near two young men I didn't know, one of whom was handsome, with light-brown hair just this side of blond. And then—

Mr. and Mrs. Fitzgerald, and their daughter, my best friend, Rose. She waved from across the room, and suddenly I was glad to be here. I hadn't seen her in weeks; she and her parents had been in Boston, and I'd missed her so much. She'd sent me a note a few days ago saying they'd returned, but I hadn't expected her here.

I would have rushed to her right then, but Aidan and I had to greet Mrs. Devlin, who gave me a hug scented—again—with roses and whispered in my ear, "Patrick's been waiting to see you both. He was so happy to hear you were coming."

I managed not to make a face and said, "Mama regrets not being here, but with Grandma being so ill—"

"I quite understand," Mrs. Devlin said. "You two enjoy yourselves."

I left Aidan to himself and hurried over to Rose.

"It seems forever since I've seen you!" Rose said, hugging me.

"It *has* been forever," I said. "Tell me you're staying in the city for a time, please."

"At least through the summer, Papa says." Rose tucked a loose strand of her red hair behind her ear and led me away from the others, into a corner near a vase full of peacock feathers. "I'd forgotten how much Mrs. Devlin loves roses. I feel quite at home. How perfect I'd be for Patrick! Then there would be a Rose in his bedroom too."

I couldn't help laughing at how scandalous she was. "You know, he might be tired of roses."

She laughed with me. "Oh, I suppose so. You must tell me what's been happening. What have I missed? Tell me everything!"

Now I did make a face. "I'm to have my debut this year. In October."

"October!" Rose clutched my fingers. "Oh, I can't believe it. I vow I'll be an old spinster before Mama allows mine. She thinks I should wait until I'm nineteen."

"I wish I could wait so long."

"You do not! Balls and suppers and walks in gardens and all the boys asking you to dance . . . Oh, it's so romantic."

"It's not romantic, Rose," I said miserably. "Not the way I must do it. I'm to find a husband this year if I can. We'll lose the house otherwise."

Rose's brown eyes warmed with sympathy. "Perhaps it won't be so bad as you think. A rich husband could take you wherever you wanted to go. Think of that. Why, you'd take your honeymoon on the Continent, of course. France and Italy and perhaps even Spain!"

She made it all seem so bearable. I had to smile. "I have missed you, Rose."

"You need someone to rouse you from your books and your boring old poets." Rose's glance flashed past me. "So what do you think of Patrick Devlin now? Three years in Ireland changed him for the better, don't you think?"

"I haven't seen Patrick yet. Aidan and I only just arrived."

"You saw him when you came in. He's never left this room."

I shook my head. "No, I—"

"I told you he's changed." Rose's voice lowered to a whisper. "Why, he's right over there with his friend Mr. Olwen, who came with him from Ireland."

I glanced over my shoulder. I knew everyone in this room but the two young men in the corner, and just then the handsome one turned, and I nearly gaped like a fish when I realized it was Patrick Devlin.

And oh, Rose was right. How he had changed.

The last time I'd seen him had been a few months before he'd left for Ireland. I'd just turned fourteen, and he'd been eighteen, and all skinny angles, coltish and gawky.

And now . . . now his broad shoulders filled out his brown coat; the face that had been all angles had become truly gorgeous. His gray-green eyes were as heavily lashed as a girl's.

He caught my glance and smiled; it was mischievous, a smile I remembered, and I realized that he'd caught me staring. I looked quickly away, and Rose laughed. "I see you like the look of him now."

"Don't," I whispered, blushing madly. "Oh dear God, tell me he's looked away."

"No. In fact, he's coming over."

"Don't tease. No, he's not. Not—"

"Why, hello, Mr. Devlin," Rose said.

And there he was. Standing beside me.

"This can't be little Rose Fitzgerald I'm seeing," Patrick Devlin teased with an exaggerated Irish accent.

"The very same," Rose said with a light curtsy. "And I'm certain you remember Grace Knox."

"Miss Knox." He dropped the accent and smiled at me.

That smile left me breathless. It was all I could do to extend my hand and say, "How nice to see you again, Mr. Devlin."

His fingers brushed mine and then held my hand too long for politeness. "The last time I saw you, you were still in short skirts."

"Yes, it's been some time."

"You've aged very . . . well."

"Thank you." And then I felt like an idiot for saying it, for not coming up with some clever remark in return. But I hadn't Lucy's charm nor Rose's talent for flirtation. Patrick Devlin's smile overwhelmed me; I couldn't think of a single thing to say.

His smile broadened as if he knew it. "Your brother tells me you'll be debuting this year."

"Yes. October."

"You'll invite me, I hope."

My throat tightened so I could hardly speak. "If you wish."

He laughed. "Don't *you* wish to have me there?"

My face must be the color of a lobster. "Yes, of course."

"Why, she'd be a fool not to, wouldn't she?" Rose's eyes twinkled. "Just returned home and already you're the catch of the season, Mr. Devlin."

He flirted right back, completely at ease. "Am I that elevated so soon?"

"I think you must know it." Rose tapped his arm with her

finger. "But I suppose you managed to find a sweetheart while you were away."

She was so bold.

Patrick said, "Ah, unfortunately I'm afraid love has quite eluded me. But I have hopes that will change." And then, astonishingly, impossibly, his gaze came to me. "I believe we're seated next to each other at dinner, Miss Knox. Might I have the honor of escorting you to the table when the time comes?"

Had Rose not nudged me—hard and not very subtly—I think I might have stared at him in shock for minutes. As it was, it seemed a horribly long time before I managed, stupidly again, "But Aidan—"

"We'll have him tend to Lucy."

I nodded. *Stupid, stupid girl.*

"Then I'll leave you for now. My mother insists I speak with everyone." He gave a slight bow and then he went off.

The moment he was gone, Rose turned on me. "Have you lost your wits, Grace? You might as well have been a statue."

"He surprised me."

"He's interested in you."

"He's just being polite."

"Oh no." Rose shook her head. "*That* was not politeness."

"Then kindness," I said. "He knows of our misfortunes as well as anyone."

"Perhaps, but I'd wager it's more than that."

"You'd see true love in a hello."

"You're worse than me when it comes to that, and you know it. Why couldn't it be true love?"

"Because it's my life. Do you see any fat old men in this room? Because *that's* my future."

Rose only laughed.

I was as nervous as a bird, waiting for the call to supper. By then I'd talked about what a lovely spring we'd had with Mrs. Lederer and Timothy, spoken with Mrs. MacDoyle of my mother's sainthood in taking care of my ailing grandmother, and suffered Lucy's prattling about her newest love—one of many, and the grandson of an Astor and no more within her reach than the moon. No matter how successful the Devlins were, it wasn't going to buy her the interest of an Astor, who were old Knickerbocker money. There was no chance they'd accept the daughter of Irish immigrants, and one in trade, no less. But it was better than Lucy's last love, who had been a gardener, and just as inappropriate.

When the call came, Lucy tapped my arm with her folded fan and whispered, "You've caught my brother's eye, Grace. How well you've played it, with no jewelry and such simple dress. Why, you stand out from the rest of us like a Quaker."

I didn't know whether it was an insult or a compliment, which was always how it was with Lucy, but before I had the chance to say anything, Aidan came to take her to supper. He had a glass of sherry in his hand, and I eyed it and said, "How nice to see you're enjoying yourself."

He raised the glass in a mock toast. "I am indeed."

Lucy gave him a disparaging look. "Are you drunk, Aidan? So early?"

"It will only make me more entertaining, my sweet."

"I should have asked Patrick to pair you with Maisie," I said, and then started when I heard the laugh behind me. It was Patrick.

"Still bent on tormenting your poor brother, I see," Patrick said.

"Always and forever," Aidan replied.

"What horrible thing has he done to deserve Maisie?"

Everything, I thought, but I couldn't say that to Patrick. While he'd been in Ireland making something of himself, my brother had been staggering about in the company of a bottle of whiskey. Not only was I not proud of him, I didn't want the world to know, which only made me more irritated with Aidan for making it so obvious.

Lucy said to my brother, "Don't trip over my gown, you lout, or I'll never forgive you."

Aidan offered his arm, and Patrick turned to me. "Shall we?"

My nervousness returned. As he led me into the dining room, I had this fleeting wish that he'd been wrong about the seating arrangements at the same time that I knew I would be disappointed if he had. How I was to keep the attention of someone like Patrick Devlin throughout dinner, I wasn't sure. My tongue already felt tied into knots.

He wasn't wrong: our name cards were next to each other.

He pulled out my chair and when I sat, leaned close to say, "I asked my mother to do it."

I looked at him and blurted, "Why?"

"Because you've always been easy to talk to."

"You mean easy to tease."

He laughed. "Aidan and I *were* obnoxious. But I hope I've changed."

The way his gaze flickered over my face made me nervous all over again.

"Three years is a long time to be away," he went on. "Things are very different."

I scrambled to come up with something to say that didn't make me seem a complete idiot. "Yes, I imagine. Have you seen how far they've got building the bridge to Brooklyn? It's very impressive."

"Impressive indeed," he agreed. "I wish I could say the same about the 'For Let' signs in every window and the tramps on every corner."

"The city's changed."

"And so have you." His eyes lit up. "When I left, you were only just becoming a beauty."

I fumbled with the napkin stuffed into its ring—a silver band with an enameled shamrock probably made especially for Patrick's return. "You're very sweet, but I'm hardly that."

"I saw that you would be, you know. Such pale skin and dark eyes. Ah, I'm embarrassing you. Forgive me. It's only that I thought of you often while I was gone."

"Of me?"

"I don't know why that should surprise you. Did you never wonder why I followed you around as much as I did?"

"Because you and Aidan lived to torment me," I said.

He laughed. The talk grew louder around us. A servant filled wine glasses.

Patrick said, "Do you still love your poets?"

Everything about him astonished me. The way he looked, his attention, that he remembered anything at all about me beyond putting salt in my tea.

"Oh yes." Here at last was something I could talk about. "I've just discovered Tennyson, as a matter-of-fact."

"Ah, Tennyson."

"Have you read him? 'The Lady of Shalott' is my favorite."

"Yes, I suppose it would be. Very romantic, isn't it? You always liked such things, I remember. Heroes and handsome knights riding to a lady's rescue."

I felt completely out of my depth. "Yes."

I waited for him to tease me for it, but instead he said, "I brought something back for you. A book. An Irish poet I thought you might like. I'll give it to you after dinner."

I think my mouth dropped open. Before I could say anything else, the woman sitting to his right asked him a question, and the conversation turned. I, too, was swept up in it, and during dinner we didn't have the chance to speak again. But his shoulder brushed mine, and I felt he was watching me even when he didn't seem to be; and I couldn't help glancing at him now and then just to assure myself that he was real, that this wasn't some illusion that would melt away.

After dinner, Mrs. Devlin rose to usher all the women into the parlor while the men stayed in the dining room to smoke cigars and drink and talk. Patrick pressed my hand as if he didn't want me to go, and I froze, so flabbergasted that Rose had to nudge me to move. I heard them discussing the plight of Ireland before we'd even left the room.

Whatever I'd expected from the evening, Patrick Devlin was not it. He'd thought of me while he was gone. He'd brought me back a book of Irish poetry. I didn't know what to make of it. But I knew I liked it.

Mrs. Devlin poured tea, and Rose came flouncing up to me. "Well?"

"He thought of me while he was gone." I couldn't stop smiling.

Rose gasped. "No—he said that?"

"Those were his very words."

"Grace, my dear, do come sit down." Mrs. Devlin patted the settee beside her.

Rose looked as surprised at the invitation as I was. She gave me a little push, and I went over to sit beside Patrick's mother, who asked, "Cream or sugar?"

"Both, please. One lump." I folded my hands in my lap as demurely as I could, squeezing my fingers together to hide the stain on my gloves.

She said, "You must tell me what you think of my son."

I glanced around the room—no one was watching us but Rose.

"I think him very nice, ma'am," I said.

"He's a good boy. He's done a fine job taking over the business, you know. He's inherited his father's eye. There was never a clever idea passed Mr. Devlin by, and Patrick's just the same."

I sipped the tea. It was too hot, burning my lip so I jerked the cup away, too fast. Tea sloshed against the rim, but thankfully I didn't spill it.

She went on, "Your own family . . . well, so unfortunate. Your poor father . . . We all feel terribly for you and your mother."

I noted that she didn't mention Aidan, though she must have known about him as well. It made me like her even better.

"You know that your father and my husband had always hoped for a match between you and Patrick."

If I'd been drinking my tea, I would have choked. "No, ma'am. I had no idea."

"A sound business idea. The Knox ready-made shop with our tailoring business. A single location for all a man's needs. Well, you can see how it would have been."

I could. A pity there was no longer a Knox Emporium. I didn't know what to say. I settled for "It would have been nice."

"The world seems to be falling apart before our eyes, doesn't it? This depression and . . . well, you know I hold you blameless for your family's misfortunes. The decisions men make . . . as women we've not much choice but to accept them.

You're a good girl, the way you take care of your mama and your grandmother. A good, solid girl, as I said to Patrick. And Lucy likes you as well. I would welcome you into our family."

It took a moment before I realized that she was giving me her blessing. She was telling me that she wanted me to marry Patrick.

This was all too fast and too strange. I'd only agreed to a debut yesterday, and now suddenly Mrs. Devlin was talking to me about her son as if everything was already decided. I felt my mother's hand in this, and I was unsure and . . . angry. Though Patrick would be perfect—too perfect—everything was moving too quickly, everyone scheming to manage my life. Was I to have no say in it at all?

I wondered if Patrick was just as caught. Was he forced into this too? It had to be the reason for his attention. Why else would someone like him even look at me?

When the men rejoined us, I couldn't remember a word of the rest of the conversation I'd had with Mrs. Devlin, and I could not look at Patrick. I wanted only to go home. But Aidan ignored my pointed glances, and when everyone sat to hear Lucy sing some silly ballad, I slipped out the French doors, which were open to let in the warm spring air. I heard the tinkling strains of the pianoforte, Lucy's light and trilling soprano, and I stepped farther away from the house and toward the rose-twined trellis separating the yard from the bordering park. I stood just at the edge, watching the strollers, the couple in the gazebo beyond who seemed oblivious to everything around them. In love.

There was no other way for me, and what somehow made it worse was that I liked Patrick. He was the perfect solution. Rich, young, and handsome. I should be happy for his attention, whether it was real or not.

But not if he felt as trapped as I did.

I heard the footsteps behind me. "Miss Knox, are you well?"

Patrick. No doubt his mother had noticed me sneaking away and sent him after me. Sharply, I said, "I'm quite well, thank you. You should go back inside."

He came up close. He smelled of something citrusy and clean—a good smell among the others that never quite left the air, no matter what part of the city you were in: manure and garbage, dust and cooking food. "How can I leave a damsel in distress?"

"With some luck, you can find a white knight to save us."

"Mr. Devlin," I said, turning to face him. "You must believe me when I tell you that I expect nothing from you. You're very good to want to help, but there's . . . there's no need. Please tell me you understand me."

Awareness dawned in his gray-green eyes. "My mother's said something to you."

I looked away, toward an elm tree, the shadow of a squirrel racing crazily up its trunk. "Our parents . . ." I could not say more. I would not cry. Not in front of him. "Things are no longer what they were; you must know that. There's no more Knox's Clothing Emporium. There's nothing at all."

"What if I told you that didn't matter to me?"

"*Patrick,*" I said, his Christian name slipping out, what I'd called him always, the boy I'd once known. "I understand you might feel some obligation. Please let me release you from it. You don't have to pretend."

"I'm not pretending," he said. "I've loved you for some time, Grace. How could you not know that? All I've been doing is waiting for you."

I felt fluttery and weak-kneed; Patrick's words pierced my heart and stayed there.

"That can't be true," I whispered.

He stepped toward me, taking my arms, a loose hold, easy to break free if I'd wished it; but just then I didn't. "It's true. My mother will tell you so. Nearly every letter I wrote asked after you. I was afraid I'd return too late, that someone else would steal you away."

"We hardly know each other—"

"'And singing still dost soar, and soaring ever singest,'" he quoted. "Do you remember?"

"That's Percy Shelley."

He nodded. "'I want to be that sky-lark,' you told me once. 'To fly ever higher and sing the entire way.'"

We'd been in this very park. Aidan and Patrick and me. Clouds skimming across a summer sky, and a breeze laden with the scents of mown grass and melting sugar from the confectioner's on the corner. "I . . . I can't believe you remember that."

"It left an impression," he said. "Everything you said. I think I know you, Grace. But I begin to wonder if perhaps you don't quite know me."

"You were always Aidan's friend."

"And yours too."

"We were children then."

"You speak as if you're a hundred years old instead of just sixteen."

"Seventeen," I corrected distractedly. "In a month."

"Seventeen," he echoed. "June fourteenth."

He knew my birthday too. "This is a dream, isn't it? Pinch me so I wake up."

"Do you really want to wake from something so pleasant?"

"How do you know I find it pleasant?"

He grinned. "Because you haven't tried to pull away."

"Oh! Oh, I . . ."

"Don't pull away, Grace," he said in a low, sinking voice, and I was mesmerized. I wanted to be in this garden with him forever. He was so much more than I had ever thought possible.

Patrick reached into the pocket of his coat, drawing out a small chapbook. He pressed it into my hands. "Here. This is the book I promised you. The poet. Read it. I think you'll like it, and I think it will tell you something about me. If you want to know it." He paused. His gaze searched mine. "*Do* you want to know it, Grace?"

And I heard myself saying, without thought, without hesitation, "Yes."

His smile was quick and blinding. "My mother plans to ask you and your mother to tea. Please say yes when she does."

"I will," I promised.

"Thank you." The relief in his voice surprised me. As had everything else about this night. How fast this was. How very fast.

Patrick offered his arm. "Can I escort you back inside before they begin to miss us?"

I nodded. But he didn't move. When I glanced up at him, his eyes were dark. His gaze slid to my mouth. I knew he was going to kiss me, and suddenly I couldn't breathe.

There was a movement in the doorway just beyond. Aidan—waiting, watching, the good little chaperone, just as he'd promised Mama. Patrick stiffened. "Well then," he said, and led me back to the house.

And I was startled by how much I wished that my brother had stayed away.

THREE

Diarmid

They brought the man in cowering and trembling. His red hair was disheveled; there was a bruise on his pale cheek where Ossian had been a bit too persuasive. He wore an old deep-blue frock coat, and his gray tie was crumpled and loose about his throat.

"Please," he begged, his voice cracking. "Please, I've done nothing. I don't know what you want. Please—"

"Quiet." Finn sat on the edge of the scarred, blood-stained table they'd raided from the Butcher Boys just last week— another gang, another fight that left them bruised and battered. But they'd won it, just as they'd won the others. They'd quickly gained a reputation as one of the most indomitable gangs in the city. Well, why shouldn't they? Even without their familiar weapons, even in this strange world called New York City, they were the Fianna.

Finn spun his dagger between his fingers while the man

watched, then stabbed the point into the wood—*a bit too much*, Diarmid thought, but Finn had always been dramatic.

Diarmid glanced away. He hated the way Finn toyed and played, like a cat with a mouse. It was that mean streak in him, one you forgot most of the time, because Finn was usually just, and generous, and he was so good at knowing what they needed that sometimes Diarmid believed Finn could read his thoughts. But Finn had a temper, too, and he could hold a grudge a long time, and if he wanted something you didn't want to give him . . . more than the others, Diarmid knew what that was like. He loved and respected Finn. But Diarmid feared him in equal measure.

Finn said, "You've nothing to be afraid of."

"No?" the man squeaked. "How is that, when you *kidnapped* me from the Luxe? There are people looking for me, you know. They'll tell the police. You think I don't know who you are?"

Finn raised a dark-blond brow. "Who are we?"

"Finn's Warriors. I recognize you. We've all heard the talk on the streets."

"What talk is that?"

"That you're the worst gang since the Whyos. You wounded more than half of them in that fight even when you were caught by surprise. Seven against twenty-five. Everyone knows it. What you want from me I can't imagine. I'm no one. I've got nothing. No money—"

"You've the gift of Sight, haven't you?" Finn asked.

The man blanched. "No."

It was a lie; even Diarmid could see that from across the room.

"Is that so?" Finn glanced at Goll. "How did you find him?"

"A boy told us about him," Goll said, tugging at the newsboy's cap that now covered his light-brown hair. "Said if we were lookin' for magic we should get Cannel the Fortune-teller over on the Bowery."

"A parlor trick," Cannel protested. "Truly. I read people's faces, that's all. I tell them what they want to hear. It's nothing more than that."

Finn snatched the broadsheet from Goll, one of the many that adorned nearly every surface in the city. Finn glanced questioningly at Diarmid, who shook his head. He couldn't read it though he was the most educated of them; he'd been fostered by the love god, Aengus Og, with Manannan—master of illusion and trickery—as his tutor. But even Diarmid found the language of this place inscrutable, and it troubled him that these people so casually ascribed their greatest secrets to paper. Did they not understand the power of words?

Finn handed the broadsheet to their captive. "Read it to me."

The man licked his lips nervously. "'Bond's Circus. Three weeks only. Come see the Circassian Women! Magio the Sword Swallower! Chief Many-Scalps and his three wives!'"

"What's a Circassian woman?" Finn asked.

"Women from a harem," Cannel said. "They belonged to Turkish sultans."

Whatever that meant. Finn grunted. "What else does it say?"

"'Antonia and her amazing, three-legged dog! The Wild Man of Borneo! And introducing Cannel the Fortune-teller!'"

"The fortune-teller," Finn said, jabbing his finger into Cannel's chest. "Why would it say that if you weren't?"

"It's all a show!" Cannel cried. "It's a sideshow, for pity's sake! The Circassian women are just girls with curled hair!"

Finn gestured to Keenan, a tall man with a chiseled face and thick brown hair tied in a queue that flopped between his shoulder blades.

"He read your hand, didn't he? What did he say to you?" Finn asked.

"That I'd cared for birds. That I had strength enough to kill a formidable enemy. Something to do with the sea, he said."

Diarmid caught his breath. In Ireland, long ago, Keenan had been charged with the task of bringing two of every kind of bird as a hostage price to win Finn's freedom. And it had been Keenan who killed Lir, the god of the sea, Manannan's father, during the Great War between the gods.

Finn's full lips curled. He turned back to Cannel. "I think you have more power than you're admitting, *cainte*. Now why don't you tell us the truth? We're in need of a Seer, as it happens. If you do the task well, we'll let you live."

Cannel swallowed hard. "I can't. I don't think I've the skill you need."

Finn asked Goll, "Did you bring his divining tools?"

Goll reached into his pocket and took out a deck of very worn, tattered-edged cards, handing them to Finn, who looked ill at ease as he touched them. He set them on the table without rifling through them—one did not meddle with another's magic.

"Tell us what you know," Finn ordered Cannel.

Cannel glanced around the room, and Diarmid saw the resignation on his face. "I need a chair."

Finn made a motion, and Ossian brought over a barrel, setting it down with a thud. Cannel flipped up the skirt of his coat before he sat and picked up the cards. His hands were clumsy and shaking. "I need a question first," Cannel said hoarsely. "Tell me what you want to know."

"Where is the *veleda*?" Finn said.

Cannel frowned. "What's a *veleda*?"

"A Druid priestess."

Cannel swallowed again. "You won't find that in New York City, I'm afraid."

But he shuffled the cards, separating them into piles, murmuring the question. They all watched. It was never quiet in their flat; the sounds of outside—horses and wagons and children playing, couples screaming drunken obscenities at each other, gang fights—echoed through the thin walls and floors, but Diarmid felt the silence of his fellows like a force, and he knew the Seer felt it too.

Cannel fumbled with the cards, laying them out in a facedown formation. Diarmid had seen oracles divine with ogham sticks and the entrails of animals, the flight patterns of birds, or the movements of the heavens, but this was new. He watched curiously, feeling the power in the little man at the table grow with every passing moment. Whatever Cannel's protests, there *was* some magic in him.

Finally, the cards were all laid out. Cannel turned them over one by one, studying them. No one said anything. They knew to be patient with Seers—interruption could be fatal.

"She's here," Cannel said. "You were right. This—What did you call her?"

"*Veleda*," Finn provided.

"Yes. This *veleda* is in the city. I can't tell for certain where. Somewhere near." Cannel bent closer. "There are others around her. A society or . . . a club."

"What kind of club?" Finn asked.

"I don't know. I can't tell." Cannel lifted another card, studied it, frowned. He looked up, scanning the room, his gaze stopping on Diarmid. Uncomfortably, Diarmid shifted against the wall.

"What?" Finn's gaze followed Cannel's. "What is it? What do you see?"

"I think it's him," Cannel said.

"Diarmid? What about him?"

"Diarmid?" Something flashed in Cannel's eyes, some troubling understanding. He looked again at the cards, turning up another, frowning more deeply. "Yes. A dark-haired young man with blue eyes. And . . . and a spear. A bad death."

Diarmid's gut began to churn.

Oscar said with a nudge, "Well, that would be you, wouldn't it, Derry? What does it say about him?"

"That he's been chosen." Cannel pursed his lips. "There's a prophecy. A promise."

Finn's gaze hardened. Diarmid's dread grew as his leader took a few steps toward him. "What prophecy would that be, my friend?" Finn asked very, very softly. "What promise?"

"Something about this *veleda*." Cannel looked up from the cards. "His aspect surrounds her."

Diarmid's mouth went dry. He'd faced a hundred warriors alone, warring kings and thundering gods and vengeful men shape-changed into angry boars. But Finn's measuring expression was worse than all of them.

Diarmid wanted to turn away, but he pulled himself off the wall, standing straight. "There was a prophecy. Manannan told it to me. There was no *veleda* then—it didn't matter. I'd forgotten it."

Finn waited.

"He—he told me that it was by my hand that the *veleda* must die. That if I didn't do this, we would fail, even if she'd chosen us."

"I see." Finn's expression was grim. "And you didn't think it important enough to tell me before now?"

"Do you see a *veleda*?" Diarmid asked evenly. "Where is she? Even he"—Diarmid pointed to Cannel—"can't see where she is. I would have mentioned it once we found her. Once she chose."

"I should have known this before."

"How does it matter if we don't find her?" Diarmid asked.

"And if we do?" Finn countered. "Can you look into pretty eyes and wield a knife, Diarmid?"

It was a fair question. Girls were his weakness. They had always been. "She's a *veleda*," Diarmid said. "She'll know what has to be done, won't she? 'Tisn't as if I'll be killing an innocent."

"Killing an innocent?" Cannel's voice went high. "You mean to *kill* her?"

"Can you do it?" Finn demanded again.

Diarmid heard the challenge. He met Finn's gaze. "Aye. I can do it."

Cannel rose. "Look, I want no part of this. Not killing. I don't know what you need with this *veleda*, but—"

Finn set his hand on Cannel's shoulder, pushing him down. "Shall I tell you who we truly are, *cainte*? You're a Flannery, aren't you? Have you heard of the Fianna? Of Ossian and Oscar? Diarmid Ua Duibhne?"

Cannel's eyes widened. "Yes, of course I have, but—"

"We are the Fianna," Finn declared.

"*The* Fianna? The warriors of the High King? But . . . it's a tale told to children."

"Called back from undying sleep, tasked with helping Ireland in her hour of need," Finn went on. "The prophecy is laid: when we're called, the *veleda* must decide whether our fight is worthy. And then she must sacrifice herself to her choice. If she does not choose us, we fail and die." He paused. "And so we find ourselves in a confusing state. No caller or *veleda* in sight. We don't know why we were summoned or why the horn brought us to this place instead of to Ireland. These are things we must discover. And we need your help for it."

Cannel looked at each of them. Diarmid felt the truth land on the Seer—settle, stay.

"Help us find her," Finn said. "So we can win her power. So we can discover why we're here and return to Ireland. Once we're gone, you can go back to your life. We won't hold you."

"You're the Fianna," Cannel murmured. "It can't be true. This isn't some . . . this is impossible."

"Is it?" Finn asked. "What do your cards say?"

"I don't need the cards." Cannel glanced back to Finn. "You're Finn MacCool. Truly Finn MacCool."

"In the flesh. And I've made you a promise, Seer. I've never yet broken a vow. Help us find the *veleda* and our task, and we'll release you."

Cannel nodded. Hero worship was in his eyes now, an expression Diarmid had known well once upon a time, and one that he was just beginning to see again since they'd defeated the Whyos and the Butcher Boys. When they passed, little boys turned to their friends and whispered, pallid-faced girls tendered hesitant smiles. Diarmid had to admit that he never grew tired of it—though he tried to remember that pride had been their undoing.

Cannel fingered the cards. He turned over another. And then he noted, "It says here that we haven't much time."

"What do you mean?" Finn demanded.

"This card signifies the Otherworld. The door between worlds."

"This we know. The sacrifice must take place on Samhain, when the veil between worlds is thinnest," Finn said. "We have until then to win the *veleda*'s choice."

Cannel nodded. "That's October thirty-first. It's already May. Only five months."

"And if we don't find who called us?"

Cannel looked back at the cards. "Death. Disaster. Chaos. I can't see you past this. Any of you."

"You're certain of it?"

"I'm rarely wrong."

"That isn't what you told us when you arrived," Finn pointed out.

Cannel flushed. Finn turned to the rest of them. "Well then, it's quick work, but nothing we can't handle."

"I'm betting a week or less before we find her," Ossian boasted, tossing his white-blond head. "We'll be in the hills of Ireland before we know it."

The others cheered.

Only Diarmid was quiet.

This was a place of marvels. Messages traveled through wire, paper so common—and printed, no less—that it fluttered from every post and wall. Ships ran on steam, and streetcars raced on rails. Houses were piped with light, and black stones burned for hours to heat even the largest rooms. Miracles.

Though few of those miracles seemed to reach this part of the city. Even the streetlamps seemed dim here, as if the light were afraid to reach out into the darkness. Just now, the moon was full, and its brightness barely sneaked past the tall buildings leaning together to block the sky. Darkness was always the way of it here; the warrens of dead ends and alcoves were always shadowed, where men too drunk to walk—or dead—huddled. Dust rose in clouds and hazed both sun and moonlight. Narrow, unlit hallways and stairs so dark they were impenetrable even at noon, hazardous and slippery with wet and slime and sometimes other things. Piles of garbage in the streets that came to Diarmid's knees, riddled with rats.

He missed the green hills of home. More than that, he missed the peace of it. Here, even at night, the streets were full, people camping out on the flimsy landings of fire escapes, trying to flee the stink of the tenement flats and the heat—only late spring, and the rooms were already too hot and suffocating to bear. There were people on the rooftops too: women doing laundry in the cool of the night, children shouting and racing, couples courting, and men and women drinking and talking. From down the street came raucous yelling from some stale-beer dive or a two-cent lodging house.

Diarmid sat on the stoop, leaning back against the wooden rail. He tilted his head, trying to see the sky, instead seeing people leaning out of their windows.

"Going out tonight, Derry?"

"I heard you boys was going after the Black Hands next. I got a wager on ya!"

"You look lonely, lad. Want some company?"

The last was from Mrs. Mahoney, who never failed to give

him a grin and a wink when he went by. Diarmid called up, "When I do, you'll be the first to know."

She laughed, and he looked down at his legs, covered now with coarse trousers and his boots, which were dirty with dust and manure. They'd traded their grave raiment for modern dress. It had bought enough to clothe all seven of them and to buy food for a time. But now the money was mostly gone. Dry and moldy bread yesterday, purloined from ash cans and garbage piles. A few limp and rat-bit carrots. There would need to be more coin and soon, especially with the challenges they faced: rival gangs wanting to test them, simply surviving. Not to mention the task they'd been brought back for, which they didn't yet know.

He heard footsteps behind him, felt the heaviness of a hand on his shoulder, and he looked back to see Oscar, whose hair—the same pale blond as his father's—shone like a beacon in the night even without any light shining upon it.

"You didn't want any ale?"

Diarmid shook his head. Conan had managed to find a small keg somewhere, and the others were celebrating that they'd found a Seer who'd agreed to help them—not that he'd had much choice.

Oscar sat beside him, settling his forearms on his knees, letting his hands dangle. "What are you doing out here?"

"Nothing. Thinking."

"I'd give almost anything for a good bed and decent mead. Last night I dreamed of a roast. I was chewing straw when I woke up."

"We'll have those things again," Diarmid said.

"Aye."

Diarmid wasn't surprised when Oscar asked quietly, "Was it a *geis* Manannan put on you? To kill the *veleda*? Or just a prophecy?"

Prophecy could change as events changed. Where there was free will, nothing was absolute. But a *geis* was something altogether different. It was a spell of sorts, a condition, a prohibition. To refuse it meant shame and death.

"A *geis*," Diarmid said.

"Ah. You didn't even tell *me*."

Diarmid shrugged. "I never thought any of this would happen, did you? Called back to help Ireland . . . a pretty dream it was, I thought."

"I hoped for it," Oscar said. "But no, I didn't really think it would happen."

"I'll do what's required. You know I will."

"I don't doubt you."

"Finn does."

"Well. Aye." Oscar chuckled. "Can you blame him? When it comes to you and the lasses—you've the softest heart of all of us. But I guess that's what comes of being fostered by Aengus Og."

"I won't give Finn another reason to doubt my loyalty."

Oscar sobered. "It's been a long time since Grainne, Derry."

"He'll never forget it."

"He regretted it. Letting you die. He won't risk losing you a second time."

"I wish I had your faith. But I promise you: if something comes between us this time, it won't be some lass."

Oscar nodded. "Speaking of which, how about the two of us go out and find one or two? The others won't miss us for a while."

Diarmid smiled. "You never learn."

"Come on. Don't tell me you don't long for a soft breast to lie your head upon. It's been what . . . two thousand years, give or take?"

"There are ten saloons at least on this block alone," Diarmid pointed out. "Take your pick. I'm sure you'll find a lass or two among them."

"I haven't time for wooing. 'Twould be easier if you were along to flash that lovespot."

Diarmid's hand went to the spot on his forehead, the *ball seirce* a fairy had bestowed upon him because he'd been the only one of them to recognize her magic. It felt as it always did—a raised scar like a burn. He kept his hair long, falling in his eyes, to cover it. He'd enjoyed it at first—any lass who saw it fell in love with him, and he'd liked having anyone he wanted. And then he began to feel . . . empty. Now it was more a curse than a gift. He'd stopped being able to tell—was it really he those girls had loved, or was it just the spell? Even with Grainne—especially with Grainne. He swept his thick, dark hair forward again to cover the spot.

"Excess, if you ask me," Oscar grumbled, as he had a hundred times before. "You're handsome enough already."

"The *ball seirce* wouldn't help you anyway. It's me they'd want, and I don't want to have to fight you over jealousy."

"Ah, but what kind of a friend would you be if you didn't throw one my way?"

"I don't even know if it works in this world."

"Why not try it out? What can it hurt?" Oscar asked.

"We've trouble enough without courting more."

Oscar sighed. "Aye. I suppose you're right. But any bed would be a sight better than that pile of straw."

"Ask Conan to borrow his sheepskin."

"By the gods, I swear I'll throw that thing from the window before the week is done. If it gets much hotter, the smell of it will make us all sick."

Diarmid laughed.

"That's better," Oscar said. "All right then, no lasses. But how about we go on down to the Bowery and see the sights? I've a wish to be out and about tonight instead of locked up in that flat with a bunch of sweaty soldiers."

The Bowery was a street of theaters and pleasure houses, saloons and dance halls and shops, lined with gaslights of colored glass globes unlike anything Diarmid had ever seen. Gang boys roaming and drinking, girls sashaying, pickpockets and thieves and very rich men with top hats and polished boots and everyone having a good time. Tonight it sounded fun, something to lift his mood, to ease the dread that had settled in his chest and didn't seem to want to let go.

He smiled and rose. "To the Bowery it is."

FOUR

May 22

Patrick

The streetlamps cast a soothing yellow glow through the haze of dust as Patrick Devlin walked up Broadway. The chaos and congestion that usually clogged the street during the day had given way to one or two wagons making night deliveries, carriages heading to the opera or the theater or a supper party, men going to their clubs. There were couples walking and tired newsboys and vendors making their way home, but no tramps and vagrants—not in this part of town. Here the rich were still rich. Here there were no empty shop windows and warehouses given over to auction marts selling off the goods of those who had gone bankrupt. When he was in this part of town, Patrick believed all things must still be possible.

He reached for the bag looped over his shoulder, patting it as he had many times since he'd left the house, reassuring himself that the stone was still there. Tonight would be different from the last time. Tonight they would not fail. He knew it.

He'd chosen to walk instead of call for the carriage because he didn't want anyone to know where he was going, not so late. Lucy and his mother were used to his comings and goings. As long as he kept the world right for them, they hardly cared what he did. The thought irritated him. They had never embraced the cause that he and his father lived for. For them, Ireland was far away, a place to come from but never to return to. And perhaps once he'd felt the same way. Before he'd spent three years there and seen such poverty and despair. Though he supposed even that would make no difference to Lucy, who was as self-absorbed as she'd been when he'd left.

Not like Grace.

The way she'd said *yes* when he'd asked her if she wanted to know him. That breathy and yearning sigh. He had dreamed about that voice, about her face, for three years. It was his father's wish that one day the Devlin and Knox businesses would be combined, but Patrick had never cared about that. She'd always been around, throughout his childhood, a little sister for him and Aidan to tease. But then, one day, only months before he'd left for Ireland, she had come to the house to see Lucy, and he had been . . . struck. Grace had been just fourteen, thoughtful and clever and romantic. He'd realized then that he wanted her in his world.

But she was too young, and Ireland was waiting. He'd assumed he would forget her. There were too many other things to think about: keeping the business afloat after his father's death, reassuring their suppliers, tending to his mother and sister. But he'd been unable to stop thinking of Grace. Even when things had settled and he'd got involved in the Irish side of the Fenian Brotherhood and it had taken over everything, thoughts of her haunted him. He saw her in a dark-haired girl on a Dublin street, in a pile of dusty books, in a pretty ribbon dangling from a vendor's cart. When his mother had written to him of her father's death, he'd wanted to return home, but it was impossible. And then he'd heard of the Knoxes' troubles, and Grace's likely early debut, and he had rushed home as soon as he could. The rebellion he'd helped organize had failed, and he was depressed and angry. He'd wanted someone to care.

Yes, she'd said.

Now, finally, it looked as if he might have everything he'd ever dreamed of.

The brick clubhouse of the Fenian Brotherhood loomed before him. Patrick clutched the bag more tightly and climbed the stairs. Before he reached the door, it was opened by Rory Nolan, a solid and craggy-faced man with graying temples.

"Patrick," he said, ushering him inside, closing the door behind them. "The others are already here."

Patrick's pulse raced as he followed Rory past the second-floor offices and club room decorated in greens and golds, to the meeting room on the top floor. There was a table in the center of the room, but all the chairs had been cleared away. A lamp stood on the table. A long, slender piece of wood, carved with what looked like runes, rested on a cloth of green velvet.

The men around the table were haloed in the lamplight, the rest of the room shrouded in darkness. All of them were older than Patrick. Only Jonathan Olwen was close in age. They had been in Ireland together, and had returned together too. Now, as Patrick approached the table, Jonathan shoved a nervous hand through his thinning brown hair. His smile of welcome was strained. Jonathan had argued against what they were doing tonight, but in the end he'd reluctantly agreed.

Gray-haired Simon MacRonan came forward. His blue eyes glittered as he reached out a hand.

Patrick offered the bag to Simon, who opened it eagerly, taking out the flat piece of stone called an ogham stick because it was etched with the ancient Druid writing, ogham. Simon looked reverently down at the stone, and then he made a noise like a yelp and dropped it to the table.

"What is it?" Patrick asked. "What's wrong?"

"It burned," said Simon. Then he smiled. "And that's good, lad. That means it's real."

"It didn't burn me."

"There's no Druid blood in your family, as we've learned already, much to our dismay."

Patrick flushed. He tried not to think of that night three weeks ago, the certainty he'd felt as he'd dripped Lucy's blood from the little vial onto the horn. It had cost her a pinprick—nothing more, and he'd done it while she'd slept. The blood of the *veleda*, he'd hoped, as they all had. It was his heritage—his father had often said that the Devlins were descended from the Druids at Allen, the seat of the Fianna. And when the horn had come to Patrick and they'd discovered it was the *dord fiann* of the prophecy, Patrick had known the spell already—it had been in a story passed down through his family. The *dord fiann*, the blood of the *veleda*, the incantation, and then the blowing of the horn three times. They'd done it all in this very room.

But something had gone wrong. The Fianna had not appeared.

"Your sister's no veleda," Simon had snapped. *"Has your family any Druid blood?"*

A lifetime of believing, of knowing he was special, gone in a moment. Patrick couldn't help hating Simon for it, though he also needed him. They all needed him. Only Simon could read ogham, and he was descended from Druid priests and had the Sight too—another thing that should have been in Patrick's family and wasn't. Just looking at Lucy should've told Patrick she wasn't the *veleda*. She was too vain and silly. He wondered why those stories had been in his family at all.

Simon hovered over the ogham stick, pushing at it quickly with his fingers, as if it were burning hot, moving it into place beside the rowan wand.

"Are you sure we want to do this?" Jonathan asked quietly. "It's not too late to stop."

Patrick glanced up, frowning.

Rory Nolan said, "The rebellion failed. There's no money coming in. We need something to convince people a new rebellion will succeed."

"Perhaps we should wait a little longer," Jonathan insisted.

"It's only been a few days. Perhaps the Fianna will still come."

"It's been three weeks," Patrick said. "How long should we wait? People are dying over there. Families starving. You saw it too. Will you be the one to explain to them that we were waiting for a spell we already knew didn't work?"

Jonathan looked wary. "But the Fomori . . . surely there's someone else——"

"Who else? These things fell into our hands for a reason. We need an army that won't fail. We were meant to use them."

"And we can't delay further," said Rory. "It could take years to stumble upon another spell."

"The Fomori enslaved the Irish once before," Jonathan noted. "Our ancestors went to war *against* them. Then we had the old gods on our side. That's who we need: the Tuatha de Dannan."

"If you can find a spell to summon them, by all means do so," Rory said. "Thus far there doesn't appear to be such a thing. But there *is* a spell to summon the Fomori."

"The world has changed, Jon," Patrick said as reassuringly as he could. "Do you really think we can't control the Fomori now? We're civilized men——"

"We've weapons, money, and politicians in our pocket," added Rory. "We'll make them do as we bid instead of the other way around."

"And there's no other way. We need them," said Patrick.

He believed it too. His disappointment over the Fianna failure tormented him. Then Simon had found the rowan wand, half of the Fomori spell—they only needed the ogham stick—and Patrick had remembered the relic his father had brought from Ireland ten years before, which was in a display case in his study. That it had been *the* ogham stick they needed seemed a sign. The Fomori, the Children of the goddess Domnu, who had fought the old gods, the Tuatha de Dannan, and their allies, the Fianna, for the rule of Ireland—battles that had been fought over and over again throughout history. The stories said that the Fomori were the gods of chaos, but history was written by the victors. It was in the interest of the Fianna and the old gods to depict the Fomori as evil. Enemies were always so. *Thus are legends made,* thought Patrick.

Simon glanced up. "Well? Shall we continue?"

There was a murmur of ayes, Patrick's among them. Jonathan hesitated, but then nodded.

Simon bent over the items again. He began murmuring, and then his voice grew louder, words in Gaelic that Patrick translated in his head: "Darkness and thunder, blood and fire. The eye of one who slays. As one is bid, so come the rest. The rowan wand and virtue gone. A blood price paid. Now come the Children of Domnu."

Simon said them once, and then again. The third time, he picked up the rowan wand, grasping it high above his head, and strode counterclockwise around the table.

Patrick watched, the hairs on the back of his neck rising, the magic in the room growing and pulsing. The wand brightened as if the lamp shone on it, and then he realized that no, it wasn't the lamplight at all—the wand was *glowing*. Glowing ever brighter, brighter and brighter until its light pierced the room, and he had to close his eyes and look away because it was like staring at the sun. Simon's voice rose into a high and keening wail, a near scream, as he said in Gaelic, "And now the Erne shall rise in rude torrents, hills shall be rent. The sea shall roll in red waves. Now come the Children of Domnu!"

The last words were a cry like thunder, loud and roaring so that Patrick wanted to cover his ears against it. The magic was paralyzing and horrible. The lamp puffed out, the wand leaped to terrible brightness and then died. Simon collapsed onto the floor. Darkness fell hard and complete.

Silence pounded in Patrick's ears, and then he heard the room breathing, the faint in-and-out hush of the walls, the shivering of the floor as if he stood on something alive. They all stood as if held in place; Patrick was afraid to move. *What have we done?* But then someone lit the lamp again, and as Patrick blinked in the sudden light, Simon was helped to his feet.

"Now what?" Rory asked. "Did it work?"

"It felt like it worked," Patrick said.

"So did the Fianna horn," Jonathan reminded them.

And it had. There'd been the same sense of the room coming alive, the magic growing and ebbing like a tide.

"We'll wait until midnight," Rory said. "Then we'll all go home and see what happens."

There was a knock on the front door.

Patrick started. They shouldn't have been able to hear it from the third floor. But this was loud and urgent, again a sound like thunder. The whole building seemed to reverberate.

His heart climbed to his throat. He glanced across to Jonathan and saw the same fear tightening his friend's face.

No, not fear. He didn't want to feel fear. This was the answer to a prayer. A sign. Everything he'd ever wanted.

"Well," Simon said with a smug smile. "It seems we have our answer."

He headed for the stairs, and they all followed. Patrick was caught up in the excitement. The spell had worked. The magic was real!

At the bottom of the staircase, Simon paused. They gathered behind him like children waiting for someone to throw candy. Simon grinned—it reminded Patrick of the illustration of the Morrigan, the Irish war goddess, he had in his study.

Simon opened the door.

Standing on the threshold was a man. He was soaked to the skin, dark hair dripping lank to his shoulders, his clothing—an embroidered linen shirt, a scarlet cape—clinging to him. He stood in a pool of gathering water, though the night was dry and hot. There hadn't been rain in days. Other than that, he looked like any man. He was of medium height and muscled. A thin scar slashed his cheek.

He looked at Simon and then past him, to where the others stood on the last few stairs.

"Hello, lads," he said. "'Tis Daire Donn, King of the World and ally of the Fomori. I am their messenger. I believe you called?"

FIVE

Earlier that day

Grace

I felt I moved in a dream those next days. I thought about gorgeous Patrick Devlin and the way his gaze had lingered on my mouth—I must have relived that moment a hundred times. He could not really have said *"You were only just becoming a beauty."* Or he *had* said it but he hadn't meant it. None of it. Not the *"I've loved you for some time,"* nor the *"Do you want to know me, Grace?"*—or at least he hadn't said it in that way that clutched my heart and made me answer "Yes," and in my head, *Yes yes yes.*

I told myself he would think better of those things. There would be no invitation to tea, and nothing more would come of it.

But the invitation for me and my mother arrived, delivered by a messenger boy who stood on the stoop and said to Mama, "I'm to wait for an answer, ma'am"; and I began to think that perhaps my dreams of romance might come true after all.

My mother turned to me with a knowing look. "Now why, I wonder, would Sarah Devlin be so anxious to have us to tea, Grace?"

"I believe she thinks her son and I would make a good match."

"Patrick," Mama mused.

"Don't tell me you didn't know," I accused. "You've already spoken to Mrs. Devlin. The two of you conspired—"

Mama swept my words away with "Are you averse to such a match?"

"No," I admitted.

"Then it hardly matters how it came about."

I'd been reading the book Patrick had given me that he'd said would tell me something about him. The poet was James Clarence Mangan. An Irish poet, as Patrick had said, and at first all I'd seen were pretty poems about Ireland and ancient heroes.

But the more I read, the more I saw what Patrick must have wished me to see. The poems were pretty, yes, but they were much more than that. "Lament for Banba" held the lines: "For the hour soon may loom / When the Lord's mighty hand / Shall be raised for our rescue once more!" And in "Dark Rosaleen": "'Tis you shall reign, shall reign alone, / My Dark Rosaleen!" I remembered what Aidan had said about Patrick being a member of the Fenian Brotherhood, and I understood. These were poems of war, about Ireland rebelling against British rule. Patrick was telling me of his passion for Ireland and her politics.

I closed the book, looking out my window onto the street below, and tried to decide how I felt about Patrick's involvement. I thought of the way he looked at me, the things he'd said. Ireland didn't matter to me, but I liked the passion it inspired in him. I liked that there were things that mattered to him beyond himself. He wasn't like the other boys I knew, who talked only about horses and drinking. He was like those men in the stories I loved: heroes riding into battle because the world needed saving. Patrick *was* a white knight.

I rubbed my thumb across the worn cover; clearly Patrick had read this book many times, and suddenly I could not wait to discuss it with him, to discover more of him.

——∞— *May 25* —∞——

It wasn't the butler who opened the door for us when Mama and I arrived at the Devlins' for tea but Patrick himself. "You're here at last," he said, looking at me, making my heart flutter. "Come in, please. Mama and Lucy are waiting."

"You won't be joining us?" I asked, trying not to sound disappointed when he led us to the parlor.

"I've business to attend to first, I'm afraid. But it shouldn't take long. I'll be with you shortly."

I couldn't help smiling like a fool, and he smiled back; and it was a moment before I realized we were just standing there smiling at each other while everyone looked on. I ducked my head, and Patrick said, "I'll be quick, I promise," and left.

"How wonderful that you could come," Mrs. Devlin said

as she poured tea. "Dare I hope that this means your mother is feeling better?"

"I'm afraid not," Mama said. "But we've left Aidan with her, and I trust she's in good hands."

I said nothing, though Mama and I both knew it would be a miracle if Aidan were still there when we returned. I watched as Lucy smiled distractedly and wandered to the window.

Mrs. Devlin said, "Lucy, my dear," and then, to us, "I'm afraid my daughter is not herself this afternoon."

"I'm quite myself," Lucy disagreed. "More myself than ever, I believe."

I knew that tone. Lucy was in love. The Astor boy still, or someone new?

Mrs. Devlin said in a low voice, "You must forgive her. She's been in a state. Now, Maeve, you must tell me—" She was off then, speaking again of Grandma's health, and Mama and she were soon engaged in conversation.

I went over to Lucy, following her gaze. Nothing but the park beyond the windows, fully leafed trees trembling in a warm breeze. I said, "We're blocks from the Astor house. You couldn't hope to see him from here."

"The Astor house?" she asked blankly, and then, "Oh. Oh no. I'm done with him."

"I suppose that's best, as you had no hope of him." It was a bit harsh to say it, but there was something about Lucy that brought out the worst in me.

She threw me an annoyed glance. "Yes, I know. And he's a callow boy anyway. Nothing like—" She broke off.

So Lucy had another secret love. If she wouldn't even tell me his name, he must be equally inappropriate. I sipped my tea and tried to ask casually, "Nothing like whom?"

"You wouldn't understand."

"Why do you say that?"

"Because all you care about are your poets and your stories. Why, until Patrick, I've never even seen you look at a boy."

"I've looked," I protested.

"You're so innocent sometimes, Grace. You think love is chaste and sweet and *romantic*, and it's not. It's burning and overwhelming and . . . and *messy*. It never does what you want."

Messy, yes, Lucy would think that, given that she'd never once fallen for anyone she could actually have. I said, "Well, you should know, given how often you're in love."

"This time it's *real*."

As it had supposedly been every time before. "If that's so, then you'd best tell me who it is, as I'll no doubt be seeing you with him."

"I can't be with him." A sigh. "We're like Romeo and Juliet."

"Your families are bitter enemies?"

"No, but . . ." Lucy glanced toward her mother. "But Mama would never accept him. Nor would Patrick."

"Why not?"

"Because he's a stableboy."

I choked. "A stableboy?"

"Keep your voice down."

"Oh, for goodness' sake, Lucy. You can't be serious."

"Why shouldn't I be?"

"Because he's a *stableboy*. He's even less acceptable than that gardener you liked."

"Sometimes I think it's a curse to have money," she said mournfully.

I wanted to hit her. "You don't mean that, Lucy."

"But I do. All these *things* . . ." She pulled at the lace on her bodice. "If I were poor, who I am wouldn't matter. We could be together."

"I think you'd miss your fine feather bed."

"I wouldn't," she said, almost viciously. "I would give up everything for him."

"You're mad," I said, thinking of bill collectors and furniture going out the door never to be seen again and my family in the poorhouse on Blackwell's Island. "You have no idea what you're talking about."

She ignored me. "And the most terrible thing is that it must be secret. Patrick would dismiss him in a moment if he knew. I had to beg him to hire Derry as it was."

"You begged Patrick to hire him? Since when have you had anything to do with the stables?"

"Derry needed a job. It was the only position Patrick had for him."

"I see. Wherever did you meet this paragon of manhood?"

"He was in the park. I saw him and he was . . . he's the most handsome boy I've ever seen, Grace. He's . . . Well, there's no describing him. I just looked at him, and I knew."

"When was this?"

"Two days ago."

I wanted to laugh. Trust Lucy to fall in love so quickly and deeply. And then I remembered Patrick, and suddenly it didn't seem so stupid. There *was* something magical about Madison Square in the gaslight.

"Well, I'm certain everything will work out," I said to soothe her, but I didn't really believe it. Lucy was right: her family would never allow her to be with a stableboy.

She gripped my arm. "You mustn't say a word," she whispered urgently. "If you tell a soul, I'll be ruined. Promise me. Promise me you'll say nothing."

I shook off her arm. "You're hurting me."

"Promise!"

"All right," I said.

She looked past me. Patrick had come into the room, and I felt warm when I saw the way his eyes came directly to me.

His mother said, "Patrick, my dear, is your business done?"

"For now," he said.

Lucy hissed in my ear, "Especially not to Patrick."

"We're hardly—"

"Promise."

I nodded.

She drew away. "You're so lucky, Grace. You don't know what it's like to want what you can't have."

How little she knows of me, I thought bitterly. I heard Patrick say to his mother, "Would you ladies mind if I took Miss Knox away for a few moments? Just outside, where you can see us."

My bitterness faded. When he stepped over to me and said "Would you take a stroll, Miss Knox?" I forgot all about Lucy and her stableboy.

"I would be delighted, Mr. Devlin." I ignored my mother's relieved smile, and Mrs. Devlin's doting look, as I went with Patrick out into the garden. Blooming roses in peach and pink bordered the walk that led the short distance to the park, and I remembered their scent—sweet and heavy—from the last time we'd come here. Their fragrance brought that night sweeping back, and the way he'd said, *"I've loved you for some time."* I grew hot, looking down at my boots where they peeked from under the hem of my gown—my second best— of sage-green twill.

He stopped a little ways out. "I think I shall always remember the last time we were out here as the sweetest night of my life."

I felt nervous and excited at the same time. I wanted the way he looked at me, but feared it too. I wasn't used to it. I still didn't quite believe it. "Patrick, this is all so quick."

"Not for me." He looked at me quizzically. "Am I rushing you, Grace? Would you prefer to go more slowly?"

He overwhelmed me. I wanted to go slow. I wanted to go faster. I hardly knew which.

He added, "I know it's been a difficult time for you. Your father's death was hard enough, and now, with all the rest . . . what a struggle it must be. But you've been so brave. When my own father died so suddenly, I felt as if the world had ended."

My father's death had been sudden too. His heart had

simply given out. I remembered how terrible it had been, the messenger at the door, my mother's white face. "Yes. It felt exactly like that."

"One moment everything's fine, and the next, everything is different, and there's nothing you can do to make things the way they were. I never thought I'd recover."

How well he understood. His smile was so sad and tender I wanted to put my arms around him. "But you did recover, Patrick. You've done so well for your family. Your father would be proud."

"Your father would be proud of you too, Grace," he said, and I could tell that he meant it. "I know he would."

Impulsively, I took his hand, weaving my fingers through his. The moment I did it, I was horrified at my boldness, but the look that came into his eyes made me not want to draw away.

Again, I was afraid of what he would say and how much I wanted. I said quickly, "I read the book you gave me."

"And what did you think?"

"I think you're very . . . passionate. Aidan says you belong to the Fenian Brotherhood."

"For some time now."

"Is that why you went to Ireland?"

He hesitated. "Partly. My father had business interests there. But yes, I was there because of the Brotherhood as well."

"I hadn't realized you had such a love for Ireland."

He laughed. "Really? You haven't noticed the relics all over the house?"

"Well, those, of course." I flushed at his teasing. "But I thought that was your father's collection."

"It is. It was. But it became ours together. I'm as interested in antiquities as he was."

"What I meant to say was that I didn't know you harbored such a love for the land itself."

"The people—*our* people—are oppressed there, Grace. They're dying beneath British rule. The rich landlords are taking everything, leaving poverty and hopelessness. Our only hope is for rebellion." He spoke so intently, with a restless fire in his eyes. He was suddenly not the Patrick I knew, but I realized this was his true self. I thought of the poem I'd read, "Dark Rosaleen."

I quoted, "'O, the Erne shall run red, with redundance of blood.'"

He looked stunned. "You did read them."

"Of course I did. I wanted to know you."

Our hands were still linked. He tugged lightly, so I nearly fell into him, and then he kissed me—my first kiss, and it was just as I'd imagined it would be. His lips were soft and warm, tentative at first, and then he pressed harder, parting my lips, and at the brush of his tongue, I felt something drop inside me. I wanted to pull him closer, but before I could, he drew away, leaving me breathless, overwhelmed. I didn't want it to be over.

He whispered against my mouth, "I must be the luckiest man alive."

We were both lucky.

———

I felt as if I danced on clouds. There was nothing that could trouble me, not even the fact that Aidan wasn't home when we returned, just as I'd predicted. I couldn't even bring myself to be angry or annoyed as I went upstairs to check on my grandmother, who was sound asleep.

I turned to go, but then I heard her whisper, *"Mo chroi."*

I looked over my shoulder. "It's all right, Grandma. I didn't mean to wake you."

With a frail and withered hand, she gestured for me to come close.

"You're happy," she said—it was almost an accusation. "That boy."

"Patrick Devlin. Yes."

"No. The other one."

"There is no other one. There's only Patrick. Always and forever."

Grandma grabbed my hand, squeezing it hard. She was surprisingly strong. She looked confused, and my heart fell. "Don't trust him."

"Who? You mean Patrick?"

"He will keep you safe."

More and more confusing. I pulled my hand gently from her grasp. "Sssh. It's all right, Grandma. You should rest."

"They are coming. It's you they want."

"And Patrick will keep me safe, as you said." I pretended

to understand, wanting only to soothe her back to sleep. "Shall I give you some laudanum?"

Her eyes closed and then flickered open as if she was struggling to stay awake. "They're coming. That boy. And the *sidhe*. You must remember."

The *sidhe*. The fairies. *Again.* My joy of the afternoon faltered. "I know. I will remember. I promise."

My words seemed to comfort her at last. She closed her eyes. Her breathing became deep and even.

Carefully, I tiptoed to the door. My grandmother was fading quickly. Today I'd spent more time listening to illusion than to reality. I doubted it was something a doctor could fix, even if we had the money to pay one.

Another thing I needed Patrick for. It wasn't a pleasant thought. He had so much, and we had so little, and I wished I could be certain that he wanted me for myself and not out of some obligation. *A white knight.* Would Patrick still have wanted me if Papa were alive and everything was as it had been? Or was it only that I needed his help?

I went to my room and undressed and got into bed, closing my eyes, thinking of his kiss, breathing deeply of roses. But when I finally fell asleep, it wasn't into sweet dreams of the boy I thought I could love, but into another nightmare—a piercing glow and the world streaked with fire; the Erne flowing red with blood; my ears full of the fierce and terrifying caws of ravens and thunder and my grandmother's words:

They are coming.

SIX

May 26

Diarmid

Diarmid was brushing a lovely mare named Erin, whispering in her ear as he did so, Gaelic words, sounds like music, when he heard the light tap of a boot. He paused to see Lucy Devlin come into the stable and tried to ignore his sudden surge of loneliness. It didn't matter, did it? He had a duty, and Lucy Devlin was part of it.

She was the reason he was in the Devlins' stable to begin with. He'd met her three days ago, after deliberately searching her out. Finn's orders were clear: Cannel had said the *veleda* was surrounded by a club of some kind, and logic said it was the club that had called them. The Fianna were Ireland's heroes, so it made sense that they should look for Irish clubs in the city.

There were many: The Clan na Gael, the Ancient Order of Hibernians, the Fenian Brotherhood, and a dozen other charity and church groups. The Fianna had split up for efficiency, and Finn had assigned Diarmid the Fenians. *"Infiltrate their leadership. And quickly. We haven't much time. Use any means necessary"*—here a quick and meaningful glance at Diarmid's forehead. *"Find their chiefs and the rest will follow."* Orders not much different from those they'd routinely followed in battle. Disarm the leaders first; the rest will fold.

Diarmid's instincts told him it was either the Brotherhood or the Gael that had need of them. He'd heard rumors: men who spoke of Irish independence, Irish rebellion. Britain ruled Ireland now. He hadn't believed it when he'd heard it, and he hated the idea of it. He was more than willing to fight for whoever wanted to change that.

It hadn't taken him long to determine who was important among the Fenian Brotherhood. A few men: Rory Nolan, Simon MacRonan, and young Patrick Devlin. Of them, Devlin interested him most, and not only because he'd just returned from Ireland.

Patrick Devlin also had the easiest way in. Pretty Lucy Devlin, his sister.

Infiltrate.

Diarmid had watched her for days. Golden hair and big blue eyes and a flouncy, flirty way about her. A restless gaze and a heart that wouldn't settle. She was the type of girl he understood. Fickle and vain, a bit ruthless. She reminded him of Grainne, which was the best assurance he knew that he could keep his distance.

Infiltrate.

There was a path through the park behind her house, one

she used often, and almost every afternoon at five o'clock, she paid a visit to the confectioner's at the end of it. She liked ice cream, which he'd never tasted, though it looked and smelled delicious. Sometimes she'd eat it in the shop, sometimes she would walk out with one of her friends and eat from a paper dish as they talked, dipping a tiny wooden paddle into the mound of cream, licking at it with a darting pink tongue.

All he needed was for her to see him, to really *look* at him. So he leaned against the wrought-iron lace of the gazebo and crossed his arms over his chest and waited for her to be alone. He needed a few moments to talk with her without anyone else noticing.

Two days he'd waited, and each time she had been with other girls. Then, the third day, he'd watched her emerge from the mass of climbing roses at her gate. She wore a yellow gown trimmed in pink and a hat with ribbons tied in a bow at her chin.

It was time.

She'd walked slowly, as if she were in a dream, and he'd wondered what she was thinking about. Some other boy perhaps, and he felt a tug of shame, of reluctance that faded the next moment when he heard Finn's voice in his head: *Use any means necessary.* She was closer now, only a few yards away, then a few feet. He'd raised his hand to get her attention. When she glanced at him, he'd shaken back his hair.

She'd gone still, dropping the handkerchief she'd been patting delicately to her throat. Her gaze riveted to his forehead, her lips parted prettily, a rush of breath. He had her. It had worked.

Again. There had been a part of him that hoped the power of it was gone, that it was a relic of another world. But no, of course it still worked, a gift and a curse as always. He had to fight his exhaustion and the urge to walk away. He thought of what was at stake, and he gave her the best smile he could muster—it wouldn't matter how false it was; she was bespelled. She would see only what she wanted to see.

"I believe you dropped this." He bent to retrieve the handkerchief.

"Oh." She'd taken the handkerchief, her cheeks pink. She leaned forward as if to touch his forehead. "Oh, are you hurt? That burn—"

The same reaction always. How tired he was of that look in their eyes, that shining, feverish love that was as unreal as a dream. "An old scar," he'd told her, backing away from her touch. "I've seen you before. You walk here nearly every day."

"How do you know that?"

"I've been watching you," he admitted.

"You've been watching me?"

"Aye. Do you mind it?"

"N-no," she'd said, and then "No" again. "Not in the least, in fact."

Infiltrate.

She was so easily led he hardly had to think. Within the hour, she'd gone to her brother to ask him to hire a new stableboy. If there was one thing that hadn't changed in all the time that had passed, it was stables. They reminded Diarmid of his old life, of a horse he'd loved—a beautiful bay named Siofra. The Devlins had four horses, matched chestnuts, and the stable was better furnished than any building in the slums where Diarmid lived. Walls wainscotted in walnut. Straw sweeter and fresher than that he slept on. But the smells were the same stable smells: hay and the musk of horses and manure and the dry dust of oats. The sounds were sounds he'd lived with most of his life: soft nickers, the swish of a tail, the buzz of flies. He felt comfortable there; he was glad to be around horses again.

Now he suppressed his resentment at the sight of Lucy and what he had to do and said, "Over here, *milis*."

She hurried over. Strands of fair hair straggled from her pins. Her eyes sparkled when she saw him. "I love it when you speak Gaelic to me. *Milis*. What does it mean?"

He was surprised. "You don't understand it?"

"No one I know speaks it anymore. Well, my father did a bit. Only what he knew from my grandfather. No one can even read it any longer except for Patrick."

"Your brother reads Gaelic?" Something interesting, though Diarmid wasn't certain exactly what to make of it.

She tilted her head at him flirtatiously. "He loves these Irish poets. It's all he talks about. 'Kincora,' 'Dark Rosaleen.'" She made a face. "He read one of them to us the other night. I hardly understood it."

He smiled and kept brushing the mare. "Really? They sound interesting."

"Oh, don't tell me you're obsessed with rebellion too?"

"I don't suppose you could bring me one of your brother's books—just to borrow for a bit." Finn believed Cannel could divine whether Patrick had called them, and for that they needed something of his. A book would do.

Lucy pouted. "I don't know. He'd notice it was gone, I think. And you still haven't told me what *milis* means."

"Sweet. Like candy. Or ice cream." He flashed her a teasing look.

"Mmmm. I like ice cream."

"I know."

"I'll bring you some the next time I go. Though I don't know how I can get it here without it melting."

"I've no need of it," he said. "You're sweet enough for me."

She smiled, looking at him from beneath her lashes. He wondered if she knew how alluring that look was, and decided she probably did. "Come out," she said. So imperious.

He said, "One moment," and gave the final brush to the mare. When he put aside the brush and stepped from the stall, Lucy threw herself into his arms so hard he stumbled back.

"Kiss me," she demanded.

He obliged. She was sweet and willing—more willing than she should have been. Bespelled. *Don't think of it. Do what you must.* He kissed her pouting lower lip, then kissed her more fully, once and then again before she sighed and drew away, laying her head against his chest. "I can't bear to be away from you."

"You weren't about yesterday," he said—a question, as subtle as he could make it. His goal wasn't just to get something of Patrick's but to discover what he could about him, and so far he hadn't been that successful. Lucy didn't like to talk about Patrick. What she'd told him already today was the most she'd said since he'd met her. She claimed her brother and his politics didn't interest her in the least. All Lucy cared about were the latest fashions—and him, but he'd known that would happen the moment he showed her the lovespot.

"I had to be at a tea." She made a face again. "With my brother and the girl he intends to marry."

It was the first Diarmid had heard of it. "He means to marry?"

She nodded. "Grace Knox. He's loved her for . . . oh, I don't know. A hundred years at least."

He raised a brow.

"Well, not a hundred years. But he used to moon about her, and she hardly looked at him. She was too busy with her poetry."

"Poor Patrick."

"Yes. But now she suddenly finds him *riveting*. I don't wish to be uncharitable, but I'm not the only one who's noticed that she finally sees Patrick just when her family's fallen on hard times."

No, not uncharitable at all, he thought wryly. "I thought your brother had been gone a good while."

"Three years."

"Then it's been three years she can't have looked at him."

She flushed. "I'm sorry. I know it's unfair of me. Grace is perfectly lovely, it's only . . ."

"What?"

She met his gaze, though her cheeks grew even rosier. "She can have who she wants, while I can't."

He felt guilty. Too softhearted, Oscar would say, and that was true. But he couldn't look at a girl without wanting to protect her in some measure. Lucy was no different, even if it was himself he wanted to protect her from.

It was just a spell. This wasn't real. *Infiltrate.* He sighed and whispered, "Come now, lass, let's not think of that, shall we? Tomorrow's a long time away. What's to keep us from having a little fun right now?"

He kissed her again. She pressed against him, pulling on his shirt, jerking it from his trousers so she could touch his skin. He let her do it, though he would stop it soon enough. There was no point in hurting her more than he had to. Just so far and no further.

Because as soon as he learned what he needed about her brother, he'd be gone.

SEVEN

June 1

Grace

I woke with a headache almost every morning now, pain colored with the lingering memory of my nightmares: battles and blinding light, violet lightning and fire. It was a relief to wake to the sun streaming through my thin curtains, to hear the familiar sounds of the city instead of war cries and the hoarse, strident caws of ravens.

Mama had given her first lesson to Mrs. Needham's daughters, and she came back pale and nervous, her mouth tight, the shadows beneath her eyes darker. "Mrs. Needham has requested Mademoiselle Paulette make your debut gown."

Requested. More than a suggestion, then. I saw how much my mother hated this. I hated it too. "I've never heard of Mademoiselle Paulette."

"Nor have I," she told me. "But Mrs. Needham says she's a talented seamstress. And apparently not too expensive."

"Why should she care how much it costs? We're paying her back, aren't we?"

Mama sighed. "Oh, Grace. How can I tell her it's not her concern when she's lending the money?"

"Then I can go to Stewart's. Or Lord and Taylor," I said resentfully. "Ready-made is good enough if it's money she's concerned about."

"Go to Mademoiselle Paulette. At least to see what she's offering. I would go with you, but I'm afraid I'm not feeling well." Mama put a fluttering hand to her temple. "Perhaps you could go with Lucy. Or Rose."

This was all so ridiculous. "Mama, there's no need for a debut. Not with Patrick—"

"Of course there must be a debut. What will people say if you marry Patrick Devlin without one?"

"I don't care what people say."

"I won't have rumors that there are . . . reasons for the rush when you're a respectable girl."

I felt myself redden. It was only made worse when I remembered Patrick's kiss and how much I'd liked it.

She continued, "If Patrick does propose, as his mother and I both believe he will, then we will announce it at your debut. But you *will* have one, Grace. On this I must insist. Go to the dressmaker's. Now I truly must rest. Where's Aidan?"

I hadn't seen my brother since that morning, when he'd stumbled in, unshaven and haggard. It was clear he'd been up all night. *"Where have you been?"* I'd demanded, and he had waggled his fingers at me and said, *"Nowhere you want to know."*

"Probably sleeping. But I can wake him up if you like." *Which he deserves,* I thought, hoping Mama would give me the satisfaction. But she shook her head and said nothing— what was there to say anymore?

Rose lived just down the street, and there was no one to send with a message, so I walked to her door to invite her along.

"We'll take Lucy too," Rose said with excitement. "She's moping about her stableboy, so this will give her something else to think about."

I didn't really want Lucy there, but I supposed if she was going to be my sister-in-law, I should make her a better friend. Rose sent a message around to the Devlins', and Lucy was free. The day was pleasant and not as hot as the last few had been, and so we walked to the square. Lucy had said we could take her carriage.

"It gives her another chance to see her stableboy," I noted.

Rose dimpled. "Exactly. And we'll want her in a good mood for shopping."

I hoped to see Patrick, but when we got there his mother said that he was at the shop. "He'll be so sorry to learn he's missed you, my dear. But I'm grateful you're taking Lucy with you this afternoon. She's been most . . ." Mrs. Devlin spoke as if hoping I would understand, and I did. Better than she knew.

"Hopefully, Rose and I can change her mood."

"I've already ordered the carriage for you, and it should

be here in a few moments." She glanced up the stairs. "I'm certain Lucy won't dawdle."

Rose said, "Perhaps we should go up and hurry her along."

"Oh, please do. And you girls must stop at the confectioner's after. Have them put it on my bill."

"You're very kind, ma'am," I said.

She smiled and hurried off; Rose looked up the stairs and sighed. "Well then. Into the lion's den."

I shuddered. "Perhaps we should go without her."

"And give up a visit to the confectioner's? You must be mad."

"You know I won't be able to help at all. She doesn't like me that much."

Rose grimaced. "Coward. But if I'm gone more than fifteen minutes, you'd better come rescue me."

"Fifteen minutes," I agreed.

She took a deep breath, squared her shoulders, and went up to Lucy.

I walked outside to wait on the stoop. There was a small bench that looked out at the cast-iron railing and the raised brick beds with their yew hedges. Promenaders trailed from the park, women with their veiled hats, elegant men seeming not to sweat despite the warmth, a few children with their parents.

I reached into my pocket for the book that Patrick had given me, opening it to "Dark Rosaleen," soaking up the words because they belonged to him, because somehow I could see him so clearly when I read them.

I was lost in thoughts of Patrick when I heard the thudding creak of carriage wheels, and I looked up as the Devlin carriage came to a stop before the house. I closed the book and stood, going down the steps to tell the driver that Lucy and Rose would be there in a moment. Then the boy who'd brought the carriage jumped down from the seat.

My first thought was that he was stunningly beautiful.

My second was that he was glowing. *Glowing.* Not just limned by the sun, but glowing as if he *were* the sun. The light began at the very center of him and spread, an aurora that pulsed and radiated, and suddenly I was struck with blinding pain, a spike driven hard into my temples, so I gasped and dropped Patrick's book, and the whole world tilted and spun and I was falling—

Arms caught me, holding me close. "Careful now, lass. Careful. I've got you." A deep voice, a heavy Irish accent in my ear, an arm like an iron bar around my waist. I grabbed his hand, and the world righted; the pain in my head abated as if it had only been waiting for his touch—there and then, just as suddenly as it had come, fading nearly to nothing, to a dull throb. I closed my eyes. When I opened them again, I felt shaky but no longer light-headed.

His face was only inches from mine. He looked to be eighteen, or perhaps nineteen, and that he was Lucy's stableboy there was no doubt. She'd said he was handsome. He was much more than that. Dark, shaggy hair fell into his face, nearly covering his black eyes so I had to resist the urge to push it out of the way. He had a long face and a strong chin with a bit of a cleft. A wide mouth. Full lips and a blade of a nose—big enough that it should have marred his beauty, though it didn't in the least. My breath seemed to lodge in my chest. My heart set up this rapid beat. I thought: *Oh, here you are at last.*

As if I knew him, as if I'd been waiting for him, though I'd never seen him before in my life. He was not someone you could forget.

He frowned at me, drawing back. "Have we met?" His voice was much deeper than such prettiness should allow.

I heard myself say, "You must be Lucy's stableboy."

He replied bluntly, "And who are you?"

Arrogant, a little superior. Startlingly impertinent.

"Grace Knox."

"You're Devlin's lass."

Devlin's lass. Patrick. Now I was aware of the fact that we were standing in front of Patrick's house, and that this boy hadn't released me and I hadn't asked him to. And worse, that I didn't want him to. He held me so tightly that every inch of me pressed against him. And my skin tingled as if it had stopped being numb after a very long time.

No. Oh no, no. This could ruin everything.

I tried to push away. His arms only tightened. I said, "Please. Please let me go."

"I'm going to take you inside. Can you walk, or do you need carrying?"

"No." I shook my head, trying to bring my thoughts into some kind of focus. "You were glowing in the sun, and . . . just let me sit. I'm all right. Truly."

He looked as if he didn't believe me, but he let go. He appeared as reluctant to stop touching me as I was for him to do so, and I was startled at how cold I was when he released me. I felt for the brick ledge of the flower bed and sat on its narrow edge, leaning back against the springy yew.

"Are you sure you don't want me to take you inside?"

That accent was so strong he must have just come off the boat. *Oh God.* I put my hand to my head. Only the memory of pain remained. "I'm all right," I said again.

"You'll pardon me if I say you don't look it." He smiled; a long dimple creased one cheek. It made him more attractive than ever. I swallowed hard and then was irritated with myself for being so affected. *Patrick!* I reminded myself.

"I told you I'm fine," I snapped. "And I don't know how you can see anything with that hair in your eyes."

"You've a sharp tongue for a girl who was swooning in my arms only moments ago."

"You're very arrogant for a stableboy."

He shrugged. Cocky and confident. Again that grin. "And that was a quick recovery you made, lass. Perhaps the quickest I've ever seen."

"My headache's gone already. It's never been so—" I understood then what he'd meant. "You think I swooned just so you would catch me?"

"'Twouldn't be the first time."

"Well it wasn't *this* time. It had nothing to do with you. It was the glow."

"So you said."

"You *were* glowing. You were." I realized the moment I said it how absurd it sounded. And the truth was, now that it was over, I didn't quite believe it myself. It had been so strange. "I don't know. I haven't had anything to eat this morning. Perhaps it was only that."

"No doubt."

That smile of his dropped right though me. I jerked to my feet—too fast; the blood rushed from my head. I flailed uselessly for the railing.

He grabbed my arm to steady me, close enough that I saw that his eyes weren't black at all but a deep, deep blue.

He didn't even try to hide his laughter. "A trick stops working when you try it too often, lass. Next time I'll let you fall."

"Why, Grace, there you are!"

Lucy's voice, almost shrill. I glanced over my shoulder to see her standing on the stoop, Rose beside her. Lucy's expression was quietly furious. I realized that her stableboy still had hold of my arm.

He must have realized it at the same moment, because he let go, quickly. Lucy came down the stoop, her pale eyes blazing. She grabbed his arm, pressing herself against him. "Tell me you're driving us."

He glanced at me. He looked uncomfortable as he carefully disengaged himself from Lucy. "I just brought the carriage up. Leonard's on his way."

As if Rose and I weren't standing right there, she whispered, "I've missed you so. We're going to choose Grace's debut gown now, but will you meet me later?"

"Lucy, you're in the middle of the walk," Rose said in a low voice. "People will see."

"I don't care," Lucy said, but she stepped away from him. She gave him a pleading look that was far too obvious. "Please, Derry."

A shiver swept me at the sound of his name; again I felt that familiarity, that sense that I'd known it already. *And you did*, I reminded myself. *Lucy told you at tea.* But I couldn't escape the feeling that it had nothing to do with that.

He leaned to whisper something in Lucy's ear, and I went hot with . . . jealousy. *What's got into you, Grace?* I looked away. When I looked back, Lucy was smiling.

"Here's Leonard now," Derry said.

The driver came hurrying. He touched the brim of his hat, deep-green livery—the Devlins' color—and said to Lucy, "Forgive the delay, Miss Devlin."

She didn't even look at him. Her gaze was fastened on Derry.

"You'd best go, lass," Derry said gently, pushing her a little.

Lucy flashed him a brilliant smile, and then she said brightly to Rose and me, "Shall we?"

The driver helped her into the carriage, and then Rose. I couldn't stop myself—I glanced back at Derry. He was watching me with a thoughtful look that made me stumble on the carriage step.

The driver closed the door, and we were off.

Lucy played with a loosened ribbon on her shawl, tucking it neatly into place as she said to me, "I do hope my brother hasn't misjudged you, Grace. He'd be so disappointed."

I didn't pretend to misunderstand her. "I tripped coming down the walk. Your Derry was only helping me to my feet."

She shot me a glance from beneath her lashes.

Rose said, "What color do you think Grace should choose for her gown? I've told her pale green, but perhaps pink would be better?"

Lucy said, "Oh, it depends upon what style she chooses. I vow I . . ."

I hardly listened. Instead I thought of that strange and persistent glow, the pain that had disappeared at his touch. The way he'd held me and the leap of my heart and my sense that I knew him. How foolish that I should feel this way. I didn't want this. I'd never seen him before and I doubted I would again, and so this feeling that I'd been waiting for him . . .

It was nothing. An illusion brought on by no breakfast, just as that strange glow had been. And yet the glow hadn't been completely strange either. There had been something familiar in it too. Something I'd seen somewhere—

Then it came to me. My nightmares. Flashes of intense, blinding light. Pain and ravens.

I shuddered and reached into my pocket for Patrick's book of poems, for the reassuring feel of something belonging to him, something to remind me of who I was and what I wanted.

But the little book was gone.

The entire time we were at Mademoiselle Paulette's—discussing patterns and fabrics, ribbons and buttons—I wished to be home. I remembered dropping the book on the walk the moment the headache came upon me. No doubt it was still there. Or Lucy's stableboy had picked it up. Perhaps he had taken it to the house. Patrick had written his name on the flyleaf, so there would be no mistaking where it belonged. Perhaps it was waiting for me. I didn't want Patrick to know I'd lost it, to think I had been so careless with something so very important to him.

It was all I could do to smile and laugh with Rose and Lucy. I agreed with them on the choice of pattern, though I had trouble remembering afterward what it was. A scooped yet modest neckline, puffed sleeves decorated with lace and ribbon and . . . flowers. There had been flowers. And . . . and pink. Yes, definitely pink.

Lucy mooned about Derry the whole hour we were at the confectioner's, sitting at a small round table with curved legs, eating ice cream with sugared violets that Lucy held between her lips and sucked upon until her mouth was delicately tinted purple. When Rose teased her about it, Lucy said, "Oh no! What will Derry think?"

Rose said, "I imagine he'll like licking you pink again."

Lucy blushed.

I pretended I didn't feel sick at the thought. "Rose!"

"Don't tell me you'd say no to him," Rose said, dragging her spoon through her melting ice cream. "*I* wouldn't, that's certain. He's gorgeous. Too bad he hasn't a penny to his name."

"I'm partial to fairer coloring," I said.

"Well, you would say that now, wouldn't you? But I

remember when you couldn't tear your eyes from Bobby Sullivan. Dark hair and dark eyes. He looked like Derry, didn't he?"

"Derry's eyes are blue," I said, dipping my spoon into the ice cream, scooping up a violet. I had crunched it between my teeth before I realized they were both staring at me. "What?"

"You noted the color of his eyes?" Lucy asked.

"I could hardly help it," I said. "He was holding me closer than was proper. He's a bit of a flirt, Lucy. Even you must admit it."

"He flirted with you?"

Stupid, Grace.

"I'm certain he was just being kind, isn't that so, Grace?" Rose provided.

I nodded. "Yes. Yes, of course. He couldn't let me fall to the ground, now could he?"

"Whatever made you swoon, Grace?" Lucy's voice was light, but I heard her suspicion.

I opened my mouth to tell them about the glow, but what exactly was I to say? That he'd been afire like the sun? That it had been very like the dreams I'd been having? That his touch made it go away? It seemed ridiculous even to me. I settled on "I'd eaten nothing all day. I was a little light-headed."

"It was lucky he was there then," Rose put in. "You could have been hurt."

"Yes. And he knew about Patrick. He said I must be Patrick's girl."

Rose laughed. "No, did he? I imagine you liked that."

"He sounded just off the boat. He's probably Catholic as well, and you know how clannish they are. I'd watch out for him, Lucy. He probably wants a dozen children and an obedient wife."

"Sshh." Rose giggled. "You are so bad, Grace."

"I don't care if that's what he wants," Lucy said, raising her chin. "I would be perfectly happy with a dozen children."

"Not if you're raising them in the slums," I countered.

"I have money."

"But he doesn't. And you're mad if you think your mother will allow it. Or Patrick."

"My brother's a romantic too."

"Not enough of one to marry his sister to a stableboy."

Lucy's eyes narrowed. "You think you know Patrick so well. But you don't. Why, you didn't speak to him for three years."

"I know him well enough," I said, a little more angrily than I should have. "I know what matters to him. I know how he feels about Ireland. I know he cares about oppression and poverty and want. Things you know nothing about."

"And neither do you," Lucy said, pointing her spoon at me. "You think that just because your family's fallen on hard times you know everything about being poor. But you've just paid a dressmaker to make a gown for your debut, and my brother is preparing to go down on his knee to save you, so don't go all high and mighty on *me*."

She was right. I felt the sting to my pride, a shame that made me look down into my dish, stirring little violets into whirlpools of melting ice cream, my appetite completely gone.

Rose said, "Must we argue? Come now, both of you. It's been a perfectly lovely day. Let's not spoil it."

"Of course," Lucy said. "I'm sorry, Grace. I shouldn't have said those things. We're to be sisters, after all."

"I'm sorry as well," I said sincerely.

"There," Rose declared. "Isn't that better?"

Lucy stood. "Let's go back to the house. It's hot and I'm tired."

And no doubt she wanted to run off to visit her stableboy. But I didn't say that. We said little on the way to the Devlin house.

In the too-warm parlor, Mrs. Devlin looked up with a smile. "Did you choose a gown? Is it lovely?"

"It is," Lucy said curtly. "Pink."

"I believe that's Patrick's favorite color," Mrs. Devlin said.

"Really? I would have said he preferred green." Lucy threw me a smug look.

Her mother said, "I thought he would have returned by now. I do know he would want to see you, Grace."

"You'll excuse me if I retire?" Lucy asked. "I'm afraid I'm quite exhausted."

Rose and I both murmured good-byes. When Lucy flounced from the room, I turned to Mrs. Devlin. "Ma'am, I think I dropped a book earlier. Outside, while I was waiting for the carriage. Did anyone retrieve it?"

"No, I don't think so." She bustled into the hallway, calling for the butler. But he hadn't seen it either.

"Perhaps it's still outside," I said. "Rose and I will look for it as we leave."

"I'll be sure to tell Patrick you were here. And to give him your regards," Mrs. Devlin said.

Outside, Rose asked, "Did you really drop a book, or was it just an excuse to leave?"

"I really dropped it. And it's Patrick's, too, so I must find it." I bent to look beneath the bench.

"It's Patrick's?"

"A book of Irish poems." I hurried down the stoop, searching at the foot of the railing. Nothing.

"And you just dropped it?"

We were at the end of the walk. Where I'd first seen the glow and had the headache. "Yes. I was reading it and then the carriage came up and my head . . . it was the worst headache I've ever had."

"Not just hunger then?" Rose asked.

"I don't know. Perhaps. But I've never felt like that."

"You don't want to get between Lucy and this boy, Grace. Not if you want Patrick."

My stomach tightened. "Who says I'm going to get between them?"

"The way he was looking at you . . ."

"He's a flirt, as I said," I told her impatiently. "And an irritating one too. He's just perfect for Lucy. Together they can pretend they're king and queen and rule the world."

Rose laughed. "However are you going to hold your tongue when you're Lucy's sister-in-law?"

I sighed. "I don't know that I will be, Rose. Perhaps Patrick won't propose."

"Oh, I think he will. But not if you keep picking at Lucy. She has his ear, you know."

"I'll try to be good." I let the yew branches fall back into place. "It's not here. What am I going to do?"

"Tell Patrick you lost it."

"I can't! It means so much to him. How am I to tell him that I was so careless I just dropped it in the street?"

"Well, perhaps it will turn up."

I followed her back to her house. The book hadn't been kicked aside. It hadn't fallen into the bushes. Which meant it would've been lying here on the walk, obvious to anyone. Obvious to the stableboy who'd been standing right there. He must have it. And he had to know who it belonged to. But he hadn't turned it in to the house. Why not?

Unfortunately, the only way to find out was to ask him.

When we came to Rose's door and she asked me to come in for some lemonade, I told her I had to check on my mother. But instead of going home, I doubled back. I knew where the Devlin stables were—two blocks over from the park, only a short walk from here.

I was nervous as I went there, my pulse racing. *Stupid!* There was nothing to worry about. This morning had been odd, and those things I'd felt . . . whatever the cause, I had no wish to see Derry again. And who knew if Lucy was there right now, lying to her mother, sneaking out. . . . He'd whispered *something* to her; doubtless it had been a time to meet him later. Wouldn't *that* be perfect, to run into her there.

But I needed that book. And I knew Derry had it.

The stables were on the corner. As beautiful as any mansion—probably just as well appointed, too, though I'd never been inside. The brougham we'd taken to the shop was parked outside, and the driver was polishing it until it gleamed in the sun. He started when he saw me.

"Miss?"

"I think I might have left a book in the carriage," I lied. "I wondered if perhaps you'd found it. A small book. Of poems."

Leonard shook his head. His hat was off, his dark-green coat lying over the carriage wheel. "No, miss. There was no such thing."

"I must have dropped it. Perhaps the stableboy found it on the walk."

He jerked his head toward the open stable door. "He's just inside. You could ask him yourself."

I knew that he believed this was just what I'd come to do, and I hated it, especially because it was true, even if not for the reason he thought.

The inside was as beautiful as I'd expected. Polished walnut stalls and gleaming leather tack hanging from the walls, porcelain troughs of water, a barrelful of oats so fine I would have been glad to eat them myself. The stable smelled like any other, of oil and leather, hay and horse, but the air here seemed more rarefied somehow, as if the scents of sweat and manure were not allowed but kept hovering outside, waiting to sneak in.

I hesitated just inside the doorway. I saw no movement anywhere but for the horses: a swish of tail, a stomped foot. And then I heard a noise, a muttered voice, and Derry emerged from a stall. There was no glow this time—not that I'd thought there would be. He held a currying brush, and his shirtsleeves were pushed up to expose muscled forearms, his shirt mostly open, revealing far too much of his chest, which gleamed with the fine sheen of sweat. His dark hair was still falling into his face—irritating me all over again. How could he even see through it?

I wished I hadn't come. But before I could retreat, he saw me.

He straightened, then I saw that mocking expression again. "Miss Knox," he said—there was not the slightest surprise in his voice, and that was irritating too. "Let me know if you mean to swoon, will you? I'll wash my hands. I wouldn't want to get you dirty."

"I've no intention of swooning."

He put aside the currying brush and leaned against the stall. "Am I still glowing?"

"No. Not since . . ." *Since you touched me.* I swallowed those words, knowing already what he would make of them.

"Not since when?"

"Since you caught me," I admitted.

His grin grew, exactly as I'd thought. "I've been told I have a healing touch."

"I doubt *healing* was the word."

He inclined his head as if to acknowledge that was true

and propped his elbow on the top railing of the stall. "So what brings you here, miss, if 'tisn't 'healing' or catching you want?"

"You may be the most arrogant boy I've ever met. I'm here because I want my book."

"Your book?"

"I dropped it. When I . . . when I swooned. And now I can't find it. I thought you might have it."

"Why would I want your book?"

"I have no idea. I doubt you can even read."

"You're a bit arrogant yourself, Miss Knox."

"Am I wrong?"

He crossed his arms over his chest and gave me that thoughtful look that had stolen my breath outside the carriage, as if he saw something in me that belonged to him, and I felt it, too, as if something in *him* belonged to *me*. That strange recognition made me step back, suddenly—and again—afraid. He noticed it. His voice was very soft when he said, "I don't have your book."

I didn't quite believe him, but I didn't know how to call him a liar. Still, I needed that book. "It was Patrick's book. Please. He lent it to me, and I really must have it."

He said nothing. Just that *look*.

"Please. If you have it, you must—"

"Did you choose your gown?"

The question startled me enough that I answered him. "Yes, as it happens."

"What color?"

"I don't know why it should concern you."

"It doesn't. I'm just curious. What color?"

"Pink."

He nodded. "You're Irish, aren't you? I'm not mistaken?"

This odd conversation was getting odder. "Yes."

"Black Irish." He smiled, again that dimple.

Just as my grandmother used to say. *"There's good to come of that,* mo chroi." I couldn't think of how to respond. The moment stilled. Finally, I said, "Well, I—" at the same time he said, "Pink's a good choice for you. Devlin won't be able to look away."

His voice was quietly reverent, and I heard Rose in my head, telling me not to come between Lucy and this boy, and my fear—of myself, of him, of losing everything—grew. I thought: *Leave now.*

I said lamely, "I should be going. I only wanted to ask you about the book. If you're certain you don't have it . . ." I let the words dangle, a hint, if he wanted to take it.

He didn't. Again the impertinent grin. "D'you need an escort home?"

"No." Too quick. Too much. I knew it the moment I said it. His grin broadened, and I turned away, nearly tripping over my skirt as I hurried from the stable. He didn't have Patrick's book, and I'd humiliated myself for no reason. I wanted nothing to do with him. Not now and not ever.

I told myself that all the way home.

EIGHT

Diarmid

Diarmid handed the book to Finn as he stepped through the doorway. "It's Devlin's."

"You're sure? It needs to be something that belongs to him," Finn said.

"It's his. His lass said so."

Finn raised a brow. "His lass?"

"She dropped it this morning in a swoon. I happened to be there."

"Let me guess: she took one look at you and fainted out of pure desire." Oscar came up beside Diarmid. "What'd you do, show her the lovespot?"

"One at a time," Diarmid answered with a smile, though the thought of Grace Knox troubled him. He didn't want to talk about her. "I've my hands full with Lucy."

"That never stopped you before."

"She's not to my taste."

Surprise flickered in Oscar's green eyes. "Not to *your* taste? Now there's something I've never heard before. You even like the ugly ones."

Diarmid shrugged.

"What's wrong with her? Is she warty?"

Diarmid wished he'd said nothing at all. He hadn't been able to forget Grace Knox all day. At first he'd thought her the same as any other lass. She liked the look of him, he knew, but she wasn't going to admit it—well, she would be a fool to, wouldn't she, when she was near betrothed to Devlin and Lucy was her friend? And that swoon this morning . . . he'd known girls to do worse things to get his attention, and all her talk about glowing didn't convince him otherwise. But after that she'd been . . . sharp-tongued, actually. And that *was* a first. And a relief. He hadn't been able to resist needling her. He'd even enjoyed it. It was so different from the usual simpering and flirting that only filled him with bone-deep weariness.

But she unsettled him. There was something about her— something his instincts told him to stay clear of. He felt drawn to her, and she intrigued him, and that was dangerous enough in itself. But when you added to that his sense that he somehow *knew* her—and it was more than the fact that she reminded him of someone . . .

"Not warty, no," he told Oscar. "She's pretty enough. But snappish and prickly. Self-important too."

"And you like them blithe and laughing."

"There are plenty of girls. Why waste time on one who doesn't like me?"

"She doesn't *like* you?" Oscar laughed. "Ah, there's my explanation right there. What's wrong with the lass?"

Finn had been watching them thoughtfully. "Do you think she's involved with Devlin's politics?"

Diarmid's first thought was *maybe*. There was fire in her. But he didn't say it, because the truth was that he didn't know her at all. He could be misjudging her completely, if only because something about her troubled him. There was no point in making Finn more curious than he already was.

So he answered, "I couldn't say. I've never seen them together. But she seemed distressed to lose the book."

Finn nodded and handed the book to Cannel. "What's in it, *cainte*?"

Cannel opened the cover. "Diarmid's right; it is Patrick Devlin's. He's written his name on the flyleaf." He ran his finger across the scrawled signature before he turned to the next page. "It's a book of poems by James Clarence Mangan. Anyone heard of him?"

Finn looked at Diarmid, who shook his head, as did the others.

"'Dark Rosaleen,'" Cannel read the titles. "'Lament for Banba,' 'Kincor—'"

"'Lament for Banba'?" Finn's voice was sharp.

Diarmid understood why. Banba. Another name for Ireland. It had been common in their time, one of the three goddesses who had begged to be honored with the land's naming. Éire and Banba and Fotla. But he hadn't heard it said at all in this city. Not until now.

"Read it," Finn ordered.

Cannel started at the urgency in Finn's tone, but he cleared his throat and read, "'O my land! O my love! / What a woe, and how deep, / Is thy death to my long mourning soul! . . .'"

The poem compared Ireland to a tree felled by an ax, and talked of thrones usurped and the proud people of Banba held in thrall, until the lines, "'For the hour soon may loom / When the Lord's mighty hand / Shall be raised for our rescue once more!'"

Cannel's words were followed by silence, broken by Keenan's soft "By the gods. It talks of rebellion."

Ossian added, "Devlin must be our man."

Finn said to Cannel, "Do a divination."

"I've told you. I don't know that I can."

Finn said nothing, but he wouldn't look away. One didn't refuse Finn when he wore that expression. Cannel took the deck of cards from the table and put them on top of the book. Then, moving his lips soundlessly, he shuffled the cards and laid them out. Diarmid waited with the others.

Finally the Seer looked up from the cards. "Devlin's involved in something, that's certain. Very involved. Whatever it is consumes him."

"Is he our man?" Finn asked.

"Difficult to say. But I think it's a real possibility." Cannel pointed to a card. "You see this one? It means there's something dark looming."

"Dark? How so?"

"Not wicked, but perhaps unsavory. Something that could

turn. Indecisiveness. Fear. He hasn't got the control he believes he has. And here—" Cannel pointed to another card. "Here I see a need to protect and a willingness to sacrifice."

"To sacrifice what?" Diarmid asked.

"Anything," Cannel said.

Diarmid couldn't help thinking of Grace Knox—and that unsettled him even more.

Finn asked, "Why did the lass have this book?"

"She didn't say," Diarmid answered. "Perhaps Devlin gave it to her."

"Find out what she knows."

"It might be better done by Oscar."

"You're already there, and I need Oscar to keep on with the Clan na Gael," Finn said.

Diarmid was relieved—until he realized why: he didn't want Oscar near Grace Knox. It puzzled him. He'd barely met the lass, and he felt he should keep his distance from her, so why should he care? He didn't understand the contradiction. He didn't know why he felt any of it.

Finn said, "What about Devlin's sister? Did you get something of hers?"

Diarmid reached into his pocket for the ribbon he'd snapped from Lucy's gown just before he'd come. He handed it to Cannel, though he knew already they'd find nothing in Lucy, nothing to do with Patrick's plans. "Do we still need the book, or can I return it?"

Finn scowled. "Why does it matter?"

"The lass came looking for it. She suspects I have it."

"Give it back to her then," Finn said. "It will be a good chance for you to find out what she knows. And I want you to get into the Devlin house. Search it. Without getting caught. If Patrick Devlin is the one who called us, the horn will be there somewhere."

Diarmid nodded and tried not to think about why he felt breaking into the Devlin house was less of a risk than asking Grace Knox a single question.

NINE

That night

Patrick

When the Fomori's messenger, Daire Donn, had arrived ten days ago, Patrick had been reassured. Daire Donn had been impossible not to like. He had come into the clubhouse like an old friend, smiling and shaking hands, and before he'd reached the stairs he'd been dry, his linen shirt sparkling with gold thread and embroidery of the deepest purple, his cape of fine scarlet wool swirling about his boots.

"So why did you call us, my friends?" he'd asked as they sat on padded leather chairs in the clubhouse meeting room. Daire Donn's dark eyes had gleamed as he looked at Patrick. "'Twas you who led this charge, aye?"

Patrick had been surprised to be noticed. And then flattered. "We've called you for Ireland's sake. She's been under British rule for centuries now. Her lands are fallow, her people starving. We're the Fenian Brotherhood—"

"Fenian?" Daire Donn had paused as he lifted his tankard of beer.

"We're named for the Fianna," Rory put in.

"Ah, I see."

"Like them, we plan to be the heroes of Ireland," Jonathan said.

Patrick had winced. A misstep. He remembered the legends well. The Fianna and the Fomori had always been enemies, and Finn MacCool had fought more than one vicious battle with Daire Donn when he was called King of the World and allied with the Fomori. There would be no love lost there. Patrick had rushed in with "We're asking for the help of the Fomori. We want an uprising, a rebellion. Our other attempts have—sadly—failed. But with the Fomori as our allies, we think we can succeed."

"To throw off the rule of Albion," Daire Donn had said. Albion was the ancient name of England.

Patrick nodded. "Yes. To give Ireland back her pride and her power."

"Ah." Daire Donn smiled broadly. "Well, I think perhaps we can come to an agreement. I know my fellows well; they cannot like to see their lands in the hands of Britons. But they will want something in return."

Patrick had leaned forward eagerly. "Yes, of course. Once the rebellion succeeds, we'll need leaders to guide the people, to write a new constitution. There will need to be a new government formed—a democratic one—and we can offer you a place within it."

Rory said, "There will be opportunities for good men to shape a new world."

"A new world?" Daire Donn took a sip of beer. "That sounds promising. I will have an answer for you in ten days' time. Will that be acceptable?"

Patrick let out the breath he hadn't realized he'd been holding. "Yes."

After that, the talk had been filled with stories and laughter as Daire Donn recounted the Fomori's exploits, which had eased Patrick's worry. It was as he'd thought: the Fomori had an entirely different way of looking at events. The Fianna were not quite as heroic as they'd been portrayed. They had moments as bloodthirsty and cruel as those told of the Fomori. And Daire Donn's love of Ireland was obvious, as was his enthusiasm to help.

But now it had been ten days, and they'd heard nothing. Patrick stood over one of the glass cases in his study, staring down at the things inside, the ogham stick safely locked in place, separate from the rowan wand, which Simon had hidden elsewhere. Patrick felt a shiver of excitement when he looked at the stone. Daire Donn had been everything he'd hoped. The old King of the World had been a charismatic man. Patrick understood why people followed him.

And most importantly, he seemed a reasonable man.

Tell me, Patrick thought impatiently. *Send the message.*

He tapped his fingers against the glass. Impatience was his failing, he knew, but he couldn't help himself. He could be patient with some things: with the business, with his mother, with Lucy, though she tried him often, as when she'd come begging him to hire some poor boy who needed a job—and who had thought Lucy capable of such finer feeling? It made Patrick wonder if perhaps he'd been wrong; perhaps his sister wasn't as shallow as he'd thought. And despite the depression, the business was doing well—rich men knew how to stay rich, and they always needed tailoring and hats—so what was another stableboy if it made his sister happy?

He turned from the display case, striding to the window, looking out on Madison Square, at promenaders and tinkling fountains, the smell of roses from his mother's garden wafting through the open window. He thought of Grace in the reflected light of the garden: the softness of her mouth against his, the way she'd quoted "Dark Rosaleen" to him. He'd been struck then with the urge to tell her everything. Everything the Fenian Brotherhood had done, everything he wanted. The old magic and the failure of the Fianna to show and the calling of the Fomori. Daire Donn.

But there again, he was too impatient. He would tell her eventually, because he knew she would share the passions of whomever she loved. It was that romance in her, her love for the Irish legends: the tale of Finn, who'd saved the life of High King Cormac of Ireland and was made the head of the king's elite fighting force as a reward; the love story of Grace's namesake, Grainne, and her Diarmid; and the tragedy of the fair-haired Etain's love for Oscar. Grace understood his passion for their homeland.

But he'd also seen her nervousness. He'd had to remind

himself that she was still so young. Almost seventeen, but there was so much she didn't know about the world, and at twenty-one, he'd seen so much more. He wanted to teach her. He wanted to see that fire in her eyes burn for him. But he had to go slow. Waiting was the key.

He gripped the windowsill hard. He pressed his head against the glass.

He hated waiting.

When he heard the knock at the front door, he jumped. But then he realized that Daire Donn was unlikely to send a messenger to his house. No, the Fomori's answer would come to the Brotherhood, where Rory Nolan was waiting.

Patrick heard the opening of the front door, the maid's voice. He heard her footsteps down the hall. When she knocked at his study, it was all he could do to school his face into a pleasant smile.

"A note for you, sir," she said, giving him what looked like a scroll tied with a ribbon before she left.

It wasn't paper, but parchment. Real parchment, made from scraped hides. Thick yet pliable.

Patience, Patrick cautioned himself. It could be nothing, an invitation to a costume ball. A themed supper. Some foolish waste of time.

But he knew it wasn't. He felt the magic pulsing from it. He was amazed that the maid hadn't seemed to feel it as well.

He stripped the ribbon from the scroll and unrolled it, his fingers trembling.

The note was written in Gaelic, in thick, flowing ink. He'd been reading Gaelic since he was ten, and this was no trouble.

> *We agree to your proposal. Together we will make the Eire run red with the blood of Albion. We come by ship. We will arrive with the summer solstice.*
>
> *Daire Donn, on behalf of the Fomori, also known as the Children of Domnu*

They had agreed. They were coming! The summer solstice—that was June twenty-first, only a few short weeks away. It had been so easy after all, just as Patrick had hoped. The Fomori were coming, and together they would save Ireland. And the answer had come to *him*. Daire Donn had chosen *him*.

Patrick smiled.

The scroll turned to dust in his hands and disappeared.

TEN

June 2

Grace

My dreams that night were filled with death and destruction, screaming ravens and fire. Aidan shouting *No, Grace!* as purple lightning flashed. And then there was a river, and sunlight, and a blond young man standing on the bank beneath a tree laden with red berries. He turned—Patrick—his face lighting in that irresistible smile, and I ran toward him; but as I did, he changed. He wasn't Patrick—but Derry, and I knew I looked into the face of my own destruction.

I woke with my head pounding and the fury to forget him, and was relieved when I heard my grandmother call for me. When I stumbled to her room, she was twisted up in the bedcovers, her nightcap completely turned about so that the ribbons trailed into her face.

"Grainne," she croaked when she saw me, which was odd in itself, as she almost never called me by my given name.

"Look at you," I said, trying to smile, to ignore my headache. I leaned to straighten her cap.

She grabbed my wrists so suddenly and tightly I cried out. "You must stop him," she said. "It can only be you."

"Grandma, please—"

"Is she all right?"

It may have been the first time in weeks that I was truly glad to see my brother. He stood barefoot in the doorway rubbing his eyes, his clothes so wrinkled it was obvious he'd slept in them. I thought of my dream, his shouting.

He said, "I heard her call out."

Grandma released me as suddenly as she'd grabbed me. She leaned back against the pillows with a groan. "That boy."

Aidan came into the room. "What boy?"

"I don't know," I said. "She's been saying it for days. I think she means Patrick."

Aidan sat on the edge of the bed. I wanted to say something cutting, but he didn't seem drunk for a change, and he gave me a sweet smile as he took Grandma's hand, murmuring calming words. He was so good when he wanted to be.

"There you are, my boy," Grandma said, herself again.

My boy. I wondered if I'd got it wrong. If that hadn't been what she'd said before, instead of *that boy.* Perhaps it was my brother she'd meant and not Patrick. It made sense. *Don't trust him,* she'd said, and *He will keep you safe.* Both things could be true when it came to Aidan. But to say that only I could stop him . . . I had no power over Aidan. I could not guilt him into seeing what he was doing to us, and my anger had no effect. His charm worked on me as well as anyone.

Now I watched as his charm worked on Grandma too. She'd seemingly forgotten me. I hesitated, not trusting to leave her to him, but he said, "It's all right, Gracie. I'll stay for a bit. Go on and do whatever needs doing."

"The dishes, you mean?" I could not keep from being cutting after all. "As there's no kitchen maid?"

Aidan's eyes darkened. "You're learning a valuable skill. We could hire you out if need be."

I rolled my eyes and went back to my room to get dressed. My headache lingered, not strongly but there, the kind of thing you forgot until you turned your head just so or saw too bright a light. And that reminded me of Derry and that blinding glow, the stabbing pain. I still didn't know what had caused it. But it seemed better to forget it.

My mother had gone to give pianoforte lessons again, and I was in the kitchen, up to my elbows in greasy water, wearing my oldest dress, with my hair straggling into my face, when there was a knock on the back door. I meant to ignore it, but whoever it was kept pounding. Probably a peddler looking for the cook we didn't have. I pulled my hands from the water, wiping them on the hem of the apron, and I yanked open the door.

"You took your time." Derry leaned against the wall near the door. Last night's dream whirled back, as if his dark-blue gaze wasn't enough to unsettle me on its own. "I see it wasn't to fix yourself up."

My face flamed. I told myself I didn't care. He was a *stableboy.* What did it matter if he saw me in my oldest dress, with my hair falling every which way? I raised my chin and met his gaze. "What do you want?"

"You're not going to invite me in for tea?"

"I'm busy, as you must plainly see."

"Doing what?" He craned his neck to look past me.

"Washing dishes."

He raised a dark brow, barely visible through that thick hair. "Do you never comb your hair out of your face?"

"I like it that way," he said. "Most girls do too."

"Don't you have something else you should be doing rather than bothering me—like mucking out stables or twisting Lucy about your finger?"

"Twisting Lucy—is that what you think I'm doing?"

"Aren't you?"

"You don't think much of me, do you?"

"You've given me no reason to think otherwise."

"You're very sure of your position for a lass who's washing her own dishes."

I grabbed the edge of the door, meaning to close it on him.

He stuck his foot in the gap and pushed the door open. He came into the kitchen, making me step back. "Don't send me away so quickly. I've come to give you this." He reached into his pocket and pulled out something.

"Patrick's book!" I reached for it, and Derry pulled it away, just out of my reach. When I reached for it again, he put it behind his back.

"What will you give me for it?" he asked with a too-sure smile that said he'd played this game many times.

"I'm not Lucy," I said. "And I don't like being teased. If you think I'm going to give you a kiss for it, you're sadly mistaken."

"A kiss? What makes you think I want one from you?"

I tried to pretend my face wasn't burning *again* and drew away. "Keep it then."

His smile softened—it was even more humiliating to see that he realized how much he'd embarrassed me.

This time when he held out the book, I didn't take it.

"I'm sorry, lass. I shouldn't have teased. You bring out the worst in me, I'm afraid. Go on, unless you want me to drop it on the floor."

Warily, I took it. I'd been worried over losing it, but it wasn't until I had it in my hands that I realized just how worried. "Thank you. Where did you find it?"

"On the walk." He grinned. "Where you swooned."

"You *did* have it! You lied to me!"

"I wanted to read it."

That surprised me. Both that he'd wanted to and that he could. "Oh. Did you?"

"'Alas, alas, and alas! For the once proud people of Banba!'"

I clutched the book. "You did."

"You know what the poem's about?" he asked.

"Ireland's oppression."

"You care about such things?"

"Why shouldn't I?"

"Safe here in your little house," he said, gesturing. "Choosing pink dresses for a party. You'll pardon me if I say it doesn't seem that Ireland's troubles *trouble* you."

"You don't know me at all," I said. "I care very much."

"Do you? For yourself? Or for Devlin?"

My heart was pounding, though I didn't know why. "It's Patrick's mission. And so it's mine too."

"How involved are you, lass?"

"Involved? Involved in what?"

"The Fenian Brotherhood."

"Why, not at all. It's a club for men. That's why they call it the 'Brotherhood.'"

"What else do you know of it?"

"If you have questions about the Fenians, you should ask Patrick. Though I don't guess they'd have you as a member either, if that's what you're wondering."

"They only want rich men, is that it?"

The way he was looking at me . . . I thought of yesterday, how I'd been pressed against him and then how he'd stared at me in my dream, and I wished he would leave. I said meanly, "They want heroes, not stableboys."

But he didn't even react. He just kept looking at me as if he couldn't look away. "What has Devlin told you, lass? What are their plans?"

"Why would he share them with me?"

"Because you're to be his wife."

"That's not . . . yes. Perhaps." It flustered me that he'd said it. That he knew it. "It's not settled yet."

"So still time to back out?"

"Why would I want to back out?"

"You're young yet to bind yourself."

"I'll be seventeen in twelve days. Which is *not* too young to be married, not that it's any of your concern. And if I have to marry, then why not Patrick? He loves me. He *knows* me."

"You have to marry?"

And I felt this urge to tell him all of it, as if he would understand, as if he always had. *Always?*

"What makes you so sure he knows you?" he asked intently, stepping toward me.

He was too close. He was solid and stunning and I wished he would touch me, and that thought shocked me so much I said forcefully, "Why are you asking me these things? My life has nothing to do with you."

He went still. I saw a flicker of recognition in his eyes. "You know, you remind me of someone. Someone I lived near in . . . I guess 'twould be County Kildare now."

"My family is from Allen."

"Ah. Perhaps a relation then."

"Perhaps. My grandmother once said we were related to nearly everyone there."

I waited for him to say something else, but he only gave me a look that made me want to look away.

"Thank you for returning the book," I said carefully, stepping back. "Now I think you should leave. I've things to do, and I can't believe the Devlins would appreciate you being here instead of in their stables."

He started. "Aye. I should go. Stables to muck, girls to twist about."

I couldn't help smiling.

"You should smile more often, you know."

Then he turned on his heel, and was gone.

—∾— *June 6* —∾—

Dinner was intimate: Patrick and his family, me and mine. Mama had asked a neighbor to watch over Grandma, so she and Aidan were both here, and even the fact that Aidan reached far too often for the wine couldn't mar my happiness.

"Have you decided on the venue for Grace's debut?" Mrs. Devlin asked my mother.

Mama said, "Oh, I think someplace small."

"Small!"

"Grace needn't have a large one, Mama, if she's already got a beau," Lucy put in.

Patrick smiled warmly at me. "I agree with Lucy. It should be small."

"In any case, I'd thought a violinist enough music," Mama said.

"There must be room for dancing," Aidan said, taking another sip of his wine. "Or no one'll come."

Mama said firmly, "Small is better."

I glared at my brother, who seemed oblivious to what my mother wasn't saying—that small was all we could afford, even with Mrs. Needham's *kind* support.

Lucy said, "Half the boys we know are terrible dancers anyway. They'd ruin Grace's toes before the night is out."

"My dear," Mrs. Devlin murmured.

"Well, it's true. And I don't know why a debut should matter so much. Wouldn't we all be better off if we didn't display ourselves like so much . . . horseflesh?"

I stared at Lucy in amazement. She'd spent the years leading up to her debut going through every *Godey's Lady's Book*, debating the cut and color and embellishment of her gown, worrying over what flowers should decorate the tables and where the candles should be placed to show her blond hair to its best advantage. I had never known anyone who cared so much for debuts as Lucy Devlin.

"It's all so old-fashioned, don't you think?" Lucy went on relentlessly. "We should be free to choose a husband from the whole world instead of those few who deign to answer an invitation."

Now I understood. It was about Derry, of course. I opened my mouth to make some comment about horseflesh and stableboys. Then I remembered how I'd felt standing so close to him in my kitchen, and I let the words die on my tongue. I hadn't told her about his visit, and I didn't intend to. She would think only the worst—of me, not of him.

Patrick threw his napkin aside and rose. "Mama, Mrs. Knox, if you don't mind, I thought I'd take the opportunity to show Grace the collection." He looked at me. "That Celtic horse you mentioned."

I'd mentioned nothing of the kind, but gratefully I pushed

aside my thoughts of Derry. "Oh yes. I'm eager to see it. Mama, do say yes."

"We'll just be down the hall," Patrick added.

Mrs. Devlin said, "Patrick's obsession—and his father's. I vow those relics consumed Michael's every waking moment. You must not encourage Patrick, Grace."

"I only want to show them to her," Patrick said, laughing.

Lucy said wryly, "Shall I chaperone?"

I flashed her a glare, which she ignored, and then I looked pleadingly at my mother, who said, "No need, I think, if it's just down the hall. I do hope I'm not making a mistake in trusting you, sir."

Patrick pressed his hand to his chest. "I'll be on my best behavior."

He took my hand, tucking it into the crook of his arm as he led me out of the dining room.

His warm breath tickled my ear as he whispered, "I thought we should never escape."

"You mean you haven't a Celtic horse to show me?" I teased.

"I've something better," he said, taking me into the study. Once we were there, he started to close the door, and then he left it ajar. "Perhaps we shouldn't give them reason to think poorly of us. Though if it were up to me, I'd lock it tight— Ah, what's this? Don't tell me I've made you blush."

There was no point in denying it.

"Who knew that Grace Knox could go so pink?"

"If you tell anyone, I'll murder you in your bed."

"I wouldn't dare. Especially because I can think of a few things I'd rather you do there."

I had walked right into it. Now my face felt on fire. I looked away, and then his fingers were at my jaw, forcing me to look at him, and his expression was so full of longing, the heat in my cheeks spread to the rest of me. He bent to kiss me, and again I shivered as his lips touched mine; again I wanted to pull him so close he couldn't escape.

His mouth moved to my jaw. "I'm sorry," he whispered. "I shouldn't tease. It's only that I'd despaired you would ever think of me as anything more than a friend."

"You know I do," I said, marveling at the truth of it. "But I think friendships, too, are important, don't you? I would hate to be the kind of wife who plays no part in her husband's real life."

He drew away. "His real life?"

I wished I'd said nothing; I wanted him to go on kissing me. But he was looking at me in a way that made me want to answer honestly. "I would want to know how he feels about things. What he thinks of the world. What his passions are."

"It's what I want as well." He released me. "Now look about you, and you can readily see what my passions are."

The study had been his father's, and I had been in it as a child. It seemed much the same, dark with leather and the smell of tobacco and old wood; there were piles of books lying about, which had not been true when his father was still alive. At one end was a fireplace of cherry and black marble, flanked by fat leather chairs and solid tables with clawed feet.

The curtains—deep-brown velvet with heavy tassels—were drawn back from windows that let in the evening, and the brass gas sconces glowed warmly. The room was welcoming and comfortable; I felt at home in it, even though it was purely a man's room.

A large desk was at the other end, and beside it were the display cases—at least four, and above them box frames, each holding a piece of Celtic antiquity. One held a hammered bronze mask, another a silver torc—a crescent-shaped neck-lace—with a bull's head decorating each end. There was a small stone relief carved with the goddess Brigid, showing her trinity: maiden, matron, and crone. Beside it was an illustration of the Morrigan, the Irish goddess of war. Like Brigid, the red-haired Morrigan had been depicted in her three aspects. She was the Morrigan, but she was also Badb the battle crow; Nemain the Venomous, the inciter of frenzy; and Macha the Hateful, the collector of souls. There were ravens perched on her shoulders and severed heads, death and destruction all around her—

"It's beautiful, isn't it?"

Patrick had come up behind me. He leaned over my shoulder, pointing at the picture, so close I felt his warmth and smelled his clean, citrusy cologne.

"Beautiful and terrible," I said.

"See the severed heads? The Celts believed the soul resided in the head, and so taking the head of an enemy not only gave them power, but kept that soul from reaching the Otherworld."

I shivered. "What did they do with the heads?"

"Displayed them on stakes, mostly. As warnings to their other enemies." His voice lowered. "Sometimes I dream about the Morrigan."

I turned to him. "So do I! Terrible dreams. Lately quite often, nearly every night. I think it might be because my grandmother—" I broke off the moment I realized what I'd almost said.

"Your grandmother?" he prompted. "I heard she wasn't well."

"Yes. She's . . . she's quite ill."

"I'm sorry to hear that."

I saw the compassion in his eyes, and I wanted to tell him about her madness. *And if you do, it will ruin everything.* "Oh, let's not talk of this now. What did you want to show me?"

"All of it. Everything I am. Some of these things have been in my family for generations." He touched a bronze statuette resting on the top of the case. "This is the horse I told you about. And there, inside, see the serpent bracelet? It's perfectly wrought, even for how primitive it is. And that raven statue too." He smiled ruefully at me. "Though I wouldn't want to see it in my dreams. And this—do you know what this is? I think it might be my favorite." He pointed to another framed drawing, one different from the rest—not paper or parchment, but what looked like tree bark, very thin and a bit shredded. On it was painted a man with dark hair holding a pile of red berries, which he was offering to a woman who knelt beside him, her blond hair cascading over her shoulders.

The painting was faded and hard to see, bits of the bark missing altogether.

"It's very old," Patrick went on. "Do you recognize it?"

"No." I shook my head. "Should I?"

"It's your namesake. Grainne. And Diarmid, offering her berries from the magical rowan tree in the forest of Dubros."

"Oh." I caught my breath. "Oh yes, of course."

Patrick's gaze held me. "Grainne was the daughter of Cormac, the High King of Ireland, and she agreed to marry Finn, the leader of Cormac's band of elite warriors and bodyguards. But at the great betrothal feast, she became frightened of Finn and so she asked his lieutenant, Ossian, to take her away. He refused. So she went to Diarmid Ua Duibhne, the most handsome of the Fianna. He refused as well. But Diarmid had a gift that had been given to him by one of the children of the *sidhe*, a lovespot that made any woman who saw it fall in love with him."

I let him tell the story I knew very well—it was one of my favorites. I loved the sound of his voice, the way he looked at me. "The *ball seirce*," I breathed.

"The *ball seirce*. And even as Diarmid turned Grainne away, she saw it and fell in love with him. Grainne laid a *geis* upon Diarmid that compelled him to take her away from Finn. That night, she put a sleeping potion in the wine of all the warriors but Oscar and Ossian, and with their help, she and Diarmid stole away.

"Finn was furious when he discovered the theft of his betrothed. He followed Diarmid and Grainne zealously, for years, determined to win her back and destroy the one who had been his friend. Finn sent all manner of magical beings after them. He called on every alliance he had. But Diarmid defeated them all: the three sea-champions and their armies at the hill of Curra Ken Amid, the evil hounds of Slieve Lougher, the giant of Dubros. Ossian and Oscar, troubled by Finn's temper, did what they could to help Diarmid and Grainne, and sometimes they were aided by Diarmid's foster father, the love god, Aengus Og."

Patrick's voice kept me captive. I'd always dreamed of my own Diarmid, the white knight of my fantasies, who would fall in love with me and spirit me away, braving all threats and evils to be with me. A fantasy, yes, but Grainne *was* my namesake. It was easy to imagine how it had been, how breathless and exciting.

Patrick continued, clearly enjoying himself. "Finally, Finn tracked them to the magical wood of Dubros, but Oscar said that any man who would harm Diarmid would have to get through him first. Oscar was the greatest of Finn's warriors; even Finn was no match for him. So Finn went to the Land of Promise, to his old teacher, a witch, who said she would help. She hunted down Diarmid on a flying water lily and tried to kill him with poison darts. But Diarmid was the best spearman alive—he slew the witch with a single hurl of his Red Spear, and Finn was forced to abandon his quest. When Aengus Og asked for peace, Finn agreed, and Grainne and Diarmid were exiled and married.

"But after a time, Grainne grew lonely. She wanted to see her father, and so Diarmid agreed to take her to the High King's feast. There, Diarmid was awakened in the night by a terrible sound, and when he went to investigate, Finn told him that it was a wild boar; Diarmid was under a *geis* by Aengus Og never to hunt boar because Diarmid's half brother had been turned into one magically when they were youths. Diarmid asked for Finn's assistance, which Finn refused, and Diarmid went alone into the night.

"And there, on the plain of Ben Bulben, Diarmid was slain by the great boar that was his half brother, and as he lay dying, Oscar and Ossian pleaded with Finn to save him, because water drunk from Finn's hands was healing. Finn brought Diarmid water, but before he reached him, he remembered what Diarmid had done and so he let the water slip through his fingers. Three times he did this, and three times Ossian and Oscar begged for him to heal their friend. At last, Finn agreed; but by then it was too late, and Diarmid died."

"It's so sad," I said, as overwhelmed by the story as I always was.

Patrick smiled gently. "Not so sad really. Aengus Og took Diarmid's body to his home and brought his soul back now and then so he could talk to him."

"But Grainne married Finn then. So it *is* sad."

"I suppose she didn't really love Diarmid."

"I like to think she did. And that when he died, Grainne

had no choice but to marry Finn. I like to think she mourned Diarmid the rest of her life."

"You don't think she loved him just because of the lovespot?"

I shook my head. "Perhaps at the start. But then I think it became real for both of them. He was an honorable man. How could she not love him?"

"Honorable? For stealing away his captain's betrothed?"

"He was under a *geis*. And even when they ran away, he resisted her for Finn's sake."

Patrick stared at me. "How do you know that?"

"Grandma says so. The way she tells it, Diarmid left bread behind each night to signal to Finn that he'd not yet . . . well—you know."

"I've never heard that part of the story."

"It mattered to him—his loyalty to Finn." I looked again at the illustration, Grainne's long golden hair.

"I guess that loyalty bought him something. Aengus Og gave Diarmid's body back, so he's supposed to be sleeping now with the rest of the Fianna, ready to return when the *dord fiann* blows. It's all just a legend, but I wish . . ." Patrick sighed, and then he said softly, "Perhaps I could be your Diarmid, Grace."

There was something slow and searching and familiar in his eyes, and my dream flitted back, Patrick on the riverbank and then . . . not Patrick.

I pushed the image away. "What would we be running from?"

Patrick glanced at the display case. "Why couldn't we be

running *to* something? The stories are important, Grace. And these relics are too. They're our heritage. My father told me we're caretakers. That our job is to keep them safe until they can be returned."

"You mean to return them to Ireland?" I asked. "But how valuable they must be."

"Some are. The most valuable pieces aren't here. They're in safekeeping." He reached into his pocket, pulling out a key, which he inserted in the lock of one of the cases. He opened the glass and picked up a long flat piece of stone carved with markings that looked like bird feet—runes. He held it reverently. "But this may be the most important piece I own, though it's worth little in money." He held it out to me. "It's an ogham stick. Take it."

"Are you certain? I don't want to break it."

"You won't. It's stone. You'd need the strength of Cuchulain." Another legendary Irish hero.

I took the stick from Patrick. I expected the feel of cool stone, but it was warm, as if it had been resting in the sun. And growing warmer. Almost . . . hot. Scalding. *Burning.* "Ouch! Oh—" I gasped and thrust it back at Patrick so hard he nearly fumbled and dropped it. I looked down at my fingers, expecting to see blisters form, but there was nothing. The skin wasn't even red, and yet it had been so hot. . . .

Patrick frowned and looked down at the stone in his hands, asking sharply, "What did you say?"

"I— Nothing."

His frown deepened.

I worried that I might have offended him, that he would think me somehow not the girl he wanted. "It's fascinating, Patrick. Truly."

His expression cleared. "I've arranged the cases so sunlight hits them every day near sunset. I like to come in here and look at them then. They look as if they're glowing. Magical." He set the ogham stick carefully back into the case. "Some of these things . . . the old magic's still in them. You can feel it."

I didn't know what to say to that. He wasn't joking, and there was that reverence again in his voice, along with an odd excitement. I thought perhaps he meant magic as in *presence*, the way some things seemed to hold their history within them. My grandmother's horn had been like that. Sometimes when I held it, I could have sworn I *heard* the battles it had been in, the cries of men, the clash of swords, and the *swoosh* of spears rushing to their targets.

"They're so full of history," I agreed.

"They are, but that's not what I mean. I mean . . ." He hesitated. "I mean magic."

"You can't mean real magic."

"Don't you believe in it?"

"I believe some things feel almost alive," I said. "They're so old, and they've seen so much that I think they just become . . . imprinted."

"Yes." His gray-green eyes were lit with an inner fire. "Though it's more than that too. Grace, can I tell you something without you thinking I'm mad?"

"Of course."

He clutched my fingers as though he was afraid I would dash away. "You know I'm involved with the Fenian Brotherhood."

The echo of Derry's words, his questions, came into my head. "Yes."

"We've raised money for the rebels in Ireland, but the last uprising was a disaster. Things have grown desperate. I was there, Grace. To see such a loss of hope . . . I remembered something my father had told me, about the old magic, and I thought: What could it harm?"

"The old magic?"

"We've done something amazing, Grace. In only a few weeks, everything will change. *Everything.* I can't speak of it now, not yet, but it's real. It's real, and it's as alive as it always was. And soon the whole world will know of it—"

"I think if the two of you don't come to the parlor, Mama might call for the police," Lucy said from the door.

Patrick released my hands and sprang away in a single moment.

I was dazed, still captured by the things he'd said. *The old magic. Something amazing. Real and alive.* I didn't think him mad. I didn't know what to think, except that I wished Lucy had stayed away a few moments longer, because Patrick gave me a quick glance, a shake of his head, and I knew that what he'd told me was to be kept secret and that he would not speak of it before the others.

"Of course," he said to his sister. He turned to me with a

smile. "I've kept you to myself long enough. Go on with Lucy. I'll be there as soon as I lock these up."

I nodded. He met my gaze, that glow still in his eyes, and I felt as if the two of us were together in something bigger than ourselves—and I liked the feeling.

When we left the room, Lucy gave me a simpering smile. "How close you were. Why, it's almost scandalous."

I said nothing. My mother would hardly mind, and I didn't think hers would either, given that the two of them were conspiring to get Patrick and me together.

Lucy put her hand on my arm, stopping me. "Grace," she said urgently, all nastiness gone. "I need a favor."

"You have a funny way of showing it."

"I'm sorry. Truly I am. It's only . . . well, you must know how jealous I am of you and Patrick. You must know—"

"What do you want, Lucy?"

"Derry wants to take me to a parish fair," she rushed on. "He said to ask you to come as our chaperone. He's worried for my reputation."

"Is he? How good of him. Is that what he was telling you before our shopping trip? That he couldn't meet you alone because he worried for your reputation?"

She at least had the sense to blush. "That was different. Other people will see us. It's a *parish* fair."

"He's Catholic then, as I thought. Lucy, surely you must see how useless this is? Your mother—"

"I don't need a lecture from you, Grace. You needn't be so

self-righteous. It's not as if I'm asking you to accompany us to a dance hall. Will you come or not?"

"It's not seemly even if I do. It will just be the three of us caught in a compromising position, and I cannot afford it."

"Then ask your brother to come too. He'll be chaperone enough for all of us."

That was true, though the thought of asking my brother to go, or trying to keep him away from liquor or cards if I did, was exhausting.

"Please," Lucy whispered fervently. "Please. I'll do anything you ask in return."

It was truly the last thing I wanted to do. A provincial parish fair. My brother. Derry with Lucy. I felt a flash of jealousy that unnerved me. *How ridiculous you are.* I'd just left Patrick. It was *Patrick* I wanted. *Needed.*

Lucy kept going. "It will be fun. There will be games, and food. Puppets, he said. A magic lantern show. I hardly ever see him. You must help me, Grace. I'm quite desperate."

It was that, finally, that made me give in. Lucy was going to be my sister—*hopefully*—and she would go with Derry whether or not Aidan and I were there. I could protect her this much.

Reluctantly, I nodded. "Very well. I'll try to convince Aidan."

"There will be drink there," she said.

"Then I'm certain he'll come."

Lucy laughed. I didn't know whether it was at my joke or in relief that I'd said yes.

I asked, "When is it?"

"Derry has Thursday evening off."

I sighed. Evening. Of course. It was not only the hardest time to think of an excuse to leave the house, it was the worst time to go anywhere with Aidan.

"Oh, thank you. Thank you," Lucy said. "I'll make certain you don't regret it. I promise."

I regretted it already. *Derry. Watching me. Waiting.*

I looked longingly over my shoulder, back to the study. I thought of the things Patrick had said and that fire in his eyes. *"Perhaps I could be your Diarmid, Grace."* And I told myself I wished to be nowhere else but with him, listening to his talk of Celtic history and magic.

ELEVEN

June 11

Grace

W hy would I want to spend the evening with you and Lucy Devlin and her new boy?" Aidan asked, lolling on my bed, tossing about the worn pillow that Mama had embroidered with daffodils.

"Put that down," I said, grabbing it from him. "There will be plenty of drink to be had, I understand. And what else have you to do?"

"Plenty more than playing nanny. There's a card game at the Bucket with my name on it."

"What will you gamble away this time? Mama's shoes?"

"Perhaps this," he said, grabbing back the pillow. "It's a pretty thing."

"*Aidan.* Truly, this must stop. You're bankrupting us; surely you know it. Mama's already forced into giving pianoforte lessons, and—"

"Mama loves playing the pianoforte. And she's doing it

for your ridiculous debut. Why you've need of it with Patrick Devlin sniffing around, I don't know."

"Must you be so selfish? Why can't you see——"

"Hell, Grace, you've turned into as big a fishwife as Mama," he said, covering his face with the pillow.

The words stopped me short. As far as I knew, Mama had never even raised her voice to him.

"I don't understand how you can do it," I said desperately. "How you can just let everything go. Everything we have."

He lowered the pillow, and in his blue eyes was a fear I had never seen before. "You don't know anything."

"Then tell me. Explain it to me."

He looked away. When he looked back, he was again the self-deprecating, devil-may-care brother I knew. "What kind of drink did you say would be at this fair?"

"Aidan, *please*."

"Leave it, Gracie," he said, rising from my bed, tossing the pillow so it skidded across the bare floor. "I'll go to the fair with you if you're so hot to do a favor for Lucy Devlin."

"Thank you," I said.

He only grunted and left the room.

Mama agreed the moment she heard that Lucy meant to go and Aidan would chaperone us. I didn't tell her that Derry was coming——she would see it then for what it was: a chance for Lucy to be alone with her beau. And as she didn't ask me if anyone else was going along, I didn't have to lie outright. "I'm glad to see you and Patrick's sister growing so close," was all Mama said.

Aidan was sober when we went to get Lucy.

"It would be nice if you stayed that way," I told him.

"Don't count on it. So is Lucy's newest really a stableboy? She's certainly coming down in the world."

"She'll hear nothing against him either," I said. "So don't bother to tease. You'll only rile her. And he's irritating enough on his own without adding her to it."

"You've met him?"

"Once or twice. In passing."

"Long enough to know he's irritating?" Aidan cocked his head.

"It's obvious within moments."

My brother laughed, and then we were knocking on Lucy's door, and Lucy came hurrying out, calling behind her, "Here they are now, Mama! We shan't be late!"

She closed the door before her mother could respond. Lucy was breathless and bright eyed and beautiful, in a blue-striped dress trimmed with silk pansies, a fringed paisley shawl, and a white straw hat with a ribbon that matched her dress and her eyes. I felt plain and coarse beside her—there'd been no point in wearing either of my best gowns, as Patrick wouldn't be here to see. I remembered how Derry had last seen me, wearing stained brown and an old apron. I told myself I didn't really care what he thought of me, but at the sight of Lucy my heart sank. My lavender gown trimmed in black with jet buttons was so simple and unadorned that I would be unnoticeable. *Which is just what I want.*

"Hurry." Lucy glanced down the street. "Patrick should

be on his way home now, and he'll want to come along if he sees us."

I wished he would. But of course, if Patrick came, Lucy wouldn't get to see her Derry. "What did you tell your mother?"

"That we wanted to take a promenade and get ice cream, as the night was so pleasant and warm." She made a face at Aidan. "I do hope you'll say nothing to make her think otherwise."

He turned a pretend key against his lips. "I am well locked, milady."

Lucy let out a long-suffering sigh.

The evening was still very warm, but there was a breeze coming off the river. When we reached the stables, Derry was leaning against the outside wall. His shirt was buttoned, I was glad to see, but he wore no coat and no hat. He probably had neither. When he saw us he pushed off the wall, but Lucy was already racing toward him, throwing herself into his arms.

He bent to kiss her, a rather long and passionate kiss, and I looked away, right into my brother's eyes.

Aidan grinned. "Well, well, it seems Lucy has herself a man instead of a boy."

"Don't be an ass," I said. "He's younger than you."

"But he has quite the style, don't you think?"

"I would hardly know."

Aidan laughed.

Finally, Derry pulled away, leading Lucy over by the hand. His eyes—like Lucy's—were sparkling.

"Miss Knox," he said with a smile—how could he make

me feel like the only girl in the world when he was holding Lucy's hand?—"'tis good to see you again."

Two seconds with him and I was already flustered. "This is my brother, Aidan. He's agreed to accompany us. Aidan, this is Derry . . . I'm sorry, I don't know your—"

"O'Shea," Derry provided.

"Think of me as nonexistent," Aidan said, frowning and squinting as if the light were too bright as he shook Derry's hand. Probably laudanum again, I thought, though I would have sworn he was sober. He glanced at Lucy, who clung to Derry like a limpet. "I'm here merely for propriety's sake, and I shall safely disappear the moment the ale's in view. But Grace will serve better as your conscience anyway."

Lucy simpered, "Grace has never broken a rule in her life."

"Really?" Derry looked at me. "You're truly such a saint, Miss Knox?"

It sounded like an insult coming from him. I said quickly, "They're both exaggerating. I've broken plenty of rules—" I stopped, wondering why I said it. It wasn't even true. Well, not the *plenty* part.

My brother laughed again. "So she fed her peas to the dog a time or two. Or stole a tart from the pantry. Believe me, man, it's best to be bad when she's not looking."

"I'll keep that in mind," Derry said, still smiling that arrogant, mocking smile. Lucy wrapped herself around his arm as if she meant to grow there.

Why had I come?

"So where is this fair?" Aidan asked. "I've a dry throat."

"Not far," Derry said. "The Sisters of Charity school."

Lucy and Derry set off, with Aidan and me following. Lucy snuggled into Derry's side, and he looped his arm around her waist and held her close—very close—and I said, "You'd best be careful, Lucy. We're not so far from home."

She threw me a look but didn't pull away. Derry seemed to have some common sense; he tucked her hand by his side instead. Only Lucy could make even that appear obscenely close.

My head began to ache.

It wasn't long before we approached a large brick school with painted wooden trim. The windows were open, the light from within glowing in the twilight. I heard laughter and talk and music as we went up the stairs. There was a table just inside the door where two women sat collecting the admission fee of twenty-five cents and selling raffle tickets. Lucy dug into her little purse, but Derry had enough coin to pay for all of us. "I'm the one who invited you," he said, and I thanked him and hoped I didn't sound too relieved, as I hadn't thought to bring a single penny—not that I had one to bring.

"What's the raffle for?" Lucy asked.

"Why, a hundred different things," replied one of the women. "There's a sewing machine and a parlor organ and a real Swiss clock and a fishing pole . . ."

"Two stuffed birds in a cage," said the other. "And some beautiful china painted with gold-edged harps. Oh, too many things to name."

"I'll take a ticket," Lucy said.

"I'll take one as well," Derry added.

The woman looked expectantly at me, and I elbowed Aidan, who said, "I assume you fine ladies will be selling ale?"

I wanted to hit him.

"Oh yes, just inside," one of the women said, and he smiled at them and passed by without buying a ticket.

"Thank you very much," I whispered to my brother.

"It'll be all I can do to pay for the ale," he whispered back. "And what would we do with an organ but sell it?"

"Selling it would be just fine. It would bring more than the ticket cost."

"We'd probably end up with the stuffed birds," he said.

We stepped into the main room. It had been decorated to its very last inch to look like a night garden. Hanging from the ceiling were banners declaring the names of the donating businesses and bunting in two shades of blue, along with dozens of phosphorescent stars and moons. Potted plants were in every corner, the scents of cut irises and roses and urns full of jasmine mixed with those of ale and sweat. There were real canaries in cages, singing and chirping to join laughter and talk, the crack of balls at a nearby billiards table, roars of applause from another booth. Tables lined one side, each showcasing things for sale: embroidered handkerchiefs and linens, china dolls, painted pen wipes. At a makeshift stage at the far end, children sat giggling as a puppet with a long nose pummeled another. There was a sign reading "Magic Lantern Show," with an arrow pointing into a hallway. Another said "Smoking Room," with another arrow.

Booths sold food of all kinds: oysters and sardines, chicken and salmon, candies and jellies and towering cakes, petits fours wearing sugared violets and icing roses, crosses shaped of nougat. Another booth sold claret punch, ale and lager, and my brother touched the brim of his hat and said, "If you'll excuse me, I see my quarry now. If you've need of me, I shall be just over there."

Which left me alone with Derry and Lucy.

"I want to see the Magic Lantern," she said breathlessly to him.

He glanced at me. "What do you want to see?"

What I wanted was to go home, but I was here, and it was too soon to leave. "That would be fine," I said with a wan smile.

Lucy gave a not-so-subtle hint—"You seem tired, Grace. Why don't you have a lemonade and sit for a bit?"

Because the room would be dark, of course, with no one to see or care about her kissing Derry if I wasn't there. My headache blossomed. Why should I care? Let Lucy ruin her life. And so I said, "Why, what a good suggestion, Lucy. I think I will."

But Derry shook his head. "Come with us." He grabbed my hand so quickly I had no time to react, and a shiver went through me at his touch—what was worse was his glance that said he knew it as he pulled Lucy and me together in the direction of the Magic Lantern.

Lucy glared at me from behind his back, and the moment we got into the darkened room and took a seat—Lucy and I on either side of Derry—I pulled away, clasping my hands in my lap so he couldn't grab one again.

It was dark except for the glow cast on the audience from the screen at the front of the room and the pyramid of gauzy light streaming from the magic lantern at the back. A man stood by the lantern, adjusting the slides against the bright arc light. "Presenting images of Ireland for your viewing pleasure!"

The show began, photographs painted over with water-colors: the flat-topped Hill of Tara, fields with stone fences and herds of sheep, ruined castles, picturesque rivers and salmon jumping. The audience *ooh*ed and *ahh*ed. I glanced at Derry and Lucy, fully expecting them to be locked in each other's arms, but while Lucy was nuzzling his throat and trying her best to climb inside of him, Derry was staring at the paintings on the screen as if he'd never seen anything like them. His eyes glittered in the reflected light. The planes of his face were stark, almost brutally limned, taut with . . . with yearning.

I turned to look at him more closely.

As if he felt my gaze, he looked at me. He smiled—very small and wistful, but perhaps that was just the lack of light that made me think it, and I turned away again, just in time too, because it seemed Lucy had finally got his attention.

When the show ended, and the applause still didn't have them separating from each other, I nudged Derry hard with my elbow. "The lights are coming up, for pity's sake," I hissed, and he pulled away from her just as they did.

The lights were only just bright enough for us to find our way out of the room, but even so, Lucy looked dazed and well kissed; it was all I could do not to snap at her as we filed out, stepping from near darkness into fully bright gaslight. I blinked and squinted, and just then Derry passed beneath the light, and my vision blurred—that glow again, glancing off his skin as if he were made of gold.

My headache came on fully. I stumbled, pressing my fingers to my eyes. I heard my whimper from somewhere far away, felt someone bump into me, a muttered "Excuse me," and then another as the exiting crowd jostled me. Blindly, I reached for the wall.

"Here, lass." Derry grabbed me, and I stumbled against his chest as he led me to a nearby bench. Lucy hovered, a worried look on her face.

"Grace, are you all right?" she asked.

"I . . . I think so. I just . . . just for a moment I felt sick." But the pain was fading nearly as quickly as it had the first time I'd seen that glow.

"When did you last eat?" Derry asked me.

"I don't know. This morning, I think." A small piece of toasted bread with no butter, as it was too dear.

His arm was still around my shoulders. I heard myself make a little sound of protest as he shifted to reach into his pocket—I didn't want him to draw away. He glanced at me, tightening his arm as he drew out a coin and handed it to Lucy, saying, "Get her something, Lucy, will you? And fetch her brother. We'll go."

"No," I said. If we left now, Lucy would never forgive me. "No, I'm fine. Truly. I don't want to go."

I didn't mistake the relief in Lucy's eyes. She hesitated.

I said firmly, "Leave Aidan to his drink. I'll be fine."

"At least get her something to eat," Derry told Lucy.

"I don't want you to spend your money," I said.

"'Tis mine to spend as I like," he replied, giving a nod to Lucy, who hurried off. Then, "Are you truly all right, lass, or were you just saying so to soothe Lucy?"

My headache was gone. "I'm truly all right."

"What happened?"

"The light was so bright for a moment. . . ."

"More glowing?" There was a light tease in his words. He tucked a loose curl behind my ear. My breath seemed to squeeze from my chest.

I looked down at my hands.

"There was," he said, the teasing gone. "Me again? Or someone else?"

I covered my eyes. "This is so stupid——"

He took my hand and lowered it, forcing me to look at him. There was real concern on his face. "Was it me who was glowing?"

"Just a little," I admitted. "It was the way the light hit you, I think."

"Describe it to me."

"It wasn't as strong today. More like . . . there was a fog of light about you, and then the pain, and——"

"A sudden pain? And now it's gone?"

"Mostly."

"What made it go?"

This I truly didn't want to admit. "When you . . . touched me."

I expected mockery. A flirtatious comment. But he only looked puzzled and concerned. "Very like before," he murmured. He drew away; I felt a chill where before I'd been warm.

"But the last time it was stronger. As if you were the sun."

"In the sun?"

"Not *in*. As if you were the sun itself," I corrected. "As if the glow . . . Oh, this sounds so ridiculous."

"Tell me."

"As if it came from inside you. There was just this ball of light where you stood."

"Did that disappear, too, when I touched you?"

I nodded.

He muttered something beneath his breath. Gaelic, I realized. Though I heard it rarely now, and I understood even less.

"How long have you been here?" I asked.

Derry jerked. "What?"

"In America. How long have you been in America?"

"I suppose . . . since Beltaine."

That he mentioned the ancient Celtic festival made me smile a little. "You speak Gaelic. You say Beltaine as if I must know it when no one talks of such things anymore. And I saw the way you watched those Magic Lantern pictures. As if you might jump through the screen to go where they are."

He frowned as if he was trying to make sense of my words.

"It's obvious you miss Ireland terribly," I explained gently. "Why did you leave it if you love it so much?"

"There was no choice," he said.

Now I frowned. "No choice? What do you mean?"

Derry hesitated, and I found myself holding my breath.

In the main room, someone was making an announcement in a very loud voice. There was a host of cheers.

Derry glanced toward the sound, and when he looked back at me, he said, "It doesn't matter. I'm here now. There's nothing to do but make the best of it."

I was disappointed. It wasn't what he'd been about to say, I knew. It was the kind of answer he might give to a stranger, to Lucy, and then I realized how odd it was I'd thought that. Lucy was no stranger to him. She was closer to him than I was.

I looked down at my hands again. The truly odd idea was that he might tell me anything of importance at all. Odder still was why I should care.

Derry said, "Tell me, lass, this glow . . . have you seen it before? Before me, I mean?"

"No. Just you," I said.

"And the pain? Anything else like it?"

"I've been having headaches lately. Not so bad as this, but they come with the dreams." *Dreams. Oh, very good, Grace. Why not just say dreams of you?* "Nightmares," I blurted.

"Nightmares?"

"Storms of fire and lightning and a strange light, like the one around you. And ravens."

"Ravens." Derry was very somber, all traces of his teasing, arrogant self gone.

I nodded. "I know. Ravens are harbingers of doom. My grandmother says it all the time."

"Beyond that, anything else? Anything you've seen that affects you the same way I do?"

"Nothing affects me as you do," I muttered.

He gave me a half smile. "I heard that, you know."

"You shouldn't take it as a compliment."

"I don't," he said. "Do you mean to answer me?"

"There's nothing," I said. "The nightmares and you, and . . . oh, there was an ogham stick Patrick gave me to hold that burned my hand. But I think it was only that it had been in the sun."

He went very still. "An ogham stick?"

"A piece of stone with . . . well, they're words of a sort, carved into it. The Druids used them to cast spells and . . . I don't know, read fortunes, I suppose. It's quite ancient."

"Where did Devlin get such a thing?"

"Patrick collects Celtic relics. So did his father."

"What kinds of relics?"

"Statuettes and torcs, stone reliefs, drawings, that kind of thing. He has four cases in his study, and that's not even all of it. You should see it. . . ." I trailed off as I realized that there was no chance Derry would ever be invited into Patrick's study. "He says he means to return them to Ireland one day, where they belong."

"Does he?"

There was something funny in his voice. "Is something wrong?"

He stared at me as if he couldn't look away. Then he smiled, and it was like a sign saying *We're done with all this now. Back to the usual.* "Are you feeling better, lass?"

Again, I felt disappointment. "I am."

"My healing touch." He waggled his fingers at me. Just then Lucy returned, bearing a little plate full of petits fours. She was licking icing from her fingers. "I hope you don't mind," she said as she gave me the plate. "I couldn't resist trying one."

The white icing gleamed in the gaslight, piped roses a moist and glistening pink, sugared violets twinkling. My mouth watered.

"It'll just make you sweeter," Derry said, rising, pulling her laughing and squirming into his arms. Very deliberately, he licked a bit of icing from her lower lip.

"You're so *bad.*" Lucy giggled in the moment before he kissed her, deeply and thoroughly. Her arms curved languorously around his neck; she buried her hands in the waves of his thick dark hair.

And I was jealous. Terribly, horribly *jealous.* Miserably, I looked into the plate of petits fours. The smell of them was sickly sweet, the sugared violets melting purple, the piped roses wilting. The thought of biting into one turned my stomach. I put aside the plate and sat there, waiting until Derry and Lucy unknotted themselves. And then once they had, the way Lucy looked . . . as if she'd just risen from bed; no matter that she was fully dressed—everyone in the place must know exactly what she'd been doing. Derry was no better. His dark hair was sticking up where she'd tangled her fingers in it.

"I saw a man over there with a machine that makes paper flowers," Lucy said, straightening the bow beneath her chin, gesturing for us to follow as she turned. "He's giving a demonstration now. Let's go see." She hurried off.

Derry held out his hand to help me from the bench. I ignored it. "She ran her fingers all through your hair."

He leaned close to whisper, "How would you know that unless you were watching?"

"I know because it's a mess," I snapped back.

He grinned. "You seem to care a bit too much about my hair, lass, if you don't mind my saying so. But I suppose if you're very nice to me, I might let you comb it."

Whatever truth had passed between us when Lucy was gone had completely disappeared. He glanced past me to the bench, to the plate with the petits fours. His grin faded. "You didn't eat."

"The two of you made me so sick I lost my appetite," I said, and then I marched away, following Lucy into the crowd.

TWELVE

Diarmid

Aidan Knox was very drunk when they left the fair, and somehow drunker still when they dropped Lucy at her house. Diarmid realized then that Grace was keeping her brother upright. "D'you want help to get him home?"

She flashed him a look of pure fury, and he knew she must be overcome with shame. "Thank you, no. Good night."

"Yer a strange 'un, aren't you, Derry-erry-erry?" Aidan slurred before he began laughing helplessly, falling over his sister's shoulder.

Diarmid caught Aidan's arm, helping him upright again, but when he began to walk with them, Grace said, "Good *night*, Derry," and he stood back and watched them go.

For a block. Then he followed, discreetly, just to make certain they made it home without someone robbing them or worse. There were desperate men about in these times and wilding boys who roamed the streets looking for prey, which a girl and her drunken brother surely were. It wasn't until she manhandled her brother up the steps and into their house that Diarmid relaxed and went back to the stables.

The night was too warm; it set his mind turning. He thought about her obvious distress tonight and how fiercely he'd wanted to ease it, to touch her, to tangle his fingers in *her* hair. He wanted to believe it was no different from the way he felt about girls in general, but it was, and he knew it.

He thought of how she'd seen his homesickness during the show, and her question about why he'd left that he'd wanted to answer. But he couldn't say: *I was called. It was a spell. A prophecy.* And so he'd said nothing, and seen her disappointment when he'd put her off.

And twice now she'd seen him glowing. Twice it had caused pain that left her weak and helpless. An ogham stick—*by the gods, Patrick Devlin has an ogham stick*—had burned her hand.

Once he was back at the stables, he went to the little tack room he shared with Jerry, the other stableboy. Jerry was hardly a boy, closer to thirty than twenty, but jobs were hard to come by now, and he said he'd rather be paid to be a stableboy than not be paid at all; and Diarmid saw enough tramps in the streets, sleeping on stoops and in dank corners, to agree. Diarmid took off his shirt and lay on his cot, listening to Jerry snore, feeling the sweat prickle on his skin and promising himself that everything about Grace Knox could be explained away. She'd said it herself: he'd stepped in the light just the right way, and she'd been faint again from not eating. The ogham stick had been in the sun.

But . . . her nightmares. Nightmares about storms of fire and ravens. Still, everyone had nightmares. And it was only because he'd been on battlefields where the Morrigan's Badb had sent her ravens descending in a cloud of screaming terror that he'd felt such an anxious dread when Grace had said it.

Yes, easy to explain. But for one thing:

He'd realized who Grace reminded him of: Neasa, who'd been Finn's adviser and Seer and sometime lover. A Druid priestess with the gift of oracle and spell casting. She, too, had dark and dancing eyes and thick, curling hair and skin pale as milk. Diarmid had seen that hair of hers swirling as if it were alive as she called up storms that chased and blistered in their fury. Storms of wind and thunder and crackling lightning.

Neasa, whose daughter had been the *veleda*. Who'd been given the care of the *dord fiann*. Who'd lived at the foot of the Fianna stronghold, Almhuin. The Hill of Allen.

"My family is from Allen," she'd said.

The *veleda*.

Diarmid pushed the thought away the moment he had it, the same way he'd been pushing it away all night—really, since she'd told him where her people were from, though he couldn't deny it was why he'd asked Lucy to bring her along to the fair. He was trying not to spend much time with Lucy now—it only made him feel terrible. He hadn't wanted to spend another evening watching the lovespell shine in her eyes, but there had been no other way to get close to Grace Knox. It had been his whole reason for the fair: to ask Grace questions, to discover . . . what? Something, anything. He hoped to find that she was no one. Just a girl whose family had fallen on hard times, who hadn't eaten and had swooned from hunger.

And that wish troubled him too. Because the only reason he was working in the Devlin stables was to discover who had called them and why. To find the *veleda*. Without her, they were dead. Samhain would be here soon enough; it was already June. They needed the *veleda*.

He should be overjoyed at the idea that he might have found her.

"When she makes the choice, the sacrifice must be at your hand," Manannan had said. *"This is the* geis *put upon you, lad. 'Tis you who must kill her. If you refuse this, the Fianna will fail and be no more."*

He'd thought that the *veleda* would know the prophecy, that she would know her role and the sacrifice that must be made. He had no wish to kill a lass, but the Druid priestesses he'd known had been as strong as any man, and as determined. There was no weakness in them, no hesitation. They would have been trained to die. But here was Grace Knox, with her worn gowns and dancing eyes and the blithe way she told him that her soon-to-be fiancé collected Celtic relics, as if she didn't understand the significance of that at all.

Because she didn't.

She was an innocent.

She could not be the *veleda*.

But he felt in his heart that she was.

—◦⊙— *June 12* —⊙◦—

He woke the next morning to heat that made him sweat before he even moved, and a dread that lodged in his chest. He buried himself in work, in mucking stalls, trying not to think. In the light of day, nothing seemed quite so dire; it was easy to feel that he wasn't certain, to decide merely to watch Grace Knox for a while until he was sure. Then he would tell Finn. Finn was charming and charismatic, but he was also ruthless, and—Diarmid had to admit this troubled him even more— he doubted Finn would miss her resemblance to Neasa. What Finn would do about the fact that Grace looked like his old lover Diarmid didn't know, and didn't want to guess.

So he would watch. And while he was watching, he would get into the Devlin house and look at these relics. Ancient Celtic torcs and statuettes, she'd said, and he wondered if there had been a horn among them. If Devlin had been the one who called them.

And if he had, what did he know about the *veleda*?

It seemed too big a coincidence, Diarmid's suspicions about Grace Knox along with the very sudden attention Devlin was now paying her. But perhaps it *was* a coincidence. What had Lucy said? That her brother had loved Grace for years. Per- haps so. Diarmid could see why.

Still, it made him uneasy.

Finn had ordered him to search the Devlin house anyway, and as it was, he'd delayed long enough. Grace had said the collection was in Devlin's study—not all of it, she'd said, but perhaps he would find what he was looking for. Finn's hunting horn had been a working one, without a great deal of ornamentation. So many years later, it would only look old and not especially valuable. Perhaps it would be in one of those cases. And Diarmid wanted to get his hands on that ogham stick. He wondered what Cannel would see in it, if anything.

When twilight passed and night fell, and the steward said the horses wouldn't be needed tonight, Diarmid told Jerry he was going to take a walk.

The other stableboy chuckled. "You'd best watch yourself with that Devlin girl. Ya know you're playin' with fire."

Diarmid said nothing to that. It was true. A few more days and then he would walk away, and after a week or so of not seeing him, the lovespell would fade, just as it always did. Lucy would think of him with fondness if he was lucky, or bitterness if he wasn't, but even that would disappear eventually. Because her love for him had been compelled. It wasn't real.

It never was.

Diarmid shook off his sadness at the thought and put Lucy from his mind as he strode the two blocks through the lamplit streets to the well-kept houses of those rich enough to live in this part of town without being so rich they had mansions and summer homes. Once he was at the Devlins' back gate, he leaped over the cast-iron arrows and into the narrow strip of yard, past a marble bench and a small fountain and rows of rosebushes, their fragrance sweet and heavy in the evening air. He peered stealthily into the windows until he found the study. There was no outside door, but there was a window.

The only light came from a lamp burning on the desk, a dim glow. The study was empty, but for how long?

He grasped the sill, pulling himself up—a two-thousand-year sleep hadn't taken away the strength he'd honed in battle and in spear practice. Once he had a good hold, he put his hand to the sash. It slid open easily, soundlessly—thank the maids. He leveled himself up and through, dropping as silently as he could to the floor, which was thickly carpeted—another blessing.

There he paused, listening. He heard voices from another room, more than a few. Music from a pianoforte, inexpertly played. So the Devlins had guests, which he hoped meant Patrick Devlin would be busy entertaining.

Diarmid made a quick scan of the room. Display cases lined the wall to his right. Framed shadow boxes held the things Grace had mentioned. A bull-head torc like those he'd seen a hundred times—not one meant for kings, but worn by a warrior, perhaps even one of the Fianna, though he didn't recognize it. Statuettes, a stone relief, some drawing on bark he could barely make out in the dim light, another of the Morrigan. He shuddered at that and looked away, into the cases, and then it was as if his other life washed over him in one dizzying wave—the world he'd known: fortresses and rolling green hills and the wind blowing through his hair as he hurtled with his fellows toward an advancing army, a battle cry in his throat, the sword called Liomhadoir, the Burnisher, in his hand, and the Red Spear at the ready. The things in this case had belonged to warriors and kings—that bowl there, the one cast with wrens, had been Neasa's. He'd seen her drink from it a hundred times, some foul potion that helped her find her visions. There was a crystal Druid egg the size of an apple; a few amulets—two on a necklace, green stone threaded through with red; another blue and set in a ring. A bronze shield with arms he didn't know. There, a silver goblet that reminded him of those he'd seen on the table of the High King. The sheer number of things was astounding, but there was no horn. Then he saw the ogham stick.

The ogham runes were chipped, hard to read, and it was too dim, but there was no time to study it now. Better to take it and be gone. He tried to lift the case lid—it wouldn't budge. Locked. He glanced around, saw the paper knife gleaming in the lamplight on Devlin's desk, and grabbed it, working it in the lock. Too broad. He turned back to the desk, saw the letter opener, and tried that instead. A few twists and the lock was sprung.

Diarmid pried open the lid and took the ogham stick, which was as cool as any stone should be. He tucked it beneath his arm and closed the lid again, a little too hard. He froze, listening for any pause in the conversation, anything to tell him that someone had heard. The music continued. He breathed a sigh of relief and then left the cases and went to the bookshelves, looking at each and every ornament that decorated them, hoping for the horn. Statuettes, mostly, another Druid egg. No horn.

He glanced toward the window. He should go, except that she'd said there were other things too. This wasn't the entire collection, and who knew when he would have another opportunity? He should be sure. Where else would Devlin keep valuable things?

Perhaps his bedroom.

Diarmid hesitated. It was too risky. But Finn would ask him if he'd searched the house, and when he confessed that he hadn't, he'd be sent back. And this felt too *right*. All these relics, Patrick Devlin's obsession with Ireland, the poems about rebellion and oppression. *Patrick's mission*, Grace had said, and Diarmid's instincts screamed that the horn was here somewhere.

He leaned out the window, tossing the ogham stick onto the ground below—best not to get caught with it if he was going to get caught, and the chances of that were rising every moment. Without it, he could lie that he'd been meaning to visit Lucy—which would be bad enough but wouldn't be as bad as being arrested and hung as a thief. He went to the door of the study, opening it just a crack, peering out. No one in the hall. The music was louder now. Diarmid eased from the room, looking warily toward the servants' stairs near the kitchen.

He dashed for the stairs, hiding himself in the shadows of gaslight turned low. When he reached them, he took the first five to the turn of the landing and drew back, waiting. He heard no one, but the stairs creaked beneath his step. No one would think twice about sounds on the servants' stairs, he hoped. The next floor was empty, a hallway lined with closed doors. He went down the line, knocking quietly at each one in case someone had taken to bed with a headache or dyspepsia or something, opening each when there was no answer. Mrs. Devlin's room was marked by the scent of roses. Then Lucy's—a lace-testered bed, an abandoned gown, scattered shoes. He smiled; the room was so much like her. It felt like an invasion of privacy, too, and he liked that less. He shut the door again.

He thought the next room might be Devlin's. It was a man's room, in deep blues and dark woods, but it felt empty— nothing there to show that anyone inhabited it. Diarmid went to the next. This was the one he wanted, he knew immediately, and he slipped inside. It was like the study below: leather chairs by the fireplace, a bed with heavy curtains in brown velvet. A dressing table littered with cuff links and a tangle of silk ties, a brush with strands of dark-blond hair.

Diarmid looked for anything that might house the rest of the collection. He went through everything: the dresser drawers, the huge armoire. Only clothes and more clothes—by the gods, Devlin must have a different shirt for every day! Under the bed, the desk near the window. Nothing.

Diarmid had canvassed the entire room. Wherever Devlin kept the rest of the collection, it wasn't here. Diarmid had been so certain. But now he was tempting fate.

He left the room and crept again down the hall, down the stairs. He was at the first landing when the applause started. He pushed himself back as far as he could into the shadows. If the party was over now, there would be no place to escape except back up, and he didn't relish the thought of somehow having to manage a drop from a two-story window. Or he could wait in Lucy's room and pretend he'd come to see her and enlist her help in getting out. Except that what she'd want once they were alone in her bedroom, what she would think he'd come for . . . that would be harder to manage than the window drop.

The pianoforte started again. Not over yet, thank the gods. He eased down the steps. The hall was clear; he was halfway to the study.

Then he heard footsteps coming from the parlor.

Diarmid froze against the wall. All he could hope was that the light was dim enough. But it wasn't; he knew that the moment he saw her coming toward him. She stopped. He heard the soft catch of her breath. She looked right into his eyes, and his heart jumped.

Grace.

Her hand went to her throat, a pretty little startle. "Der—"

He shook his head and pressed his finger to his lips, and she went silent. Then he took his chance. He went to the study door, with one last glance at her before he opened it. Her skin looked white in the dim light, her eyes like black pools. She said nothing as he slipped into the study, closing the door behind him.

He didn't wait to hear her call the others. He raced to the window, pushing it open, throwing himself out, then closing it again behind him. He grabbed up the ogham stick where it lay in the grass and then hurtled to the gate, launching himself into the park and the darkness.

He was blocks away before he realized no one had come after him. It was too much to hope that she had said nothing. She didn't like him; no doubt she'd take the first opportunity to turn him in. Unless she thought he was there to see Lucy, in which case perhaps she'd keep quiet. She'd kept Lucy's secret until now, but she might not continue once the ogham stick was discovered missing. She was no fool. She would know who had taken it.

Which meant he had to do something to make sure she kept her silence.

THIRTEEN

Later that night

Grace

Patrick lifted my shawl from the mass of cloaks and hats in the butler's arms and put it around my shoulders, his fingers brushing my skin so lightly it raised little shivers. He leaned close, whispering, "I wish we'd had a chance to speak alone."

I told him, "I haven't forgotten the things you said the other night at dinner." And I hadn't. His talk of old magic and whatever amazing thing the Brotherhood had done. I'd wanted all night to ask him more.

But we hadn't been alone the entire evening. I'd caught him watching me, staring at me thoughtfully and sometimes impatiently, and I felt impatient too.

He murmured, "Later. Sleep well," and kissed my temple, so sweetly and tenderly, as if I were this precious thing he meant to keep close, and I felt the strain of what I'd been keeping from him for an hour or more and thought of telling him. Just saying, *"Your stableboy was sneaking about the house tonight."*

But I didn't. Just as I didn't think about the way I'd felt seeing Derry standing there and knowing why he was here: for Lucy. I shouldn't care. *I would not care.*

I smiled and said, "Good night, Patrick," and my mother thanked the Devlins for the lovely evening—which *had* been lovely, if for no other reason than that the O'Daires and the Nolans now knew about me and Patrick. He'd made no secret of it, attending to me with the dedication of a husband, and Mrs. Devlin often had made little hints: "How fine the two of them look together, don't you think, Maeve?" and "I hope very soon to be looking into the faces of my own dear grandchildren." Patrick had smiled at me in a way that made me blush.

When Patrick left me to say good night to the others, I cornered Lucy. "You should be more careful," I whispered to her. "Do you want the whole world to know what you're doing?"

She frowned. "I've no idea what you're speaking of."

I rolled my eyes. "Don't worry, I'll keep your secret. But if you're so foolish as to get caught for taking such a risk, don't blame me."

She just stared at me blankly. She was much better at lying than I'd imagined, and I'd done enough of it myself to recognize it.

The O'Daires took Mama and me home in their carriage, and once they left us off, my mother said worriedly, "Wherever do you think Aidan could have got to?"

My brother was supposed to have come to supper tonight,

but he'd been nowhere to be found when it was time to go, and Mama had spent the evening fiddling with her handkerchief, glancing out the window.

I said, "No doubt he had another card game to attend. We haven't lost the house yet; there's something to gamble away before the lawyers get it."

"Oh, Grace, what shall we do with him? If the Devlins were to discover . . ." She trailed off hopelessly.

Too many things could finish that sentence: The extent of our debt, how very much Aidan drank and gambled, the fact that I expected the doctor's lawsuit any day, or the madness my grandmother was slowly falling prey to. Any of those things could destroy my chances with Patrick. I'd told him that Grandma was ill, but madness . . . that was something else altogether, a stain on our family. The Devlins knew that we'd lost the business and the stocks—the whole world knew that. Lucy had said herself that Patrick was saving me, and so they also knew how very much his suit meant and how disposed I was to accept it.

My pride hurt at the thought; again I felt the weight of everything I must accept. I closed my eyes and made myself think of Patrick's fingers lingering on my skin, the whisper of his voice against my ear. *"Perhaps I could be your Diarmid."* I liked him so much, and I knew I could love him. Perhaps I already did. What was not to love? He was so handsome that it was hard to look away from him, and his kiss . . . yes, I had liked that, too, very much. I felt safe with him. Again I told myself how very lucky I was.

The house was dark. The gas had been turned off for lack of payment, and when we stepped in I lit the oil lamp we'd left just inside the door. The emptiness of the house felt eerie in the wavering light.

Mama said, "I'll check on your grandmother and then I'm going to bed. It's been a long evening."

Together we went up the stairs. I watched her go down the hall, stooped and wan looking now that she'd dropped the merry mask she'd put on for the Devlins.

I remembered how happy she'd been when Papa was alive, how she'd enchanted. Her teas and suppers, her light fingers over the keys of the pianoforte, the shine of her red hair in the gaslight, and the sparkle of jewels against her throat. I could give her those things again. Once I married Patrick, I would make certain she never wanted for anything.

I went into my bedroom, closing the door. The only light came from the streetlamps outside. I didn't bother to light a candle. Instead, I unbuttoned my gown and stepped out of it, laying it over the back of the chair. I took out the ribbon and let my hair fall, too tired to braid it. I would regret it in the morning, but just now I didn't care. When I took off my boots and stockings, the cool wood floor felt good against my swollen feet. The release of my corset was a relief, and I let it fall and kicked it aside. I reached to pull off my chemise.

And then I felt something. Or heard something. I froze, listening. Perhaps Aidan coming home. But no, there was no noise at all but for my own breathing. Still, it seemed that the eeriness I'd felt downstairs had followed me here. As if the room itself were watching me.

My nightmares flashed through my mind. Still wearing my chemise, I climbed between the sheets, looking about the room, trying to peer into shadows. I took a deep breath to calm myself. There was nothing frightening here. Mama and Grandma were in the next room. I lay down, pulling the blankets to my chin, telling myself not to be a fool.

A shadow surged toward me, a weight on my bed. I gasped and jerked up, but he pushed me back, a hand clasped over my mouth, whispering harshly in my ear, "Don't scream. Don't make a noise. I'm not here to hurt you, lass. I just want to talk to you."

I tried to thrust him off, but his hands tightened on my arms, his whole body against me, hot and heavy.

"Grace, don't," he whispered, and I knew then who it was. Derry. His face was so close to mine that I felt the brush of his hair against my cheek. "I don't mean to hurt you, d'you understand?"

I nodded. He was so strong that it was hard to move against him.

The pressure of his hand lessened. "You won't scream? You promise?"

Again I nodded.

"All right. I'm going to take away my hand. I'm trusting you, lass. Don't make me regret it."

Slowly, he lifted his hand. I did as he asked; I didn't cry

out. Aidan wasn't here, and Derry must know that already. My grandmother and mother would be no help. And the truth was that I was no longer afraid now that I knew it was him.

He'd only lifted his hand; other than that he hadn't moved. I felt him breathing, the warm weight of him, and my own breath came fast.

I whispered, "Get off me."

He rolled, stretching out alongside me. The light from the street passed over him; I saw his silhouette as he went up on one elbow to look down at me, though I couldn't see his face.

"What do you want?" I asked angrily. "Or do you just have some disgusting penchant for watching girls undress?"

"I wouldn't call it disgusting. And you'll note I made a noise before you took off *everything*."

"How good of you."

"I've some scruples."

"Perhaps they should extend to not sneaking into girls' bedrooms. Do you know what the Devlins would have done if they'd caught you there tonight?"

"I have a good idea," he said drily.

"I would have thought Lucy more than willing to come to you at the stables. You shouldn't have taken such a risk."

"Careful, lass, it sounds as if you care."

"I care for *Lucy*. She's Patrick's sister. I don't want her hurt."

"I'd prefer to avoid that myself," he said, and there was a resignation in his tone that alarmed me, as if he knew she would be hurt eventually.

"You know she's in love with you."

He sighed. "Aye."

"And your intentions—"

"Are none of your business." He leaned closer. "Just now I'm more curious about *your* intentions. Did you tell anyone you saw me tonight? Devlin?"

"No. I didn't want to get Lucy in trouble."

"Good. I'll thank you to keep my visit a secret, if you would."

"I would have done so anyway. You didn't have to come and scare the life out of me."

He was quiet for a moment. Then he said, "There's another thing."

I felt a little flutter of . . . not fear exactly. "What?"

"Devlin will find something gone tomorrow. When he does, I want you to keep quiet. I'll bring it back in a few days."

He'd gone into Patrick's study, I remembered. Where the collection of relics was. "What did you take?"

He hesitated. "The ogham stick."

"The ogham stick?" I leveled myself up on my elbows too. "The one I told you about? But why?"

"Ssshhh." His hand came to my shoulder as if he meant to push me down again, then lingered before he pulled away.

I swallowed hard and asked again, more quietly, "Why did you take it?"

"There's someone I want to show it to, that's all. Then I'll bring it back."

"But who? And why? What has it to do with you?"

"Nothing," he said in a soft, soft voice. My skin felt too

sensitive, I was too aware of him—his breathing, his heat. "'Tis nothing to do with me. Devlin will have it back before he knows it. I won't damage it, Grace; I promise."

"Miss Knox to you," I said, hoping he didn't hear the waver in my voice. "Why should I keep your secret? You're a thief. Why shouldn't I tell Patrick everything?"

"Because I'll be arrested if you do."

"Perhaps it's what you deserve."

"Perhaps." He leaned forward, planting his hand at my other side so he hovered over me, and I fell back against the mattress to avoid him. His eyes shone, but the rest of his face was all in shadows. "Tell me what I can give you in return for keeping quiet. You have me in your power—command me as you will. Miss Knox." He whispered my name mockingly against my ear. Then he drew back, just enough. His mouth was only an inch from mine.

I turned my head away. "What can you possibly give me that I want? Can you change the world? Can you cure Aidan of his drunkenness and turn him into the brother who once cared about his family? Can you erase our debt? Can you ease my mother's worry and save my grandmother from her madness?" I turned to look at him again. I felt the bitterness rise in me so it seeped into my every word. "Well? Can you do any of that? Because those are the things I want."

He went still.

I pushed at him, my palms against his chest. He was unmovable. "Just go, Derry. I'll keep your secret. Just leave me alone."

"What if I can't do that?" His voice was low, almost hoarse. It had the strangest effect on me. I felt suspended, expectant. My hands were still pressed to his chest. I felt his breath against my lips. I only had to raise my head the slightest bit to kiss him. I knew it was what he wanted me to do, and it was suddenly what I wanted too.

Then I remembered. *Patrick.*

I pulled away. Derry moved then, as if my touch had anchored him and now he was free. He was no longer hovering, no longer touching me at all, and again, as when he'd taken his arm from my shoulder at the fair, I felt cold.

"You're not as powerless as you think, lass."

I laughed harshly. "Is that so?"

"Aye." He rose, the mattress lifting. He stepped away, only another shadow in the darkness. "I know it, and someday you will too."

I heard him move to the door.

"Good night, Miss Knox."

And then he was gone, and both the eeriness and the warmth I'd felt were gone with him, leaving a hollowness in my chest, and a memory of him, lips close enough to kiss, like a long-ago dream.

FOURTEEN

That same night

Patrick

She was beautiful and sweet, and Patrick was still burning at the way she'd looked at him tonight. He'd wanted nothing more than to continue the conversation Lucy had interrupted the other day, to tell Grace that he'd managed to bring the legends alive. But there hadn't been an opportunity, not with so many people about, and tonight had been about convincing others to invest in the Fenian Brotherhood. Soon, the Children of Domnu would be here, and with them an army ready to rally to Ireland's cause. That was what he should be concentrating on.

Patrick closed the study door behind him. He took off his frock coat and laid it over a chair, and then he went to the display cases, pressing his hands against one. The lamp on the desk behind him cast his shadow over the case so the amulets inside went dim. He looked over the relics with satisfaction, as he often did. The bowl with the carved wrens there, the serpent bracelet over there, the ogham stick—

Patrick looked closer.

The ogham stick was gone.

He lifted the lid. Unlocked. In disbelief, he searched the case, pawing over the items even though he knew the stone was not hidden among them. *Gone.* He looked at the lock, which had been forced, and then he ran to the window, jerking it open, thinking that somehow he would come upon the thief. There was only the faint laughter of someone still out in the park so late.

Who could have taken it? Someone here tonight? No. They were investors. But for Rory Nolan, they knew nothing of the Brotherhood's secrets. The others had been Grace and her mother, and the thought that one of them might have sneaked in here during the evening and stolen it was laughable.

Which meant it had to be someone else. But who? Who would have known its importance?

It's not important anymore, he reminded himself. The stone needed the rowan wand. And the Fomori had already been called, so it wasn't as if someone could call them again.

Still . . .

Best to take precautions. Patrick went to his desk, scrawling a note to Rory Nolan and another to Simon, to ask if the rowan wand was still safely hidden. He woke a servant to take the messages off immediately, with instructions to wait for answers.

Within two hours, he had both. Nolan hadn't taken it. Simon still had the rowan wand.

Patrick sank into the chair at his desk. He looked toward the display case, the scratched metal of the lock, and he could not keep from asking *Why?* Why the ogham stick when there were other things in the case more valuable? That meant it hadn't been an ordinary thief but someone who could read ogham.

Patrick was seized with a grim foreboding. Whoever had taken it had a reason.

But what?

The question kept him staring into the darkness.

FIFTEEN

June 13

Grace

That night I dreamed of Derry again. He was bare chested, bruised and bloody, as if he'd been in a fight, his arms braced on the pillows behind him, laughing as he teased me. I pushed him, and he caught my hand and pulled me down with him. His eyes were so dark I felt lost in them; the longing I saw there matched my own. All I wanted to do was kiss him, but as I leaned to do so, the dream shifted, ravens screaming over narrow, dark streets. Clubs and knives flashing purple with the lightning crashing above, and Aidan saying, *"Don' run off with him . . . Don' go. . . ."*

I woke shaken—not just because of the dreams but because of the way Derry's visit seemed to have inspired them. The warmth of his skin, how close he'd been—the things I'd told him that I'd never said to anyone. I made myself think of how desperate Patrick would be when he found the ogham stick missing and how great a risk I took in keeping quiet, in trusting that Derry would return it as he'd promised.

It turned out that I was right to be worried. That afternoon as I sat with Mama in the parlor, reading while she embroidered, there was a knock on the door.

A bill collector, I assumed, and I put my book aside.

Mama glanced up. "Is Aidan home?"

"As if he would be any help," I muttered.

But it was no bill collector. Patrick stood on the stoop, looking distressed, and behind him were two policemen.

Patrick smiled at me, though he seemed distracted. "Miss Knox—" Spoken like a caress, as if he wanted to say my Christian name but didn't dare in front of the police. "Forgive me for intruding this way, but there's been an incident, and the police want to speak with you and your mother."

Pretend you don't know. I hoped I only looked concerned. "What is it? What's happened?"

"Something's been stolen, miss," said a policeman with heavy muttonchops and a full mustache. "We're speaking to everyone who was at the Devlin house last night."

"Just questions," Patrick assured me. "It's nothing to worry about."

"I see." I stepped back to let them in. "What was taken?"

Patrick's mouth tightened; a haunted look came into his eyes. "The ogham stick."

"But surely you don't think—"

"You're not under suspicion, miss," said the same police officer.

"My mother's in the parlor," I said, and then I realized there would be nowhere for them to sit—only the ancient settee and the chair—and Patrick would see how we truly lived.

As I reluctantly ushered them in, my mother rose to greet them, looking alarmed, and I tried not to see the way Patrick peered about the room.

Whatever he thought, I couldn't see it in his expression. He said courteously, "Mrs. Knox, I hope we haven't come at an inopportune time."

"No, of course not. You're welcome always, Patrick; you know that." She stared questioningly at the police.

Patrick introduced officers Moran—the one with the sideburns—and Stoltz, who was clean shaven with close-set eyes.

Moran said, "Please, ladies, sit down. This won't take long."

I took the settee, and Mama sat again in her chair. Patrick seated himself on the edge of the windowsill—again I saw the way he glanced around, and I looked away in shame. Something else to blame Derry for. I hadn't considered this at all, that the police would be involved or that Patrick might come here. The next time I saw Lucy's stableboy, I would tear into him for it.

"I trust you ladies are familiar with Mr. Devlin's collection of relics?" Moran asked while Stoltz stood behind him, silently taking notes.

I nodded. "Yes, of course. I've seen them."

My mother said, "I know of them."

"When was the last time you saw them, Miss Knox?"

"A few days ago," I answered. "Mr. Devlin showed them to me himself."

"Not since then?"

I shook my head.

"Apparently, at some point last night, something was taken. The lock was picked, but we don't believe it was an expert job. The relic taken was worth little—" Here he looked at Patrick for confirmation.

"Its value was more sentimental," Patrick said, but that it mattered to him was obvious.

"Mr. Devlin says he last saw the item, an—"

"Ogham stick," Patrick put in.

"Aye. Earlier that evening. Did either of you ladies have occasion to go into Mr. Devlin's study that night?"

"Of course not," Mama said.

I shook my head again.

"Did either of you see anything odd during the evening? A servant where he or she shouldn't have been, for example, or perhaps a door left open that should have been closed? Anything at all out of the ordinary?"

"I'm afraid not," my mother said.

I thought of Derry in the shadows, pressing his finger to his lips. I thought of him leaning over me on my bed, whispering, *"You have me in your power—command me as you will."*

I met Moran's gaze and tried not to look as guilty as I felt. "I saw nothing unusual."

Patrick rose. "I'm certain someone would have told me if they had."

Moran gestured to Stoltz, who closed his notebook. "But we have to be sure now, don't we? Thank you, ladies, for your time. I'm very sorry to have disturbed you with such a matter."

"It's quite all right," Mama said. "I completely understand."

We saw them to the door. I hung back, as did Patrick. He touched my arm just before we went into the hall, and when I turned to look at him, he said, "Tomorrow's your birthday."

I would be seventeen. It seemed suddenly both too old and not old enough. "You remembered."

The warmth of his gaze enveloped me. "I've something special for you."

"You shouldn't."

Mama was ushering the police out. Patrick whispered in my ear, "We'll see each other soon," before he left with the police.

Mama leaned her head against the closed door as if her strength was gone. "Well, that was unfortunate."

"Yes. But I'm certain they'll recover it."

"That Patrick came with them, I meant."

I thought of our empty parlor. Then I remembered his words. "I don't think it mattered. He said he had something special for me for my birthday."

Mama raised her head. "He said that? Something special?"

I nodded.

Her mood lightened immediately. "Do you think it could be a proposal?"

I hadn't thought of that. "Oh. I don't know."

"Well, we can only hope it is, and that this"—a limp gesture at the house—"hasn't changed his mind."

"Yes," I said, though now I didn't know which I felt more: dread or excitement. "We can only hope."

——∽— *June 14* —∾——

My seventeenth birthday dawned cloudy and humid, promising thunderstorms. I spent the day waiting anxiously for a message. I jumped at every sound until my mother said, "Goodness, Grace, you're restless as a cricket."

But I knew she was waiting too. I knew she was worried that Patrick's visit had changed his mind about me.

That wasn't really what worried me. Today could be the day I went from being just myself to being a fiancée, the day my future was truly decided, and I didn't know what to feel— one moment cursing how everything in my life had conspired against me, the next remembering Patrick's kiss, the warmth of his eyes.

And I couldn't stop thinking about my dream of Derry laughing, the longing I'd felt for him. Just a dream, thank goodness, but . . . *"You're not as powerless as you think."*

I didn't want to think of him at all. It was possible that he had ruined everything for me.

The day passed slowly. In the far distance, I heard thunder, and it made me think of blood and fire and ravens, so I couldn't concentrate on my book. I put it aside and went to the window.

Aidan wandered into the parlor and came up beside me. "I suppose you've plans with Patrick today."

I turned to glare at him. "Nothing's been settled."

He looked surprised. His blue eyes were bleary, red rimmed. "Really? You mean you aren't to see him? I thought he meant to propose today."

"What do you mean? Did he say something to you?"

Aidan shook his head and then squeezed his eyes shut as if the motion hurt. "No. I just thought . . . the way he looks at you . . . and it's your birthday. It's the kind of romantic gesture you'd like. Patrick knows that well."

I couldn't answer. I felt close to tears, which was ridiculous. Just then a delivery wagon drove up, with "Davis's Flowers" painted on the side. The door opened and a man stepped out—a messenger bearing a huge bouquet of flowers and a small package.

"Well, that must be from Patrick now," Aidan said.

I went hurrying to answer the door, my mother and Aidan just behind. When I opened it, the messenger said, "Miss Grace Knox."

"That's me."

He placed the bouquet into my arms—it was so large I could barely grasp it. The whole world was suddenly perfumed with pink roses and lilies. Aidan stepped forward to take the other package the man held out and closed the door.

"Just flowers?" Mama sounded disappointed. "Is there a card, Grace?"

I searched for the card and plucked it from the stems, handing the bouquet to my brother. My fingers trembled as I opened it.

Grace—no flower can compare to you, and there's no gift I could give you that could show the extent of my esteem. But please accept these in honor of your birthday, and know I am thinking of you.
Yours, Patrick

"Well?" Mama asked.

I tried to smile as I handed it to her.

Aidan said, "There's this too," and thrust the package at me.

I knew the moment I took it that it was a book. I opened the paper. The cover was smooth and unblemished—the book was brand-new, the pages uncut. I opened it to the flyleaf, where Patrick had written:

To my Sky-Lark, in honor of her seventeenth birthday (and who will know me best on page 111).
With my deepest affection, Patrick

It was a book of poems by an Irish poet, J. J. Callanan. I said to my brother, "Hand me your knife."

He pushed aside the lily tickling his nose and gave me the knife. I turned the folded, uncut pages to where Patrick had indicated, and then I cut the folds to reveal a translation of an Irish poem called "The Lament of O'Gnive": "How dimm'd is the glory that circled the Gael. / And fall'n the high people of green Innisfail / The sword of the Saxon is red with their gore / And the mighty of nations is mighty no more!"

Another poet who spoke of oppression in Ireland. *"Do you want to know me?"* Patrick had said, and now I wondered: was this all there was to him? Only Ireland?

"What makes you so sure he knows you?"

"No jewelry, eh?" Aidan said disapprovingly.

"That would hardly be appropriate," Mama said. "But I hoped for a proposal. Oh, what he must have thought yesterday . . . What is that book he sent you, Grace?"

"Poems," I said. "An Irish poet."

"More gloomy talk of rebellion," Aidan said. He peered at me around the flowers in his arms, and I was surprised to see compassion in his eyes before he shoved the bouquet at our mother. "You'd best put these in water, Mama, before they wilt. I suppose we'll have to smell the things for the next week. They're making me sneeze already."

Patrick had told me this would be something special, and I supposed it was special that he wanted to share his passion with me. But I'd wanted something more. Even Aidan understood my wish for romance. *"What makes you so sure he knows you?"*

I pushed Derry's words away. Patrick *did* know me.

"Perhaps I could be your Diarmid," he'd said. Patrick understood that I'd felt we were moving too fast. But things could not be delayed much longer. My family could not afford the luxury of waiting.

My mother was tight-lipped the rest of the day, more wan and distracted than usual. She did her best with a birthday supper. Soup with decent bread and a dessert of applesauce and cream. But she ate almost none of it, and her hand went to her head often, as if she were in pain, which was something I could understand. I felt the start of my own headache. "You'd best push him along if you can, Grace."

"Why?" Aidan asked, taking a spoonful of applesauce—the only thing he'd eaten. "I promise you he'll ask her to chain him soon enough. There's no point in rushing it."

I kicked him under the table.

"Oww," he cried out. "What'd you do that for?"

My mother sighed. "We can't wait much longer. I expect a summons any day."

"A summons?" Aidan asked.

"From the doctor's lawsuit," I told him. "Come, Aidan, you know all about it."

He went silent. Then he put his spoon on the table, deliberately, as if the world depended on him doing it just right. He rose. "If you'll excuse me. Happy birthday, Gracie."

He went out of the room. But not before I'd seen the misery in his eyes and felt his terrible despair. I stared after him, my anger with him replaced by sudden fear. I'd known something was wrong with my brother, but this was the first time

I'd thought that perhaps he was as afraid as I was. I heard his footsteps down the hallway, and then the opening and closing of the front door.

My mother put her face in her hands.

I had no idea what to say to her that hadn't been said a hundred times. I rose, gathering the dishes, putting them into the washing tub. "I'll take Grandma her supper."

I took the bowl of soup and some applesauce upstairs. I forgot my brother when I saw Grandma out of bed, wavering as she stood in her bare feet at the window, her nightgown fraying about her bony shins.

"Grandma." I set down the food and rushed over to her. "Whatever are you doing out of bed?"

I tried to help her back, but she shook me off. "I'm fine, *mo chroi*." She was as clear-eyed as I'd seen her in days.

"I've brought your supper. Won't you sit to eat it?"

She sighed and shook her head. Her cap lay abandoned on the bed, and her gray hair straggled from its braid.

"Then sit so I can brush your hair?"

"Bring the chair here," she commanded.

I pulled the chair to the window, and she sat, staring outside. The air was still and heavy, the leaves on the trees not stirring. The sky was gray, and I heard thunder in the distance.

I took up her brush and felt her relax beneath my touch as I undid her braid.

She said, "'Tis your birthday today."

"Seventeen," I said.

"I heard a knock."

"Patrick Devlin sent flowers. And a book of poems."

She grunted. I brushed her hair in silence for a few moments before I said, "There's a storm coming in."

"Not yet. But the *sidhe* are everywhere already. And the ships are on their way."

I had to bite back a sigh. I expected her next comment to be something about *They are coming*, or *That boy*, another slip into dementia, but instead she said, "Do you remember the old stories, *mo chroi*?"

"The old stories?"

"Cuchulain. The Battle of Magh Tuiredh. Lir's children."

"You know I do." She used to hold me upon her lap, her words seeming to unfold before my eyes like vibrant, glowing visions. "The Children of Lir made me so sad. Turned into swans for nine hundred years."

Grandma's shoulders bowed in relief so palpable I could feel it. "Thank God for that," she whispered.

"Thank God for what? That the Children of Lir were swans for nine hundred years?"

"No," she said, so quietly I had to strain to hear. "That you remember the stories. What about Lochlann's son?"

It was the story of a famous battle between the Fianna and those gods of darkness and chaos known as the Fomori.

"Of course I remember," I told her.

"You see it in your dreams," she said, and I started—how did she know of my nightmares?

She went on in the storytelling voice I remembered, quiet

and intent. "It began when the King of Lochlann decided to invade Ireland and take back what was once under Fomori rule. The attempt cost him his life and left his young son orphaned. It was Finn MacCool himself who took the young Miogach to foster, and the son of Lochlann was raised to manhood in the Fianna's fortress and given every comfort.

"But Finn did not realize how much Miogach hated them all, nor did he know that Miogach had secretly gathered together the Fianna's enemies: the Fomori and their allies.

"One day Finn and some of his men were out hunting, and they came upon Miogach, who invited them into a room with soft silk hangings, comfortable pillows, and polished wood floors. The Fianna left their armor and weapons at the door, as was the custom, and Miogach left to get food and wine."

"But he didn't return," I said, plaiting her hair.

"No. The walls became rough planks, the silk tapestries decaying rags, and the floors cold, wet earth. The Fianna were imprisoned in the House of Death. Finn and the others called for help in the hopes that some of their fellows might hear their cries.

"Finn's son, Fia, was out searching for his father when he saw Miogach's mighty army gathering to cross the river. Miogach called, 'You slew my father. I will have my vengeance.' Fia said, "Twas your father who decided to invade Ireland. Don't seek vengeance for what is just, or vengeance will rebound on you.' But Miogach advanced.

"Diarmid and Keenan arrived at the river just in time to see Fia on his knees, soldiers dead all around him, his weapons and his shield crushed, while Miogach raised his mighty sword to take Fia's head. Diarmid threw his spear, but it only struck Miogach in the side, and Miogach killed Fia. In a rage, Diarmid slew Miogach. Then Diarmid heard the cries of those in the House of Death and followed them. But he could not release Finn and the others, who were dying of hunger and thirst.

"When Diarmid returned to the ford for help, he found that Keenan had fallen into an enchanted sleep. It was left to Diarmid to fight the three kings and their six hundred men who were the advance riders for Daire Donn, the King of the World, who had come with the Fomori to aid Miogach. Keenan finally woke to help, but by then Diarmid had killed them all. He took the heads of the three kings to Finn, who rubbed the blood on himself and the others, freeing them from the spell. But there was not enough blood to rub on Conan, and they had to pry him up from the floor, leaving some of his skin and hair behind so he was forever bald.

"They were joined by the rest of the Fianna and met Daire Donn and his two thousand men in a battle to end all battles, with thunder and lightning from Druid stormcasters and the screams of the Morrigan's ravens. At last, the Fomori and their allies were defeated, though the Fianna lost many of their own as well, thus ensuring that the hatred between the Fianna and the Fomori will never die."

"But it was Miogach's fault," I protested. "His vengeance rebounded on him just as Fia said it would."

"Aye. But do not be so quick to think truth holds to only

one side, *mo chroi*. Vengeance is a bitter cup to drink from, but perhaps it would have been avoided had Finn not assumed his kindness to Miogach would make up for killing the boy's father. 'Twas Finn's arrogance at fault nearly as much."

"Well, thankfully those battles are long over," I said.

"Battles are never over, and nothing stays gone. Everything circles 'round and 'round about, over and over again. The end is only another beginning."

I assumed she spoke of my father's death and our losses, of Aidan. "I haven't lost hope, Grandma."

"You will need more than hope." She gripped my hand where it rested on her shoulder, squeezing my fingers tight. "It will take all your courage, Grainne."

"I know, Grandma."

"You don't know! You don't know, but you will. Your mother must help—"

"She can't help, Grandma. She's getting weaker. She's so worn out by all this. I'd call the doctor, but . . . it's up to me, I'm afraid."

Grandma ignored me. "Aidan will know what to do."

I snorted. "Aidan only knows how to get his next drink." Then I thought of what I'd seen in his eyes today, and I wished I hadn't said it. It all seemed so hopeless. Mama and Grandma, and Aidan too—how was I to save them all?

"There is so much for you to learn. So little time, *mo chroi*. Ah, that thunder—do you hear it?"

She was slipping away again. Wearily, I said, "Yes. I hear it."

"That boy . . . and . . . the children of the *sidhe*—there are more every day. They will not rest until they have you. You must be careful . . . find the truth—"

"Come, Grandma. You should eat. You should rest."

She twisted to look at me. "Promise me." Her eyes were dark stones, but *she*, my grandmother, wasn't there. She was back in the world of her imaginings, where the Fianna and the Fomori fought battles in lightning, fire, and blood. I knew what those visions looked like. But the difference between my grandmother and me was that I knew they were only dreams.

"I promise," I said, though I had no idea what I promised, and I was certain she didn't either.

I helped her to the bed. Her gaze was distant, and she said little more as I tucked her in and fed her spoonfuls of soup and applesauce. But she shuddered at every crack of thunder, and I knew she heard in it the battle cries of the Morrigan, and that instead of the thin yellow coverlet on her bed, she saw fields of blood.

SIXTEEN

June 15

Diarmid

Diarmid couldn't take the ogham stick to Finn and Cannel right away. When he'd returned to the stables after visiting Grace Knox, the whole place had been in a flurry—Devlin had needed the carriage, and Jerry was snarling *"Where the hell were you?"* and Diarmid had been unable to sneak out the rest of the night. Instead, he lay in the darkness and thought of her, the curves of her body beneath that flimsy shift—it had been all he could do to make the noise that kept her from drawing it off. He needed her silence too much to make her angry. But now he was haunted by how familiar it had felt to lie beside her, as if he belonged there, as if he already knew her every breath and sigh. He had not wanted to leave, and the urge to touch her, to keep touching her, to kiss her, had shaken him. He'd fought himself with every breath. If she was the *veleda* . . . he did not want to finish the thought.

Best to keep his distance, he knew, and her despair had only settled his intentions. He made himself stop thinking of her and focus on getting the ogham stick to Finn.

But the next day was no better; no chance to escape at all. Leonard came back from driving Lucy to some social call, saying, "Devlin's in a panic. Police all over this mornin'. I guess somethin' went missin' from his study."

The police. Already. Diarmid had hoped it might be longer before the theft was discovered. He'd hidden the ogham stick in the pile of manure and dirty straw from mucking the stables, and he tried to keep from constantly checking it. He hadn't even had the time to look at it or to decipher the ogham runes, and he didn't have the chance the next day either, nor the one after that. Diarmid chafed with anxiety and impatience, but he couldn't risk losing the job by just leaving—and he didn't want to raise suspicion either.

But that night, finally, things calmed enough that he had the opportunity he needed. When darkness fell—bringing with it distant thunder and air that felt thick and swollen— Diarmid was up at the sound of Jerry's first snore, pawing through the filthy straw until the stone was in his hands. He washed it and his hands, shoved it into a saddlebag that he threw over his shoulder, and stepped into the sweltering night.

He nearly ran to the tenement. Keenan and Goll were practicing parries and feints in the yard, and he waved for them to follow as he raced up the pitch-black stairs. His boots slipped on something wet—by the gods, *wet*. Garbage or drink or blood?—and he rapped out the code they'd devised on the door and was through it in a single motion, breathless and sweating.

Finn was laughing as he tore a hunk of bread from the loaf on the table. His pale eyes darkened when he saw Diarmid, with Keenan and Goll coming in a rush behind.

"What is it?"

Diarmid slung the saddlebag off his shoulder, removing the ogham stick. "It's Devlin's," he said. "I stole it."

"You stole it? Does he know it's gone?" Finn asked.

"Aye. The police know it too."

Finn put aside the bread and made a quick, commanding gesture to Cannel, who'd been standing against the wall, laughing with Ossian as he drank a mug of ale. The whole room smelled of it, and now Diarmid saw a keg dripping into a small puddle on the floor and more than bread on the table: apples and meat. He caught the scent of roasted pork, and his mouth watered.

"What's all this?" Diarmid asked.

Oscar came up to him, smiling. "Keenan's working at a saloon up the street. Goll got a job at a butcher's. Ossian's won two boxing matches. All in all, a good week."

"You should come around more often, and you'd know," Finn said, faintly chiding as he took the ogham stick and turned it in his hands.

"He's too busy with his girls," Oscar said, tousling Diarmid's hair.

Diarmid dodged. "Too busy stealing relics from Patrick Devlin and evading police, you mean."

Cannel reached out to touch the stone in Finn's hands and then recoiled as if it had burned him. He turned to Finn. "How can you even hold it? It's hot as an oven."

"It burned my hand," Grace Knox had said. Diarmid's gut tightened.

Finn tossed it from one hand to the other. "I don't feel anything." He looked at Diarmid. "You?"

"It's just stone," Diarmid replied, not saying that he knew someone else the stick had burned.

"Can you read it?" Finn asked Cannel.

The Seer shook his head. "What is that? Runes of some kind?"

Finn crooked his finger at Diarmid, who came over. The smell of the roasted pork was making him sick now. Without a word, Finn handed him the stone.

The runes were worn; in some places entirely chipped away. Diarmid ran his fingers over them, feeling the cut in the stone, reading the language he'd been taught when he was only a boy, hearing the voice of Manannan's Druid, Tadg, in his head: *"Only the strongest spells and curses are committed to stone or wood, lad, and those cannot be undone, not by the strongest heart."*

And this was a spell; he knew it the moment he looked at the first rune. *Darkness*, and *thunder. Blood. Fire. The eye of one who*—Diarmid squinted, trying to make out the next symbol, which had been rubbed thin at one side—*slays*, he thought. *The eye of one who slays. As one is bid, so come the rest.*

The thunder in the distance seemed to grow louder.

The something *wand. Rowan. The rowan wand* and *virtue*—he thought it was *virtue. Virtue gone. An eric*—blood price—*paid. Now come the Children of Dom*— Here the rune was completely gone.

Diarmid let out his breath in a rasp. *Domnu.* It had to be that. The Children of Domnu. "The Fomori."

Finn froze. "What?"

"The Fomori." Diarmid looked up at his leader. "It's a spell to call the Fomori."

"By the gods. Are you sure?"

Diarmid nodded.

"Tell me what it says."

"Wait," Cannel said, putting up a hand. "If it's an incantation, he shouldn't be speaking it."

"I'm no Druid," Diarmid told him. "I don't know how to say it." And that was what mattered, the *saying* of it. How each word was emphasized, the cadence. "And I don't think 'tis complete either. It mentions a rowan wand. I think you need that too."

"They would be fools to put the whole spell on a single stone," Finn agreed. "To call the Fomori . . . 'tis a serious thing."

"You mean a disastrous thing," Ossian said, pushing past Conan, who had paused in the middle of grabbing a piece of roast.

"Aye." Finn looked again at Diarmid. "What exactly does it say?"

Diarmid read, "'Darkness and thunder, blood and fire.

The eye of one who slays. As one is bid, so come the rest. The rowan wand and virtue gone. A blood price paid. Now come the Children of Domnu.'"

They all went quiet as if they were waiting for the sky to crack open and the Fomori to rain down upon them. Diarmid's memory of Fomori destruction and desecration was as heavy as the smell of roast pork in the room.

"Do you think Devlin knows what this is?" Finn asked him.

Diarmid shrugged. "I don't know. Probably not. 'Twas in a locked case, but it wasn't hard to get to."

"Even if he does, he doesn't know how to say it," Cannel added.

"Do you?" Finn asked him.

Cannel hesitated. "Perhaps. When I touched it, it burned. Then when Diarmid was reading it . . . well, I knew how it must be said. At least, I think I knew."

It had burned when she touched it. What would she know if he said the words to her? Diarmid felt cold.

Cannel went on, "But Diarmid's right. It needs the rowan wand. No one could call the Fomori with this alone."

"You didn't see a rowan wand?" Finn asked.

"No," Diarmid said. "But she said the collection in the study wasn't all of it."

"Who said? Devlin's sister?"

Diarmid cursed himself. "His lass. That's how I knew about it. She said he had the relics, so I went to see for myself."

"Ah. Well done."

Diarmid knew how foolish it was, but he felt warm at Finn's praise.

"No horn, either, I'd guess?" Ossian asked.

"No horn," Diarmid confirmed. He nodded toward the stone. "I'll have to take that back. What with the police all over looking for it." And him.

Finn shook his head. "'Tis too dangerous to return it. You know this."

"But if he's the one who blew the horn, why would he call both us and the Fomori?"

"Because he wants a war?" Conan guessed.

"That makes no sense. He wants to liberate Ireland from Britain," Diarmid pointed out. "Why would he call us *and* our enemies?"

Ossian said, "Sometimes men are fools."

Finn rubbed his chin. "We must keep it."

As much as Diarmid didn't want to say it, there was no choice: "She saw me take it. Devlin's lass. She's promised to keep quiet as long as I return it."

Oscar laughed. "Well, she's a girl, isn't she? I'm guessing you can talk her into keeping her silence whether you return the thing or not."

Down the table, Conan laughed in agreement and stuck fingers already shiny with pork fat into the roast, pulling loose a piece to pop into his mouth. Diarmid felt increasingly ill.

"She's loyal to Devlin," he managed.

"So make her loyal to you," Oscar said.

Diarmid glared at him. Then he noticed Finn was

watching the both of them, and he tempered his anger. " 'Twould be better if I could return it."

Finn said, "I'll think about it. For now, find out where the rest of the collection is. If it turns out there's no rowan wand, this won't matter, and Devlin can have it back. But we can't take the risk that he knows what he has, Diarmid. If he has the means to call the Fomori . . ." None of them needed him to complete the sentence.

Diarmid's heart sank, but he nodded.

Finn gestured toward the roast. "Have some meat with us then, and some ale. You've been too long away."

And Diarmid recognized that as an order too. Not that he didn't want to be with his friends. He'd felt the strain of being away, of living in a world where he wasn't himself, where a girl could disdain him for being a stableboy and he was unable to say: *In my world, there wasn't a lass who didn't want me. In my world, I could have anything. I could give you anything you wanted; I could make your troubles disappear.*

The thought startled him. He had too soft a heart when it came to girls. And her plaintive desperation had moved him. That was all it was.

Finn had turned back to the food, as had most of the others, and the talk and laughter returned, though with an edge to it this time. The ogham stick had changed everything; Diarmid felt the tension in the room, the fear that the thought of the Fomori raised in anyone who had ever known them.

Oscar clapped his shoulder. "Come, Derry. Have some ale. You look bedeviled."

Which he was, there was no denying. He went with his friend to the keg. Oscar poured ale into a broken mug. "We'll have to share. No one's thought to buy crockery yet."

"Except you," Diarmid said.

"Well, yes, I've *thought* of it. But I haven't actually *bought* it, as you can see. And Da won't part with a coin. He's stingy as a virgin."

Diarmid followed Oscar to the fire escape. The bolts that fastened the flimsy metal to the mortar grated; the whole thing creaked as if it were complaining of their weight. Diarmid sat beside Oscar, leaning against the brick wall. The rest of the world was on the fire escapes tonight as well, people talking and laughing, their faces moving in and out of the light coming from their windows. Someone sang a melody he thought he recognized, though the words had changed considerably over the years.

Oscar said, "The air's hot as Senach Siaborthe's kiss."

A demon allied with the Morrigan. Diarmid smiled.

"So tell me about Devlin's sister. Since I've no female companionship for myself, I'll have to live through your tales."

Diarmid took a long sip of the beer, which was warm and strong. He didn't want to think of Lucy. "She's sweet and she likes ice cream, and that's all you'll hear of it."

"Then what about the other one?"

Diarmid tensed. "What about her?"

Oscar looked at him. "What's wrong with her?"

"What d'you mean?"

"You get riled as a nasty boar when she's mentioned. I

thought you would take my head off in there." Oscar grabbed the mug of beer from him and took a long draught. "So tell me why."

Diarmid realized that getting Oscar's opinion was part of the reason he'd come tonight. "She troubles me," he admitted, taking the mug from Oscar.

"She's loyal to Devlin, you said. Does she know about us, d'you think?"

"I don't think so. She makes a lot of noise about Devlin and his plans, but I don't think she truly knows them. She's an innocent, but . . . you saw the way the ogham stick burned Cannel?"

Oscar nodded as he took back the mug.

"It burned her the same way."

Oscar's brow furrowed. "You saw it?"

"She told me. She thought it was because it had been in the sun."

"Had it been?"

"There's something else." Diarmid lowered his voice. "I told you the first time she saw me she swooned."

"Hardly unusual," Oscar said wryly.

"Not for the reason you think. She said I was glowing."

"Glowing?"

"As if I were the sun itself. That's what she said. It gave her such a headache she collapsed with the pain of it. And not just once. There was a second time too. Not so strong, but the same."

"And the ogham stick burned her the way it did Cannel. Who's got Druid blood." Oscar's voice was flat.

Diarmid nodded. The ale settled badly in his stomach.

"The *veleda*," Oscar whispered.

"I don't know."

"But you suspect it might be so."

"I don't *know*. I'm still trying to work it out. If she is, she knows nothing about any of this. She doesn't even realize what she is. By the gods, Oscar, I thought at least she would know."

"You *like* this girl," Oscar said slowly.

"I like all girls." Diarmid heard her voice in his head, a nagging whisper, *"What can you possibly give me that I want? Can you change the world?"*

If she was what he believed, he would do much worse than change her world. He would destroy it.

Oscar said, "You'll have to tell Finn."

"Not yet. Not until I know for sure. I'll have your word that you won't say anything either."

"By the gods, Derry, if she *is* the *veleda*—"

"Your word," Diarmid said roughly.

"You have it. But you'd best discover soon whether she is or not. If Devlin knows what he has, if he's the one who called us . . . There's something in the air, Derry. I can *feel* it."

Diarmid didn't disagree. "I want you to come with me to see her. I wonder if she'd see a glow in you too."

"You think the *veleda* in her is seeing the Fianna in you."

Diarmid nodded.

"When? The sooner the better."

"I'll have to think of how to get Grace alone."

"Grace?" Oscar said.

"Miss Knox," Diarmid corrected. *Miss Knox to you.*

"Why not just pay her a visit?"

"I'm a stableboy, Oscar, remember? She wouldn't invite me into her house." Which had been nearly empty, he remembered. Only a few pieces of furniture, and her bedroom so plain he'd wondered at first if it was a spare room. "And I don't want to take the chance that her brother might be there. Though I suppose he'd probably be too busy sleeping it off."

"Ah. He likes his liquor?"

"A bit too much."

"Then where?"

Diarmid thought. Finally he said, "Meet me at the stables the day after tomorrow. Midmorning. I'll figure out some way."

"And then all I need do is step into her path?"

"All you need do," Diarmid said, "is glow."

SEVENTEEN

June 17

Grace

The morning was sweltering, thunder still rumbling in the distance, so that my grandmother tossed and turned in her bed and my mother paused often in her embroidery to flinch and then gaze unseeingly out the window, asking vacantly, "Where does that come from, do you think?"

I had no answer. I curled up with the book that Patrick had given me for my birthday, immersing myself in poems of rebellion and blood until it seemed my nightmares had come alive on the page.

Just before noon there came a knock on the door, and Mama sighed and put aside her needle.

I jumped off the settee. She looked unable to manage much of anything today. "I'll get it."

"You are so good, my darling." She sagged back into her chair.

I prepared myself to meet whatever new bill collector or

policeman had decided to visit, but when I opened the door I found a newsboy standing there. He touched his billed cap and gave me a quick grin. "I'm to ask for Miss Grace Knox."

"I'm Miss Knox."

He held out a piece of paper. "This is for you."

Whatever hope I had that it was from Patrick disappeared the moment I saw that it was only a broadsheet folded into quarters, an advertisement for Madame Pompadour's Kidney Remedy on the outside.

"What's this?" I asked, but the boy was already disappearing down the block without waiting for a tip.

I stepped back into the house. Mama called, "Who was it, Grace?"

"No one. A boy looking for his dog."

The lie came so easily to my lips. Slowly, I unfolded the paper.

The handwriting was unfamiliar. Flowing and rounded, almost pretentious in its ornamentation. Blotched, as if it had been folded hastily, before it was dry.

> *Meet me on the Battery.*
> *One o'clock, at the flagstaff.*
> *I must speak with you about*
> *the other night.*
> *Derry*

I stared at the note. The handwriting was so completely at odds with what I knew of him that I could hardly believe it was really from him. But it had his sometimes imperious air about it, as if I must have nothing better to do than drop everything to meet him.

Which, actually, I didn't.

I must speak with you about the other night.

When he'd laid beside me in my bed. When he'd been close enough to kiss. When I'd confessed the things I shouldn't have confessed.

My dream. His skin against my fingers. That yearning.

I wanted to ignore it. But then I remembered the ogham stick and how furious I was with him, and nothing could have kept me away.

My mother would never allow me to walk to the Battery by myself, but if I took Rose . . . Well, the day was hot and unbearable; why shouldn't we promenade on the Battery to enjoy the cool breezes off the harbor? In the middle of the afternoon, there were certain to be plenty of people about. We couldn't be safer.

I folded the note into a small square, stuck it in my pocket, and sauntered into the parlor. I sighed and picked up one of the handkerchiefs Mama had just finished, pressing it to my forehead as I went to the window. "It's so warm."

Mama made a noise of agreement.

"I think I might ask Rose if she'll go for a walk."

"A walk?" Mama's pale forehead creased.

"Perhaps down to the Battery."

"That's such a long way." Mama bent again to her sewing. "Perhaps Rose's mother will let you take the carriage."

"I'll ask." Impulsively, I bent to give her a hug—which was too much, I knew immediately. She looked at me with a frown.

I said, "I'll be back before supper."

I left the room nearly before I finished speaking. I walked as quickly as I could to Rose's, just short of running, and by the time I arrived, I felt the trickle of sweat at my hairline, and my corset felt almost unbearably tight.

The maid opened the door, but before she could get a word out, Rose, who'd been coming down the stairs, rushed past her. "Grace! I had just thought to send for you. D'you want to get some ice cream? It's so damned hot."

The curse made me smile—it was so at odds with Rose's pert prettiness, though I knew she did it just to shock people.

"What about a walk on the Battery instead?"

She wrinkled her nose. "There'll be a hundred people there at least."

I pulled the note from my pocket and handed it to her.

"What's this?" She unfolded the paper. "Derry?" She looked at me in concern. "Grace, what did I tell you? He's Lucy's boy. And what's this about the other night? You haven't been seeing him?"

I said, a little too hotly, "Of course not. I've no idea why he wants me to meet him."

Her brown eyes were suspicious.

I sighed. "Oh very well, I might have *some* idea. I told him about Patrick's relics when we were at the parish fair. I think he might want to ask me about them."

"He's interested in relics? Why doesn't he ask Patrick then?"

"Please, Rose. Come with me, or I shall have to go alone."

"No, you certainly will not," she said sternly. "I'll come with you. If only to be sure this is nothing more than you say."

"Believe me, I'd rather embroider a dozen handkerchiefs than spend another moment with him. But if it's about Patrick, I should find out what he wants."

Rose snorted inelegantly and went to ask her mother's permission. "We're to take the carriage down," she said when she returned, which meant we had to wait for it to be brought around. "No good can come of this," Rose muttered. "Lucy will have your head if she finds out."

"And if she finds out, you can tell her there was nothing in it," I said.

Finally, the carriage came, and once it did I wished it hadn't. The constant jerking and swaying of the springs in the sweltering heat nauseated me. When we pulled to a stop at the entrance to the park, I stumbled out, taking deep breaths until I realized it wasn't just the motion of the carriage that had made me queasy, but the thought of seeing Derry again.

Battery Park was twelve acres of broad stone paths twined with shrubbery and flowers. In the center was the flagstaff where we were to meet Derry, near the empty bandstand. The park was as full as predicted, all sorts of people, not just the well-to-do, wandering about the elms, lifting their faces to the nearly nonexistent breeze coming off the harbor; others standing near the huge stone wall where granite stairs led to the water. I heard the waves from passing steamers slapping against the wall. Beyond was Brooklyn, and Governors and Staten Islands, and the bridge to Castle Garden, where immigrants first came into the city.

What a horrible idea this was. I must be mad. If Lucy discovered this—I didn't want to see him again, not even to rage at him. Whatever Derry wanted to tell me about the other night, I had no wish to hear.

But Rose was grabbing my arm. "The flagstaff—isn't that where we're to meet him?" She pulled me down a stone path, past three men lolling on the ground as if they had nowhere else to go and a little boy and girl sitting restlessly on a cast-iron bench, looking longingly at the children playing tag.

The flag at the top of the staff fluttered limply, and dark clouds hovered ominously near the horizon. But the thunder seemed to have quieted for a while. I hadn't realized how disconcerting it was until it was gone.

"It's after one," Rose noted as we reached the flagpole. She put her hand to her eyes, searching the crowd. "Didn't he say one?"

"Yes." I didn't see him anywhere. Perhaps he hadn't been able to get away from the stables, or we were too late. I took Rose's arm. "He's obviously not coming. We should—"

A young man stepped from the crowd. Blond-haired, handsome enough to make me gasp, and then . . . a screeching, searing light pulsed from him. *Like Derry,* I thought in the moment before the pain slammed into my head and I cried out, my legs collapsing beneath me. I heard Rose's "Grace!" and then I fell.

Derry was there before I hit the ground, arms around me, murmuring, "Steady, lass," low in my ear, but this time the pain did not go when he touched me. It hurt so much—someone was moaning, keening. . . . I heard his voice as if it came from miles away, harsh and urgent, "Touch her. Now! Get over here and touch her."

I felt a hand on my shoulder. A voice I didn't recognize. "Like this?"

The pain eased. The blinding light faded to a red pulse and then left completely. I heard my own gasping breaths, and I felt Derry's arms tight about me, his chest against my back as I sagged against him, the brush of his thick hair against my cheek as he leaned over my shoulder to say "Are you all right now?"

I nodded. "I think so."

His arms didn't loosen. I opened my eyes to see Rose staring at me and the handsome golden boy beside her, his arms folded over his chest, looking at me as if I were some animal in a zoo, fascinated and wary at the same time.

"What happened?" Rose asked.

"I . . . I don't know. I felt a little faint." How warm Derry was—*bare chested and laughing . . . No.* I pushed at his arms so he would release me. "I'm all right."

He let go with obvious reluctance, grabbing my arm again when I wavered.

"It must be the heat," I said, trying to smile.

Derry looked at me searchingly, and then he gestured to the other young man. "This is my friend Oscar."

"And this is Rose—Miss Fitzgerald," I said.

"You didn't trust me enough to come alone, I see."

"You didn't come alone either," I pointed out.

"Pleased to make your acquaintance, Miss Knox," Oscar said, stepping forward. He smiled at Rose. "And yours, Miss Fitzgerald." He had green eyes to go with his white-blond hair. His face was chiseled, his mouth set in what looked like a perpetual smile. His Irish accent was as heavy as Derry's.

And Rose, I saw, was taken. "Oscar," she said with a flirtatious smile. "How do you know Derry?"

"We came over together," he said. "On the same boat, eh, Derry?"

"Aye. The same boat."

"Do you work in the stables as well?"

Oscar's eyes twinkled. He glanced at Derry and then at Rose. "I leave the horses to Derry. Just now I'm at my leisure."

"I see." Rose's smile widened. "Well, if you're at your leisure, you've time for a promenade. Shall we walk where it's cooler?"

Rose was absolutely shameless.

"The two of you go on. We'll catch up," said Derry, and I remembered why I'd agreed to meet him. The headache that had faded took up residence again in my temple.

Rose said, "Are you certain you're all right, Grace?"

I nodded, thinking how easily she meant to leave me alone with Lucy's beau, no matter how much she had warned me. But then again, Oscar was gorgeous. Not so much as Derry, but still . . . Rose gave me a can-you-believe-this? look as he offered his arm and the two of them set off down the path, her skirt swaying with the exaggerated movement of her hips.

"Your friend seems to like him," Derry noted once they were away.

I swirled on him so quickly my skirt caught on the toe of his boot. "Who is he? Why did you bring him here?"

"You saw the glow in him too. I know you did."

"He was in the sun."

Derry glanced at the sky. "It's pretty overcast today, don't you think?"

I put a hand to my eyes. "Who is he?"

"Let's sit down," he urged.

"I don't want to sit anywhere with you."

"You'd rather I have to catch you again? You like the feel of me that much?"

I felt the blood rush into my face. "I don't like you at all," I lied.

"I know." He gestured to a nearby bench. "But sit with me anyway."

"Why did you ask me here today?"

"Sit down and I'll tell you."

I glanced back to Rose and Oscar, who were moving toward the seawall. The way Oscar had glowed, the way his touch had restored me . . . just like Derry.

"Grace." Derry's voice was very soft. "Sit down." I didn't resist as he took my hand and led me to the bench.

Once we were there, he didn't release my hand. His fingers were long, almost elegant, I noticed, staring down at them, thinking I should pull away, that I should tell him not to touch me. But the throbbing in my temples was gone, and I knew that if he took his hand away, it would come back.

He said, "I wanted to tell you that I'm not returning the ogham stick just yet. I will, just . . . it's taking longer than I'd thought."

I looked at him in alarm. "The police are looking for you. They came to the house. Patrick came with them. He saw . . ." *how poor we are.*

"He saw what?"

"You might have ruined everything."

"You think Devlin won't want you once he sees how far your family's fallen?"

His perception stunned me.

He smiled a little grimly. "That won't happen."

"How can you possibly know that?"

"Because—" He looked away, taking a deep breath. "Because I know it. What makes you think he'd abandon you now that he's seen how you live?"

"I don't. I'm just . . . afraid."

"Why wouldn't he want to help you?" He was still looking away. "I would, if it were me."

"That's even more humiliating," I whispered.

He turned to me, his hair falling forward to obscure his dark-blue eyes so that I felt again the urge to push it away, to really see what he was thinking. "Aye. You have your pride. 'Tis no small thing."

He understood.

"It's an honest thing in a world where there aren't many honest things. You should hold on to it. Don't let anyone tell you 'tisn't worth keeping."

"Holding on to my pride means my family goes hungry. It means we lose everything else we have—everything Aidan hasn't already lost for us. If it were just me . . . but it's not. I've my mother and my grandmother to worry about."

"Your brother's fault. Not yours. Why do you pay the price for it?"

"Because Aidan won't. Or can't. Everything belongs to him, and there's nothing I can do to make him care about it." Again I thought of that look I'd seen in my brother's eyes. "I don't know what's wrong with him."

Derry squeezed my hand. "Perhaps Devlin could—"

"Patrick doesn't know," I said, horrified. "He *can't* know. If he found out about Aidan's debaucheries, or how much we owe . . ."

"You think he won't find out? Or are you just hoping to keep it from him until he's married you?"

I heard the censure in his words.

"Not a good way to start a marriage, though I suppose not . . . unusual."

I had not thought of it that way. I felt suddenly dirty. I pulled my hand from his and buried it in my lap.

"But 'tis none of my business," he said.

"No, it's not," I said coldly.

"Do you love him?"

"That's none of your business either."

He nodded. "Where I'm from, the age of choice for a girl is fourteen. She can choose anything, but few choose marriage. You've so much before you—"

"You talk as if you're ancient. What are you—eighteen? Nineteen? Not much older than I am."

"Ah, that's right. You had a birthday since I've seen you last, haven't you? Happy birthday."

"You remember that? Thank you."

"So, seventeen. I suppose I've got to take back everything I said. Why, look at you"—he pressed a finger to my forehead lightly, a quick touch that burned—"wrinkles already. You're very nearly an old crone."

I laughed, and he looked surprised for a moment before he laughed with me. I liked the way his laugh sounded, as if it was real and true, and *so familiar.* I liked the way it looked on him too: his sparkling eyes, that long dimple creasing his cheek. *Just like in my dream . . .*

My laughter died.

His own smile faded. It was another moment before he looked away. "So do you know what you're getting into? Binding yourself to a man whose whole life is dedicated to Ireland?"

"What is that supposed to mean?"

"Only that it's the life Devlin's chosen. Is it really the one you want for yourself?"

"It has to be." I knotted my fingers together. "You know, I've always wanted a white knight to take me away. And now, here's Patrick, waiting to do just that, and I . . . well. It isn't what I thought it would be."

"Things never are, are they? If it's not what you want, why not just run away? Be your own white knight. There's an entire world out there."

"For you, perhaps. But I'm not a boy— What would I do?"

"Anything you wanted."

"Oh, Derry, I think you don't live in the same world I do."

He looked at me as if he knew me better than I knew myself, and the images from my dreams felt too vivid—not dreams but memories, though that wasn't possible. It couldn't be possible.

He said, "Maybe not. But I would do what I could to help you, lass. Whatever I could. If you wanted to run . . ."

It was tempting. To run away. To leave everything behind. Like the first Grainne.

"Perhaps I could be your Diarmid."

I swallowed. "I'm not that girl, Derry." It felt as if I were putting something away, something I meant never to take out again, and I was suddenly, horribly sad. "I'll marry Patrick when he asks. I'll help him with the Fenian Brotherhood—"

"You should keep your distance from them." His expression changed into one that chilled me. "That ogham stick . . . 'tis a dangerous thing. Did Devlin say any of that to you? When he offered it to you, did he ask you to say anything or to—"

"No, of course not. He wanted me to see it, that's all. How could it be dangerous? It's just a stone with some writing on it."

"One that burned you, you said."

"It had been in the sun. I told you that too. Patrick put the cases where the sun could reach them. He says they look as if they're . . ."

"Glowing," Derry finished.

"I remembered something my father had told me, about the old magic . . . We've done something amazing . . . It's real, and it's as alive as it always was. . . ."

"You said that wasn't all of the collection in his study," Derry went on. "Do you know where he keeps the rest of it?"

I shook my head, lost in my thoughts. The glowing and the burning stone, Patrick's words, and now Derry . . . and Oscar . . .

"Has he shown you anything else? A wand, perhaps? It would look like the stone, with carving, but made of wood. Of rowan."

"No. No, I don't know what you're talking about."

"Or a horn. Has he ever shown you a horn?"

A horn. I stared at him.

Derry sat back. "You've seen it."

"Patrick's never shown me a horn. But I used to have one."

"You?"

"An old hunting horn. It had been in my family a long time. But then Aidan lost it in a faro game. I don't know where it is now."

"What did it look like?"

"Just old. My grandmother told me it was ancient. It was cracked on one side. And it had a hammered silver band."

"Silver. But that . . . you're sure 'twas silver?"

"Yes. I know it so well I think I could tell it from a dozen others in the dark. I used to lie on my bed and imagine all the places it had been. Why does it matter? Why should Patrick have a horn?"

"I don't know that he does." Derry glanced up; whatever trouble had been in his eyes cleared. "Here comes Oscar with your friend. Don't say anything to her about this."

"Another secret you're asking me to keep."

"Another secret." He caught my gaze and held it. "Do me a favor, lass. Don't rush into anything with Devlin. Can you do that for me?"

"Why should I?" I laughed incredulously. "I've just told you how I need to marry. Why should I wait? What has any of this to do with you?"

He glanced beyond me. Urgent and low, he said, "Use your good sense, Grace. Think about all this—" He broke off with a sudden, charming smile. I looked over my shoulder to see Oscar, with Rose clasping his arm, her round cheeks flushed, her eyes shining. What was it with my friends and these Irish boys? It was as if their sense had been stolen clean away. *Though I'm no better, am I?*

"I thought you were going to join us," Oscar said with his own charming smile.

"We got distracted." Derry rose, holding out his hand to me, and I had no real choice but to take it.

"I think we should go." I looked at Rose, who was studiously ignoring my pleading glance.

She smiled up into Oscar's eyes. "Oh, but we just got here, Grace. No one's expecting us for hours."

Which was hardly an intelligent thing to say when we were with two boys we hardly knew, neither of whom could claim to be a gentleman. I felt Derry watching me; when I looked at him, his eyes glittered, with warning or something else, and I shivered, the things we'd talked about clashing like swords in my head.

From the harbor came the thunder again.

I started, and Derry's fingers tightened on my hand, which he hadn't released and I hadn't drawn away. "I need to get back to the stables before they miss me." He glanced at Rose in apology. "Some other time, maybe."

Sighing, Oscar added, "Aye, some other time. 'Twas a pleasure meeting you both."

"Just remember what I said," Derry told me as he let go of my hand. Then that arrogance again, the flirt. "Try not to miss me too much."

"It's hard to miss someone you don't think about!" I called to his retreating back as he and Oscar walked away.

He threw me a teasing grin over his shoulder.

Rose said, "Lucy is going to murder you."

"Not if she doesn't know. And if you say a word, I'll tell your mother you were meeting some immigrant boy in Battery Park. She'll never let you out of the house again."

"Why, Grace Knox, I never realized you could be so devious."

But she didn't know, of course, just how devious I'd learned to be. Bill collectors and angry doctors. Men bearing promissory notes signed by Aidan. *"Are you just hoping to keep it from him until he's married you?"*

"So what did he want to talk to you about? Did he declare his undying love? Has he thrown over Lucy for you?"

"Even if he had, I'm in love with Patrick."

"Of course you are," Rose said. "I suppose you're right. He's hardly appropriate."

"Hardly," I said. I turned back again, searching the crowd for glossy dark hair and white-blond that turned golden in the light.

But Derry and Oscar had already disappeared.

EIGHTEEN

The same day

Diarmid

S he looks a bit like Neasa," Oscar said as they went back to the stables. "Have you noticed that?"

"I noticed," Diarmid said. "She said her people are from Allen."

"Allen? How can that be a coincidence? By the gods, she *must* be the *veleda*. She must be. And that swoon . . . I've never seen anything like it. She saw me glowing, too, didn't she?"

"Aye."

"You have to tell Finn."

Diarmid had known that was true the moment she'd put her hand to her head and collapsed before Oscar. He didn't think he'd be able to get the sound of her keening from his head. Or her helplessness, the way she'd gripped his arms, that made him feel he would do anything to protect her.

Run away, he'd told her.

He was a fool.

"Cannel can divine the truth of it," Oscar said with assurance. "And if she is the *veleda*, Finn will never forget 'twas you who found her."

"There's something at least."

"'Twould be good to see the two of you on solid footing again," Oscar said, slowing, looking at him with a concern that told Diarmid exactly how much his rift with Finn had wounded the Fianna. And that made him feel even guiltier, that he was hesitating. It was about all of them. The prophecy.

They were nearly at the Devlin stables. Diarmid said, "I'll tell Finn tonight."

Oscar nodded. "I'll say nothing until you do. Maybe it won't be so hard as you think, Derry. Maybe the lass knows more than you believe."

"Maybe." Diarmid thought of the confusion in those dark, dancing eyes.

"Even if she doesn't, you've a smooth tongue. You can convince a lass to do anything, even without the lovespot."

Diarmid snorted. "Smooth tongue or no, this one won't stay still enough to listen. You saw her today. She could hardly wait to be rid of me."

Oscar considered him thoughtfully. "I've never known you to be wrong about a girl's heart. What is it about this one that blinds you?"

"What do you mean?"

"'Tis obvious she wants you."

Diarmid stared at Oscar, dumbfounded. "Which was it that addled you so, the heat or the little redhead?"

"And I'm thinking you want her too," Oscar went on, ignoring him. "So show her the *ball seirce* and be done with it. Then you'll both have what you want."

"And what if she *is* the *veleda*?" Diarmid asked. "What if I have to kill her?"

"Well, at least she won't die a virgin."

Diarmid hit him. Hard, in the stomach, hard enough that Oscar doubled over. "What was that for?" he gasped.

"For being an ass. No wonder Etain took a club to you all those years ago."

"She had a vicious temper." Oscar moaned.

"You can hardly blame her, given that she was wedded to you. This is a different world, Oscar. We can't just take what we want the way we used to. Here we're no better than . . . than stableboys. You'd best remember it." Diarmid walked to the stables, leaving a silent Oscar behind him.

When he went inside, Jerry muttered, "About time. You owe me a bottle for this one."

Work felt good, sweat and effort, as good as it had felt to hit Oscar, though Diarmid regretted it now. He didn't believe what his friend had said. Whether or not *he* wanted Grace Knox—and he did, he might as well admit it, even though he knew how foolish it was—he didn't think she felt the same.

Though a few times he'd thought perhaps she was growing to like him just a little bit. In her bedroom, for example, when she'd looked up at him with those eyes shining in the dark and told him the things she wanted. *"Can you change the world?"*

Or today when he'd seen her consider running away and he'd nearly fallen over himself to help her. The way she laughed—such a familiar sound, which was strange, as he would have sworn he'd never heard her laugh before. She rarely even *smiled* at him.

And then there was the fact that she'd come to meet him in the first place. He hadn't been at all sure that she would, though he'd hoped what he'd asked Leonard to write for him would raise her curiosity.

"Can you change the world?"

He forked hay into the feeding troughs. He refused to think of Grace Knox for the rest of the afternoon. When night came on, he made his way through the moist and heavy air to the tenement—not rushing this time, smiling at the whores he passed, stopping to have a word with a passing newsboy or a man who recognized him.

"I heard the Black Hands was coming for you boys," said Tommy Royce, who ran with a gang called the Alley Boys, as he spat tobacco into an already overflowing, fetid gutter.

"You put much credence in it?" Diarmid asked.

"Heard it from Little Nose himself."

"You boys willing to fight with us?"

"Aye. Send the word," said Tommy, slinking again into the darkness, and Diarmid went on his way. He glanced involuntarily at the black sky. The world felt uneasy; he would welcome something to make the feeling go away. A good fight would relax him.

Finn and Ossian were in what passed for a yard—dust

and baking sewage, stinking and miasmic—training a group of neighbor boys by the light of an oil lamp placed on the ground. Finn was saying, "If you can fight in the darkness, lads, you can fight anywhere."

"We're forming our own militia," Oscar had told Diarmid that morning. *"And it keeps those boys out of trouble too. Something to think about besides hunger and no work."* Diarmid liked the idea. These people needed real heroes. For a moment, Diarmid wished, as he often did walking these streets, that the Fianna could be those heroes.

Conan sat watching from the stoop, his sheepskin around his shoulders despite the heat. The lamplight from a nearby window shone on his bald head.

"I could smell you a block away," Diarmid said as he approached.

Conan glanced up. He had a cup of ale in his hand. He motioned to Finn and the others. "Black Hands are coming for us. 'Twould be good to have you in the fight."

"I heard. I'll be here."

Conan belched and wiped his mouth with the back of his hand. "So what've you been up to, Derry? Kissing lasses and squiring them about town while the rest of us live in this wretchedness?" He kicked at the rail.

Diarmid remembered when they'd been in the Fianna stronghold—living like kings, with fine things and enough food and wine to feed them all four times over, and lasses for all, even Conan—and still Conan had been dissatisfied, a soul that always wanted more. But he was amusing and good to have in a fight, and he'd never failed them, no matter his complaints.

"I'd rather be here with the rest of you," Diarmid said, catching Finn's eye.

Finn nodded back to him, put up the stick he was parrying with, and said, "That's it for tonight, lads. Tomorrow we'll try it again."

The boys dispersed in a mass of excited grumbling, and Finn and Ossian came over.

"You've found the rowan wand?" Finn asked.

"Maybe something better," Diarmid said, stepping through the open door. He heard them clumping behind him up the stairs. The door to the flat was open.

When they were all inside, Diarmid said, "I think I may have found the *veleda*."

The room went silent. Finn said, "The *veleda*?"

"I think she may be Devlin's lass. Grace Knox. When she first saw me, she said I was glowing. It hurt her enough that she swooned. And then . . . I took Oscar to see her this afternoon. The same thing. The ogham stick burned her when she touched it. The same way it did Cannel."

"You saw this?"

"She told me. And—" Here was the worst of it, the part he didn't want to say. "She reminds me of Neasa, Finn. She looks . . . There's a resemblance. Her people are from Allen."

Finn's gaze went razor-sharp.

Diarmid forced himself to continue. "And Grace had a horn. Her brother lost it in a bet. I don't know that it's the *dord fiann.* She said it had silver on it. Did yours have silver? I didn't remember that."

Finn shook his head. "Bronze."

"Then it isn't the same one." This, anyway, was a relief.

Finn glanced at Cannel. "The *cainte* can do a divination to tell for certain. But we'll need something of hers. And I want you to bring her here."

Diarmid said, "She won't come. This part of town—she's not like the lasses around here. She's a lady, Finn."

"Bring her tomorrow."

"I don't know if I can," Diarmid said in exasperation. "'Twill be hard enough to convince her—"

"You're a soldier of the Fianna. Are you telling me you can't manage to persuade a lass to go somewhere with you?"

"Finn—"

Finn grabbed the back of Diarmid's neck, pulling him close. "I want her here, Diarmid. Time is passing quickly. Have you forgotten? Samhain grows ever closer. I don't care how you get her here. Carry her off. Show her the lovespot. Just bring her."

Because she resembles Neasa. Diarmid knew that was the reason, and he wished he'd said nothing about it.

Finn released him. "Cannel can do the divination while she's here. Then we'll know what should be done with her."

"Done with her?"

"She has to choose us, Diarmid. Do you not remember the prophecy? No one here's going to hurt her."

Which was true enough. Diarmid wasn't afraid of that. He was afraid of . . .

"'Tis you who must kill her."

NINETEEN

June 18

Grace

I spent the day reading the birthday book of poems from Patrick. I hadn't seen him since he'd come to the house with the police five days ago. Mama was right. I would have to push. I had a vision of myself on my knees, proposing to *him*, and it was humiliating just to think it. I tried not to remember Derry's words: *"Do me a favor, lass. Don't rush into anything with Devlin."*

His talk of the ogham stick and the horn, Oscar glowing . . . And on top of everything else, Derry was still in my dreams. Last night I'd seen him in battle, his hair flying behind him, a spear in one hand and a sword in the other. Then the scene changed, again the pillows, his laughter, that near kiss—Oh, this was bad. Very bad. I wished I'd never laid eyes upon him. I would give anything not to see him again.

And you don't have to, I told myself. *Leave him to Lucy. Think about Patrick.*

The plans for my debut were progressing, though the cost was one more thing I didn't want to think about. Mama had gone twice more to give the Needham sisters pianoforte lessons, and each time she came back more drawn than before, as if they were sucking the life from her.

"I think we'd best go with daisies," she'd told me just this morning. "They're less expensive, and just a few bouquets should be enough, don't you think?"

She looked so fragile now. I hated to do anything to upset her. I knew she had headaches, too, like mine, though she never admitted it. She was as tense as I was, watching the window all the time, waiting for the doctor's lawsuit or a messenger from Patrick.

The weather wasn't helping. It stayed sultry and heavy. I needed a breath of air, no matter that it was fouler outside than in. Without a breeze, the smells of the city had gathered into one great, stinking fog. But it did not smell of desperation, which was a scent I'd grown heartily tired of, and so I stepped out into the tiny backyard bordered by the alley. I'd planted a garden this year, but I had no talent for growing things, and so the flowers and the vegetables had withered and died. I let the door close behind me and sagged against the wall. It would have been nice to have something green to eat. I closed my eyes. There'd been lettuce, I remembered. And carrots, and radishes—

"Lass, might I have a word with you?"

I started, opening my eyes to see Derry leaning against the gate, looking about warily.

I felt a little shiver of something I didn't want to

understand. "All I wanted was some air. Where did you come from? Wait—are you *watching* me?"

He smiled, that dimple again. His hair, as always, was flopping into his face. He gestured to the gate. "Can I come in?"

I came down the stair, away from the house and my mother's ears. He stepped inside, catching the gate before it could clang shut, making only a soft *click*.

"I thought I told you to leave me alone," I said.

"That was days ago. You said nothing of it yesterday."

"I'd hoped I wouldn't have to."

"I don't remember things well." He tapped his head, still smiling. "Best to keep reminding me."

"Then I'm reminding you now. Leave me alone. Why are you here?"

The smile faded. "I'm afraid I need another favor."

"Another favor? Why is it you're always coming to me? Why not ask Lucy? She's the one in love with you. She'll do anything you say."

"She's busy. Tea parties and such. And you seem at your leisure."

"I'm not. In fact, I'm quite busy planning my debut."

"Aye. What is that exactly?"

"A party that announces that I'm old enough to be married. So you see, I've a great many things to do. If you don't mind—" I turned to leave. He caught my wrist, drawing me back. So warm. My pulse leaped.

"I've a friend in Bellevue Hospital," he said bluntly. "He's in bad shape, but they won't let me in to see him. I need someone respectable to get me through the door. Lucy said she can't. I'd hoped you would help."

I stared at him. "They won't let you in?"

"Not without someone like you."

"But that's ridiculous. Why would they ask such a thing?"

He shrugged. "I'm guessing I look as if I might cause trouble."

"I can't argue with that."

"Will you help me or not?"

"Well, I—"

"Please," he said. "You're the only other respectable person I know."

An innocent visit to the hospital. Why not? It was better than sitting around the house being driven half mad by the smell of desperation and my own anxiety. And Derry had asked Lucy first, so she couldn't complain if I went instead. "Your friend . . . you don't mean Oscar?"

"Someone else."

"Well then, I suppose it couldn't hurt. When did you want to go?"

"Now, if you can. 'Tis my afternoon off. But if you'd rather wait an hour or so . . ."

When it would be near dusk. My mother would never let me go with night so close. Not that she would let me go with him anyway, if she knew the truth—and here I marveled again that I had become so adept at lying that I no longer hesitated to do so.

"I can't go so late. It won't take long?"

"No. You'll come to no harm. I'll see to it. We'll have to walk, but it's not far."

"I walk everywhere, Derry. We sold the carriage a year ago. Wait here."

I went back inside. The house felt more oppressive than ever. "Mama, I'm going to see Rose. She wants to get ice cream."

My mother waved me away. "Go on. Enjoy yourself. Is Lucy going?"

I shook my head. "Lucy's at some tea or something."

"Be home before dark," she said.

I glanced at my shawl hanging on the hook. It was sweltering, so I left it. I wanted to leave the gloves, too, but I tucked them into my pocket in case I needed them to pass the hospital's requirements for respectability. I grabbed my hat—no lady went anywhere without one—a small and plain brown bonnet that had once been decorated with silk cherries. Those were gone now, popping their seams when I'd worn it once in a drenching rain, and now there was only the pink silk ribbon, very faded, which I tied beneath my chin. If I tied the bow just right, you couldn't see the way the edge of one ribbon had begun to fray.

When I went outside again, Derry was lingering by the gate, waiting restlessly, flipping the catch up and down, staring at his boots. It seemed unlike him; he'd always appeared so self-possessed, and I hesitated. Something was not right. . . .

But then he looked up and smiled, and whatever it was I'd seen disappeared. "You're kind to do this."

"If you don't have me home before dark, Mama will never let me out of the house again."

He didn't attempt to take my hand, nor did he offer his arm as we set off down the potholed alley, and I was grateful for that. I didn't want to touch him. I remembered how I'd felt when he'd grabbed my wrist. The temptation in my dream . . .

No.

He said nothing for a long while, something else that was unlike him. Nervously, I said, "You're awfully quiet."

He glanced at me. "Worried about my friend, that's all."

"Is he very badly off?"

"I don't know," he said pointedly. "I haven't seen him."

"But you said he was in bad shape."

"Did I?" He kicked a pebble into a pothole. "I imagine he is. He was in a fight. The other lad had to be carried home, so . . ."

"It's nice," I said. "That you care for your friends that way."

"My friends are my family. I'd do anything for them."

The intensity in his voice made me look more closely at him. "Oscar seems nice."

"Nice," he repeated. "You've said that twice. It's *nice* that I care for my friends. Oscar seems *nice.*"

"What's wrong with *nice?*"

"Nothing." He shook his head. "Nothing. I'm sorry."

"It's all right. I imagine I'd be upset, too, if one of my friends was in the hospital."

A small smile again. "Aye. I imagine you would. You're good to your friends as well. Rose. And Lucy too—even though you don't seem to like her much."

"Oh, Lucy's all right. But we were never close. She's older, you know, and I think she tolerates me only because I'm useful."

"Useful?"

"She knows I'll do what she asks because of Patrick. So I make a good chaperone when she wants to see you."

"Ah yes. The rule follower."

"If I were truly that, you wouldn't have been kissing her at the parish fair."

"Something to thank you for, then."

I remembered how he'd licked icing from her bottom lip, and again I felt that little drop in my stomach, which startled me into babbling, "Well, how surprising."

He gave me a questioning glance.

"This. You and me. Having a conversation where you're not flirting. It's nice—oh, forget that—I mean I don't mind talking to you when you're not."

He smiled again.

"Don't start," I admonished. "I'm happy to be your friend, Derry, but I wish you'd leave the rest of it for Lucy, or for girls you're truly interested in."

"What makes you think I'm not interested in you?"

"It wouldn't matter if you were," I told him frankly. "It's not you I want."

"Because you've got Devlin dangling."

"And you have Lucy. I can't have you complicating things. I can't have anything to do with the ogham stick. I can't afford for Lucy to be angry with me for things she's . . . imagined."

"You think she might be upset to find I'd been in your bed, you mean?"

Heat rushed to my cheeks. "She's no one to trifle with,

Derry. She's no Astor, but her family's rich enough, and Patrick knows important men. She'll never be able to have you, but if she thinks you've wronged her—you'd best take care."

"You've no need to worry. I know what I am."

"Then you know she's not for you. If you pursue this—"

"I told you I know what I am," he said brusquely.

"I'm sorry. I don't mean to pry, not really; it's just that—"

"I see how it concerns you, lass. And I'll try not to make your life more difficult than I have to."

"Than you have to?"

We had reached the corner to the hospital, but when I started to turn, he took my elbow, steering me lightly in the other direction.

"Bellevue Hospital is that way," I said.

"We're going another way around."

"But it's directly—"

"He's in a separate wing. The poor wing. You know it?"

The truth was that I'd never actually been to Bellevue, and he probably knew it better. "No."

"Then it's this way," he said.

I followed him, though it seemed to me we were moving in a distinctly bad direction. The shops we passed gave way to empty stores, their windows papered with signs that read "For Let" or "No Irish Need Apply." There were more and more men lingering idly in doorways. The vendors selling plump oranges and bright peppers became those selling small, wrinkled apples and day-old bread. No longer were people clad in silks and summer muslins but in ragged clothes, too many of them milling listlessly about as if they had nowhere else to go.

I glanced at Derry, who was staring straight ahead. "This is the right way?"

"Aye." Short and to the point. His hand crept to my elbow again, this time a tight hold. "Stay close, will you?"

The big Belgian paving stones of the streets gave way to broken cobblestones and potholes. Horse piss ran in rivulets down the gutters, trash piles grew higher, the smell of onions and ale stronger. There were dogs everywhere, sniffing in the garbage, fighting in the middle of the street. And so many people. Children shouting and racing about. Women splashing in the muddy puddles that gathered beneath the spouts of the green public pumps as they filled their buckets. Men wandering out of saloons. A group of girls lingering on the corner narrowed their eyes at me and called out, "Good day to you, Derry!" He ignored them.

This could not be the way to Bellevue, could it? "This is certainly the long way 'round."

"'Tis a bad part of town," he admitted.

A little too true. The walks in some places were crumbling away. The buildings and streets grew closer together, and when I looked down the crossing alleys, they appeared full of dead ends, warrens of endless buildings. There were saloons everywhere—there must have been seven on one block alone. Derry steered me around a rooting pig with a muttered "I don't like pigs." His fingers tightened on my arm so I thought he might leave a bruise.

And I knew for certain that he'd lied to me.

"We're not going to see your friend at Bellevue Hospital."
He was quiet.

"We're not going to any poor wing."

"I'm sorry, Grace."

I tried to pull away. He was so strong I couldn't budge.

"Let go of me. Take me back this minute or I swear I'll scream."

"There are four lads on that corner," he said to me in a low voice. "D'you see them?"

I followed his gaze. Four young men, ill-clad, two barefoot. I saw when they caught sight of me, of Derry, their speculative glances, their too-careful attention.

"You don't want to pull away from me here, Grace. Or scream. Trust me on this."

He was right. I felt a prickling fear and cursed myself for coming with him—how well did I know him anyway? All my talk of being friends, all my well-meant advice . . . What a fool I was. I'd lied to my mother. It would be hours before she was worried enough to send a message to Rose, and even then Rose would pretend we were together to save me from trouble. I would have done the same for her. No one knew where I was. Or who I was with.

"Where are you taking me?" My voice sounded too high.

"I told you. To visit a friend."

"Another friend like Oscar?"

"Aye."

"And you couldn't have just told me this? Instead of tricking me this way?"

"There's no reason to be afraid. 'Tis a few questions he wants answered is all."

"Questions?" Men lay in corners, some looking up blearily as we passed, others not moving, not even seeming to breathe. Children with torn pants and no shoes. A woman going through the garbage, tossing out a dead rat by its tail. "About what?"

He hesitated. Then he said, "The ogham stick."

I stopped so suddenly that he stumbled. "Derry, no. I told you. I want nothing to do with it. If Patrick were ever to find out—"

"He won't find out." He pulled me after him. "Best to keep moving."

"He has the police looking for it."

"They won't find it here." He turned a corner, ducked through a corridor between two tall brick buildings, over planks that sank and wobbled, set as they were over a swampy, green, festering *something*; and then we were in a warren of four buildings surrounding a central yard with more planks spread over a cesspool and a row of tottering privies that looked as old as the world, ready to collapse upon themselves. The stench was remarkable. I fumbled with my handkerchief, pressing it to my nose. I saw his bitter smile as he took me to a back door. Black metal fire escapes tangled up the sides of the buildings like knotted laces. There were two small boys playing, rolling a ball back and forth, and one of them looked up as we approached, jumping to his feet. "Play ball with us, Derry?"

"Not today, Wills," Derry said. "Soon, though, I promise." Then he took up the ball and threw it, and they chased after it like puppies, shouting in joy.

"What is this place?" I asked in a horrified whisper.

"Home. At least for now." He turned to me, taking my face between his hands before I had time to move or protest. "Just answer his questions. You've nothing to be afraid of. I'll be there. I promised to keep you safe, and I will."

His words only frightened me more. I jerked away from him. The bow of my hat caught on his hands, the knot sliding, loosening. "You've already lied to me. Why should I believe a word you say?"

"Grace, I—"

"Let's just get this over with. But don't ever ask me for another favor. I swear I'll never do another thing for you. Not ever."

His mouth tightened. "Take my hand. It's very dark."

"No."

"Then don't touch the walls," he said matter-of-factly. "I don't know what's dripping down them today. Slime or blood or something else."

"Blood?" I shuddered. He took advantage, grabbing my hand, holding it in a grip I could not break, and pulled me after him.

Once we'd turned the first landing, away from the light of the open door, it was so dark I couldn't see anything. I had no idea whether it was a wall or emptiness I stepped into. It could have been the middle of the night on these stairs—*the middle of the night in hell,* because it was that hot too. And the smell was indescribable. Sewage and drink and smoke and sweat. Something gamy and rotten. Derry made his way carefully, now and then saying, "Watch this one" or "Step to your right."

We passed open doors that lent a little light; I glimpsed men smoking and shirtless, women yelling at whining children. It seemed a long time until we reached the top.

Derry paused before a door. "Close your eyes."

"Why?"

"'Twould be best, I think."

"I'll keep them open, thank you."

"Suit yourself." He rapped hard on the door—three short, one long, a code—and the door opened.

I saw Oscar, and a tall man with thinning red hair, and then I was blinded, as if there were stars in the room, each pulsing, each bright as a burning sun. My knees went wobbly. Derry grabbed me as I crumpled. And the pain . . . dear God, the pain was worse than ever. Derry's arms were all that held me up. I heard him shout, "By the gods, touch her!"

A familiar voice—Oscar's—saying, "Do what he says. Quickly now, lads. No sense making her suffer."

My head felt as if it would explode. Moaning, I closed my eyes—no help; the light blared through my eyelids, as red as blood.

"Hurry," Derry growled, and then there was a hand on my shoulder; another, one by one, and with each the pain lessened a little, the light faded. A final press, and the last bit of it melted away, leaving me weak. Something was wrong with me. Something was terribly wrong. Why did this keep happening? And always around Derry. *Always.*

"It's you," I heard myself whisper. "It's because of you, isn't it?"

He said nothing except a rough "Get her a seat," and I heard the scrape of something across the floor, and then he was helping me onto something—not a chair, a barrel. I opened my eyes and the room spun, and I closed them tightly again, putting my face in my hands. "I'm going to be sick."

Another scrape across the floor. "There's a bucket to your right," Derry said in my ear, and then, "Is there any water?"

"Just ale," said someone.

But the nausea was fading. "It's all right. I . . . I'm fine. . . ."

"This happens every time?" Another voice, commanding but also melodic.

"Until she's touched." Derry's hand was on my arm. "'Twas a hard one this time, lass. Too many. Are you sure you're all right?"

I opened my eyes.

The room was small and dingy, with a doorway in one wall and a window at the far end, letting in some light. A large scarred table sat in the middle of the room. Scattered throughout were barrels and piles of straw, and on all of these sat young men—though three of them looked a bit older, perhaps in their early twenties. They were all watching me, gray eyes and brown, blue and green. Blond hair and brown, one who was bald. And they were all astonishingly good-look-ing—except perhaps for the bald one, though he wasn't ugly.

I looked at Derry. "Where am I?"

He swallowed and gestured to the others. "These are my friends. Finn's Warriors—that's what they call us. There's Oscar, who you know, and Cannel"—the red-headed man, the only one who hadn't glowed. Derry named off the rest, each of whom nodded in turn. Keenan, wiry, with thick brown hair and eyes warm as chocolate; Goll, one of the older ones, perhaps Patrick's age, with a hawk-like nose and a newsboy's cap. Ossian, also older, with white-blond hair and a face so like Oscar's that I assumed they must be brothers. Conan, the bald one, wearing a heavy, graying fleece. The names sounded familiar, though I couldn't bring my thoughts together enough to know why.

"And this is Finn," Derry said finally.

Suddenly I realized why I knew the names. Derry's friends were calling themselves after the mythical Fianna. The conceit might have made me laugh if I hadn't been so uneasy.

Finn rose. Like Ossian, he was a few years older than the others, and he was . . . beautiful. Golden hair chased with red. Eyes of a startlingly pale color. Sharp cheekbones and a full mouth. He wasn't as classically handsome as Derry, but his presence filled the room as he came toward me.

He looked me over. "You're right; there is a resemblance." That haughty yet melodious voice.

"Aye." Derry sounded miserable and resigned.

"Resemblance to who?" I asked.

"I told you," Derry said, not looking at me. "A friend who lived near us in Ireland."

I remembered then. County Kildare. Probably a relative.

Finn stepped closer. I felt as if there were things about him I should know, and not knowing them was dangerous. "Grace Knox," he murmured. "Patrick Devlin's lass."

"What do you want with me?" I demanded, and then wished I hadn't when Finn turned to Derry and smiled.

"She's spirited too."

"I'd also like to go home, so can you please do what you will and be done with it so I can leave?" Which may have been the most stupid thing I could have said, I realized in the next moment.

Derry sighed. "You see."

Oscar laughed. "Well done, Miss Knox. Well done indeed."

Finn waved a hand at the others. "I'll take a moment with Miss Knox."

The others moved as if they'd been held suspended and Finn's command had released them. There was a keg in the corner, sausages on the table, and they went back to drinking and talking.

I looked at Derry, panicked.

Finn said to him, "You too. Leave us."

Derry glanced at me. "Finn, you—"

"I'll return her to you in ten minutes," Finn said. "If she still wants me to."

Derry had said he'd protect me, but Finn felt formidable, and I thought that any war between them would not end in

Derry's favor. I felt his wariness as he left me with Finn and went to the keg with the others. He stood in the corner with Oscar, watching over the rim of his cup.

Finn came even closer to me. "What do you know about the Fenian Brotherhood?"

Answer his questions, Derry had said. "Nothing. My friend Patrick Devlin is a member. That's all."

"You know nothing about their activities?"

"I'm not privy to their secrets."

Finn grasped the edge of the barrel, a hand on either side of me. The pure maleness of him made me swallow nervously. "You're lying," he said.

"They mean to free Ireland from British rule. Patrick . . . Mr. Devlin . . . told me that they'd helped raise a rebellion in Ireland, and it was a failure. That's all I know."

"Devlin collects relics. You've seen them?"

I nodded. "Torcs and statuettes. The ogham stick. Which I believe you have."

"Have you seen a rowan wand? Or a horn?"

"Why? Why do they matter?"

He backed away. I glanced past him to Derry, whose eyes looked black.

Finn made a quick gesture. "Bring the ogham stick," and almost before he got the words out, Goll hurried up with something in a rag. He handed it to Finn, who unwrapped it and held the stone before me. "Touch it."

I recoiled. "I'd rather not."

"Why?"

"I'd just . . . rather not."

He smiled, more gently. "Please, Miss Knox."

Again I glanced at Derry, who nodded, and I laid my hand upon the stone. It was as warm as it had been before, growing hotter with every second—burning. I jerked away, expecting to see blisters on my hand that weren't there. Something else I didn't understand.

Finn chanted, "Darkness and thunder, blood and fire. The eye of one who slays. As one is bid, so come the rest. The rowan wand and virtue gone. A blood price paid. Now come the Children of Domnu."

The words unfurled in my head as if another voice said them to me. The verse Finn spoke felt wrong; it wasn't how it should be said, though I had no idea why I thought that. "No," I couldn't help saying. "No, you're saying it all wrong."

He lurched back as if I'd hit him. He held out the ogham stone to Ossian, who took it from him without a word, and I felt foolish and afraid. I wanted to go. Finn reached out, taking a strand of my hair between his fingers, staring at it with longing. It was all I could do not to yank away. Finally, he looked up with a sad smile that pulled at my heart, though I'd been afraid only moments before.

He let go of my hair. "Thank you, Miss Knox. You've been very enlightening. Now please, you must be hungry and thirsty. Join us for a bit, if you will, and then I'll have you escorted safely home."

I hadn't realized I'd been holding my breath, and now I let it out. "That's all? That's all you wanted to know?"

"Why, is there more you can tell me?"

"No. That is, I don't understand. I have nothing to do with this."

He gave me a slow bow. "You're welcome here, Miss Knox."

It was a signal. Derry was at my side in seconds.

"Get Miss Knox something to eat and drink," Finn said. Before he left us, a look passed between them. I knew it was an order. *Join us for a bit,* he'd said. I knew already Derry would do whatever Finn asked of him. He'd brought me here at Finn's request, no matter how reluctantly.

I felt Derry's tension ease. Whatever he'd been afraid of hadn't happened.

"D'you want something?" he asked me. "There's not much—sausage and bread—but I can—"

"I think I would be sick if I ate anything," I told him, which was true.

"I'm sorry. There was no other way. What did he say to you?" He glanced over to the table where Finn had gone to speak to Cannel. "Never mind. You can tell me later."

"I don't know what's happening to me," I said. "I don't understand any of this. Not the glowing, or . . . I must be going mad."

"I don't think so, lass."

He held out his hand, and I took it without a thought. The others watched as he led me across the room. Finn and Cannel huddled over a deck of cards on the table; Ossian eyed us as he drank from a cup of ale.

Oscar came bounding up. "You can't take her away yet, Derry. Why, she just got here. What do you think of our humble abode, Miss Knox?"

He was so charming it was hard not to smile. "I think it could use a woman's touch."

"What, you don't think that stain in the corner a good enough decoration?"

"I suppose, if you embellished it a bit."

"Ah now, why did we not think of that? Embellish how? A bit of blood perhaps? Or mud?"

I couldn't help laughing. "That wasn't exactly what I'd imagined."

Oscar's green eyes sparkled. "No? I've been told I have a talent for art. Many a lass has commented on it."

"Have they?"

"D'you think that might impress your pretty friend Rose?"

Just then Goll came up, bearing a cup of ale, which he offered to me with a shy smile. "'Tis good to have a lass about the place for a change."

I took the ale, though it smelled strong and bitter, and I hadn't the stomach for it. I thanked him, and then Oscar nudged me, trying to get my attention again and spilling his ale down his shirt in the process. I offered him my handkerchief.

"Pansies," he said, looking at the handkerchief. "You do some fine needlework, Miss Knox."

"I don't, but my mother does. You have a good eye."

Keenan stepped up and said, "A good eye? Oscar?"

I listened while the three of them went back and forth about who had the sharpest vision. Only Derry said nothing. I felt his impatience growing until he interrupted Keenan in the middle of his boasting with "She'll judge a contest between you later. Just now she's wanting some air."

I didn't miss Oscar's frown as Derry pulled me to the window. He let go of my hand, pushed the sash all the way up with his shoulder, and stepped over the sill to the fire escape below. "'Tis cooler out here," he said, turning to offer his help. Careful of my skirts, I sat on the sill, trying not to show any ankle—not very successfully—as I twisted to follow him out. From behind us in the room, I heard catcalls.

"They're savages," Derry muttered. "Ignore them."

He helped me onto the platform, steadying me as I sat, and then he sat beside me and handed me back the cup of ale that Goll had given me. Tentatively, I tasted it—as bitter as I'd thought, even more so. Warm and rather nasty. My stomach slipped, and I put the cup aside.

The fire escape looked out onto a crowded street. I'd never been up so high—five stories, perhaps six. It seemed a long way down, but everywhere people lounged on their fire escapes, one or two men shirtless, women shouting at children playing in the street below.

"It won't fall, will it?" I asked, testing the rail.

"It hasn't yet."

"That's hardly reassuring."

"It's held four of us at one time. Only a little creaking."

"Very funny. You've probably loosened it."

"Probably," he agreed, drinking. "Now tell me what Finn said to you."

"He asked questions about the Fenian Brotherhood. And the ogham stick."

"That's all?" He looked dourly into his cup.

"What else should there be? You said there'd be questions and nothing more."

His mood puzzled me. Distracted and tense and . . . and angry. I looked at him, trying to see his expression, but those dark-blue eyes were half hidden beneath the heavy fringe of his hair. In frustration, I reached to push it out of his face.

He recoiled so sharply he banged his head against the wall. His hand was quick as lightning, grabbing my wrist, stopping me before I could get close. "Don't."

I wrenched loose. "Your hair's in your eyes. I can't see what you're thinking. It's annoying."

"Why not just ask me what I'm thinking?"

"Because you won't tell me the truth."

"Why would you say that?"

"Because I don't think you ever do. You lied to get me here, for one——"

"I said I was sorry for that."

"And you're not telling me everything. You're not telling me why you brought me here when you could have answered those questions of Finn's. I told *you* everything I told him. And you're not telling me why . . . why . . ."

"Why what?"

I looked away. "Why *anything*. Why people glow only

when they're around you. Or why the ogham stick burned me. Or why the things Finn said . . ." I didn't know how to explain, not about the verse, or the way it had sounded wrong in my ears, or how Finn had looked at my hair with such longing, as if he wanted me, or not even that, exactly, but something *within* me, but couldn't think how to ask for it.

Derry didn't give me any answers. "Do you like him? Finn?"

"I hardly know. He's very . . . overwhelming."

"What about the others? Oscar? Goll? Keenan?"

"They're charming."

"Charming."

"Yes. And not at all annoying. You could take a lesson from them, I think."

"Could I?"

"Yes. I doubt any one of them would have dragged me here under false pretenses, or sneaked into my room, or stolen anything at all—"

He laughed. "You don't think so? Any one of them would have done so if Finn had asked it. And when they were in your bedroom, they would have stolen a kiss—or more. Which I haven't done, I'd like to point out."

"Well, you have Lucy for that, don't you? And you said you didn't want to kiss me."

"I did?"

"After you stole my book. Patrick's book. When you brought it to the house."

"Ah. So I did." He was staring at me strangely. The falling sunlight hit his eyes; they were the color of the deepest part of the Sound. He brought up his knees, resting his forearms on them, letting the cup of ale dangle in his hand. "And you have Devlin."

I thought of Patrick's kiss and how I'd wanted more.

"So the two of you can sally forth together and save the world." The irony was thick in Derry's tone.

"You don't like Patrick. Why?"

He shrugged. "I don't know him."

"Then why do you say such things?"

"Perhaps because he's playing with things that should be left alone. Or perhaps because he's got you wound about like the string on a top. The things you say you want—do you really believe he can get them for you?"

"Yes." I remembered the weight of Derry on my bed, the shine of his eyes in the darkness. "He can save me."

"Can he? Or better yet, will he? Or will you just find yourself in a different prison? Can he change the world?" Derry laughed lightly and took a sip of his ale. "Maybe not."

"Can you? Can anyone?"

"Some things are hard to change, I know. When I see all this . . . despair . . . I don't know how anyone can bear it. How do you live without seeing green? How can you go up and down these stairs every day and hear your children cry with hunger and . . . Well, I don't know how to fix it. But it seems wrong not to try."

"What a tender heart you have," I said, astonished to hear such sentiment in him.

"When people say that, it means they plan to do nothing themselves."

"It's harder for me. It *is*," I insisted when I saw his raised brow. "You're a boy; you can at least try to change the world if you want."

"One minute you're on top of the world," he said, lifting his cup in a mock toast, "as rich as a king or prince, and the next you're living in a room with seven others and eating moldy bread. But life's a gamble, isn't it? And we all have to wager. Still, you get to choose what that wager will be—whether you'll take a risk, and whether 'tis faith or fear that guides you." His gaze challenged me. The blue of his eyes seemed to shimmer.

For a moment, I thought of him on a riverbank. Watching me. Waiting.

And then, from below, I heard a shout. A child screamed out, "The Black Hands! The Black Hands is coming!"

Derry jerked to attention, spilling the ale from his cup. His face tightened in a way I didn't recognize. I followed his gaze to a group of young men coming around the corner below us. Each of them had smeared one of his hands with soot. Some had striped their faces with it as well. They stopped beneath us. Thunder cracked as one of them called up, "Hey, Warriors! The Black Hands is waitin' for you!"

TWENTY

The next moment

Grace

D erry dropped the cup, and it tumbled to the platform below. Someone yelped as it hit. Finn leaned out the window, his hands braced on the sill, forearms taut with muscle. He shouted down, "Better have your coffins ready!" and then he nodded at Derry and said, "Come on."

Derry grabbed me by the shoulders. "Stay here. D'you understand me, Grace? Don't move from here, no matter what happens. I'll be back for you."

"What are you talking about—you can't mean to go down there. Why . . . that's a gang, and . . ." *A gang.* I went queasy again. The Black Hands was a gang.

Just as Finn's Warriors was a gang.

Finn's Warriors. What had I been thinking when Derry introduced them that way, that it was just some club name? They'd styled themselves after the famous Fianna for a reason.

I touched his arm as he rose. "Don't. Don't go."

He pulled away. "I'm a Warrior, Grace. This is what I *do*. You'll be safe if you stay here. Promise me. *Promise me*."

I nodded mutely, and he was through the window and back into the flat. Inside there was a shout, a laugh, the sound of boot steps. I'd heard of gangs, of course—who hadn't? The river pirate gangs. The Baxter Street Dudes and the Whyos—who it was rumored would hurt or murder anyone for the right amount. They even had a price list. My father had complained about them every summer, and now, with the depression, the gangs had grown braver and more ruthless, waylaying express wagons in broad daylight, picking pockets on every crowded streetcar, robbing those who walked alone on city streets. Stay away from this part of town—how often had I heard that? And yet here I was. With a stableboy who wasn't a stableboy. *"I know what I am."*

A member of a *gang*.

I pulled back into the corner of the fire escape, wanting to disappear as Finn and Derry and the others—all but Cannel—streamed out through the doorway below, their boots raising clouds of dust. There were seven of them, and twice that many Black Hands—even more. The sky seemed to darken. I heard the thunder again.

The charming boys I'd seen laughing and joking only minutes ago were grim and menacing now. People gathered to watch on the fire escapes, so many that the platforms and ladders creaked and sagged. Young boys gathered stones, shouting, "You get 'em, Finn!" "I got an extra knife if you need it, Oscar!" An older woman above me called, "Watch yerself, Derry m'love!" Mothers pushed younger sons behind their skirts; girls with excited faces watched as if this were some fine entertainment. I could hardly think for my fear.

But I watched, just as everyone else did, as the two groups advanced on each other. I watched Finn circle their leader and then engage, fists flying and muscles flexing and dust pillowing up in the scrabble, scrimming the whole scene with a brown fog. Then Derry rushed in, grappling with some tall boy who was all arms.

People cheered, frenzied. Little boys threw rocks at the Black Hands. Finn wrestled his opponent to the ground, his boot on the leader's throat, kicking viciously while the Black Hand tried to cover himself, and then the two disappeared in dust. Two of the Black Hands were on Goll, who shrugged them off seemingly without effort, and Conan's dirty fleece swirled as he fought off one and then another.

The Warriors should have been hopelessly outmatched. But there was a mesmerizing efficiency to their fighting. They relished this; they were *smiling* as they fought. An excitement rose in the crowd that gripped even me. I found myself on my feet, grabbing on to the railing of the stairs above, my fingers grazing the bare foot of a boy who clung to the fire escape as he shouted, "Get 'em, Finn! You got 'em, Oscar! Kill 'em !"

And then the wooden clubs appeared. Pulled from belts or pockets by the Black Hands as if in unison, and they went after the Warriors in earnest. I began to see blood. Streaming down Ossian's face, and then Conan's. A Black Hand clubbed Oscar's shoulder, and he fell to his knees before he twisted and grabbed the club, slamming it into his attacker's knee. The boy screamed and collapsed.

I tried to find Derry in the melee, but the dust was so heavy now it was hard to see anything. Then I saw the glint of metal.

And Derry. Circling one of the Black Hands, who held a long knife, slashing once, twice, and each time Derry dodged, crouched. He knew how to fight; he was good at it. Very, very good. It was like watching a stranger as he feinted, falling back, ducking the knife thrusts, his dark hair flying. He came in close; the Black Hand thrust again, and I screamed as the knife plunged into Derry's stomach. All I could think was *No, no, no*—

But then, impossibly, Derry twisted. Unharmed. Now he had hold of his opponent's wrist, and the knife was between them. He jerked the arm of the Black Hand backward, the knife poised above them both, glinting lethally before Derry twisted again, dodging and at the same time wrenching his opponent's arm until the Black Hand screamed, this terrible, terrible scream that made me press my hands to my ears. The knife that had almost gutted Derry was now in his hand. Derry didn't hesitate; he plunged the knife into the boy.

I couldn't possibly have heard the Black Hand gasp from where I stood and yet I did. He grabbed for support, for Derry, who jerked the knife loose and stepped back with satisfaction; and the boy fell to his knees, clutched his abdomen, and pitched forward, lying motionless in the dust while blood pooled beneath him.

Derry had killed him. Derry had killed him, and what was worse, he'd done so with such deliberation. I told myself it was a fight. The Black Hand had attacked him first. But the cold wouldn't leave me, nor the trembling. The scene below seemed a horrible dream. Finn slashing at another boy. Oscar and Keenan brandishing the clubs they'd taken from their enemies.

And Derry with a bloody knife and that boy sprawled in the dust, blood thickening in the heat.

The cheers and shouts receded to a dull roar in my head. I turned numbly to the window. My hands shook as I pulled myself over the sill. I raced through the room, past Cannel, who was laying out the cards on the table. I thought I saw him look up. I thought I heard him say, "Miss Knox—" but I kept going, to the door and out, down the stairs, feeling my way. *Don't touch the walls.* Something slimy and wet on my fingers, something thick and stinking. I half fell on an unseen landing before I caught my balance. I couldn't see, not just because of the dark but because of tears, and all I wanted was to be home. To be home in my own bed, reading Tennyson. Not here. *Please God, not here, not anymore.*

I stumbled out the door. The shouting was deafening. I pushed my way through the crowd. Someone grabbed my arm; I jerked loose. I choked on dust, the air pressed in.

I tripped over a board; fetid liquid splashed on my skirt, and I ran on, not thinking, wanting only to get home. I heard someone call out "Grace!"

Derry.

I ran harder. Just . . . get home. Ignore him. Don't think of him. *"I'm a Warrior. This is what I do."* He killed a boy and he was in a gang and he was a liar and I did not belong here. I belonged in my safe house on Twentieth Street. I belonged with Patrick Devlin, who would never look like a warrior as he gutted a boy with a knife. Who would never appear in my dreams in battle, bearing a spear—and it seemed now as if that was the real Derry. Not the arrogant boy with the teasing smile and the way of seeing things in me he should not have been able to see.

I kept running.

"What a tender heart you have," I'd said. I grabbed up my skirts and ran faster. The light was fading; the sun had set. It was dusk, and I wouldn't be home before dark after all. I wouldn't be home, and I couldn't think what excuse to tell my mother, and I hardly knew where I was going. Just dodging alleys, pushing past other people, one or two calling out "Miss—" or "Watch out, girly!"

And then someone stepped in front of me. I slammed into his chest, and he grabbed my arms.

A young man, straggly hair, stubble on his cheeks.

"Look at this, boys," he said as three others stepped from the shadows of an alley. "And there you was, Bobby, just sayin' you was bored."

I tried to pull from his hold.

"Where're you off to in such a hurry, miss?" He clicked his tongue against his teeth. "And without an escort too."

I jerked away. This time he released me. But when I turned

to run, another of them was in front of me, blocking my way. I turned—another one. They had surrounded me.

The one who'd caught me said, "Why don't you come with us? We'll all have some fun."

"No, I . . . I have to get home." I was too frightened to do more than whisper.

"I tell you what—we'll take you there. After." He glanced at his fellows. "Won't we, boys?"

There was a chorus of ayes.

I tried to run, to push through. But one caught me and laughed as he released me to try again. A pointless game, cat and mouse, and still I tried. Once, twice, and each time caught, pulled back, and their laughter echoed in my head along with my own panicked heartbeat.

"Let me go, damn you!" I cried.

The leader stepped forward. He grabbed my arm. "Come on now."

He dragged me toward the alley. People hurried past, doing nothing, and I pulled at him and stabbed my fingernails into his wrist, screaming, "Help me! Please help me!" and no one did. People just looked away as if they'd seen such things a hundred times before. I set my heels, and he just dragged me harder, the others following. Dear God, why was I even here? *I shouldn't be here. I shouldn't—*

"You'll want to leave this one alone, Billy."

The voice came from behind me, deep and quiet.

The boy dragging me stopped and looked over his shoulder. "Derry! We heard you boys was fighting the Hands."

"'Tis nearly over." Derry vibrated with battle energy. His skin was gray with dust; there was a streak of blood on his face. One sleeve of his shirt was red, one hand. "If you hurry, you might see the end."

"Well, now we got us another entertainment," Billy said. "Care to join us?"

"I would. Except I don't feel much like sharing her tonight."

Billy released my wrist. "She belong to you?"

Derry held out his unbloodied hand to me. "I thought I told you to stay put, lass."

"I saw what you did," I whispered.

"Ah, I see." He looked at Billy and the others, his mouth curved in a thin smile. "This one has a soft heart, I'm afraid. Not much for fights."

"Some girls is like that," Billy said.

"Well, I'm here now. Nothing to worry about, lass. No need to run." Derry flexed his fingers. *Come.*

Billy and the others stood back to let me go to him, but warily, as if they weren't certain they should. Derry pulled me to his side, sliding his arm around my waist.

Billy's brow furrowed. "You sure she belongs to you? If you don't mind my sayin' it, she don't look too happy to see you."

"She likes to save her affection for more private moments, don't you, lass?" I felt his lips against my hair, the brush of them against my temple. He gripped my waist, a warning, and I forced myself to nod, to smile.

"Yes," I managed.

Derry kissed my jaw, moving to the hollow beneath my ear. "You wouldn't know it to look at her, but she's a wild thing. And 'tis all for me, isn't it, lass?"

Billy looked at me. I tried again to smile. "Yes," I whispered.

Billy motioned to the others. "Then we'll leave her to you. Too bad, though. She looks to be a tasty piece."

"Another time, maybe." Derry kept me against him as we walked away. After a few paces, I tried to pull loose, but he said forcefully in my ear, "Finn's made an alliance with Billy's Boys. We need them. I don't want to fight them over a girl. Put your arm around me. Make them believe this."

I put my arm around him—all muscle through his shirt— though I could not relax. We went a block like this, and then another, before he looked over his shoulder.

"Are they gone?" I asked.

"Aye."

"Then take your hands off me." I pushed away from him, tripping in my haste.

He caught my arm to steady me and then let me go again. "Don't blame me. I told you to stay put, didn't I? You're lucky I saw you run off or they'd have you in the alley already."

"You killed that boy."

"Aye."

"You were so . . . It was as if you didn't even care."

"He would have killed me. And they came after us. They knew the risks."

"Who *are* you?" My voice rose.

He looked uncomfortable. "I told you. Finn's Warriors."

"You're a filthy gang boy. I suppose you have some kind of price list. Like the Whyos."

"A price list? What are you talking about? Grace——"

"What was so important to die over?"

"You wouldn't understand."

"I believed you. I trusted you. And you lied to me and tricked me and dragged me to this place, and that . . . that boy you killed, and . . ."

"I told you I was sorry for it."

"Sorry isn't enough! That boy is dead, and I don't *belong* here! You should never have brought me."

"I said I'd keep you safe. I have, haven't I?"

I felt the hysteria bubbling up in my chest. "You're the one who put me in danger in the first place. If not for you I never would've been in this part of town, and I . . . I . . ."

I didn't know what I wanted to say. All I knew was that I had to get away from him. But it was growing dark now, the lamplighters coming around bearing flames on their long poles, and I didn't dare run away from him, not after what had just happened.

He touched my arm. "Grace, let me explain——"

"Don't *touch* me. You're covered with blood."

I moved away from him, a few paces ahead. I wiped at my eyes, smearing away tears, though why I should be crying I had no idea. He was nothing and no one. He'd killed someone without a second thought. Once I got home I would never see him again.

I felt him behind me, following silently. The neighbor-hood changed, the streets becoming clean and well cared for again, the stores bright, the people no longer ragged. I rehearsed what I would say to him when we finally reached my home.

And then, there it was: my house, a lamp glow from a lower window, the rest dark. Mama in the parlor, no doubt, worrying. *"Before dark,"* she'd said, and I must think of a lie to tell her, and I hated him for that too.

When we reached the gate, I spun around. Here now, the lines I'd rehearsed, delivered just so: "Leave me alone. If you come near me again, I'll call for the police. I want nothing to do with you, or any of Finn's Warriors."

Letting the gate slam shut behind me, leaving him speech-less and motionless on the walk—that was what I'd imagined.

But he grabbed the gate as I went through, following me. I broke into a run. Halfway up the stoop, he caught me. "By the gods, Grace, let me explain, will you?"

He pulled me to the side, up against the wall, anchoring me there, his hands gripping my wrists. I fought to get free, and he said, "Be still. Be still and listen for once."

"Listen to what? What will you say—that you're sorry again? I don't want to hear it. I want nothing to do with you. Can you at least understand that?"

I glared up at him. His face was etched in the light from the window above. He was pressed against me, unyielding, that energy still coursing through him, exhilaration and anger and something else now. I heard a sound like a little gasp—me, I realized, in the moment before he bent his head and kissed me.

It was like an arc light bursting into full power, the glow I'd seen in him spreading to me, setting me afire. His mouth moved on mine, soft at first and then more urgently, his lips urging mine open and then pressing harder, more intimately, his tongue searching, tasting. The world fell completely away, leaving only him and the sense of something opening inside of me until I felt I might burst, too, and I knew this was what I'd wanted from the moment I'd first seen him, standing on the walk in front of Lucy's—

Lucy.

Patrick.

I jerked away, and he fell forward, his whole weight on me before he caught himself. He was breathing as roughly as I was.

"Let go of me."

He did, lifting his hands from my wrists, palms out. He stepped away, only an inch, perhaps two. It was enough.

I slapped him as hard as I could.

He staggered back, bringing his hand to his face, and I dodged past him, my palm stinging, tripping over my skirts as I bounded up the stoop. I was almost at the door when I heard him say, "Grace—"

I wrenched open the door and fell inside, turning to twist the key in the lock, and then I leaned against the door, pressing my forehead against it. *Don't knock*, I begged him silently. *Just go. Just go.*

I didn't hear him. Eventually, I straightened and went up the stairs, and then I remembered that he had waited for me in my room once. I could not keep him out if he wanted to come in. The thought terrified me. Terrified and . . . *Don't be there, Derry, please. Please leave me alone—*

"Grainne Knox, what exactly is the meaning of this?"

Mama. I turned to see her standing at the bottom of the stairs, the oil lamp in her hand.

"We lost track of time," I said dully. A terrible lie, but in my confusion I could think of nothing better. My palm tingled. My lips burned. I wondered if she could see how well I'd been kissed. "But Rose's stableboy walked us back, so there was no need to worry."

She eyed me carefully. I knew she thought I was lying, and I hoped she wouldn't press it. I didn't know what I would do if she did. "What's that on your face? On your cheek?"

I touched my cheek. "Dirt?" I guessed. "I don't know. It's . . . it's very dusty outside."

"Patrick Devlin sent a messenger while you were gone," she said in a voice that told me how angry she was. "To ask you to supper tonight."

My heart flipped. "Oh."

"Yes. Oh. I think perhaps you should find an excuse to see him tomorrow, Grace. And reassure him."

"I will. I'll send him a note first thing in the morning."

"Good," she said.

She was going to let my lie stand.

"Good night, Mama," I told her, and then I went into my

room. It was empty. I walked over to the window that overlooked the street, pushing aside the curtain to see into the yard half lit by a nearby streetlamp, staring down into the shadows.

He was gone.

I let the curtain fall back into place. I went to my trunk and the mirror above. I lit the stub of candle pooling in a dish, and I saw what my mother had seen: a slash of something dark over my cheek. I put my fingers to it and leaned closer to the mirror to see. *Blood.*

I looked down at my wrists. One of them was streaked with blood as well. Blood that had been on his face and on his hand. Blood from a boy who died in the dust outside a tenement on Mulberry Street.

I poured water from the chipped ewer into the basin and picked up the cloth I kept there, scrubbing at my cheek, at my wrists, scrubbing at the blood that stayed until I thought it would never come off, that it would mark me forever, so that everyone who looked at me would know what I'd done, how I'd let him kiss me until I felt the pulse of him in my blood, how I'd kissed him back—a gang boy, a boy who glowed, a boy who'd lied to me and tricked me.

I dropped the cloth into the bowl and put my face into my hands.

TWENTY-ONE

That night

Diarmid

The girl was impossible. A sharp tongue and too-quick temper. She rarely smiled. He'd only seen her laugh twice—and the second time was today, in fact, when she'd laughed with Oscar and Goll and Keenan, and he'd gone mad with jealousy. When was the last time he'd felt such a thing? Never. Not once. Or . . . perhaps once, in those years after he'd died, when his foster father had brought his soul into his body now and again so they could talk awhile, and he'd learned that Finn had taken Grainne as his wife and that she'd gone to him willingly—*"Take me away from him, Diarmid. I can't marry him. I love you. Save me from him."* And then the moment Diarmid was dead, she'd turned around and married the man that he'd ruined his life to save her from.

But even then his jealousy hadn't been as strong as that he'd felt today. And he'd never felt such cold and penetrating fear as when he'd seen Grace run. He didn't think she knew how close she'd come to tragedy—which he'd saved her from, by the way, and all he'd got in return was her anger.

She was maddening. He couldn't get her out of his head, and the whole side of his face hurt because she had a fearsome right hand—she was stronger than she looked, which he might have admired any other time. But not now when she had his blood racing and his whole body just . . . humming. That kiss . . . his elation when he realized she was kissing him back, that she wanted him, too, and with it that burning, consuming fire . . . He'd never felt anything like that. Never. Not even with Grainne.

Cursed, tormenting girl. *Filthy gang boy*, she'd called him. Diarmid Ua Duibhne. The pride of the Fianna. No girl had ever refused him, whether she'd seen the lovespot or not. And she had *slapped* him, and it had hurt and stung his pride and done nothing, not one single thing, to keep him from wanting her.

He was more than half in love with Grace Knox, and that might be the most foolish thing he'd ever done in a life that had been full of foolish things. And almost every one of them due to a girl.

Stay away from her, he thought. *Do what she wants. Leave her alone.* It would be better for both of them. Her life didn't include who he was now. A stableboy. *Filthy gang boy.*

He was at the tenement before he knew it. Dim light from windows sent the yard below into shadows, but still he knew the evidence of the fight had been cleared away. The police left the gangs alone for the most part unless they were pressed into action by public outcry. It was best not to antagonize them. The bodies of the Black Hands—not just the one he'd killed, because the others had done their share—*and she hadn't complained about the two Finn had killed in those first minutes, had she?*—had been hauled away. They would be found squirreled in hidden alcoves throughout the city or floating in the river. None close enough to implicate the Warriors, though the Irish would know they'd done it.

The moment he stepped inside the flat, he saw what was happening—the cards spread, Cannel's formation, and in the middle Grace's handkerchief, stained with ale from mopping up Oscar, the purple and yellow silk threads of the pansies glimmering in the sputtering lamplight.

He'd forgotten the reason he'd brought her here.

"She's the *veleda*," Finn said to him.

Diarmid just stood there staring blankly.

Grace is the veleda.

Cannel frowned over the cards. "Though there's something else here too. I don't quite understand it, but . . ." He lifted one card, moved it about.

Diarmid cleared his throat. "Are you sure?"

The Seer nodded. "And you're all around her, as always. But here are two cards I don't understand."

"What do you mean?"

Cannel held up one—illustrated with a full moon and

dogs howling. "This card, where it's come up, means vision, but it's removed from her. Separate. And this one—" Another card lifted, this one painted with a winged, horned creature and a naked couple. "Terrible power."

"Terrible power," Diarmid heard himself saying. "As in, she has terrible power?"

"Of course she does," Ossian said. "She's the *veleda*."

"Yes. It's just the placement is odd. Again, it's removed." Cannel met Diarmid's gaze. "But she *is* who you're looking for. And you surround her, just like in the first divination."

You surround her. Pressing her against that wall. Feeling her breath and the beating of her heart against his chest. Burning to cinder with her kiss. Diarmid closed his eyes and squeezed the bridge of his nose.

"Well, now we know who she is, and we can proceed," Finn said with satisfaction.

"We don't even know who called us or why," Diarmid objected.

"Whatever the task, she'll have to choose eventually. Which reminds me—we'll need the incantation for the sacrifice. The *veleda* should know it. Do you think she does?"

Diarmid laughed miserably. "She doesn't know *anything*, Finn. Not what she is. Nothing. Whatever the *veleda* was supposed to know . . . it's all been lost."

Finn's confidence didn't waver. "Question her again. Perhaps she knows something she doesn't realize. Even if we don't know who called us and why, we must persuade her to choose us. So start persuading her."

"She told me tonight that if I came around again, she'd call for the police. Perhaps Oscar should try."

Even Diarmid heard the despair in his voice, and he saw by the way Finn looked at him that his captain hadn't missed it either.

"You have a weapon Oscar doesn't have," Finn said. He looked at Diarmid's forehead. "Use it."

To them it was easy. Shake aside his hair, show Grace the lovespot just as he'd done with Lucy. He'd never hesitated before, and they wouldn't understand why he was so reluctant now. And the truth was that he wasn't certain he understood it himself. Except that he heard her voice in his head: *"Can you change the world?"* Except that for the first time he had harbored a hope—foolish yes, especially after tonight, but there nonetheless—that she could be the one who might love him for himself. And the thought of seeing the spell in her eyes, watching her bend to him, wanting to do whatever he asked, the fire in her muted—

It startled him to realize how much more he wanted. And that he wanted it from her.

Finn's eyes narrowed. "Or would you rather *I* try to persuade her?"

Diarmid's whole body tightened.

"I didn't think so," Finn said in a tone that stung. "Women choose where they love. If she loves you, then that's one thing in our favor. We need the advantage, Diarmid. And 'tis best that you win her anyway. Then she won't hesitate to bare her throat to your knife when the time comes."

'Tis you who must kill her.

"Well?" Finn asked. "Will you do this?"

Diarmid saw them watching him. All of them. Waiting for his agreement, which he must give, because the *veleda* must choose them. And he must kill her in order to release her power to them, and it must be done on Samhain or they would fail and die. Gone forever. No return.

It was more than just his life at stake. He was Fianna. His brothers were counting on him. Finn was counting on him. And he knew already what it felt like not to be part of them, to be separate. He didn't ever want to feel that way again. Not because of a girl. Not because of anything.

Diarmid nodded. His voice when it came was hollow, but it was there. "Aye. I will."

TWENTY-TWO

June 19

Grace

I tossed and turned all night, restless and yearning, falling asleep only to find nightmares of fire and ravens and my brother's voice—*Listen to me, Grace. Don't go!*—as purple lightning forked through dark skies. And then I was lying beneath Derry, and I felt breathless and alive as he kissed me, his fingers dragging at the drawstring of my chemise, and then . . . the flash of a knife above me. A scream, and there was only terrible pain and . . . darkness.

I woke in a cold sweat. Why were these things happening to me?

I had never been so afraid. But now I knew what I must do.

It was a betrayal, of that there was no doubt. Lucy would never forgive me. Then again, she hadn't seen that boy collapse or Derry's hand red with blood. Derry was dangerous, a liar and a thief and a murderer. He belonged in jail. Lucy would survive it. She'd been through more "loves" in a summer than most people had in a lifetime. And as for me . . . I was afraid of him—yes, that was true. I was afraid of the bloodlust I'd seen in him. Afraid of the wariness I'd seen in those boys who'd had me cornered and how quick they'd been to release me to him. I was afraid of the ruthlessness with which he'd plunged his knife into that boy.

But mostly I was afraid that I would forget all that if he kissed me again.

I sent a note to Patrick asking to see him, and the relief on my mother's face convinced me that this was the best course. I took breakfast to my grandmother, murmured soothing words to her as she muttered "They're coming" and "That boy," and then I woke Aidan, who was sprawled across his bed wearing yesterday's clothes and smelling of a distillery, and told him that he must chaperone me.

He moaned into his pillow. "Take Mama."

"Mama's not well. Which you would see if you cared to look. And Grandma's getting worse. Mama needs to watch over her."

"I'll watch."

"You can't do it from your bed or a tavern. Get up, Aidan. Give me an hour, and then you can go off wherever you like."

"Just pretend I'm there," he said, barely moving.

"As I did the last time you chaperoned, when you spent the entire time at the drinking booth?"

"It was what Lucy preferred anyway. She only wanted to kiss her stableboy."

I hit Aidan's shoulder. "I need you to do better than that

now. I can't afford talk the way Lucy can. And I must see Patrick."

"God save me from lovebirds," my brother said, but he rolled onto his back and blinked in the late-morning light. "Go on. I'll be out in a moment."

My stomach felt tied in knots. It seemed forever before Aidan came out of his room, looking crumpled and bleary. I was halfway out the doorway before he made it to the stairs.

The sky was brightly overcast, the air still and heavy, that thunder ominous and hovering, though this morning it seemed louder, closer. Aidan grimaced at the sky, shielding his eyes from the glare. "God, I wish to hell that storm would come in. That thunder—my head is killing me."

"It couldn't be the drink," I noted. "Or whatever else you're taking."

"Laudanum," he admitted. "When I can afford it. Last night was decent. I won a few dollars."

"You could pay the gas with it, so Mama wouldn't have to sew in lamplight."

"There's not enough for that."

"You mean there's not enough to pay it *and* buy your next bottle."

He gave me a piercing look—one so unhappy I could only gape at him as he said, "You think you know what you're talking about, Grace, but you don't. So be quiet."

I felt the urge to comfort him, which was even more surprising, because the last thing I wanted to do was make Aidan feel *better* for ruining us. So I said nothing more as we walked to the Devlins'. I found myself looking for the carriage, for Derry, wanting to see him at the same time I didn't want to lay eyes on him again. *Grace, stop!*

We went up to the door, Aidan looking about as if he'd rather be anywhere else and me steadying myself to do what I'd come to do.

The butler showed us to Patrick's study, and I tried not to think of how I'd watched Derry slip inside that night, nor everything that had happened after. The butler announced, "Mr. Aidan Knox and Miss Knox are here, sir."

Patrick had been bent over his desk, but he bounded up with an eagerness that made me realize I'd been wrong to be afraid. Just seeing him reassured me and made me feel cherished. *Yes, this is what I want.* This smile instead of another. Gray-green eyes instead of midnight blue. A kiss that made me feel treasured and loved instead of one that felt as if everything inside me struggled to break free.

Patrick smiled at Aidan and shook his hand. "It's a warm morning. Should we walk in the park?"

"The park's as good as anywhere," my brother said. "As long as it's a short walk."

I glared at him, and he raised his brows as if saying, *"What?"* and Patrick led us into Madison Square. Aidan drew back, sauntering behind us, my good watchdog, while Patrick took me ahead.

He said, "I missed you at supper last night."

"I'm sorry. I didn't return home until late. Had I known of your invitation I would have rushed."

"It's no matter. There will be plenty of other suppers."

"I hope so," I said.

His eyes lit. "Do you? Grace, I've so much to tell you. Things I meant to say before. In only a few days, everything will change, and—"

"I've something to tell you as well, Patrick," I said, wanting to get the words out before he distracted me. "It's actually why I've come. Well, and I wanted to see you, of course. But this . . . it's about your stableboy."

"My stableboy? What about him?"

I glanced over my shoulder. Aidan still followed several paces back, looking restless. He wouldn't last much longer. Patrick took my hand, tucking it into the crook of his arm, covering my fingers with his. Strong, warm fingers, like those on another hand, pressing me against the wall. *But not covered with blood.* "He's . . . he's a member of a gang. One of those terrible gangs downtown. Near Bleecker Street."

Surprise flickered in Patrick's eyes. "My stableboy. You mean Jerry or Derry?" He smiled slightly. "Ridiculous, isn't it? Like matched horses."

"Derry," I said, embarrassed at how I breathed the name. "It's Derry."

"So how do you know this?"

"I just— Aidan told me." Aidan was a good distance away now, paying almost no attention to us. A safe lie. And my brother would feign knowledge if asked—Aidan might even believe he *had* told me about the gang and didn't remember it.

Patrick glanced back, and my heart pounded, thinking he might stop and call Aidan after all.

"Derry's one of Finn's Warriors," I said urgently.

"Finn's Warriors?" Patrick stiffened.

"Yes. That's the name of the gang. Have you heard of them?"

"I don't know. Possibly. But . . . isn't this who Lucy begged me to hire? I thought it odd at the time—"

I hadn't wanted to drag her into it. Still . . . "Well, she believes she's in love with him, I think. You know how Lucy is, and he's very handsome. It's only one more reason to dismiss him—before she makes a fool of herself. Not that she has yet," I amended.

"Finn's Warriors," Patrick mused. "And you say Lucy's in love with him?"

"She says she is. She fell so quickly, though. Overnight, really. And he is . . . he can be charming, I suppose. But I think you could still save her if you sent him away now."

"She fell for him overnight?" Again that quiet, musing tone.

I frowned. "Patrick?"

"I don't think I've laid eyes on him. What does he look like?"

I didn't know where Patrick's questions were going. "Dark hair. Blue eyes."

"Anything strange about him? Any . . . deformity, I guess it would be?"

"A deformity? No. Nothing like that."

He turned to look at me intently. "*You* haven't developed . . . feelings . . . for him, have you?"

The way he'd pressed against me. The burn of his kiss and how I'd kissed him back. "N-no. Of course not!"

Thankfully, Patrick didn't seem to notice my discomfort. He looked out over the park. "Finn's Warriors. I wonder how many of them there are?"

I knew exactly, of course, but there was no way I should.

"And their leader? Let me guess: a man named Finn?"

"Yes." My relief that he was taking me seriously made me too fast. When I saw Patrick's puzzled glance, I tried to temper my eagerness. "I mean . . . I suppose that's why they're called Finn's Warriors." *They've named themselves after the Fianna,* I wanted to say, but I could have no way of knowing that either and so I said, "I think Derry stole the ogham stick too."

Patrick halted abruptly. "Why do you think that?"

"I don't know it for certain," I lied. "But I suspect so. Something he said—he asked me if you had other things."

"What other things?"

"An ogham stick made of rowan. A horn."

"Why was he asking these questions of you?"

"I think because I'd said something to him about the relics. I'm sorry, Patrick; I didn't mean to. We were just making conversation, and—"

"Why were you making conversation with a stableboy?"

"We were waiting for Lucy to come back with petits fours."

Patrick blinked in confusion. "Petits fours?"

"It doesn't matter," I said, though I felt as if I were falling deeper and deeper into a well from which I could never climb out. "I swooned, I'm afraid, one day when Lucy and I were together. The heat and"—*Derry glowing*—"and he was there and sent her for some food. We were just talking, Patrick. But he knew about the relics, and he asked me, and that's why I think he took the ogham stick."

Patrick led me off the path, out of the way of other promenaders, and turned fully to face me. "It's all right, Grace. I'm just surprised, that's all. I'm surprised he thought to ask questions of you."

"He's been very familiar," I said. "It's not just for Lucy that I ask you to dismiss him, Patrick. It's for me as well. He makes me nervous. I've asked him to leave me alone, but he just won't. I don't know what else to do."

"I see. Well, I'll have a talk with this Derry. Perhaps it isn't too late." He spoke the last as if to himself.

"Too late?" I asked.

He shook his head. "Don't worry. I'll make certain he doesn't trouble you again."

My relief was almost dizzying. My faith that Patrick would help me with this, that he was the only one who could, overwhelmed me. "Thank you. Thank you so much."

"I'll take care of everything. I'll talk to him, but I won't tell him where I learned it, if that worries you."

"I don't mind if he knows. In fact, I'd rather he did. Perhaps it will help him keep his distance."

Patrick's mouth quirked in a smile. "You've a vengeful streak. Have I ever told you that?"

"A time or two, I think. Perhaps when you put that frog down my dress—"

"And you repaid me by throwing my tin soldiers into the river."

"I was baptizing them," I protested. "They seemed in sore need of redemption. And besides, I wouldn't have done it if not for the frog."

"As I said, a vengeful streak. I'll have to remember that." Patrick glanced down the path, to where Aidan had slowed his step even further, and then he leaned close and whispered, "I know you think we're moving too swiftly, and I know I'm too impatient. It's a terrible flaw, but I . . . I have hopes . . . I hope . . ." He paused, as if gathering his courage.

He was going to propose. Everything I'd waited for, and all I could think was *No, no, not yet.* All I could think was that I must hold him off. I found myself saying, "You mustn't think of such things now. What's important is Lucy. And doing something about Derry." And then the moment I said it I wondered why I had.

"Derry, yes." He straightened, his gray-green eyes soft with a hurt that I regretted.

I said desperately, "Just now I'm afraid for your sister. All these other things . . . we can speak of them later, can't we? I want to, just . . . not now."

The joy on his face was blinding. He took my hands, lifting them, pressing his lips to my gloved fingers. "Yes, of course. You're right. Lucy is what's important now. You're so good to look after her as you do."

"You must know I love your family as my own."

"You're a better sister to Lucy than I am a brother. It speaks well of"—he broke off with a small smile—"of you."

It hadn't been what he was going to say, but I was glad, and I didn't let myself wonder why. "You'll look to this soon?"

"Immediately," he said, and then we both looked down the path to my brother. Aidan leaned against a tree as if he hadn't the strength to stand on his own, but he wasn't watching us. He was staring at a group of ragged boys across the park. Gang boys. No one I recognized, but still my heart stopped.

And when Patrick leaned close again and whispered, "I am your servant in all things, Grace. You must know it," I lifted my face to his. I let him kiss me.

And I didn't let myself compare it to any other kiss.

TWENTY-THREE

That afternoon

Grace

Almost the moment I left Patrick and started back to the house with Aidan, my guilt and fear returned. It wasn't just that I'd betrayed both Lucy and Derry, it was that I didn't understand why I'd dissuaded Patrick from proposing. I had agreed with Mama that I'd needed to push him. And yet, when the time had come, what had I said? *"You mustn't think of such things now."*

I only felt worse when Aidan said, "That was some kiss, Gracie. I hope Patrick proposed before he took such liberties."

"As if it matters to you."

I thought Aidan would make some cutting remark, but instead he stopped. "You know it does."

I wished I could say, *I don't know what's wrong with me. I want to love Patrick, yet . . .* But the years when I could speak to Aidan about anything were gone. "Really? Lately, I wonder."

He winced, and I felt terrible. But before I could apologize, he said in that devil-may-care tone I'd grown to hate, "It's only a few blocks home. You can make it on your own, can't you? I've just remembered I have an engagement."

Whatever apology I might have made was replaced by irritation. "Yes, by all means. Go hurl yourself off a bridge for all I care."

"Perhaps I will, just to spite you."

"At least you'll be too numb to feel the impact."

He laughed, but it was humorless. He touched the tip of his hat and bowed slightly. "I love you, too, Gracie."

I watched him walk off. I couldn't face going home to Mama and Grandma. Not just yet. Then I realized Rose's house was very close.

I didn't give myself time to think better of it. I hurried there, forgetting that it was her mother's calling day until I saw the carriages waiting out front. Rose would be too busy with visitors for me. I knocked on the door anyway and asked to speak to Rose privately, and in a few moments, she came to the door. "What is it, Grace? You know it's Mama's calling day."

"I know, and I'm sorry. But I need to talk to you."

Her expression turned from curiosity to concern. "What is it? What happened?"

I motioned for her to join me on the stoop. When she did, my words rushed out. "I told Patrick that Derry's in a gang."

"What? Why would you do such a thing?"

"Because he is. He and Oscar both. They're in a gang called Finn's Warriors, and, Rose, they were in this fight and I watched Derry kill this boy and then he kissed me and—"

"What? Stop! Stop right there." Rose glanced back at the house and then led me away, onto the sidewalk. "What do you mean, he kissed you?"

I let out my breath in exasperation. "I tell you that he and Oscar are in a gang and they've *killed* people, and you ask me about a kiss?"

"Because that's why you're here. Because he kissed you, and you liked it."

My mouth fell open. Trust Rose to see the truth. "He killed a boy. I watched him do it. In a gang fight."

"Why does that surprise you?" she asked. "He's a *stable-boy*, Grace, or have you forgotten? And he's Irish. It would be stranger if he wasn't in a gang. He's no more appropriate for you than for Lucy—and if she finds out you've kissed him, you'll lose Patrick."

I sagged against the cast-iron fence. "I know."

"Would you care?"

"Yes, I would care! I don't understand myself. Today when I was with Patrick . . . he was going to propose, Rose, and I stopped him. I told him we had time. But I don't have time. I *want* to marry him. I want to stop feeling this way—"

"What way is that?" Rose asked.

It was so hard to admit. "When Derry kissed me, I . . . I kissed him back."

"Has Patrick kissed you yet?"

"Yes, but what has that to do with it?"

Rose leaned against the railing beside me. "You're just slumming with Derry, and you know it. There's nothing wrong with it. We've all done it. Believe me, I would kiss Oscar, too, given the chance. But I wouldn't run off with him or marry him or anything like that. It's not you kissing Derry that has me worried. It's that he belongs to Lucy, and now you've gone and told her brother that her beau's a gang boy. . . . You'd better hope she doesn't ever discover it was you."

My guilt returned, worse than ever.

"Now, me, I've kissed . . . oh, I don't know. There was Michael O'Shaughnessy and Bobby Olson and Timothy Lederer—"

"You kissed Tim Lederer? You never told me that!"

"Well, it was *months* ago, and you were all involved with your family and everything, and it isn't as if it matters. It was just the one time. Let me see . . . there was that boy in Charleston and another in Boston—"

"Rose—"

"Listen to me, Grace. A kiss is a kiss is a kiss. I've liked all of them. But I'm not a fool, and neither are you. How did Patrick's kiss make you feel?"

"Loved. Like the world could swallow me, and he would never let me go. I wanted more."

"And Derry's?"

On fire. As if I were falling into something dangerous and exciting. As if I were meant *to be in his arms.* "Dangerous."

"Because he's forbidden," she said with authority. "And he *is* forbidden. It doesn't matter what you feel for him, Grace. *He* doesn't matter. He can't. Your mother would be beside herself.

You'd never be able to go out into society again. Everyone would cut you. Is that what you want?"

I shook my head.

"You see? It's a fun game, but Patrick is the one you're meant for, Grace. You know it as well as I. It's all right to have kissed the stableboy, but now you must let him go."

She laid it out so clearly. It was only a kiss, a small indiscretion, and now it was over. It was right to tell Patrick about him, for Lucy's sake as well as for my own. And now Patrick would take care of things, and I would never see Derry again.

I ignored the pinch of my heart at the thought and hugged Rose. "I knew you would help."

She hugged me back. "You would have figured it out on your own. I don't blame you, Grace. Derry *is* gorgeous. But then, so is Patrick. Just promise me that the next time he starts to propose, you let him finish."

"I will," I promised.

"And I'll try to find someone to throw into Lucy's path. She'll forget Derry as soon as she falls in love again, you know."

I couldn't help but laugh. And I didn't let myself think about the look in Lucy's eyes when she spoke of Derry and how well I understood it. Rose was right. Some things were never meant to be.

TWENTY-FOUR

That evening

Diarmid

It should have been easy enough. He would go to her house. When she answered the door, he would just shake back his hair and show her the lovespot. If he did it quickly enough, she wouldn't have time to remember she hated him, or to do any of the things she'd warned him she would do if he came near her again. Diarmid spent the entire day imagining it. The flash of anger in her dark eyes when she saw him at the door and then the way the anger would melt away. The way she would gasp prettily and say, "Oh! Does it hurt?" and reach to touch it the way they all did. He would take her in his arms and kiss her, and she would whisper against his mouth that she loved him, and—

And the whole vision made him sick.

Just do it, he told himself. It was as Finn said: women chose with their hearts. *"Then she won't hesitate to bare her throat to your knife when the time comes."*

Diarmid was bruised and sore from yesterday's fight; it felt as if he were imprisoned in a steam room, the air wet and hot and that wretched, constant thunder that raised the hairs on the back of his neck. Where was it coming from? It felt unnatural, like those storms the Druids used to raise during battles. Thunder and lightning, and the air turning violet and blue and black. The crackle of electricity. He'd never liked them. Those storms were terrifying, meant to instill horror, and combined with the Morrigan's ravens, that was exactly what they did. It had been only through sheer practice that he hadn't succumbed to the same frenzy, a mental game he used to play with himself through the chaos of battle—to convince himself that *he* had brought the storm, that he was in control of it, that it could not touch him.

But this thunder hadn't yet reached that intensity. It stayed distant and nagging, shortening everyone's temper. Leonard had kicked the carriage this morning after he'd scraped his hand against the brake lever. Jerry had cursed and thrown a hoof pick when a fly tormented him. Diarmid had to fight the thought: *Do it now. Do it now. Go to her.*

When he was done mucking the stalls, he plunged his head into the barrel of lukewarm water out back, not bothering to dry himself off, just shaking his hair like a dog until droplets flew everywhere and his shirt was soaked. It was the only thing that had felt good the entire day, but it didn't improve his mood. Night fell and he still hadn't made himself go to her. Another day gone. Finn would expect this to be quick; he couldn't delay long. But one day, perhaps two, he could do.

His mood was made worse by the fact that he *wanted* to see her. He couldn't get the kiss out of his head. Not the way she'd lifted her face or her soft sigh when she'd realized what he was going to do. Not the hunger in the way she'd kissed him back. Hunger that wasn't compelled, that had nothing to do with any lovespot.

All he wanted to do was forget it. But he couldn't go back to the others at the tenement—he couldn't bear their watchful eyes, Finn's questioning of his loyalty, and Oscar's puzzling over his hesitation. Tonight he just wanted to be alone.

When Leonard told him and Jerry to turn in, that neither the carriage nor the horses would be needed, Diarmid set off instead. He wandered down to the Bowery, taking in the clustered colored globes of the lamps and illuminated signs that lit the darkness with a false daylight, the organ grinders with their silly monkeys that made him laugh, street vendors selling ginger cakes and oranges, and the German bands playing waltzes on the street corners. He walked past dime museums and theaters, dance halls and saloons. There was a feeling in the air tonight, a sort of desperate gaiety raised by the strangeness of the thunder, as if everyone on the crowded streets felt the need to have fun while there was still time to have it. He heard it in laughter that seemed overly boisterous and saw it in the almost frenzied way boys dashed from saloon to saloon, the brightly yearning stares of the girls he passed.

Diarmid stayed there for a long time. Long enough that the theaters let out, their melodramas and minstrel shows over. He didn't go in anywhere but only walked, and sometimes stood watching. It was pointless, he knew, and he was tired and not good company for anyone; and being here hadn't eased his own yearning or his apprehension but had only brought them both into sharper focus. He was turning to head back to the stables, and bed, when he saw Aidan Knox.

Grace's brother was staggering, clearly drunk, wearing no hat and with his tie undone and crumpled. He looked pasty pale, a ghost beneath a shock of dark hair, as he went to the door of a gambling hell, and not a respectable one either. Aidan paused. Diarmid could almost see him thinking *Yes? Or no?*

And then Aidan seemed to set his shoulders in determination. He grabbed the door handle, nearly falling into it before he got it open and went inside.

"Can you cure Aidan of his drunkenness and turn him into the brother who once cared about his family?"

Diarmid stared at the door. Aidan's pause puzzled him. The way he'd considered and then chosen, as if he was deliberately courting destruction.

Diarmid had known men like that. Men trying to forget the horror of battle, or sadnesses too great to bear. Drowning their sorrows and their memories in mead or ale. Intentional oblivion, and if it led to death, so much the better.

And now Diarmid wondered: What was Aidan Knox trying to forget?

He thought of the way Grace had watched her brother with love and despair. Diarmid knew he couldn't cure Aidan—there wasn't a man on earth who could save another from his own destruction if that was truly what was wanted.

But perhaps he could watch over Aidan tonight. It was something Diarmid could do for her, even if she didn't know he was doing it. Some way to make up for what he had done. What he was going to do.

Diarmid went to the door Aidan had disappeared through and stepped into clouds of smoke and talk. The place was small and ill-lit—a few sputtering oil lamps set about the tables and the gas sconces on the walls black with soot. At one side was a bar, at the other a faro table with a bright and badly painted tiger on the wall behind; men crowded around both. At other tables they bent over cards or dice. Most were dressed as he was—laborers and immigrants. And among them, with his moneyed bearing and loosened tie, stood Aidan Knox.

He was at the far end of the room, drinking whiskey as he waited for a place to open at a table. Aidan was swaying. Diarmid remembered the way Grace had swooned at the fair—the glow, yes, but he knew, too, that she had been hungry. And here was Aidan buying whiskey when he should have been buying bread for his family, and Diarmid thought, *Leave him. Let him destroy himself.*

But Diarmid crossed the room. He went up to Aidan, who glanced at him once, vaguely, and then again, his gaze sharpening. "I know you," he slurred. "Lucy's stableboy."

Diarmid winced. "Aye. Derry O'Shea."

Aidan raised his glass. "You're to be congrat—gradulated. I been tryin' to kiss Lucy Devlin for five years."

"I don't think she likes the taste of whiskey," Diarmid said.

Aidan laughed. "Don' she? Have you done more than kiss 'er yet?"

Diarmid ignored that. "Come sit with me. There's a table over there." He pointed to a corner where two men were leaving.

Aidan squinted at him. "All right. What game are we playin'?"

"I'll tell you when we get there."

Aidan stumbled so badly that Diarmid grabbed his arm to keep him upright, and when he let go, Aidan fell into the chair, dropping the whiskey. The heavy shot glass bounced off the table. Whiskey went flying.

Aidan watched it go with a sort of dumb fascination, and then he raised his hand, motioning to the bar. "Another whiskey, please!"

Diarmid made a motion, too, one that told the bartender *no*. "It's getting late. Don't you think you should go home to bed?"

"Home?" Aidan grunted. "No."

"You look like you could use a good night's sleep."

"Can't stand it there."

"Why is that?"

"There are thin's—" Aidan sprawled over the table, his dark hair falling into his face, once again squinting as if the light was too bright. There was something odd about him tonight. Diarmid couldn't put his finger on it.

"There are things?" Diarmid prompted, seeing the struggle in Aidan's eyes as he tried to remember what he'd been saying.

"Thin's," Aidan said finally. He sat up again. "You wouldn't believe me if I tol' you."

"Maybe I would."

Aidan put his hand to his forehead. "I got a headache. Somethin' screamin'. D'you hear it?"

"Only thunder," Diarmid said.

"Not thunder." Aidan shook his head, closed his eyes. "Ah. God. I can't stand it. How c'n you stand it?"

"It's just too much drink. You'll sleep it off. You'll be fine."

"I'm never fine. And it's the whiskey makes it go away." Aidan opened his eyes, and the depth of misery in them startled Diarmid. There was nothing in Aidan Knox that Diarmid respected, but that despair was something he understood. It made him want to help Aidan for his own sake.

Aidan went on. "That screamin' . . . I don' know how she stands it either."

"Who?"

"M'sister. Where's the whiskey?"

"What do you mean about Grace?"

Aidan smiled crookedly and wagged his finger. "I see how you look at her, y'know. Lucy in one hand, and you want m'sister in the other."

Diarmid felt hot. "I don't know what you're talking about."

"Well, you can't have 'er. She's in love with Patrick Devlin, y'know. She's goin' to marry him." Again that misery in his eyes. "Save us all."

"Maybe not," Diarmid managed.

"Oh, she is. He's going to propose, and she'll say yes. Should've seen 'im kissin' 'er today."

The floor seemed to give way beneath Diarmid. "What?"

"No chaste kiss either. Grace'll say yes, and we'll all live happily ever after." Aidan laughed bitterly. "But he don' know, does he? We'll brin' the curse on 'im too. But no one says anythin' about it. They all preten' they don' know."

"She'll say yes." It took Diarmid a moment to hear what Aidan was now saying. "Don't know what? What curse?"

"The *curse*," Aidan said, squinting again. "There's somethin' wrong with you, isn't there?"

Impatiently, Diarmid demanded, "What curse?"

The thunder rumbled. Aidan squeezed his eyes shut. "I can't stand the screamin'. Make it stop. C'n you make it stop?"

Enough of this! Diarmid stood. "Let's get out of here."

"Not home."

"You'll only make her worry if you don't go there."

Aidan put his hand to his head. "I wish she wouldn'. She don't know, not yet; but she will, won't she? You know she will."

"What will she know?"

"I can't go home. Don' take me home."

Just nonsense after all, Diarmid told himself. *Nothing to worry about.* "Fine, you can spend the night with me."

Aidan didn't protest when Diarmid pulled him up, but he stumbled and sagged, boneless. Finally, Diarmid put Aidan's arm around his shoulders, bearing the man's weight as he dragged him from the gambling hell and back into the street.

Aidan mumbled more about the screaming in his head as Diarmid took him out of the Bowery, wishing all the time that he hadn't bothered to follow Aidan, that he hadn't thought to do a good deed for her, because she wouldn't know it anyway, and she wouldn't care.

"No chaste kiss."

It seemed an eternity before he reached the stables, hauling a semiconscious Aidan inside and maneuvering him over slippery straw and sawdust to the tack room, where Jerry was snoring away. Diarmid got Aidan to the cot and let him fall there. Aidan hit his head against the wall on the way down, moaning.

"Quiet," Diarmid whispered.

Aidan grabbed his shirt, pulling him close. "'Preciate this."

"Don't mention it."

Aidan said, "Broken up."

"Pardon?"

"We're all . . . broken up." A half-uttered sob. Aidan was crying. "Everythin' ruined."

Drunken blathering. He wished Aidan would shut up and go to sleep. Diarmid pulled away, and Aidan let him go.

"Grace too," Aidan said. "But there's somethin' 'bout you. You look like . . ." His head lolled to the side. He said with amazement, "Screamin's . . . stopped." And then he was unconscious.

Diarmid sighed. No wonder Grace was so worried. All that talk about curses and screaming. Diarmid sat against the wall, bringing up his knees and leaning his head back to look at the ceiling.

"She'll say yes."

But she hadn't yet, had she?

He closed his eyes as exhaustion washed over him. Before he knew it, he was lost in dreams where he was kissing her, and she lifted her pale throat to him, and he pressed his mouth to her pulse and felt the beat of her heart in his blood. Then a knife flashed in his raised hand, and there was a terrible scream, and his arms were empty and he was alone and waiting in darkness. He heard thunder and the roar of a cyclone wind, and she was there again, her hair alive in lightning, the air pulsing blue and violet and red, her dark eyes dancing as she swept everything in her path away.

—◦◦— *June 20* —◦◦—

He woke to an unfamiliar voice saying in irritation, "Do I pay you to sleep? And what the hell is Aidan Knox doing here?"

Diarmid opened his eyes, staring into a pair of expensive boots, slowly becoming aware that his neck had a crick in it and his shoulder hurt from being jammed up next to a boot-jack and his bruises from the gang fight were sorer than ever. He blinked and rolled—he was on the floor, he realized—and rose to his elbows, peering up at a young man with hair just this side of blond who was staring at him with a mixture of concern and annoyance.

"We haven't met," the young man said. "But I'm your employer. Patrick Devlin. Jerry tells me you're Derry."

Diarmid winced both at the silly rhyme and the pain, and struggled to his feet. "Aye. One of your twin dogs, at your service." The moment he got a good look at Patrick Devlin, he knew what Grace saw in him. *Don't think of that.* Diarmid rubbed the back of his neck. "Sorry. Late night."

Devlin glanced to where Aidan was sprawled on the cot. "Aidan was involved, I take it."

Diarmid nodded. "Though mostly it was me trying to save him from himself."

"I see." Devlin frowned.

Too late, Diarmid remembered that Aidan's condition wouldn't do much to help Grace. "I don't know that it's a common thing—"

"I need to talk to you," Devlin interrupted.

Diarmid was blurry with sleep, but even so he knew how odd it was that Patrick Devlin would want to have any kind of conversation with his stableboy. *Lucy,* he thought first. And then, *the ogham stick*—but no, Grace had promised not to tell.

But that was before he'd lied to her and tricked her. Before he'd kissed her, and she'd slapped him.

"About what?" Derry said, then realized no stableboy would speak to a master that way.

Devlin didn't bat an eye. He was looking at Aidan. He murmured to himself, "I suppose I should get him home first.

Grace will be worried." To Diarmid he said, "Come to the house in an hour. Could you do that?"

Devlin's manner was unusual. Asking, not demanding, as was his right. Warily, Diarmid said, "Aye."

"Miss Knox has told me some interesting things," Devlin said casually. "Very interesting things. About you."

Now Diarmid went cold. Grace had told Devlin something about him, but what? And why? She'd been angry. She couldn't have said anything good. But then again, she didn't know anything. Not who they really were. Not what the ogham stick meant. Not that they suspected Devlin was involved, nor that they believed it was the Brotherhood who had called them here.

Devlin gestured to Aidan. "Help me get him on a horse."

Diarmid shook Aidan awake. Grace's brother looked around blearily, moaning and grabbing his head.

"God," Aidan said, and then he noticed Devlin. "Patrick. What the hell're you doin' here?"

"You're in my stables," Devlin pointed out.

Aidan laughed—he was still a little drunk, Diarmid realized as he helped Grace's brother to his feet. Which was also odd. He must have had even more whiskey than Diarmid had thought. He had to help Aidan into the saddle. Devlin jumped in front, and Aidan made some derisive comment about riding like a girl, and they started toward the stable doors.

Diarmid was halfway to the water barrel when Devlin said, "One hour, Diarmid Ua Duibhne. Don't be late."

Diarmid froze. For a moment he didn't think he'd heard correctly. His name. His name, which no one but the other Fianna knew. Grace didn't know it. She could not have told Devlin. *How does Devlin know it?*

But by the time Diarmid had gathered himself enough to look back, Patrick Devlin was already riding out into another sweltering, thundering day.

TWENTY-FIVE

The same day

Grace

Everything went from bad to worse when I opened the front door to find Patrick supporting a disheveled and still-stumbling Aidan.

Mama put her hand to her mouth, and the only sound that came from her was a high little *eek.*

"For God's sake, don' bring me here," Aidan slurred.

Patrick gave my mother a reassuring smile and glanced past her to me. "I thought I'd deliver your brother to you, as he seems in no state to get himself home."

"Oh, Aidan." I wanted to cry.

My brother raised his eyes to me. "Grace, don'."

"It's all right," Patrick said softly. "Might we come inside?"

My mother stirred to life, standing back to let them in. Patrick released Aidan, who stumbled over the doorjamb. Patrick grabbed him again. "Shall I help him to his room?" he asked me.

I nodded numbly.

"I c'n make it on my own," Aidan said, but he fell over the first step. I followed as Patrick and Aidan made their slow way up, Aidan crashing against the wall, the banister, Patrick. Patrick took Aidan to his room, releasing my brother to fall upon his bed. Aidan hit the mattress with a garbled groan, as limp as a rag doll, his hair tumbling into his face.

Patrick was breathing hard as he turned to face me. He took my hands, pulling me to him, wrapping his arms around me while I buried my face in his shirt. A fresh, clean scent, no dust or sweat or blood. I felt his kiss on my hair.

"I'm sorry," I said. "I'm so sorry."

"It's all right, Grace, truly. I'm only glad I could bring him home to you again."

I felt the rumble of his voice against my cheek. I didn't want to pull away. In Patrick's arms, everything seemed all right. But it wasn't. Nothing was going to be all right again. I heard my mother's step and drew back. "Thank you," I whispered.

He nodded. Then my mother was there, saying, "Patrick, you've been so kind. Will you stay for tea? I do wish we had some way to thank you."

Patrick shook his head. His gaze lingered on me. "I'm afraid I can't stay. I have a meeting. But I wanted to be certain Aidan got home safely."

"Grace," Aidan murmured from the bed. "You don' know . . ."

"I suppose you'd best tend to him. I won't keep you,"

Patrick said.

"Let me show you out," Mama offered.

Once they were gone, I turned on Aidan with fury. "What's wrong with you? How could you let Patrick see you like this?"

He ducked his head as if he thought I meant to hit him—which didn't seem such a bad idea. "It wasn't my fault."

"You couldn't have picked some club where he was unlikely to go?"

"Wasn't at a club. He came to the stable."

"The stable? What stable?"

"Where I was sleepin'."

My head felt filled with static. That damned thunder! "Why would you be sleeping in a stable?"

"Derry took me there."

"Derry?"

Aidan nodded, covering his eyes. "'E was at the club."

"Derry was at a club with you?"

"Gamblin' hell. Nasty place."

Nothing about this could be good. "Why were you with Derry at a gambling hell?"

"'E found me there."

"I don't understand."

"'E was there," said my brother. "Made me come to the stable with him."

"Why would he do that?"

Aidan shrugged and then grimaced. "Made me stop drinkin' an' leave. I didn' want to come home, so 'e took me with 'im."

I stared down at my brother. It was Derry, not Patrick, who had found and taken care of Aidan. The static in my head grew louder—a buzzing, but muffled and foggy. "But why?"

"I think it was for you. The way 'e looks at you . . . Thought 'e was with Lucy?"

"He is. He was, I mean. Not anymore, I imagine. I told Patrick about them."

My brother winced again. "Wha' for? That was mean."

Yes, it had been. But it was best for Lucy, and for me. It was *best*.

"Iss all broken, Grace." He clutched his head. "God, that thunder! It hurts. . . . Don' it hurt you too?"

"The thunder isn't what hurts you, Aidan."

"Patrick called Derry somethin' strange . . . Diarmid. 'E called him Diarmid. Like the legend. You 'member? Diarmid and Grainne. Like you. Funny." Aidan's laughter turned hysterical. I waited until he calmed again, until he grabbed my hand, and I saw his love for me burning in eyes that looked too bright, feverish. "Don' run off with him, Grace. Not like the story. Promise me. I can't keep you safe then. Don' go. Don' go."

The same words from my dreams, said the same way. The buzzing in my head stopped, just like that. "What? What did you say?"

"'E'll change things." Aidan flung his arm over his eyes. "Change everythin'."

Aidan was just drunk. As always. "I think you should sleep."

"All right," he said agreeably. "Close th' curtains."

I ignored that. Let him sleep in the light. It was nearly noon. I stepped away from the bed, leaving him lying there, fully clad, filthy boots streaking the coverlet.

I had my hand on the door when Aidan said, "Somethin' strange about Derry, though, don' you think?"

I paused and turned to look at him. "What do you mean?"

"In the right light, you know . . ." Aidan's voice was barely there. "He rather . . . glows."

TWENTY-SIX

Diarmid

Diarmid went to the back door, the servants' entrance, and waited tensely for the maid to fetch Patrick Devlin.

The maid came back, surveying him with a frank—and appreciative—gaze as she said with obvious surprise, "He wants to see you in his study."

He followed her down the hallway where Grace had come upon him the night he'd stolen the ogham stick. The study was bright, daylight coming through the windows and gas flames wavering in their polished sconces.

"Here he is, sir," said the maid, closing the door carefully behind her when she left.

Patrick Devlin sat at his desk, looking rather like a boy playing with his father's things until he glanced up, and Diarmid saw that Devlin was as tense as he was.

Devlin stood. He came around the desk slowly and then

leaned back against it, crossing his arms over his chest. "Thank you for coming."

"I didn't know I had a choice, Mr. Devlin," Diarmid said.

"Oh, I think you know that you do." Devlin smiled thinly. "And please, call me Patrick. I think you'll find that we have common interests, and I'd like for us to be friends. Shall I tell you what I know of you?"

Diarmid nodded.

"Miss Knox tells me that my sister is in love with you."

Diarmid said nothing, but he felt Grace's vengeance with a little shock. He hadn't thought she would do this—he'd underestimated her. Or at least underestimated how shaken she'd been by the fight with the Black Hands and perhaps . . . the kiss too. No, definitely the kiss. She had slapped him and run from him.

"She'll say yes."

Suddenly Diarmid realized how hard she was trying to keep him away. And when he realized that, he knew she'd told Patrick everything.

"She also tells me that you belong to a gang. And she believes you have the ogham stick that was stolen from this room."

In a way, Diarmid admired the completeness of it, how willing she was to destroy him.

She might have succeeded, too, if Patrick Devlin hadn't been a member of the Fenian Brotherhood. If there hadn't been more—much more—that she didn't know.

"Finn's Warriors," Patrick said thoughtfully. "Do you know what I find interesting?"

"No idea," Diarmid said.

"That it's what the Fianna might call themselves today. Finn's Warriors."

Say nothing, Diarmid cautioned himself. *Listen.*

"Two months ago, just after I returned from Ireland, a man came to me with something to sell. He knew of my interest in Celtic antiquities. He had a horn he'd won in a wager. It was a horn that looked very like drawings I'd seen—except there was an inscribed silver band. It had been cracked, you see, in battle, and they'd stripped away the ruined bronze and repaired it with silver."

"I used to have a horn," she'd said. *"Aidan lost it in a faro game."* But the silver she'd mentioned had confused him. He hadn't considered that it might have changed over the years. *Stupid.*

"A friend of mine can read ogham. He's descended from Druids, and many of these relics still hold the old magic." Patrick's eyes were very green in the light. "But you know that already, don't you?"

"The *dord fiann,*" Diarmid murmured.

Patrick nodded. "The Brotherhood has been studying the old spells for some time. So did my father, and he passed the interest down to me. I knew there must be a *veleda* to use the horn correctly, but my father had said we were descended from her. That her blood runs in our veins, and . . . I hoped. We performed the ritual and blew the horn. But no Fianna appeared."

Patrick met Diarmid's gaze. "I don't know if you can

imagine my disappointment. All these years . . . trying everything we could to save our homeland. We were desperate, and I'd believed at last we had some way to win. For days we waited, and then we realized no Fianna were coming. You must understand . . . no one thought the horn had worked. But it had. It *had*. Just . . . not in the way I'd imagined."

"What way was that?" Diarmid asked.

Patrick laughed. "I'd thought you would appear in my parlor. The blood, the incantation, and three blows of the *dord fiann*, and—voilà!—there you would be."

"That's the way it should have worked. I don't know why it didn't."

"I see." Patrick hesitated. "Where did you wake?"

"In a tenement near Mulberry Street. We've been looking for who called us ever since."

Patrick's voice turned reverent. "Finn's here. Finn Mac-Cool. And you . . . Diarmid Ua Duibhne. That's who you are, isn't it? I knew it when Grace said Lucy had fallen in love with you overnight. My sister is prone to lovesickness, but when she begged me to hire you, she seemed oddly intent. I didn't realize . . . I thought she was turning her attention to charity work, something worthwhile at last." He laughed at himself. "But you used the *ball seirce* on Lucy, didn't you?"

"We were looking for who called us," Diarmid said again. "It occurred to us to look at Irish clubs. Those who might have an interest. The Fenian Brotherhood was one. I needed a way to get close to its leaders. You. Lucy was a way in. I'm sorry for it."

"I hardly believe it."

Diarmid asked, "What did you intend for us to do?"

"Ireland's greatest need—isn't that what the prophecy says? And she *does* need you. The Irish are leaving in droves to come here. Britain is destroying them. If this continues, Ireland will be no more. We've organized rebellions, but we aren't strong enough. We need Ireland's greatest warriors. Her heroes. We called you to go to war against the British. To win self-rule for Ireland."

Diarmid felt a rush of relief and excitement. Already the battle lust came upon him, the need to protect and revive his homeland. He wanted the fight, and the others would want it as well. Diarmid hadn't known until that moment how afraid he'd been that the task would not be an honorable one.

"So is it a worthy fight?" Patrick asked.

Diarmid hesitated. "Aye, it seems so. But 'tisn't my place to decide. If you know the prophecy, you know that as well."

Patrick smiled. "Well, Lucy can be fickle, but I think we needn't worry. She'll choose as I tell her, especially now that she's in love with you."

"Lucy?"

"It was her blood on the horn. I admit I'd begun to doubt that any Druid blood ran in our veins, no matter what my father had said."

Diarmid shook his head. "Lucy's not the *veleda*."

"What do you mean?"

"The horn belonged to Grace. Aidan lost it in a bet."

Patrick looked blank for a moment. "Grace? You don't mean—*Grace* is the *veleda*?"

Diarmid said bluntly, "She's the one who has to choose. She's not so manageable as Lucy, I'm guessing, but her brother says that you mean to take her to wife. If that's true, she's got a reason to want to choose our fight. Of course, once it's done, and the sacrifice is made—"

"Sacrifice?"

"On Samhain. The sacrifice to release her power to the side she chooses."

"I don't understand. What sacrifice?"

"She has to die. To release her power, the *veleda* has to die."

Patrick paled.

Diarmid said softly, "You didn't know."

"No. No, I know nothing of that. It isn't in the stories. My father said nothing—"

"You used the horn to call us, and you didn't know there would be a cost?"

"Not that kind of cost!"

Diarmid believed him. The shock and horror on Patrick's face were too real. "Well, 'tis too late now. Once you called us, the *geis* was in play. The *veleda*'s bound to it, just as we are."

"No," Patrick whispered. "No. It's not possible."

"It has to be."

"I know I blew the horn, but . . . but I can't . . . I can't . . ."

Diarmid felt again that sinking nausea, the reminder of what he must do. He felt sorry for Patrick. It was obvious the man loved Grace. "You won't have to lift a hand," Diarmid told him.

"Then who?"

"That task falls to me. 'Tis a *geis* laid a long time ago. If I don't take her life, we fail no matter what her choice. Fail and fade."

"This is why . . . she said you'd been attentive. That you wouldn't leave her alone. This is why."

"It must be done on Samhain. It's not much time."

"Dear God. There must be another way. A way she doesn't have to die. Or . . . perhaps you're wrong. What if it's not her? Could you be wrong?"

"We've a Druid of our own who says she is," Diarmid explained. "And there are other things about her that say it too. Things she sees."

"She's had nightmares. Headaches."

"That and more. When she touched the ogham stick, it burned her."

"The ogham stick! God. Oh, God. I forgot. . . . I didn't think. I mean, I did, but I didn't know. I didn't know she would be involved in any of this! They're coming!"

"I don't know what you're talking about."

"The ogham stick calls the Fomori."

"Not alone. Not without the rowan wand—"

"We have the rowan wand."

Diarmid's gut knotted. "You didn't."

"We *did*," Patrick said. "When the Fianna didn't arrive, we . . . well, I told you, we needed help."

"You called the Fomori?" Diarmid's dread turned to anger.

"We didn't know the Fianna were here!" Patrick sounded panicked. "But it doesn't have to matter, does it? We've talked with their messenger, with Daire Donn. We've made a deal with them. Their help in return for shared power—"

"The Fomori don't share power."

Patrick grabbed Diarmid's arm. "They've promised us."

Diarmid threw him off. "They've broken every promise they've ever made. How can you not know this?"

"It isn't like that." Patrick was pleading now. "With the Fianna's help, we'll be invincible. Grace will choose our side over the British—of course she will. We'll find a way so that she doesn't have to die. You won't have to kill her. We'll find another way. Daire Donn or one of the Fomori will know a spell."

"The only spells they know are for death and destruction," Diarmid spat. "You'll be enslaved to them. By the gods, do you know what you've done?"

"The Fianna can help us control them."

"No one can control them! And because you called them you've changed everything. We'll never join with the Fomori. They've been our enemies since the beginning of time. You'll trade British rule for enslavement. That's what you'll have when Daire Donn and the others seize power. I've seen it before."

"No, it doesn't have to be that way—"

"If you could see what I've seen . . . The Fomori don't change. They want chaos. They thrive on terror and blood. You can't hope to control them. All they have ever wanted is to ravage every Irish soul. If you bring them here, they will destroy us all."

Patrick drew himself up, his panic replaced by resolve. "It's too late. Tomorrow's the solstice. They arrive then. And you're wrong about what will happen. You're wrong about who they are. The world is no longer as it was. We have promises. They will honor them. I've met Daire Donn. I believe him."

"Then you're a fool."

"We will win this fight. Ireland will win!"

"Ireland will fall to fear. And so will you. You'll be lucky if any survive it."

"You can't make the decision," Patrick declared. "You're not the head of the Fianna. Make my request of Finn—"

"He'll be no more willing to ally with the Fomori than I am."

"—and if he refuses, then you're right: it will be a war between us. But you're the one making Grace choose."

"You sound afraid," Diarmid needled. "Why is that? Do you think she'll choose the Fianna over you?"

"No, I don't think that," Patrick said. "Grace loves me."

How sure he sounds, Diarmid thought. He wondered if Patrick would be so confident if he knew about the kiss. For a moment, Diarmid wanted to say, *I had her pressed against a wall only two days ago, and given the way she was kissing me, I doubt she was thinking much of her love for you.*

He bit off the urge. Instead, he said, "But she knows the stories, too, doesn't she? How will she feel when she discovers you're allied with the gods of chaos? Do you really think she'll choose you over the heroes of Ireland?"

"Heroes? Perhaps once you were. But there's a reason for the *veleda*. Greed and arrogance, wasn't it? The people were tired of your demands. Tired of the Fianna."

Diarmid said nothing—it was true.

Patrick tried again, "But if you fought with us, that wouldn't matter. Grace wouldn't need to decide between us. It would be all of us against the British instead of what you make it now. It's *you* who changes it, Diarmid. You're the one who makes it the Fianna against the Fomori, not me."

Diarmid felt an overwhelming, terrible grief. He turned to go. Wearily, he repeated, "You're a fool, Patrick."

And Patrick Devlin said, "Stay away from her. Stay away from her with your damned *ball seirce*! You're no longer welcome in my stables. I don't want you near her. Do you hear me?"

Diarmid knew he wasn't talking about Lucy. He looked over his shoulder. "You've started a war, Patrick. Perhaps you didn't mean to, but you did. And in wars, people die. Especially innocents."

Then he wrenched open the door and went out, letting it slam shut behind him, striding down the hall, past the older woman, who must have been Mrs. Devlin, standing in the doorway of the parlor, staring at him in stunned disbelief, and Lucy in the room behind her, calling out, "Derry? Derry, is that you?"

He was out the front door and down the stoop in moments. Once he hit the walk, he broke into a run. Behind him, the clouds darkened over the harbor.

TWENTY-SEVEN

Later that afternoon

Diarmid

P atrick's voice rang in his ears. The Fomori. The summer solstice. *Tomorrow.* Balor of the one poisonous eye and Tethra, the treacherous sea god. The beautiful, terrible Lot . . .

Sweet Danu, there was so little time. He raced through the streets, aware of nothing but getting to Finn. When he finally reached the tenement, the yard was full of young men training. Diarmid skidded to a stop, raising dust, his breath rasping.

Oscar looked up. "Derry? What in the name of—"

"Where's Finn?"

Oscar jerked his head toward the side yard, and just as he did, Diarmid spotted his leader at the water barrel. Finn's golden-red hair shone in the sun. His gaze seemed to pierce Diarmid before he looked away.

"What have we here?" Finn asked.

It was a moment before Diarmid realized that Finn was

looking at something behind him and that the others had stopped fighting to look too.

Diarmid turned.

Grace's brother stood there. Aidan was sweating, his shirt-tails untucked, his hair falling every which way, hands braced on his thighs as he tried to catch his breath.

Diarmid would have sooner expected to see a kelpie. "Aidan? By the gods, what are you doing here?"

Aidan tried to straighten. He wavered, squinting; it seemed he might collapse. And his eyes were a strange color. Blue and . . . purple, too, so bright they looked unreal. They struck a familiar chord.

Aidan said, "I wanted to talk to you. About Grace. I was waiting . . . outside Patrick's. I tried to stop you, but you're *very* fast."

"He's the swiftest of all of us," said Finn, walking over. "He should have slowed to give you time to catch up."

"I didn't know he was behind me," Diarmid said. "And I wouldn't have waited for him anyway. Finn, there's much to tell you. I spoke with Devlin this morning—"

Finn held up his hand to stop him. "Who is this?"

Diarmid felt he might burst with all there was to say, and Aidan was just wasting time. "He's no one. The *veleda*'s brother. Aidan Knox. There's more important news—"

"More important than a stormcaster?"

Diarmid foundered while his brain—focused on Patrick and the Fomori—scrambled to catch up. "A what?"

"He's a stormcaster," Finn said.

With Finn's words, Diarmid suddenly felt the hum in the air, and his skin quivered. He remembered now where he'd seen eyes like that before. Neasa calling down her purple storms. Tethra summoning his eerie blue lightning.

Electricity radiated from Aidan Knox.

Aidan looked from Finn to Diarmid, blinking and obviously confused. "I don't know what you're talking about. Derry, is there someplace private we can talk? I don't feel well. But I have to speak to you about Grace."

"You didn't see this in him?" Finn asked Diarmid. "The brother of the *veleda*, and you didn't think to look?"

Diarmid didn't know what to say. He *hadn't* seen it. Not until this moment, and now he wondered how he had missed it. He'd been with Aidan all last night. How had he not noticed?

Aidan swiped a hand across his brow. He was perspiring so heavily his shirt stuck to his skin. He looked ready to swoon. "You're . . . it's too bright."

Finn took his arm. "Come, sit down. Ossian! Some water for our good friend Mr. Knox!"

He led Aidan to the step of the building, and Aidan sat gratefully, taking the ladle of water Ossian handed him. He gulped it and then raked his hand through his hair. It stood on end. The day rumbled with thunder, and Aidan put his hand to his eyes. Diarmid recalled last night—Aidan's complaints about the screaming in his head.

"Go on home now. Nothing here to see!" Oscar dismissed

the boys. Diarmid heard their grumbling as they left the yard, one or two trying to linger until Finn gave them a warning glance, and finally, they were left alone.

Aidan looked at Diarmid. "These your friends, Derry?" It seemed to take all his effort to get the words out.

"This is Finn," Diarmid said, gesturing to his leader and then to the others in turn: "Ossian, Oscar, Goll, Keenan, and Conan."

Aidan stared at him. Then he laughed. "You're joking, right?"

"No."

Aidan's laughter died. He looked confused, and then afraid. "Patrick called you Diarmid. Not Derry. Diarmid."

"Aye."

"Diarmid Ua Duibhne. Like the legend."

Diarmid watched as the truth dawned in Aidan's eyes, and he thought of Grace. He wondered if Patrick had summoned her. If even now she was learning what she was.

"I don't understand." Aidan started to rise.

Finn put his hand on Aidan's shoulder to keep him in place. "Oh, I think you understand very well, stormcaster."

"You keep saying that. I'm not—"

"You carry the power of storms within you," Finn told him. "Like your ancestor Neasa, the great Druid priestess. You can command thunder and lightning."

Aidan laughed again, but weakly. "That's impossible."

"Tell me you don't feel lightning in your fingertips, or

hear thunder in your head. Does not fire rage in your blood?"

Aidan stared at him. "You mean . . . you know what this is? Dear God, I thought I was going mad. Or dying."

"Not mad, no. Nor dying. You are only untrained. We can help you, Aidan Knox, if you wish it. We have had many dealings with stormcasters before, and Neasa was a very strong one. Her blood runs in your veins."

Diarmid saw the relief—and dread—in Aidan's eyes. "You can cure me?"

"'Tis no sickness but a call to power. There is nothing to cure. But we can help you to control it."

"And you know how to do this because you're the Fianna," Aidan whispered. "Truly the Fianna?"

Finn bowed his head in acknowledgment.

"So all the stories are true."

"Stories?" Finn asked.

"My grandmother told us stories for years about Druids and *sidhe*. About the Fianna. Finn MacCool and Diarmid Ua Duibhne and . . . and all of you."

"Did she tell you about the *veleda*? About what she is called to do?" Finn pressed.

Aidan said, "I know the prophecy, yes. The *veleda* has to decide if the Fianna's fight is a worthy one."

"The *veleda* blooded the horn, and we have been awakened to serve Ireland. We believe it was the Fenian Brotherhood, and your friend Patrick Devlin, who called us. What we don't know is why."

"We do know why," Diarmid interjected. "'Tis what I

meant to tell you, Finn. I spoke with Devlin today. He's admitted it. All of it. 'Twas the Fenians who called us. They want us to fight with the Irish rebels against British rule."

Finn's pale eyes lit. "Against the British?"

The other Fianna murmured. Diarmid heard their excitement with a sinking heart. "There's more," he said, and then he told them about the Fomori, finishing with "They arrive with the solstice."

"That's tomorrow," Finn said.

"The Fomori?" Aidan echoed. "But Patrick knows the Fianna and the Fomori are enemies."

"So I told him," Diarmid said. "And I told him, too, that we wouldn't fight side by side with them."

"By the gods, I'd rather slit my own throat," Oscar said.

Finn asked, "Does he not understand what the Fomori are?"

"He thinks they can be reasonable," Diarmid said. "The Brotherhood spoke to Daire Donn and offered them shared power when British rule is overthrown."

Finn laughed in disbelief.

"But that makes it an easy choice for the *veleda*," Aidan said. "Surely any priestess would choose the Fianna over the Fomori."

Diarmid felt Finn's gaze. Deliberately, he avoided it. "Maybe she would. If she wasn't betrothed to the leader of the Fenians."

Aidan froze. "It *was* the *dord fiann*. Grace's horn."

Diarmid nodded.

Aidan said, "But Grace wouldn't choose them. No matter what Patrick said."

"No? What if he tells her he can find a way to save her life?" Diarmid asked.

"Save her? What do you mean, save her?"

"There's a part of the legend that seems to have been forgotten," Diarmid said.

"What part is that?" Aidan asked warily.

"She has to die," Diarmid said, hearing the harshness in his voice. "To release her power, she has to die. Devlin didn't know that. I don't think Grace knows it either."

Aidan looked stricken, which made Diarmid like him a little better. Thunder rolled. Aidan's hand went again to his head. "Grace doesn't know what she is. And everything . . . it's all a jumble in my head. Pieces I can't grasp. Like a dream . . . or a memory . . . and there's all this screaming."

The air seemed to grow heavier. Just breathing raised a sweat. They all looked to the sky, which was growing darker.

"Tomorrow," Finn said. "We must prepare for the fight."

"Is Patrick right? Is there a way to save my sister?" Aidan asked.

Diarmid didn't trust himself to speak. He didn't know what Finn might hear in his voice. Despair, or fear, or something worse. No one else answered for him.

Aidan looked at each of them. "Well, that's honest anyway."

"I'm afraid the Fomori cannot help her either," Finn said. "You're free to ask them and hear their lies, but we could use your allegiance."

"And my sister?"

Finn said, "I won't lie to you, stormcaster. We need her. She *must* choose us. And in the meantime, we can keep her safe. You do not want the Fomori to have her."

"No, I don't. I want to trust you. You were once honorable men, while the Fomori have never been."

Finn inclined his head in acknowledgment. "We would be honorable again, stormcaster."

Diarmid made himself say, "At the ritual, I'm the one who has to kill her."

Aidan's eyes riveted to him. Diarmid felt as if Grace's brother could see inside him.

Aidan said, "Is that the reason you look at her the way you do? Do you mean to seduce her into wanting death?"

Diarmid's anger leaped. "The *geis* has nothing to do with it!"

And then he remembered the others were there, watching.

Oscar laughed. "He likes your pretty sister. He'd kiss her even if she wasn't the *veleda*."

Diarmid wanted to groan, but he knew Oscar had said it to help. The yard was silent, broken only by the grumble of thunder.

Finally, Finn said, "So now you know the truth, storm-caster. Do you still wish to help us? We need your sister here safely before the Fomori arrive."

"Yes," Aidan said. "I followed Derry to tell him to stay away from Grace, but everything's changed. I don't want her in Fomori hands, even with Patrick there."

Finn nodded with satisfaction. He glanced again at the sky. "We've a great deal to teach you in a short time. We'll have much need of you before the end."

"You'll keep Grace safe? You promise it?"

"She has nothing to fear from us," Finn vowed.

Which was true enough, at least for now. The one thing Diarmid knew for certain was that Grace would be more than safe here. She would be a queen. There would be nothing she couldn't ask of them, nothing Finn wouldn't grant her. Until it came time to kill her.

Finn ordered, "Ossian, get Cannel. We'll see what we can teach our stormcaster in the next few hours. Then Aidan and Diarmid will go fetch the *veleda*. 'Tis Tethra's thunder we hear. I'd know it anywhere. The Fomori are very close. We can waste no time. Are you ready to do what must be done, Diarmid?"

The *ball seirce* seemed to burn on Diarmid's forehead.

"I am."

TWENTY-EIGHT

Later that day

Patrick

P atrick glanced out the window as the carriage lumbered to a stop. The traffic on Broadway was at a complete standstill. He knocked on the ceiling to signal his driver and then got out, shouting to Leonard, "I'll walk from here."

He wove through the wagons with their cursing drivers and the other stalled carriages on the street. The weather pressed upon him, that ever-present, unnerving thunder.

The Fianna were here. Grace was the *veleda*. *Grace.* If he'd only known . . .

He thought of the way she'd looked up at him in the park. Those dark, trusting eyes. Why hadn't the horn brought the Fianna to the club the way the spell had brought the Fomori? Why to a tenement? Why had there been such confusion? Spells weren't supposed to work that way.

Why?

He hated that he didn't know. He hated it more because

that one thing, that singular thing, had cost him everything. Had the Fianna appeared as they were supposed to, he never would have called the Fomori, and the Fianna would have joined with the Fenian Brotherhood, and the *veleda*'s choice would be clear. Patrick hadn't even considered that the cause might prove unworthy, and it wasn't. Diarmid had said so.

But still . . . *Grace.* Grace would have to choose. And she would have to die.

There *had* to be another way.

Patrick reached the redbrick building and sprinted up the stairs, wrenching open the door and racing to the meeting room. His message to the others had declared an emergency, and they were all there.

"Why have you called us here, Devlin?" Rory Nolan asked. "Have the Fomori arrived early?"

"The Fianna are here!" Patrick announced.

They went silent.

"What?" Jonathan asked finally. "They're here? How can that be?"

"The horn worked," Patrick explained. "It brought them to a tenement, where they've been posing as a gang."

Simon said, "But they should have come here, just as Daire Donn did."

"Yes, they should have come here. No one knows why they didn't."

"How did you discover them?" Rory asked.

Patrick sank into a chair, burying his face in his hands. "Diarmid Ua Duibhne is my stableboy."

Rory said, "Perhaps you'd better start at the beginning."

Patrick looked up. "The Fianna have been searching for who called them. They looked for Irish organizations. That brought them to the Brotherhood, which brought them to me. Ua Duibhne took a job as my stableboy, hoping to get close to me. I discovered the truth only this morning. I've spoken with him. Finn's here too—all of them."

Jonathan let out his breath. "Thank God. Well then, that's it, isn't it? The Fianna are here. We'll win. We'll win at last!"

Patrick said, "The Fomori are coming, too, remember? And the Fianna have refused to fight with them."

"They've refused?" Jonathan looked stunned. "But . . . we called them. *Can* they refuse us?"

"Of course they can." Simon sat down heavily. "They have free will. No one can compel them. The point was for the Fianna to learn a lesson. They can choose a side. They *must* choose a side if they want the chance to keep living." He looked at Patrick. "Did our fight not interest them? Surely you explained it? Surely they want to win self-rule for Ireland?"

Patrick nodded. "Diarmid said they were more than willing to do that. Until I told him the Fomori were involved."

"Did you tell him that things are no longer as they were?" asked Rory. "That we can control the Fomori? That Daire Donn—"

"I told him all that. He said that no one could control them. That the world would fall to devastation and despair if they were involved."

Simon sat back. "Well, then, that *is* a problem."

"So they won't fight for us," Rory said. "We have the Fomori now. We don't need them."

Simon shook his head. "I'm afraid it doesn't work that way. The Fianna have been called, and now the fight has changed. It's the Fianna against *us* and the Fomori. Which means we have to beat them. And we need the *veleda* to choose us." He looked at Patrick. "I assume your sister is the one, after all, as she blooded the horn?"

Patrick's throat tightened. "No. It isn't Lucy."

"Then who? Did Ua Duibhne know who she is? Have they found her?"

This was worse than he could have imagined. "They know who she is."

"Do they *have* her?" Simon asked. "We can't let them have any advantage."

"They don't have the advantage. Not yet anyway. We do. Or . . . I think we do. She's my soon-to-be fiancée. Grace Knox."

His announcement was met with astonished stares.

Jonathan said, "Are you certain? Does she know she's the *veleda*?"

Patrick threaded his fingers through his hair, gripping his pounding skull. "Yes, I'm certain. I don't know if she knows. I haven't spoken to her. I came directly here."

"Your soon-to-be fiancée," Simon said. "What exactly does that mean?"

"I haven't proposed yet. I would have, but she felt we were moving too quickly—"

"Will she accept your suit?"

"I believe so."

"Because she loves you?" Simon asked.

"I hope so. I think so."

"Listen carefully to me, Devlin," Simon said. "We need more than the girl accepting you because she sees the benefit of marrying a rich young man. She will have to choose between us and the Fianna. Does she love you? Do we have an advantage?"

Jonathan said, "But wait . . . doesn't Diarmid Ua Duibhne have a . . . what was that called? The thing that compelled women to love him?"

"The *ball seirce*. And yes. He used it on my sister," Patrick said dully.

"Does he know your fiancée? Has he used it on her?"

"I don't think so," Patrick said. Grace had said Diarmid was attentive, but she hadn't seemed lovestruck. Not like Lucy—

"But he might," Simon said. "Finn MacCool is brilliant and ruthless. He'll see the *ball seirce* as a tool. You need to secure her, Devlin. Now. Keep her away from Ua Duibhne. Propose to her. Win her to our side. I don't suppose you can rush the marriage?"

"I don't know. Perhaps."

"You must try."

Hopelessness swept over Patrick. "There's one other thing Diarmid told me. The *veleda* makes the choice, but she must die to ensure it. She must *die*."

Even Simon looked shocked.

Patrick went on, "That part of the prophecy was lost. It wasn't in any of the stories I knew. Why would it be lost? Why would we not know it?"

"It's been two thousand years," Simon said. "Things go missing. But even if we'd known it, would it have changed what we did? Would you have refused to call the Fianna?"

"I thought the *veleda* was my sister. Of course I would have refused."

"Would you really?" Simon asked. "It seems a small price to pay. One life for thousands."

"Goddamn you, Simon. What if it were your sister? Your fiancée?"

"I would still have called them," Simon said firmly.

Around the room, the others nodded.

"You're either willing to sacrifice everything for the cause, or you're not the man we thought you were," Simon said.

Patrick's life had been dedicated to this cause, and they were *questioning* it. He knew he wasn't weak, and he wasn't wavering. But this . . .

He said rawly, "I love Grace. How can I watch her . . . ?"

"This is for Ireland, Patrick," Rory said gently. "You said you were willing to die for her."

"That was *me*. This is different. I can't condemn Grace."

"You have no choice," Simon said. "The prophecy is already in play. The *veleda* is bound to the Fianna. There is no other way."

"Perhaps there's another spell. Perhaps she doesn't need to die. The Fomori might know, don't you think?"

Simon sighed. "Yes. Yes, perhaps. We'll ask Daire Donn when they arrive."

But Patrick saw that Simon didn't believe it.

"If there is another way, we'll find it," Jonathan reassured him.

Rory added, "We'll all study the problem. But in the meantime, Simon is right; you must secure her. We can't lose her to the Fianna, and if she loves you, well . . . we need her help. You know this."

Simon was watching him. They all were. Patrick looked down at his clasped hands. At long last, the fight was to be had, and he was at the fulcrum of it. He could make a difference. He could change the world.

And none of it would matter, because he would lose her.

"Yes," he whispered. "I know."

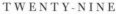

June 21—Summer Solstice

Grace

It was still thundering the next day. Aidan had disappeared yesterday soon after Patrick had brought him home, and I'd seen no sign of him since. Mama only said in a distracted voice, "Is he gone again? He shouldn't keep doing that. He has to be at your debut, at least."

I thought of how strange my brother had been, his words from my dreams, but I had no time to ponder them, because a carriage arrived bearing a note from Patrick.

"He wants to see you right away," Mama said.

I wondered if it had something to do with Derry, and then was angry that he was the first thing that came to mind. How long would it be before I stopped thinking of him, or dreaming of him—or worse, reliving his kiss?

I took my time getting ready. My nightmare-filled sleep showed in the bruised-looking shadows beneath my eyes.

There was no help for that beyond powder, which I didn't have, and so I changed into my second-best gown of green twill and fixed my hair. Mama was waiting with my shawl and hat.

When I went out to the waiting carriage, thunder erupted nearly overhead, putting me even more on edge. At the Devlins', the maid said, "This way, miss. He's waiting for you in his study."

When we passed the parlor, Mrs. Devlin looked up from the settee, where she was comforting a sobbing Lucy—and I feared that I knew what that was about. "Oh, hello, Grace. We'll have tea after," Mrs. Devlin called.

It was the last thing I wanted, but I forgot all that when I reached the study.

"Grace!" Patrick glanced at the maid and ordered tersely, "Leave us. And close the door."

Now I was worried. It was unlike Patrick not to think of propriety.

He rushed to me, taking my hands, looking me over as if searching for wounds. "You're all right?"

"Of course I am."

"Nothing's happened? He hasn't been to see you?"

"Who?"

"Diar—Derry."

"No. Why would I have seen him?"

"Thank God. Thank God. I was afraid I hadn't got to you in time."

"In time for what?"

His hands moved to my face. He kissed me—hard and urgently, possessively. It was so unlike him that I pulled away, saying, "Patrick, the door. We can't—"

"You know how much I love you, don't you?" His hands didn't leave my face. "I would never do anything to cause you harm. Nothing."

"Patrick, you're frightening me."

He let go of me and reluctantly stepped back, closing his eyes for a moment as if to muster control. He looked haunted and ill.

He said, "There are things I must tell you. About the relics. I've meant to tell you some of it before, but . . ."

I remembered our unfinished conversation. How I'd longed to hear the rest. But now, looking at him, I wasn't certain I still wanted to know.

"You look tired, Patrick," I said, trying to calm him. "There must be a better time—"

"I must tell you now!" he burst out. Then, "I'm sorry, Grace. But there's no more time to wait. Please will you . . . will you sit down and let me explain?"

I seated myself on the edge of a chair, squeezing my hands in my lap as he paced before the fireplace. For a long time he said nothing. Finally I could stand it no longer.

"I saw Lucy sobbing. I suppose you've sent Derry away?"

Patrick stopped abruptly. He dragged his hand through his hair. "Yes. And his name's not Derry. Well, it is, but that's just a nickname. His real name is Diarmid Ua Duibhne."

Diarmid. Diarmid and Grainne. "Don' run off with him, Grace.... Promise me."

Finn's Warriors had all taken Fianna names. Of course Derry had taken Diarmid. *Of course.* "Like the legend?" I asked Patrick.

"Exactly like the legend."

"He said his name was O'Shea. Derry O'Shea."

"He lied." Patrick was watching me so intently I squirmed.

He was looking for something, but I didn't know what. I wanted to tell him the name meant nothing, that it was all pretend, that they all had these names. But I couldn't think of how to do so without telling him how I knew it. "Well, it's a legend, Patrick. I hope you don't think I mean to run off with Derry because we have the same names as in the story."

"It's not just the same name. He's the same person."

Everyone around me seemed to be going mad. It was this blasted thunder. "The same person. I see. Oh, Patrick, how old is that story? Two thousand years?"

"At least that." He knelt beside my chair. His hand covered mine in my lap. "This is what I was trying to tell you the other day. I know it sounds unbelievable—or . . . mad, I suppose. I told you about the old magic, remember? That some of these relics still hold it."

"I remember."

"We've found incantations. Old spells written in ogham. Some of them, it turns out, still work."

I laughed in disbelief—and despair. "Magic? Are you joking?"

"Not at all." He rose again. "I have something to show you."

He went to his desk, unlocking a drawer with a key he wore on his watch chain. He took out a wooden box. It was plain, with no design carved upon it, nothing to mark it at all. Again he knelt beside my chair. He flipped the metal latch on the box and opened it.

Inside, lying on a pad of deep-blue velvet, was my horn.

"My horn! Wherever did you get it?"

"So this *is* yours? You're certain?"

I nodded. "Well, it *was* mine. My grandmother gave it to me for my fourteenth birthday. And then Aidan lost it in a bet. How do you have it?"

"A man came to me with it a few months ago. He thought I would be interested in buying it, and I was. I didn't realize it had belonged to you."

I reached out, tracing my finger along the silver, feeling the same little shiver I always felt when I touched it, as if something in it recognized me. "Oh. Look—it's still bloody from when I cut myself on the silver." I held out my finger for him to see. "That was weeks ago. It's long healed."

"No," he whispered.

"It's all right, Patrick. If anyone but me has to have it, I'm glad it's you."

"Grace, do you know what this is?"

"A hunting horn. My grandmother said it had been in our family for generations."

"Two thousand years at least."

"Is it that old?"

"It's the *dord fiann*."

The *dord fiann*. Finn MacCool's hunting horn, spelled to recall him and the Fianna from endless sleep to serve Ireland in her time of need. The story was very like that of King Arthur, sleeping forever in Avalon until Britain called him awake again—but my grandmother had told me that Arthur and his Knights of the Round Table were only the tales of Finn and his Irish Fianna, stolen and recrafted by the British. *"And that's not all they stole,"* she'd said.

"Really? I suppose you used it to call up the Fianna?" It was a joke, but then I saw how serious Patrick looked. "What? Are you telling me you've *tried*? Patrick, it's only a legend."

"No. It's true. It's all true."

He *was* mad. *Not Patrick. Dear God, not him.* I rose. "Patrick, there must be a doctor you can see. Someone . . . should I tell your mother? What should I do?"

He caught my arm. "Sit down, Grace."

"You're talking nonsense."

"I want you to listen to me."

His voice was so calm, and when I looked into his face I saw—just Patrick. No madness, not the way I saw it in my grandmother's eyes. Or even in Aidan's yesterday. But I couldn't believe this. I *didn't* believe it.

Patrick rushed on. "The Brotherhood called the Fianna to help us with the rebellion in Ireland. We had the incantation and the horn. But no one came. I thought it didn't work. I thought the magic was dead. But it did work, Grace. It worked! The horn brought the Fianna here, and you told me all about them."

"I told you? How could I have told you?" But I knew what he meant.

"Finn's Warriors *are* the Fianna. Led by Finn MacCool. Ossian is here. Diarmid Ua Duibhne and Oscar, Ossian's son. Goll and Conan and Keenan. Does any of this sound familiar to you? And not because of any legend, but because you've seen them yourself?"

Finn, imprisoning me on the barrel. Asking me about a rowan wand and a horn. Oscar walking with Rose on the Battery. Keenan and Goll laughing with me in a tenement room. Conan with his bald head and dirty fleece. Diarmid Ua Duibhne. Derry. Glowing. *All glowing.*

"You see," Patrick said.

"No. No. It's impossible. They're just a gang—" A gang who fought with efficiency and precision, as if they'd trained for it their entire lives. They'd dispatched twice as many Black Hands in almost no time at all. They'd moved in concert. The ruthlessly deliberate plunge of a knife . . .

"It's possible. It's real. We called them. They're here!"

I was caught in a dream. A nightmare. Where Derry carried a spear and the Morrigan howled, and . . . and I had known all this already. I had known all of it, in some place deep inside me. Finn's Warriors. The Fianna.

Diarmid Ua Duibhne. The way he'd touched me and I'd felt as if I knew him. A kiss that burned like lightning.

Dreams where I ran my fingers down his bare chest. Diarmid and Grainne.

"No." I grabbed Patrick's arm, knocking the box and the horn to the floor. "No, not him."

"There's something else," Patrick said. "I need to tell you all of it."

"I don't want to hear any more."

"You have to," he said. "It concerns you, Grace. You have to hear it."

"How could it possibly concern me? I didn't know what the horn was."

"Do you remember the story of Finn's death? How he's to be called back? The prophecy?"

"I . . . yes, I suppose." My grandmother's voice came to me as she told the story like a song: lilting, rhythmic.

"Tell me what you know of it."

I forced myself to think. "The Fianna had grown arrogant. They were demanding tributes and taking whatever they wanted. Fighting for whoever paid them most. The High King grew angry and warred against them. When Finn died, the Druids put a *geis* on them. If they were called back, a priestess had to decide if their fight was worthy. If it was not, they would fail and die. But if it was, she could give them the power to win and live again." I looked up at Patrick expectantly. "Is that right?"

"Yes. That's right. They can't win without the *veleda*."

"The *veleda*." I laughed a little. "You realize how silly this sounds, don't you?"

"Our fight is a worthy one, don't you agree? Saving Ireland?"

Weariness swept me. How could I believe any of this? "Yes. So ... Derry—Diarmid—asked me about a rowan wand. I suppose you need it to find this *veleda*."

"No, Grace. We've already found her. She's you. You're the *veleda*."

"What?"

He gestured to the horn. "The horn was yours. It was only because you'd blooded it that we could call them. The *veleda* sees; she weighs; she chooses. You've already seen all this, Grace. You know you have. Your nightmares—"

"Only nightmares," I said uncertainly.

"More than that. The ogham stick burned you."

"It was in the sun."

"No." Now Patrick sounded strangely sad. "Their Druid did a divination. You're the *veleda*. There's no doubt."

Their Druid. Cannel. Derry taking me to the tenement. Lies and evasions. His questions, and Finn's. *"Touch her."* The terrible glowing and the pain and ... I sank back. "That can't be."

But it was, and I knew it. It explained everything. *Everything.*

"You're the one who must decide."

"What is there to decide? What am I to say? Your fight is worthy, carry on?"

His sadness and misery were so palpable I couldn't look away. "There's more to it than that. The *veleda* must give up her power to the side she chooses. There's a ritual. I don't know what it is yet, and I hope to find another way. I know there must be. We'll find it, I promise."

"Another way? Why should there be? Whatever power I have—" And here I laughed, because obviously the *veleda*'s power had faded over the years. "My only power is the ability to have terrible nightmares. I hereby give it up. It's yours. Take it!"

"Grace, the *veleda* has to die."

The words were so stark I couldn't understand them.

"There must be a sacrifice," he said.

I leaped from the chair. "Patrick, this is all insane. Don't you see it? I'm no *veleda*. I can't even . . . I don't have any power over my own life, and now you're saying I have to die?"

He caught me, holding me close; I struggled against him. I was no one, just an ordinary girl who liked to read poetry and tried to take care of her family. I was no *veleda*, and this was all just another terrible dream. I pinched myself, willing myself to wake up—*Wake up, wake up*—but I was still there, still being held in Patrick's arms while he whispered, "Don't worry; I won't let you die. Do you think I want this? I love you, Grace. I love you. I won't let you die."

"Then you could end this now, couldn't you? Take it all back. Send them off. You'll find another way to save Ireland. You and the Brotherhood—"

"I would if I could. I didn't know, Grace. I didn't know. And now . . . now it's all been made worse."

"How could it be worse?"

His arms dropped. He stepped away. "We didn't know the Fianna had come. We thought the call had failed. And we were desperate. We had something else. One more thing to try. We had the ogham stick."

Darkness and thunder, blood and fire. The eye of one who slays. As one is bid, so come the rest. The rowan wand and virtue gone. A blood price paid. Now come the Children of Domnu.

The Children of Domnu.

Balor of the one venomous eye, who destroyed all he looked upon. Bres, the half Fomori king who'd enslaved the Irish and ravaged the land. Miogach, the son of Lochlann, who'd killed Finn's son. Lot with the bloated lips in her breasts and four eyes in her back.

And now I knew it was all real. Everything he said. It was *real*.

"You called the Fomori?" I whispered.

"We've made a bargain with them. Their help for a share of the power. They've agreed. They're coming to help us."

"They're coming." Grandma's words.

"Patrick, no!"

"I never would have done it if I'd known the Fianna were here! How was I to know they'd been brought to some tenement? The heroes of Ireland? Why should they have awakened there? What was the reason?"

"But—"

"The Fomori were our only hope, Grace." His eyes were beseeching. "They'll be here today. And they'll find a way, another spell. Something so you don't have to die."

"And the Fianna? Have they agreed to help you too?"

Patrick glanced away. "They won't ally with the Fomori.

Now the fight is between us and the Fianna. We have to defeat them before we can help Ireland. And if we don't—if we can't, how will we save Ireland then?"

"So I have to choose between you? Patrick, do you know what you've done?"

"What if I told you the Fomori aren't as the legends say? The Fianna had reason to paint the Fomori as evil. It made them look stronger. But I've met Daire Donn. He's a good man who loves Ireland. And the Fianna have forgotten none of their arrogance. They've *forced* this. They could fight with us, but they won't. You've *met* him. *Diarmid*." He spoke the name like a curse. "Do you think him so noble?"

How easily he'd killed that Black Hand. And how frightened the gang boys in the street had been of him.

"He used the lovespot on Lucy. Deliberately. So he could get close to me."

The lovespot. I'd forgotten that. *The lovespot.*

And suddenly I knew why I'd dreamed of touching him, why I'd been so hungry for his kiss. He'd used the lovespot on *me*. It explained why I couldn't get him out of my head when I wanted Patrick there instead. Derry had bespelled me.

I didn't know whether to feel relieved or furious.

"He's the one who discovered you are the *veleda*, Grace. And he's the one who means to kill you."

"Kill me . . . ?"

"He has to. Another *geis* was laid—he's the one who must take your life at the sacrifice on Samhain. He means to seduce you into choosing them, and then once you do, he'll kill you."

"N-no. No, that can't be true." But it made sense. All of it.

"It is true. I promise it. He was here. He told me everything. Everything he's said to you, everything he's done—it's all been in service to the prophecy."

It was all a trick. A lie.

"I want to save you. But he doesn't. He'll kill you because he has to, Grace, but before that, he'll do what he must to convince you to choose the Fianna."

It was all a plan to kill me.

"I've told him to stay away from you," Patrick said. "But there's too much at stake. I don't trust him. So I want you to stay here, where I can protect you."

"I can't stay here. What will people say? And my mother . . . my grandmother . . ."

"Marry me," Patrick said.

Everything I'd waited for. Everything I'd wanted. I just stared at him.

"I love you. And he'll try to take you from me. But I'll fix all of this, and you'll choose the Brotherhood and me, and we'll beat the Fianna. We'll be married. You'll live and you'll be my wife and then we can set Ireland free. Please, Grace. *Please.* Tell me you will."

I thought of my mother's anxious waiting. The doctor's coming lawsuit and my grandmother's growing insanity and Aidan sauntering off in search of laudanum and a card game. I thought of being pressed against the wall of my own house, Derry's heart beating against mine, and the pure thrill of his kiss.

"He means to seduce you . . . and he'll kill you."

Patrick wanted to save me. He would save my family.

But could he really promise these things? Could he change the world?

I needed to know more. About the lovespot and the *geis*. About Diarmid and Grainne and the *veleda* and my dreams. I needed to understand.

Suddenly the things my grandmother had said made sense: *"They are coming." "That boy."* She'd known what was in my dreams. It wasn't just madness I'd seen in her eyes, but something else, something more—

The truth.

My grandmother knew the truth.

And it was time I learned it too.

THIRTY

Grace

I saw the hope and fear in Patrick's eyes when I said, "I've a great deal to think about. I need to talk to my mother—"

"She'll tell you marrying me is the best thing."

"—and my grandmother."

"Your grandmother?"

"She's the one who told me all the stories, Patrick. She knew details I've never heard anyone else tell. And I think she might know something about the *veleda* too. Perhaps she might know a way—"

"To save you?" If I had ever doubted Patrick's love for me, his look now told me it was true and real.

"I hope so."

"Then you must go to her. But only her, Grace. And your mother. And then you must come right back here. I'll have Leonard drive you there. Don't go anywhere without him. Promise me."

"Yes, I—"

"Right there and right back. I'll tell Leonard to watch for Diarmid. If you see him"—his voice broke—"don't look at him, for God's sake. It would only take a moment."

"I won't." How could I say to him that it was already too late for that?

Together we went out of the study. We were nearly to the front door when Mrs. Devlin came rushing out of the parlor. "You aren't going so soon, Grace? What about tea?"

Patrick said, "Not now, Mama. We'll have it later. Grace will be right back."

Mrs. Devlin looked distraught. I didn't think she'd even heard him. "Oh, Grace, Lucy would so love to see you."

Which was never true, but Lucy had been sobbing when I'd arrived. *Your fault.* My guilt barreled back. "Perhaps just a moment—"

"There's no time," Patrick said roughly.

But Mrs. Devlin had seen my hesitation. "Just have a few words with her. Just to reassure her that the world isn't falling apart."

I couldn't tell her that it was.

"All right," I agreed with a pleading look at Patrick, and he let me go.

"Don't take too long, Grace."

Lucy was on the settee in the parlor, as bedraggled as I'd ever seen her. Her eyes and her nose were red from weeping. Her hair was falling from its pins. There were no gay flowers at her décolletage, none of her usual jewelry.

"He was here," she said as I came in. "He was here yester-day, and he ran out without stopping to say good-bye. I don't know what's wrong! I haven't seen him in forever, and I've sent notes. . . ."

I sat down beside her. "Patrick dismissed him. He can't have received them."

"I know. But this was before that. *Days* ago."

"It's not as if you could have had him, Lucy. He's a gang boy." My words were tougher than I meant them to be.

Her chin jerked up; her eyes narrowed. "How do you know that?"

"Patrick told me."

"Why was he talking to you about Derry?"

"He was worried about you."

She sighed and dabbed at her eyes with an already sodden handkerchief. "I don't care what Derry is. I love him. I think I'll love him forever. I *want* him. When he kissed me . . . I've never felt that way. Oh, I know you can't understand. Patrick's far too much a gentleman to kiss you that way."

Again, I felt the rough brick at my back. The way the world had seemed to open with his kiss and devour me.

The lovespot. It's all a lie.

I said, "If he really does love you, Lucy, he'll come for you. If he doesn't, it's better that he's gone."

She went into fresh peals of sobbing. "It's not b-better."

I grabbed her hand, threading my fingers through hers, leaning close to say in a low voice, "You think you can like that life, but you won't. You'll be dodging bill collectors and never have enough to eat. You'd hate where he lives now: in a tenement with blood on the walls—"

"You know where he lives?"

"It's . . . it's what I imagine."

Lucy pulled her hand from mine. "I see."

"All you have to do is read the papers to know what that life is like there."

"Oh, for God's sake, Grace, who reads the newspaper? And Derry's said nothing of it."

"Why would he? He's after a rich girl. Have you thought he might only want your money?"

"He loves me," she insisted.

I wanted to slap her into sense. I wanted to commiserate, to say *I know how you feel. I dream of him.*

Instead, I said, "He's a handsome boy, Lucy, but there are a hundred handsome boys in New York City. You'll find another one; I know it."

"I don't want another one. I want *him.*"

"Grace," Patrick said from the doorway. "There really is so very little time."

I nodded and rose, saying to Lucy, "I must go."

She glanced toward the doorway and made a face. "Yes, by all means go with the man you love while I sit here and die of a broken heart."

It was all I could do not to tell her that her love for him was only a spell that would wear off eventually—*I hoped*—and that he had bewitched the both of us but that I was the one who might die from it.

I had to talk to Grandma. I told Lucy I would see her later and left her to sniff into her handkerchief. Mrs. Devlin gave me a grateful smile. "Thank you so much, my dear. I'm certain she'll feel better now."

Patrick took me to the carriage. When I was seated, he leaned in. "I should go with you."

"I need to do this alone."

"You'll come back? You promise you will?"

"You can tell Leonard to drag me back if I hesitate."

Patrick's grin was small. "If it comes to that, I will. Grace, you'll give me an answer when you return? To my proposal?"

I nodded.

He let me go with a sad and anxious smile, one I couldn't get out of my head as the carriage started off.

When we arrived at my house, Leonard followed me up the stoop with an apologetic "He told me to stand here and wait, miss."

There was no point in arguing with him. In fact, it was reassuring to know he was there.

The house was dim and sweltering. Mama was nowhere to be seen. I headed for the stairs, then stopped when I heard a sound behind me, a footstep. I turned.

Derry was standing at the kitchen door.

My heart leaped and then fell, a plunging, sickening drop, and I was against that brick wall again, looking at the glow flaming to life in his eyes before he bent to kiss me.

No. No! He wasn't Derry. He was Diarmid. Everything

he'd said and done was a lie. *He means to kill you on Samhain.*

I turned and ran for the stairs.

He caught up with me before I made the first step. "Grace. Listen to me. That's all I ask."

That deep voice was as alluring as ever. "Get away from me."

"You've spoken to Devlin."

"He's told me everything."

We both stilled at a noise from upstairs. Derry touched my arm, which brought a little thrill I tried not to feel. "I need to speak with you, lass. Somewhere private."

"You're mad if you think I'll go anywhere alone with you again."

"Just to the kitchen," he said. "There are a hundred weapons there you could use if you want. You could beat me to death with a wooden spoon."

"Don't tempt me. I'd like nothing more than to bruise your pretty face."

"All right. If that's what it takes to get you to talk to me." He held out his hand. "You've never let me explain."

"I gave you plenty of opportunities to explain."

He sighed. "'Tis complicated."

"Try uncomplicating it."

"I will. I will. Just . . . not here."

I needed to know the truth, but I didn't want to be alone with him. *It's a lie. A spell. Remember it.*

"Very well," I said.

He gave me a grateful look, those deep-blue, enchanting eyes—*which you can barely see through his hair, you idiot.* I turned, leading the way to the kitchen.

"Explain," I said as the door swung shut behind us. "And quickly. Patrick's waiting for me."

"What exactly has he told you?"

"More than you have. And he hasn't lied either."

"Don't be so sure of that."

"Oh really? You knew the whole time, didn't you, what I am?"

"I suspected it," he said uncomfortably. "But I didn't know for sure until the night I took you to Finn."

The night he'd used the lovespot on me. Or no . . . he must have used it before then. All those dreams I had of touching him, mesmerized by his laughter.

I said, "You've done nothing but lie to me and trick me. You've never once told me the truth about anything."

"Because I wasn't sure. There was no point in telling you anything until I was. I meant to protect you."

"From what?" I asked. "From who? Finn? Yourself? Diarmid Ua Duibhne. That's who you really are. The Diarmid who ran off with Grainne and saved Finn and the others from the House of Death. The Diarmid who slew six hundred men in the battle with Lochlann's son."

"How do you know all that?" he asked, looking startled.

"Is it all true?"

"Well, I probably didn't kill six hundred that day. Though I suppose if you counted over a few months . . ."

His humor only enraged me further. "I've believed enough of your lies. It doesn't matter what you've done to me, I won't believe you again." I tried to push past him to the door.

He grabbed my arm, in the same moment pulling me closer, until we were toe-to-toe, only inches between us, his fingers searing through my sleeve. "What I've done to you? I've kept you safe. And I'll keep on doing it, Grace. Did Devlin tell you he's called the Fomori? They're on their way now. That thunder you hear is Tethra. Have you heard of *him*?"

He was too close. It was hard to get out a single word. "Yes."

"Then you'll know what a monster he is. You don't want to be in their hands, Grace, and that's exactly where Patrick Devlin means to put you."

"Patrick's promised to protect me."

"He can promise all he wants. They're the Children of Domnu. Gods of chaos and darkness. You can't trust them."

I heard the dread in his voice, but I couldn't admit to him that I *was* frightened of the Fomori, that I was afraid Patrick might be wrong. But Patrick had spoken to them, and he knew the legends as well as I did, if not better. "What if you're wrong? It's been two thousand years."

"It's in their nature to lie to you and trick you. And in the end they'll take what they want whether or not you wish to give it."

"Nothing like you," I said.

His fingers tightened on my arm, pulling me up against him, and I could not bring myself to move away. His gaze held me as he whispered, "No, nothing like me. You know that, Grace. You know *me*. Don't tell me you don't feel what's between us."

His voice raised a pure longing I could not let myself feel. "I *don't* know you," I whispered back. "How can I, when everything you've told me is a lie?"

"Not everything."

"No? Which part of it is true? That you're a stableboy? That you are Derry O'Shea, an immigrant boy? A gang boy?"

"How could I tell you? You would never have believed me."

The warmth of him against me was distracting, tempting. I forced myself to continue. "What about when you told me you didn't take Patrick's book? Or that we were going to visit your friend in the hospital instead of a tenement in the worst part of town, where I was nearly assaulted—"

"That was your own doing. I told you not to run."

"Kissing me when you were courting Lucy! You were lying to her too! And she's in a terrible state, by the way, not that you care."

"That couldn't be helped. But she'll get over it."

"When the lovespot wears off, you mean? How long does that take, exactly? How long does she have to suffer?"

"Do you care so much?"

"I want to *know. How. Long?*" I hit his chest with my free hand, punctuating each word. He caught my wrist before I could swing back to hit him again.

"Careful, lass. I'm a bit too familiar with your hands."

Both of which he now had in a tight hold. We were so

close. He had me imprisoned. "Let go of me. I don't want you to touch me."

"Who's the liar now?" His mouth was nearly against mine. I felt myself sinking, unraveling, *yearning.*

"I want to kiss you again," he whispered. "And maybe 'twould show you that you belong with me. With the Fianna."

I recalled what Rose had said about Derry being a game. But the tables had turned, and now *I* was the game, and he was playing me. *He means to seduce you and kill you.* That was the truth I had to remember.

As carefully and clearly as I could, I said, "Don't you dare. I don't want you, whatever you think. That kiss was a mistake. It will never happen again. I want you to leave me alone."

"Ah lass, I wish I could." There was such real sorrow and regret in his voice. He said, "I'm sorry, Grace," just as he released me and started to push his hair from his eyes—at last—and at the same moment I heard my mother calling, "Grace? Grace, is that you?" and I thought of my grandmother, my questions, everything at stake, and I wrenched away, taking advantage of Derry's surprise to shout, "I'm here! I'll be right up, Mama!"

I began to push through the doorway. He put up his arm to bar the way.

I glared at him. "Let me pass."

"This isn't over, Grace. Don't you see? It can't be over."

But I pushed again, and this time he dropped his arm and I lurched through the doorway, into the hall, trembling as I hurried to the stairs.

"It can't be over." There was still the ritual, the role he must play in my fate—something else he hadn't told me.

"You know me. . . . You belong with me." Never once the truth. *I have to kill you.*

But I was free of him now. And I meant to stay that way.

THIRTY-ONE

Diarmid

He watched her go with a sense of failure, despair—and relief. Relief most of all, because even though she was running from him again, she was still herself. Still Grace, not bewitched by love, and he was glad.

He knew Finn would not understand, however. Diarmid supposed he could say he was getting ready to use the *ball seirce* and then she bolted, which was true. But he also hadn't convinced her to come with him, and that was disobeying another order.

The back door opened, and Aidan came inside. Grace's brother looked as if simply standing was the most he could do. He was sweating profusely, his hair still standing on end, his eyes glowing. Finn and Cannel had taught him a few things in the last hours, but learning to control his power would take much longer than that. Diarmid felt the electricity coming off Aidan now; it almost hurt to be around him.

Aidan glanced around the kitchen. "Where's Grace? We have to meet the others."

"She's upstairs," Diarmid said.

"I'll tell her to hurry." Aidan started past him. Diarmid stopped him. Thunder crashed overhead—very loud. Very close.

The Fomori.

Aidan cringed, looking fearfully at the ceiling. "We can't wait. We have to get her out of here."

Diarmid said, "I need more time."

"You didn't convince her?"

"Not yet."

Aidan looked sick. "There *is* no more time, Derry. Can't you hear them?" He grabbed his head. "Aaaahhhh! That screaming! I can't stand it!"

Aidan's hair was *hissing*. Diarmid put his arm around Aidan's shoulders, jerking away again as he was rocked by a painful shock. Aidan fell to his knees, gasping. "It's time. The Fomori will come for her. We'll have to force her if she won't go willingly."

The plan had been for Diarmid and Aidan to bring Grace to meet the others a few blocks away, where it wouldn't be so unusual to see gang members lingering. They didn't want to call attention to themselves so far uptown. But now Aidan was right; there was no time for that.

Aidan's eyes shone. "Bring Finn and the others here. We'll need them to keep her safe. The Fomori are so close. I can hear them!" Aidan grabbed his head again, digging his fingers into his scalp. "Shut up! Shut up!"

Diarmid grabbed Aidan's shoulder, shaking it. "You'll have to get her to the back gate. Do you understand? Get her there and wait for us. I'll be as quick as I can. Can you manage it? Just to the backyard."

Aidan squeezed his eyes shut. "The backyard. Yes. I'll bring her."

Thunder shook the house. Aidan whimpered. With a last look at the kitchen door, a last wish that she was in his arms, Diarmid left. There was no other choice now. The Fomori were here.

He ran to get the others.

THIRTY-TWO

Grace

I hurried up the stairs. Mama waited at the top. "Oh, Grace, you're back! This thunder . . ."

As if on cue, it clapped right above the house, so loudly we both ducked our heads. *Tethra.*

"Is everything all right, Grace? With Patrick, I mean?"

"He proposed."

"Oh thank goodness! And you accepted?"

How could I tell her the truth? The Fianna and the *veleda*. Choice and sacrifice. Her face was so pale I could see the blue of the veins beneath her skin. "I told him I needed to talk to Grandma first."

"Grandma? Why?"

"There were some things Patrick said. About our family. Some questions he had—"

Her hand went to her head. "The Devlins have known our family for generations. Why, your grandmother and Patrick's were as close as sisters in Ireland. Why would he question our suitability?"

"He's not questioning it, Mama," I said. "I'm sorry, I didn't mean to distress you. It's nothing. I just need to talk to Grandma for a few moments."

"And then you'll accept him?"

"Mama, please."

"Very well. I'll be in my room if you need me. Oh, I hate this thunder!"

I stopped her, hugging her as tightly as I could. She gave me a funny little smile. "What was that?"

"I love you, Mama."

"I know, darling. Is everything really all right?"

"Yes. It's just . . . things are changing so quickly, that's all."

"Everyone feels that way now and again. But you're no longer a child. You're a young woman with a full life ahead of you. And Patrick is a good choice. I know you'll do what's right, Grace. You always do."

Tears came to my eyes as Mama kissed me and drew away, going to her bedroom.

Patrick and Derry, the Fomori, centuries of Irish legend come to life. To think I was the focus of it all—in that moment it felt even more impossible. I wanted to be the girl Mama thought I was, uncertain because of a marriage proposal and not because she had to die—

But maybe not.

I straightened my shoulders and wiped my eyes, going into Grandma's room. She was sleeping, her eyelids fluttering

with dreams. I wondered what they were. Wars and a screaming Morrigan?

I touched her shoulder. "Grandma."

Her eyes opened. She stared at me as if she didn't recognize me, and my hopes that she could tell me something, anything, about the *veleda* fled. But then her gaze cleared. "*Mo
chroi?* Why are you here? Why are you not already gone?"

"Where would I go, Grandma?"

She grabbed my wrist. "Listen—you must find him."

"Grandma, I need to ask you some questions—"

"No! I can't—" Her eyes clouded, then cleared again. A
fine sweat broke out on her skin. "No time. I cannot keep it
away. I am . . . not strong enough." Her fingers bit into my
skin. "You must listen. I will be gone—"

"No. No, don't be silly—"

"Ssshhh. He is here. The *sidhe* will help you, but you must
be very, very careful."

I stared at her. This was different. She hated the fairies—
she said it all the time. *Stay away from the* sidhe. *Fear them.* But
that didn't matter now. "Grandma, please. I need to know about
the *veleda.* Do you know what I mean? Do you remember?"

"The Fianna have found you at last."

She *did* know. My despair was so overwhelming I had to
look away.

"You must . . . 'Tis not right. 'Tis broken."

"That's what Aidan said. What's broken?"

"Aidan . . . he will know."

"Grandma, Aidan's too sick, and—"

"Listen! Remember, *mo chroi*. To harm and to protect are as one."

"Grandma, please."

"'Tis a curse. The sea is the knife." Her eyes seemed to burn. "You must find the archdruid. He can help you."

"Who is that? How can he help me? What do you mean?"

"He knows. Find the *sidhe*. But careful, *mo chroi*. You must be very careful. Your mother . . ."

"Yes, I know. I won't say anything to her. But I don't know what any of this means. What archdruid? What curse? What do the *sidhe* have to do with it?"

"There is . . . a key."

Thunder again. I flinched, and Grandma glanced toward the window. The sky was darkening.

"A key to what?" I asked.

But when she turned back to me, her gaze was faraway. "Do not fear . . . That boy." Her grip loosened.

"Grandma," I said, shaking her. "Grandma, please. Answer me. What do I do now? Please—"

Her eyes closed—no answers would be coming today. An archdruid. Curses and a key. To harm and to protect . . . Aidan . . . I didn't know what any of it meant. She'd told me nothing except what I already knew: that everything Patrick had said was true.

Thunder crashed. The whole room shook with it.

Grandma whispered without opening her eyes, "They're here now. Choose well."

Then I heard the screaming.

Dusk that day

Patrick

They came while Patrick waited for Grace to return. A terrible crack of thunder, and then the maid appeared at his study door with a nervous curtsy. "You've visitors, Mr. Devlin."

Thinking it must be Grace and her family, he stepped out into the hall to welcome her and saw the crowd of people standing in his foyer.

Rory Nolan and Jonathan Olwen and Simon MacRonan were there. Behind them stood Daire Donn and five strangers: one beautiful woman and four men, one of whom was seven feet if he was an inch, with arms the size of small logs and a craggy, scarred face that would have been frightening on a dark night and was still rather disturbing during the day. One eye was hidden behind a patch.

Daire Donn stepped forward. "My good Mister Devlin, we have arrived."

Patrick motioned them quickly to follow him into the

study. When they were all there, he shut the door. Thunder rumbled again.

Daire Donn smiled. "My companions, this is Patrick Devlin. Devlin, this is Bres, former King of Ireland"—he gestured to a man with fair hair and a patrician nose, and then to the giant—"and the good Balor. Their reputations, I think, precede them."

And they did. The fair Bres was the king that the Tuatha de Dannan, the old gods, had deposed, the one the legends said had enslaved the Irish and raped the land until it was fallow. And Balor was the giant with the venomous eye that slew every man who looked upon it.

History is written by the victors, Patrick reminded himself.

"Miogach, son of Lochlann," Daire Donn went on, introducing a dark-haired man with sharp gray eyes, "and Tethra"—the Fomorian god of the sea, whose hair hung in dense and twisted locks about his face, tangling in the ends of his thick, curling mustache. "And the lovely Lot."

She was breathtaking, with long blond hair and nearly purple eyes. Lot—whom the legends said had lips on her breasts and four eyes on her back. She was fully gowned, but still . . . Patrick thought of how horrible she'd been in the stories, and again he marveled at how history lied.

"We understand the Fianna have refused our fight," she said in a light, musical voice.

"They have refused to stand with you," Patrick corrected gently.

"And so they become the fight," she said. "Well, 'tis most disappointing. We had hoped to aid Ireland rather than battle old enemies."

"One would think old hurts assuaged after two thousand years," Bres said.

"It was disappointing to us as well," Simon said. "But the Fianna have chosen their course, and now we must defeat them before we can turn to our most righteous cause."

"Well I, for one, relish it," said Miogach. "Finn has always deserved a comeuppance. I'm happy to give it to him."

Thunder cracked. Daire Donn frowned at Tethra. "I think you can stop that now."

Tethra shrugged. "I did stop. 'Tisn't me."

Lot turned to Patrick. "Your friends tell us you have the *veleda*. Might we meet her?"

"She's at her mother's house. But I expect her here shortly."

Thunder and purple lightning struck, illuminating the study. *Purple?* "What was that?" Patrick asked.

Lot raised her eyes to the ceiling as if she could see the storm through it. "'Tis Druid fire."

"Aye," said Tethra. "Not far either."

"A few blocks south," said Daire Donn.

"The Fianna used to have a stormcaster who made lightning this color," Miogach noted. "A lass with dark hair."

Daire Donn looked at Patrick. "Where did you say the *veleda* is?"

"Perhaps more importantly, where are the Fianna?" Bres asked.

And then Patrick knew where the lightning came from.

Grace.

THIRTY-FOUR

Grace

The scream came again, harsher and louder. Grandma sat up. Her eyes were almost black. "Go to him now," she ordered. "Now!"

"Go to *who*?"

This time there was a name within the scream. "Grace!"

I knew the voice: Aidan. My grandmother fell back upon the pillows, her chest rising and falling in rapid breaths. I ran for the bedroom door, reaching it just as my mother came into the hall. She was trembling. Aidan was at the bottom of the stairs, clutching his head.

"Grace!"

"What's wrong with him? What's wrong?" Mama cried.

I raced down the stairs, grabbing my brother's shoulder. "Aidan! Aidan, I'm here. What is it? Why are you screaming?"

He lifted his head from his hands. He was sweating, his

eyes a startling, shimmering, hot blue. There was another peal of thunder. He flinched.

I called up to my mother, "It's nothing, Mama; he's just drunk again."

He said, "I'm not drunk, dammit. And you're coming with me."

"Why? Did Patrick send you?"

"Come with me, Grace. Now. I mean it. There's no time."

Grandma's words. "No time for what?"

He grabbed me, pulling me with him down the hallway, through the kitchen to the back door. Dusk had gone straight to an eerie black night. I'd never seen anything like it. I stopped, but Aidan jerked me forward. "Come on!"

He was dripping with sweat. His eyes looked electrified. His hair curled around his face—I saw it *moving* as if it were alive. I tried to pull away. "Aidan, what's happening?"

Aidan yanked me with him outside. I stumbled, nearly falling into the yard.

"Aidan, stop! I'm afraid."

He turned on me wildly, his eyes glowing. "They're coming for you. I need to get you out of here."

The Fomori. The Fianna. It hardly mattered which. Both were terrifying to me. *You must choose.*

Aidan glanced behind him, toward the alley. "Do as I say now, Grace. You're to go with them. They'll keep you safe."

I followed his gaze. There in the alley were the Fianna: Finn leading the way, Derry and the others right behind him. Derry looked up at me.

"Oh no. No!" I wrenched away from my brother, but Aidan caught me and pulled me to his chest, holding me tight, and I felt energy coursing through him. I felt it in my fingertips. When I looked up at him, his hair was moving again, Medusa-like.

I pushed against him. "Let me go. Please, Aidan, let me go. You don't understand. You don't. Let me go!"

Aidan didn't budge. He was stronger than I'd ever imagined. As strong as Derry. I could not get away. He looked down at me with a determination I hadn't seen in a long time, a look that reminded me of when we were children playing games, and he'd never, ever let me win.

"He'll protect you," my brother told me.

"Aidan, you don't know who they are!"

"They're the Fianna," he said simply.

The air crackled, and Aidan was quivering within it. "If you know that, then you know what they want from me. You know what they'll do. You're the one who told me not to go with him. Don't you remember? 'Don't run off with him,' you said. You begged me not to."

The back gate clanged as the Fianna came into the yard. Finn's voice rang out, "Keep hold of her!"

I struggled against my brother, who only tightened his grip.

Finn and Derry hurried over as I pounded on Aidan's chest. "Damn you, Aidan, let me go! I don't want this! I don't want any of it!"

"It's too late for that, lass," Finn said.

"Grace, don't," Derry said softly. "Come with us. We'll protect you."

I turned on him. "I don't trust you. I know what you did to me, and I promise you I'll fight it. I don't want you! I hate you!"

He staggered back as if I'd slapped him again. Even through my anger and my fear I felt how I'd hurt him. But I didn't care.

Finn said, "You've a right to be angry. But we mean you no harm. Come now. Come with us."

His tone was soothing, persuasive. For a moment, I almost believed him. The wind picked up. The clouds churned and boiled overheard. Thunder filled my ears and racked my brother's body, though he didn't loosen his hold on me. His hair whipped across his face. Blue lightning forked, spitting into the yard, bringing the smell of burning air and panic.

I heard the drawing of steel—a sound I knew. Battlefield swords pulled from scabbards. My brother's energy sent shivers over my skin.

Keenan said, "Here they are."

The Fianna had turned to face the alley—all but Finn and Derry, who didn't take their eyes off me. Then it was as if every light in the world blew out, and we were standing in darkness.

What came next was the most terrible noise I'd ever heard: ravens screaming, a cloud of them overhead, a moving, frenzied mass. Lightning flashed so close it raised the hairs on my arms, and Aidan began to murmur something, and then there was purple lighting, too, clashing against the blue. A window opened above; my mother screamed, "Aidan! Grace! Get inside this moment! Who . . . who's in the yard with you?"

I *felt* them coming, and suddenly there they were, in the alley. A tall man with an eyepatch, another with twisted hair rising above his head as he gestured toward the sky—blue lightning spinning from his hand. A beautiful woman. Three other men and beyond them a group of gang boys—ragged clothing and some of them lame and others with only one arm, and still they looked fast and deadly, their knives glowing with the reflection of the lightning. The Fomori. Not monsters but men, and no more or less frightening than the Fianna. *"The Fomori aren't as the legends say."*

"Ready," said Finn in a low voice. The Fianna assumed fighting stances.

My brother began to glow the same way the Fianna had glowed, but I felt no pain. His hair leaped and twisted about his head. Coldly he said to Derry, "Get her out of here. Do what you must."

Aidan thrust me away. Derry held out his hand. I recoiled, and again that hurt flashed in his eyes.

"Come with us, Grace," he said. "Please. Come with *me*."

He was a liar. He'd used the lovespot to compel me. And still his words raised a fever of longing in me.

But that fever was a lie. The truth was that he had to kill me. He had to kill me, and still I wanted him, and I was more afraid of him than I'd ever been of anything.

I wanted to be away from here. In Patrick's arms. To be

safe with him and his promises. I should never have left. I should be with him now.

Just then my mother shouted, "Patrick!" and I looked to see him rushing up the alley. Patrick, who wanted to save me. *"I could be your Diarmid."*

"Grace! Don't look at him!" Patrick yelled.

Derry reached for me. "Grace. Come with me." I heard his desperation.

"Go to Patrick, Grace!" My mother cried from above.

The men in the alley advanced in a miasma of glowing purple fog. Finn drew a dagger from his belt and another from his boot. The other Fianna crouched, knives at the ready.

"Now, stormcaster!" Finn ordered.

My brother raised his arms. Purple lightning coiled and cracked. Thunder crashed. The clouds opened with a drenching rain. Lightning shot from his fingers. *Aidan?*

I couldn't deny it—Aidan's powers lit the sky. Finn yelled something in Gaelic. The Fianna surged forward. The ravens screamed. The battle began with the flash of knives and bodies grappling in the darkness and the rain lit only by lightning. Just like in my dreams. But I couldn't wake from this. I could do nothing but stand there.

"Grace!" Patrick was soaked to the skin, his blond hair dark with rain.

Derry said urgently, "Trust me, Grace. You know you can. You *know* me. Just as I know you. We belong together."

Just as he'd said in the kitchen, and I heard hope in his words again now. I felt the spell of him.

"Time to wager, Grace," he whispered. "Faith or fear?"

Patrick grabbed Derry's shoulder, jerking him around. "Leave her alone, damn you! I told you to leave her alone!"

Derry didn't raise a hand. He looked back at me. "Your choice," he said.

There was chaos all around. Blood in the alley. Knives and clubs, violet and blue lightning, the rain crashing down and thunder like the roaring of the world. And yet all I could see were the two standing before me.

I knew what I chose between. Safety and risk. Love and desire. My family and myself. Faith or fear. Derry frightened me. I didn't trust him, no matter what I felt for him. He wanted too much of me, and I wasn't ready to make that leap of faith. Perhaps I never would be. And I believed in Patrick and his love. I believed that he would help me and my family. I had known him the whole of my life. Derry had told me *"Run away,"* and Patrick had said *"Why couldn't we be running to something?"*

"Choose well," my grandmother had said.

Derry whispered, "Now, Grace. Please."

And Patrick said, "I love you. You know I do."

I stepped toward him. He held out his arms, and I walked into them, and I felt his shudder when he closed them around me, when he murmured into my hair, "Thank God. Thank God."

I heard the rush of Derry's breath as I pressed my face into Patrick's shoulder.

When I looked up again, Derry was gone.

THIRTY-FIVE

After

Grace

The Fianna retreated. A shout from Finn, and they disappeared like shadows into the night. The Fomori dismissed their warriors as well, and the alley was as empty as it had ever been except for the woman who came into the backyard, her blond hair streaming down her back. She stepped up to where Patrick had taken me on the stoop, beneath the small roof. She smiled, touching my hand, and said, "You must be the *veleda*."

"This is Lot," Patrick told me.

"Lot?"

Patrick smiled at me. "I told you: the stories aren't the truth, Grace."

"No indeed," said Lot. "And we will do all we can to help you, my dear. We have promised it to your fiancé. And I personally promise it to you." She looked at Patrick. "Perhaps you should take her inside, my dear. It's quite wet."

The rain hadn't stopped, though the thunder and lightning had, and the street and house lights had come back on as if nothing had happened. There was no sign of my brother. He had disappeared with the others. Grandma had said, *"Aidan will know."* Where had his power come from? How long had he known of it? And why hadn't he told me? So much power—the kind of power I expected from a *veleda*—and I wondered . . . what if they were all wrong? What if I wasn't the *veleda*, but Aidan? The idea wasn't any more reassuring, and I kept silent as Patrick took me inside. I wanted to rush up the stairs to ask Grandma, but Mama was with two policemen who had just arrived. I recognized them as Moran and Stoltz, who had come with Patrick to question us about the ogham stick—it seemed forever ago.

"We'll check to be certain they've all dispersed," Moran said. "I doubt they'll return. It was odd enough for gangs to be this far north."

"But things are changing," said Stoltz. "They're not playing by the rules anymore. We'll post an officer in this neighborhood to be sure. That'll convince them to keep their distance."

"Gangs?" Patrick squeezed my shoulder. "You're certain that's who they were?"

"Nothing's certain. But we heard rumors there was a fight brewin' tonight. Somethin' in the air, you know? Thunder's got everyone on edge."

"At least the storm's broken," agreed Moran. He turned to Mama. "I don't think you'll see any other disturbances tonight, ma'am."

"I sincerely hope not," said Mama. "I'm just glad it's over."

The police went outside to investigate the alley. When they were gone, Mama looked at me, at Patrick's arm still around my shoulders. Her eyes looked haunted, and I wondered what she'd seen, if she really believed the story the police told her. Had she seen Aidan set off the storm? Had she seen him glowing, his hair on end? Purple lighting coming from his fingers?

I wished she had. I wanted her to know the truth. I wanted her reassurance, for her to soothe me instead of the other way around.

"Mama," I began, and then my words died when I saw her expression shift, that vacancy and denial returned, a door closed to questions and pain, and I could not make myself be so cruel as to force her to admit what she had seen. Not yet.

Patrick said, "It's been a strange night indeed."

Mama nodded. "And that storm . . . Where is Aidan?"

"He disappeared again," I said, watching her closely.

There was nothing to tell me what she'd seen. "Well, no doubt he'll be back soon. Who was that boy in the yard—the one talking to you? It seemed as if you knew him."

"My stableboy," Patrick answered before I could. "It's true he is a gang member. I didn't know it or I never would have hired him. He's been dismissed, but I should warn you that he's been showing Grace some unwanted attention. I'm afraid he'll return to bother her, and so I hope you won't object to me bringing Grace to my house for a few days. I can keep her safe there."

My mother looked alarmed. "You think he's a danger?"

"Probably not, but she's precious to me. I'll only worry if I can't keep an eye on her." How good a liar he was. He made it all sound so reasonable. *Were we all liars then?*

My mother said, "Well, yes, I suppose taking her to your house is best, but I expect—"

"I shall be on my best behavior," Patrick promised. "And my mother will be there, of course. And Lucy."

"I'll get my things," I said.

I went upstairs, anxious to see Grandma, my questions ready to burst from my lips. I rushed into her bedroom, surprised to find her sleeping. I touched her shoulder impatiently. "Grandma. Grandma, wake up."

She didn't move. She was deeply asleep, strangely so. Grandma was usually so restless, plagued by dreams, but now she looked . . . peaceful.

I stepped back, not wanting to interrupt that peace. My questions would wait until the morning. I kissed her cheek, murmuring, "Sleep well, Grandma," and then, reluctantly, I left, going to my room.

I paused on the threshold, staring into the darkness eased only by the shadowy light from the street. I thought of how Derry had waited for me here, the things I'd told him I wanted. Nothing was as I'd imagined it to be.

"You're not as powerless as you think."

Of course, he had known even then what I was. And now that he was gone, the effects of the lovespell could fade. I could burn for Patrick's kiss. Rose had been right. He was the one I wanted. Needed.

I packed my few things in a small bag and went back downstairs to the parlor, where Patrick stood talking to my mother. "I'm ready."

Mama came forward to give me a kiss. "I'll come by tomorrow. We've so much to plan." She gave me a knowing look.

Patrick and I stepped out into the rain. It drizzled into the puddle beneath the streetlamp so it looked like a pool of golden pebbles. Something made me look beyond it. A movement, a noise. I looked into the shadows, but I saw nothing. Still, I felt uneasy.

Patrick grabbed my hand. "Come on!"

Together we ran to the waiting carriage. When we were inside, Patrick drew me onto his lap, kissing me deeply, and I felt the same tremor of pleasure that always came with his kiss.

"We'll be so good together, Grace," he promised. "You'll see. I'll save your life. And then you and I . . . we'll save Ireland."

"Is it really the life you want for yourself?"

Yes, it was. I knew that now.

Faith or fear.

I was running *to* something at last.

But the moment I thought it, I glanced out the window. Derry stepped from the shadow beyond the streetlamp. He was haloed in its golden light. His gaze met mine through the rain-spotted window, and I felt that ache that came with his every look and touch, that terrible yearning. As much as I wanted to be the Grace of the past, who longed for a white knight to save her from debt and despair, that girl was gone. There was so much more now to be won or lost. Derry had changed everything, whether he'd meant to or not.

The choice. The ritual. The *veleda.* That was my future now.

"This isn't over. It can't be over."

"Grace?"

I turned away from the window, to Patrick. "It's just . . . there's so much to get used to."

"I know," he said. Then he smiled. "But you don't have to face it alone. I'm here now."

I nodded and said the words I had not allowed myself to say: "I will marry you."

And I did not look back.

✆ About the Author ✆

MEGAN CHANCE

is the award-winning author of several adult novels, including *Bone River.* A former television news photographer with a BA from Western Washington University, Megan lives in the Pacific Northwest with her husband and two daughters. Visit her at: www.meganchance.com.